CAPTIVE ECSTASY

Beau reached up to place a pink blossom in Alanna's hair, then gently touched a fingertip to her chin. She did not pull away or seem to find his gesture unwarranted, and, without a thought, he lowered his head to place a warm and tender kiss on the corner of her mouth.

Alanna's mind reeled, intoxicated by his nearness, his kiss, the gentle touch of his hand. And although she had promised herself never to play his dove again, she found the yearning to have him hold her in his arms overpowering. Her eyes closed, she breathed the scent of him, and turned her head to welcome his kiss. . . .

ZEBRA HAS IT ALL!

Passion's Slave

BY KAY McMAHON

ZEBRA BOOKS
KENSINGTON·PUBLISHING CORP.

ZEBRA BOOKS

are published by

KENSINGTON PUBLISHING CORP.
475 Park Avenue South
New York, N.Y. 10016

First printing: December, 1983

Printed in the United States of America

His troubled gaze searched the dimness of the room, the dancing firelight all that chased away the gloom. His heart pounded, wondering if she really waited, knowing the time for feeling disloyal, guilty, was long since past. A movement from the corner of the room jerked his attention to it, straining in the darkness to reward his hours spent worriedly that she would never come again. A muffled sob broke the impending quiet.

"Why are you crying?" he whispered, concern mixed heavily with fear in his tired voice.

She moved into the rutty glow of the hearth's blaze, tears staining her cheeks, angry dark eyes flashing up at him. "I saw the doctor today. I am with child." Shaky fingertips urgently covered her trembling lips, stifling a renewal of weeping.

He took a tentative step toward her, stopped abruptly when she raised a hand. "But you shouldn't be crying. You should be happy. After all these years, you will have a child."

Flowing black hair fell about her face, hiding the

features he had grown to love. Soft brown eyes, thin straight nose, finely boned, and a full, sensuous mouth constantly haunted his dreams, and spilled into his waking hours.

Turning, she went to the window to stare into the night. "You don't understand. It is not my husband's child I carry. It is yours." The admission of her sin brought a new flooding of tears.

Pain seared through him with her words, knowing the pretext of her discomfiture, the culpability she must feel. Cautiously, he went to her, retreating sharply when she turned to slap away his outstretched hand.

"Don't touch me. Ever again," she hissed, a virulent gleam in her eyes.

Stunned by her command, his heart aching, he stood rigidly before her, unable to fathom the cause. "If—if that is what you want, then that is how it shall be."

Tears pooled in the corners of her eyes, a sob racking her body. "Yes. That is how I want it," she choked, turning away to collapse into a chair by the fire.

Slowly, deliberately, he knelt at her side, close enough to touch her but not daring. How could this anger, this hatred have happened? Hadn't they loved each other? Hadn't they lived for each other these past weeks? Suddenly he felt trapped in his feelings for this woman. And what of her husband? He felt as if he had betrayed everything in which he had believed his entire life. He choked back an involuntary sob when he realized he had beguiled an ardent friendship, years of affection, years of service, all tainted by a single night spent in the arms of this woman. Yet, what he felt for her was just as precious, just as valuable as his relationship with her husband. Now he knew it to be only one-sided. Still, the child she carried was his, and no amount of time and no words would ever dull his love for it, though that love be veiled in his touch, his words, his guidance.

He fought the tightening in his throat, and when he spoke the words came haltingly. "I can never leave you. Or your husband. What I feel for both of you is too strong. Yet, if he knew of our love—"

She opened her mouth to condemn the word, stilled by the demanding shake of his head to have his say.

"If he knew of this, he would not turn away from you, if that be your concern. I know he could never live without you."

Pleading eyes sought his. "You won't tell him?"

A tremor of compassion raced through him. "I would never hurt him so. Nor could I hurt you."

The look of pain, of helplessness, that had claimed the golden depths of her eyes from the first moment he saw her changed suddenly and she glared balefully at him. "The guilt is yours. You took advantage of me. I am blameless."

His own grief glistening in his eyes, he moved away from her, not wanting her to know. "If that's what you believe—so be it. But promise me one thing. Promise that you will love the child twice as much since I shall be denied the honor openly."

Her tears, which had vanished with his assurance that the conception of the child would remain a secret, began once more, tears of anger and contempt. "How can you expect such a thing? To love a child that is not my husband's? Love it as if it were his offspring? That is totally, completely impossible. Be it boy or girl, I will never find it in my heart to love a child conceived in lustful sin."

7

"But I loved you," he persisted, then realized how shallow the words sounded when compared with the tirade she had unleashed. "I thought you loved me," he added weakly.

Leaping to her feet, she faced him, an arrogant, haughty nature rising to the surface. "I was lonely. I acted the fool." She brushed past him, moving toward the door. "And so did you."

His dark eyes swept over her, drinking in her physical beauty before she turned in cold aloofness to leave him. His eyes filled with tears. "Nay, I am not the fool," he whispered.

One

The endless blue-green plane of the sea flowed outward in all directions, slightly marred in perfection by the light blue of the sky where they joined and blended into one. A soft breeze played shyly with the long, black curls lying possessively against Alanna Bainbridge's shoulders and cascading to her waist as she looked out from the bow of the *Sea Wind*, anxiously awaiting the first sighting of land. A small hand, raised to shade her face from the sun, cast a shadow over the beauty she did not know she commanded. Velvety black brows arched softly against her fair complexion, now lightly reddened by the hours spent on deck, added highlights to her already rosy cheeks. Dark brown eyes trimmed with long, sooty lashes reflected the gentleness of her nature as she gazed out across the sea. Above her someone shouted, causing her to squint her eyes in hopes of seeing the reason for his herald. Then it came. Only a thin dark line at first, cutting the horizon in two, growing in size until she could distinguish the shape of land. She prayed it was the harbor of Williamsburg, Virginia and the end of her journey.

The previously unmarked cloudless blue sky grew dotted with hundreds of sea gulls circling the waters in search of food, brazenly ignoring the crowd of people storming the docks as the *Sea Wind* and its passengers sailed into port. Alanna's heart fluttered in expectation of an uncertain future. She longed to go ashore but wondered what awaited her. She looked up, letting the sun warm her face in the cool breezes of early spring, while she recalled the last time she had set foot on solid ground. Nearly six weeks had passed since she, her stepmother, and father, William Bainbridge, had boarded the English capital ship in the harbor of Liverpool, England to embark on a new way of life once they reached America. A man filled with dreams, William had promised his family they would prosper from the riches only a plantation in this new world could offer, foolishly selling what meager belongings they had to book passage on the ship and destroying any chance they had to return. Alanna pressed a knuckle to the tear racing down her cheek. Now they were dead, buried at sea.

The rattling of the gangplank being lowered to the long wooden dock brought harsh reality to Alanna. She would soon be on shore and making a life for herself would be her sole responsibility. Gathering up her small bundle of belongings, she joined the others preparing to leave.

"Miss Bainbridge," a raspy voice beckoned from behind her.

She looked back over her shoulder, a questioning expression on her face, and nodded hesitantly after recognizing the heavy-set, determined figure of the first mate walking toward her.

"You'll have to wait over there with the others," he

said, chewing on the stub of his cigar.

"Yes, sir," she mumbled, looking in the direction in which his thumb pointed. She truly didn't understand the need, but rather than cause any trouble, she stepped back without question, quietly mingling with the group of men, women, and children who appeared in no haste to depart.

She walked aimlessly among the passengers, catching various parts of assorted conversations and, without realizing it, lingered beside two men when they spoke of a topic that piqued her own curiosity as well as that of the man who listened.

"The Hawk?" he asked. "How'd he come by such a name?"

The other shrugged. "Henry guesses it's cause his eyes are so black it's like starin' into the eyes of a hawk. 'Ya don't find no sympathy in them,' Henry says."

"Well, aren't you a little worried about working on his place? He sounds like the devil himself to me."

"No. Henry says it's not too bad livin' there as long as you obey the rules. Besides, I figure I'll have paid back what I owe Remington in a couple of years. Then I can go wherever I please. How 'bout you?"

The man raised the heel of his boot to tap out the ashes from his pipe and noticed Alanna staring at them. He smiled politely, touching a fingertip to the brim of his hat.

She managed a weak smile in return, instantly feeling the heat rise in her cheeks. She turned away. How rude of me, she thought, touching the neckline of her gown with her fingers. She stole a quick glance back at the men, found them both watching, and quickly walked to the railing of the ship, hoping they had not already gotten the

11

wrong idea. With a hand resting against the thick wooden balustrade, she looked once more at the throng of people bustling about the docks below her.

In the crowd, Alanna watched an old woman approach each new arrival from the ship with a basket filled to the top with flowers in various shades of the rainbow. For the most part, everyone pushed by her, only a few stopping to examine her wares. After the exchange of a coin, she would smile gratefully and try the next couple who came her way. Two small barefoot boys, their clothes torn and soiled, their faces darkened by dirt, ran from ship to ship offering to carry the luggage of its passengers for a price. Sailors from another ship impatiently elbowed their way through the people, eagerly heading for a nearby inn and a much needed tankard of ale. An unpleasant curl to Alanna's lip formed as she thought of the possibility of working in such a place if all other efforts failed her.

She heard someone shout above the noise of the crowd and scanned the multitude, seeing two freight wagons thundering to a stop below her. Shading her eyes with her hand, she watched curiously as the driver of the first wagon climbed down and waited for his companion, instantly aware of the startling difference in size of the two men. The older wore a wide-brimmed straw hat pushed back on his graying hair and stood a full head shorter than the black man at his side. Lazily, Alanna's gaze traveled down his stocky form, her eyes widening when they spotted the huge black whip rolled up and hanging from his belt. Good heavens, she breathed, whatever would he need that for? As if sensing her thoughts, the man rested his hand upon it, and Alanna swallowed the lump that had suddenly formed in her throat. He had yet to look at her, but for some reason she

12

felt he knew that someone watched. She turned away, but only a moment passed before she was compelled to look again. To her surprise, the two men had started up the ramp of the *Sea Wind,* a dark, leather-bound book tucked possessively under the older man's arm.

Everyone around Alanna buzzed with excitement, watching the stranger talk with the captain, who presented him with a paper before turning to the first mate. A few more words were exchanged and the two men walked toward the crowd of nervous people, the clicking of their heels against the wooden deck cutting through the silence that had suddenly surrounded them all. Standing rigidly before them, the man with the whip cleared his throat, opened the book, and began to read in a deep, clear voice.

"As a representative of Master Beau Remington, this fifteenth day of May in the year of our Lord seventeen hundred fifty-seven, the following names are committed into his service: Wesley Appleton, Timothy Adams, Edward and Sarah Anderson, Alanna Bainbridge—"

She felt a sudden tightening in her chest. Who was this man? How would he know she was on board? Fear threatening to overpower her, she quickly glanced around for a friendly face and found an old woman standing near.

"Excuse me," she begged, "but do you know who that man is?"

"Which one, child?" the woman smiled.

Alanna pointed to the stranger.

"Well, I suppose he's the overseer from Raven Oaks," she said, dismissing Alanna's question. "My name is Sarah Anderson. What's yours?"

Alanna's breath caught in her throat. "Overseer?"

she choked.

"Yes, dear. Why?"

"But he called my name," she said, staring at the man, who continued to read aloud from his list.

"Really? Then I guess we'll be living together."

Alanna shook her head, unable to pull her eyes from the overseer. She knew very little about the way plantations in America were run, but she had heard enough to know an overseer meant slaves. Surely this man didn't intend to make a slave of her. Fighting back the tears, she began to elbow her way toward the captain, only to be stopped in her tracks by the big black man, who appeared from out of nowhere.

"Where yo' think yo' goin'?" he asked.

"To speak with the captain. There's been a terrible mistake."

A dark brow raised suspiciously. "What's yo'r name?"

"Alanna Bainbridge."

The huge man shook his head. "Ain't no mistake. I hear 'im call yo'r name."

"But that's what I mean," she moaned. "He shouldn't have!"

"I hear that 'fore," he grinned, the whiteness of his teeth sparkling brightly in contrast to his ebony skin. "Now if yo' know what's good for yo', yo' 'ill get back with the rest."

Alanna's eyes burned with unshed tears. How could she make this man understand? What could she do to prove to him that she wasn't one of the others? If only her father was here. He would set things straight.

"Jeremiah?" she heard the overseer call and the negro at her side snapped to attention. "Start loadin' 'em in the wagons."

"Yassuh," he answered, taking Alanna's arm. "Now come along with me, missy."

She jerked free of him. "No! I'm not supposed to—"

"Jeremiah," the overseer broke in, recognizing the signs of trouble, "don't argue with her. Tie her up if you have to."

"Yassuh," Jeremiah nodded, turning a warning frown on the girl. "If'n it really is a mistake, yo' have yo'r time to talk with Masta Beau. Right now, make it easy on yo'self and come along quietly."

Alanna glanced at the overseer, spying the whip on his belt again, and decided it would be wise to follow his suggestion. For the moment, anyway. Reluctantly, she allowed Jeremiah to lead her down the ramp and boarded one of the wagons.

From the back of it, Alanna watched the ship appear to grow smaller with each turn of the wheel as they rolled away, knowing that very soon it would disappear over the horizon.

"Oh, Papa," she whispered, "whatever will I do?"

Completely at a loss, she pulled up her knees, wrapped her arms around them, and rested her brow against the coolness of her skirt, quietly sobbing.

It took them two grueling days in the hot sunshine and cramped quarters of the wagons, and one alarmingly dark night to reach Raven Oaks. The night Alanna spent on the cold, hard ground without a blanket. Every muscle in her tiny frame ached and she vowed once she reached the plantation she would sleep for a week.

The wagons rounded a bend in the road and headed up a long drive. On each side fields of what she would discover were tobacco and cotton seemed to spread beyond imagination. The horizon, set aglow in the burning lights of dusk, silhouetted the tall, unfriendly shape of the mill. Before it stood many cabins made from logs, each identical and all remarkably tidy. Scores of people bustled about, each performing some sort of duty or another, and the ringing of an anvil filled the air. It was like a small town, nestled in a hidden valley, many miles from Williamsburg. The only thing it lacked was a general store or a dress shop. Set off to one side and segregated from all the others stood a huge white house, alone and without indication of any movement from within. It radiated a feeling of power and rule over all that lay before it.

The wagons jerked to a stop and everyone eagerly climbed down, thankful for a chance to stretch their legs. All except for Alanna. She had no idea where she had been taken, nor could she envision how she would return to the ship once she was freed. Fear tightened the muscles across her chest and belly, and she sat petrified in the back of the wagon until a firm hand gripped her elbow and forced her to the ground. She looked up into the dark brown eyes of Jeremiah. Frightened even of him, she quickly backed away and joined the crowd that surrounded the overseer, feeling a little safer masked by their number.

"My name is Joshua Cain. I'm overseer for Master Remington. In this book," he told them, holding it high above his head, "I have everyone's name listed and your time of indentured servitude. You will each be given a cabin to share with a servant who has been here for some time. They will help you remember our rules. There aren't many, but they are important.

16

"First," he began, pacing back and forth in front of them, "attempted escapes will not be tolerated by slaves or indentured servants. I say attempted because no one has ever succeeded. You will be flogged should you test that record."

Alanna's eyes widened. Now she knew the purpose of the whip.

"You each will have a duty to perform, every day, including Sunday. If you're sick and unable to work, that day will be added to your length of stay here.

"Under no circumstances will you ever go to the main house unless Master Remington has called for you. You will be docked one day's work if you do. You will not speak to him when he comes for inspection unless he speaks first." Opening the book, he began scanning its pages. "I think that's just about all. Follow me—"

The new group of servants obligingly took his lead. Every time he came to one of the cabins, he called out a name, waving them inside. The lengthening shadows of day reminded Alanna that she had not eaten, and since she had nowhere to go, she decided to wait until morning to solve her problem with Master Remington. Thus, when her name was called, she silently approached the cabin, knowing it would be only for the night.

Sparsely furnished with only a table, two chairs and a bed in one corner, the cabin reflected the care someone took in keeping it clean. A vase of fresh-cut flowers adorned the crude table, bringing a smile to Alanna's face, and she decided it would be a pleasant place to spend the night compared with the long, uncomfortable weeks she had spent at sea.

She had no sooner laid down her bundle when she heard the sound of the door latch rattling. She turned,

17

somehow expecting a twinge of guilt for entering the lodging without permission from its keeper. Haloed in the archway of the cabin's only door stood a petite, shapely young woman with beautiful auburn hair. Her delicate-boned face, sprinkled with freckles, broke into a warm smile.

"Hello," she said. "I'm sorry I wasn't here when you arrived, but I had some chores to finish. My name is Cinnamon Cockrin."

Cinnamon, Alanna mused lightly, the soft arch of her brow wrinkling momentarily. Such a different name, one she had never heard before, but so fitting for the girl's reddish-colored mane. "I'm Alanna Bainbridge," she replied, her own relaxed smile curling the corners of her mouth.

"I'm pleased to meet you. Have you had supper yet?" Before Alanna could answer, Cinnamon chuckled to herself. "Now that's a silly question. You just this minute got off the wagon and I'm sure Cain wouldn't have stopped so close to the plantation. Make yourself at home," she said, moving toward the fireplace, "while I heat up some stew."

Alanna eased herself onto the bed, grateful for a chance to sit comfortably, and untwined the laces of her shoes. "I pray I did not overstep my welcome by letting myself in while you were away." She affixed her gaze to her task, unable to meet the woman's eyes.

"Oh, of course not," Cinnamon assured her. "I was told I would share the cabin. I simply didn't know when."

She glanced up and renewed her glowing smile, one Alanna accepted eagerly. Uncertainty, as well as fear, had ruled Alanna's existence since the *Sea Wind* had docked in port, and finding someone as understanding and

18

friendly as Cinnamon was more than she had expected. "How long have you been here?" she asked comfortably.

Hanging a cumbersome black pot over the flames crackling in the fireplace, Cinnamon said, "Oh, nearly nine years. Do you know how long you'll be staying?"

"Just for the night," Alanna answered confidently as she peeled off her stockings.

"The night?" Cinnamon repeated, looking up with a frown.

"Yes. You see, I'm here because of an error. My parents and I sailed here to make a new home for ourselves, but they died of fever coming over on the ship. Apparently someone thought I was one of Master Remington's indentured servants just because I was alone." She began to rub the soreness from her legs, exhibiting a credulous smile. "But it will all be corrected in the morning after I talk with Master Remington."

Rising slowly, apprehensively, Cinnamon studied the woman sitting across the room from her, then drew up a chair next to her guest. "Did someone tell you that you would be able to talk with Master Remington?"

"Yes. The big Negro called Jeremiah. Why?"

"I'm afraid he tricked you," Cinnamon said.

"What do you mean?" Alanna demanded, tossing her legs back over the edge of the bed.

"Did you voice your disagreement at the ship?"

"Yes."

Cinnamon shook her head. "I thought so. It happens all the time. I don't mean that I don't believe you, but there are those who accept the free passage, and then once they reach the shores claim there has been a mistake, hoping to be free to do and go as they please. Jeremiah always tells these people they will have the chance to plead their case with Master Remington just as soon as they reach the plantation. I'm sorry, Alanna," she whispered with a pat to Alanna's hand, "but chances are you will never be allowed to see The Hawk."

"No!" Alanna shouted. "They cannot force me to stay here. My father sold everything we had to pay for our passage. Someone lied."

"Don't upset yourself. You'll come to like living here," Cinnamon said, hoping to sound convincing.

"How can you say that? I have no intention of staying." Alanna quickly pulled on her stockings and shoes. "I will speak with Master Remington right now."

"No, Alanna, don't even think of it," Cinnamon begged, grabbing for Alanna's arm as she flew from the bed and headed for the door.

"Thank you for your concern, but this is a matter I must solve on my own," Alanna said, dismissing the warning.

Pungent odors of burning wood stung her nostrils and the cold, crisp bite of the night air gripped her thinly clad body once she stepped outside. She shivered, looking about and wondering where she might find the master of the plantation. Surely he would be dining at this hour, she thought, deciding in which building he would be. The golden lights of dusk had all but disappeared, leaving only a single stream that raced across the darkened sky, profiling the blackened shape of a house that seemed immense and threatening as it stood alone at the top of a knoll. She shivered again, deciding it to be her goal, and hesitantly started off in its direction.

Continually she glanced about, listening to her own footsteps growing louder in the opaque stillness of night and wondering if she had done the right thing in leaving the safety of Cinnamon's cabin. She looked ahead, forcing herself to concentrate on her destination, blind to all else as her mind raced with thoughts of The Hawk's denial of her freedom. Then, with only a short distance to go, someone stepped out of the shadows and blocked her way. She gasped.

"Where do you think you're going?" he asked.

Alanna's heart raced, uncertain of the danger in which she had placed herself. "I must speak with Master Remington," she replied, shaken.

"What's your name?"

She swallowed hard, knowing her chin trembled. "Alanna Bainbridge, sir," she whispered.

"I thought so. I had a feeling you'd come. Apparently you didn't listen to the rules I set down for you."

Alanna glanced down at the man's belt and saw the black whip dangling from it. "But you must understand," she begged, pulling her eyes from it. "There has been an awful mistake. I am not one of Master Remington's servants. My father sold—"

"Come with me," Cain interrupted, grabbing for her arm only to find that she had wiggled out of his reach and was heading for the house. "Stop, damn you!" he bellowed, starting out after her.

She pounded on the door only twice before he had locked his hands in her long black hair and pulled her painfully away. She screamed and he quickly clamped a hand over her mouth as he dragged her back down the stairs. They had just reached the bottom when the door opened and spilled light on them both, outlining a tall, dark figure of a man.

"What is it, Cain?" she heard him ask.

"I'm sorry to have disturbed you, Mr. Remington. A small problem I can handle. I'm afraid she got away from me."

Panic filled Alanna. She knew Cain would take her away before she had a chance to speak, and she fought desperately to free her mouth from his hold. His grip tightened.

"Very well, Cain," the man said, and Alanna's heart sank, listening to him close the door again.

"I hope your behavior tonight is not what I will come to expect from you," Cain grumbled in her ear as he pulled her tightly between his arms. "I would hate to think you will spend all of your nights where you will this one."

Alanna struggled, but soon found it fruitless. The man who held her had unbounded strength. He half carried her and, feeling the fatigue of her journey, she unwillingly relaxed in his grip, too weak to fight anymore.

He took her to a small shed apart from the rest of the buildings and threw her inside. She stumbled and fell, feeling the bed of damp straw beneath her. Groping in the darkness, she crawled to one side and huddled in the corner, picking cobwebs from her face and hair, and listening to the door slam closed, blocking out the only chance for light to filter in. Then the heavy thud of a bar across the portal filled her ears, and she jumped at the sound, knowing he had locked her in.

"It's not a very comfortable place to spend the night," she heard his muffled voice call out, "but had you done as you were told, you would not be here. I shall return in the morning to see if you've had a change of heart."

22

She listened to the sounds of his footsteps fading and knew he meant what he said. She would spend the night in this cold, dark, musty-smelling cubicle. However, one thing was for certain. She would never have a change of heart. She hated America, and she hated Beau Remington for his part in putting her where she was now.

Two

Cinnamon stood in the doorway of the cabin fanning herself with the edge of her apron held in both hands while she stared at the cloudless blue sky, feeling the heat rise from the ground that had already soaked up the rays of an early summer. The moist, heavy air made her perspire no matter what simple task she undertook and, even now, standing in the shade of the small house, she failed to find any escape. The only things that appeared to have any energy at all were the flies constantly buzzing about her dampened hair and face, lingering on her nose until an unsuccessful swipe intended to do harm frightened them away.

"You know, Alanna," she called back over her shoulder dreamily, "someday you'll realize how fortunate you are to be here."

"Fortunate? I think not," barked the sharpened reply from inside the cabin. "I hardly think being a slave is fortunate."

"Oh, you have it all wrong," Cinnamon laughed, not at all affected by her words. "The Hawk does not think of his people as slaves."

Looking up from the table dusted with flour, Alanna set aside her dough and stared at Cinnamon's back. "No? Then why are we not free to go if we so choose?"

"Because we are indentured servants. You know that. We owe him the coin it took to bring us here."

"I owe him nothing. And yet I dare not leave for fear of being dragged back in chains. Is that not slavery?" Alanna added with a slam of her fist against the table.

Cinnamon casually turned around, leaning a shoulder against the doorframe. "It's not the same," she said. "As soon as you have paid your debt you will be free to go. Negro slaves are never free."

Alanna shook off Cinnamon's argument with a toss of her dark curls and resumed her duties without another word.

"Have you ever seen a plantation with Negro slaves?" Cinnamon continued, wiping a trail of sweat from her face with a finger.

Alanna's shoulders dropped in annoyance. "No."

"Then how can you stand there and judge if you don't know what you're talking about?" Cinnamon asked, instantly detecting Alanna's resentment toward the subject by the way she glared up at her. The muscles of her small frame tightened with an instant of regret, realizing how truly upset their discussion made Alanna. "I'm sorry, but I've been here longer than you and I should know," she added defensively, watching Alanna wipe the flour from her hands on the edge of her apron with an odd smile parting her lips. She frowned, wondering what was going through her head.

"How long did you say you had been here?" she asked.

"Nine years," Cinnamon hesitantly volunteered.

"After nine years, you have still not paid back your debt and you can honestly say that's not slavery? Really, Cinnamon," she said with a shake of her head, "you're a fool."

"I am not," Cinnamon argued, rounding the table to come to Alanna's side. "I paid off my debt years ago. I chose to remain. I like it here."

"You like it?" Alanna gasped. "You're not a fool. You're insane."

Cinnamon's chin dropped in surprise and hurt with the embittered words of her friend. "Go ahead and call me names. I don't care. But where would I go if I did leave?" she asked, the tears of injured pride glistening in her eyes. "I'm just like you. My parents died of fever on the ship coming here and now I have no one. Only Raven Oaks."

Alanna refrained from making a comment, knowing her friend spoke the truth. They had nowhere to go, and during the short time they had shared a cabin, they had never gone any further than the mill. They did not know the land that surrounded them or even if they could find a new home outside its boundaries. Alanna had not been granted an audience with its master or, in fact, even seen him. How many others were forced to live as she was? Condemned to a life they did not want because of a lie someone had told. Fighting back a tear, she realized that no matter how grave her situation, she was fortunate to have found a friend in Cinnamon Cockrin.

"Why not go home to England?" she asked, trying to soothe over her sharp, thoughtless words.

"To what? I have no family there. And besides," the bright-eyed girl sang in a sudden change of mood, "I've heard rumors."

27

Rumors? What rumors in this God-forsaken land could possibly make someone as happy as they had this poor unmindful creature? The only thing that could bring joy to Alanna's heart was the knowledge that Beau Remington was dying of an incurable disease and planned to free everyone. "All right, I'm listening," she concurred, certain the girl would not speak another word unless begged to do so. "What have you heard?"

"Do you really want to know?" Cinnamon smiled, taking Alanna's hands in hers.

Alanna laughed. "Of course, silly, or I wouldn't have asked."

"Well," she began, pulling her friend to the bed that they shared, "some of the other women have been talking. They said they heard that The Hawk was going to inspect the cabins soon."

"So?"

"Oh, don't you know what that means? He's decided to pick a new housemaid," she grinned with a lift to one brow.

"A new maid? Whatever are you getting at?"

Cinnamon sighed impatiently. "He always uses that excuse to look over the women who work for him. He isn't the type just to come to one of our cabins to ease his male needs. He conveniently brings her to him. Discreetly, of course. Isn't it grand?"

Alanna straightened and wrinkled her nose. "Not hardly."

Crushed by her disapproval, Cinnamon frowned, watching the dark-haired woman leave her side and return to her work at the table. Cinnamon couldn't understand why anyone, including Alanna, wouldn't want to be chosen as Master Remington's maid. She

28

certainly did. It meant living in comfort and luxury, and the price in return for it sparked Cinnamon's interest. Other than a few stolen kisses behind the mill, she had never been held in a man's arms, not the way she was sure Beau Remington would hold her. A thought struck her.

"Have you ever seen The Hawk, Alanna?" she asked, cocking her head to one side.

"Not really," Alanna replied, remembering her first night there and how she had really only heard his voice. "I'm sure I'd spit in his eye if I did," she admitted, punching the dough with a little more zeal.

"Then that explains it."

"Explains what?" Alanna asked, looking up with a frown.

"If you'd ever seen him, you'd be just as anxious as the rest of us."

"Just because a man is handsome is no reason to give yourself to him," Alanna said, wiping the sweat from her brow with the back of her wrist.

"Oh, but it is. In this case, anyway. There's so much to gain," Cinnamon exclaimed.

"A fat belly, I'm thinking."

"Maybe," Cinnamon hummed, leaving the bed to return to her spot at the door. "But what better hold would a woman have on a man than his child in her womb?"

"Cinnamon!" Alanna cried out, leaning her weight upon her hands, which were resting on the table top.

"Oh, I know I sound wretched," Cinnamon admitted, looking back at her. "But with me it would be different. I'd do for him as no other could. I'd make him fall in love with me."

"You're a fool. He'd tire of you as he has all the others

29

and you'd be back here with me a tainted woman that no other man would have. Stop this nonsense and pray his eyes never fall on you." Alanna went back to kneading the dough.

"Then bend your own knee in prayer, Alanna Bainbridge," Cinnamon chided, "for should his eyes fall on you, his choice will be a simple one."

Alanna's dark brown eyes widened in fear at the thought. "Surely this will not happen."

Cinnamon shrugged with an air of indifference. "Possibly. If you care to run the risk," she said.

"Then he shall never have the chance," Alanna declared.

"How will you stop it? Hide beneath our bed from morning light until the dark of evening?"

"No," Alanna smiled impishly, "a simpler way."

"What, pray tell?"

"I will leave this fair plantation and seek a ship sailing for England."

"You mean run away?" Cinnamon asked, her eyes growing into wide circles.

"The first chance I get."

"But Alanna," Cinnamon warned, the seriousness of her plight unfolding. "He'd come after you. He may not treat us as slaves but you owe him and he'll see you pay."

Alanna shook her head. "Not if he can't find me," she said.

"That's ridiculous. He knows every inch of this land. He'd track you down long before you reached the ocean."

"He doesn't even know I'm here. How could he miss me?" she asked, wiping the flour from her hands again before going to the hearth. Silently, she sprinkled tea leaves into a cup and poured steaming hot water over them. "I wish I had a little lemon. Tea always tastes better with lemon," she murmured before taking a sip. "Would you care for some?"

Cinnamon impatiently shook her head. "You know the man called Cain," she said, noticing how Alanna's lip curled with the mention of him. "And you know he keeps records. Once a week he and his ledger go to Master Remington. Just staying out of sight will not help. The Hawk already knows you're here. He just hasn't put your name to a face. Yet!"

Alanna studied the tea leaves in the bottom of her cup for a moment, a thoughtful frown darkening her eyes. "It would seem then," she replied devilishly, "that I must see that my name also disappears."

"Oh, Alanna," Cinnamon moaned, "Cain keeps that book with him night and day. Don't you think others have tried before you? Please, Alanna, forget this foolishness."

"No," Alanna said angrily, walking to the window of the cabin to stare outside. "I shall not be owned by anyone."

Cinnamon sighed, not bothering to argue. She had known Alanna long enough to realize that she was stubborn to a fault. Once she got an idea in her head, nothing would change it. "All right, have it your way. But don't tell me your plans. When your disappearance is discovered, they will certainly question me. And if I don't know anything, I can't do you any harm." Defeated, she shook her head and turned away to busy herself with washing dishes.

Nearly a week had passed since Cinnamon's announcement of the inspection, and the much dreaded appearance of The Hawk had not materialized, much to Alanna's relief. However, she noticed Cain every time she turned around; always watching and writing, writing and watching. If only she could get her hands on that book!

The sun shone brightly overhead as Alanna walked to the mill to replenish her supply of flour in the large pot she managed to balance on her hip. Even though she resented every moment of her imprisonment, for that was how she thought of it, she relaxed whenever she walked among the people of Raven Oaks. There were no people in chains, no beatings, no mass illnesses such as she had heard about happening on plantations where Negroes worked, and yet these people seemed to be content to live their lives under the rule of another, never free to go unless authorized to do so. She couldn't understand why. Surely, they must realize that this was a form of slavery.

Nearing the stone building bustling with workers, she spied a group of men standing outside and passed by unnoticed. They were too busy discussing the efficiency of its production to warrant a look in any direction other than that of the papers one man held in his hands. She breathed easier once she realized no one had noticed her, knowing that if her chance came, and she made good her escape, it would be to her advantage to have a face no one could recognize. Feeling as though she had won a small victory, she stepped lightly inside the mill doors.

The air hung heavy with moisture and she could feel the perspiration beading across her face, down her back and between her breasts as she scooped up heavy pails of fresh flour and poured them into the clay pot. Trails of sweat ran down her face, matting her long hair against her neck and brow, and she paused a moment to brush a stray tendril from her nose, thinking all the while how she would much prefer a cool swim in a pond. With her job completed, she straightened, wiped her face dry with her apron and hoisted the pot once again before heading to the door.

She could feel the muscles across her back tighten with the extra weight she had to carry, and she wondered if she would make it back to the cabin without dropping it. Awkwardly maneuvering the pot to one hip to free a hand with which to open the mill doors, she clumsily stepped outside into the bright sunlight. Before she could side-step him, one of the men in the group she had passed earlier suddenly turned around and collided with her, knocking the pot of flour from her hands. The piece of crockery crashed to the ground, shattering into a thousand pieces as a cloud of white billowed upward, covering both of them.

"You blithering idiot! Look what you've done," she exploded.

Her hair, arms and chest were covered, and, no matter how many times she tried to wipe it off herself, she failed, since the flour had turned to paste after having quickly absorbed the moisture from her skin. Never before had she been so furious. And the dandy standing in front of her now was to blame. She didn't know who he was and right then she didn't care. She doubled up a tiny fist, waited for him to look up, and then landed a blow to his mouth, instantly feeling as if she had broken every finger of her hand.

The unexpected assault sent him reeling backward and Alanna grinned triumphantly, seeing a small trickle of blood appear in the corner of his mouth. She flashed him a challenging glare, having soothed her own pain at noting his, and lifted her skirts to stomp off toward her cabin.

The men who witnessed the attack stood paralyzed in fear, watching the man stare after the rapidly disappearing woman. None of them said a word, each afraid of what he might do.

Finally, in a tone nearer a growl, he demanded, "Who is that woman?"

"I'm not sure, Master Remington," one of the men offered, stepping forward, "but I'll find out."

"Do that!" he stormed, shoving them aside and angrily heading for the big house on the hill.

Alone in her cabin, Alanna relaxed in the round wooden tub of cool, sudsy water, not caring what price she might pay for neglecting her duties should she be found out, wanting only to remove the flour that seemed to be stuck over every inch of her. With her freshly washed hair wrapped tightly in a towel, she climbed from the tub and got dressed. She felt a little better having cooled herself in the water and a smile returned to her lips as she brushed the dampness from her hair. Then Cinnamon came bursting into the room.

"Did you hear?" she asked breathlessly.

"Hear what?" Alanna laughed, amused by the girl's exuberance and knowing she always managed to make things appear more urgent than they really were.

"About what happened at the mill."

The smile disappeared from Alanna's face. "The

mill?" she asked, a feeling of doom starting to rise within her.

"Yes. A woman actually *hit* Master Remington!"

The blood drained from Alanna's face and she staggered to the bed. "Oh, no," she wailed.

"What's wrong? Are you ill?" Cinnamon asked, coming to her side.

Alanna numbly shook her head.

"Then what is it?"

"I had no idea who he was. Oh, why did I lose my temper? All this time I've been so careful to avoid him and I not only run into him, but I hit him. And I drew blood," she moaned, rising from the bed to pace the floor.

"You mean it was you?" Cinnamon cried, one hand pressed to her cheek. "What are you going to do?"

"I don't have much of a choice. I'm leaving." Vigorously, Alanna tore the thin blanket from their bed. "I'm sorry about this," she added, nodding to the coverlet in her hands, "but I'm going to need it more than you."

Cinnamon stood by helplessly watching Alanna pile an extra dress, several loaves of bread and dried beef in a gunny sack, a hairbrush, and a shawl into a neat stack before binding them all in the blanket. It made quite a bundle and proved awkward for her, but there wasn't a single item she felt she could do without. If only she had a few coins.

"Running away won't help, Alanna. He'll come after you. Only he'll have two reasons. Please don't go."

"I have to. He'll probably have me beaten if I don't," Alanna assured her. Nervously, she ripped a strip of cloth from her apron and bound her hair in back with it.

"But how will you leave here without someone seeing you?"

"Oh, I'll be seen. But no one will suspect anything," she smiled, tossing her bundle in a pot very much like the one that had brought about her downfall. "I'll simply appear to be on my way to the mill."

"And then what? No. Don't tell me. I don't want to know," Cinnamon muttered, turning away with her hands pressed against her ears.

One more time Alanna found herself lifting a heavy pot to her hip. When she reached the door, she turned back. "Good-bye, dear Cinnamon. I'll miss you."

The young girl returned a weary smile, went to the window and watched the deliberate gait of her friend crossing the yard, praying Alanna Bainbridge had made the right decision.

Three

Keeping the smile from her lips proved nearly impossible for Alanna once she reached the mill and realized how easy her escape would be. Very few workers roamed outside and she didn't recognize any of them, making her plan that much better since she appeared to be one of them. Each busy with his duties, no one looked her way, and she passed without notice, quietly rounding the corner of the mill and starting off through the field of corn behind it. Several times she glanced back over her shoulder to confirm the fact that no one followed. Feeling secure, she discarded the clay pot and ran, setting her goal on the cover of trees several hundred yards ahead.

The afternoon air, quiet and heavy with heat, closed in around her, forcing beads of perspiration to form on her brow and upper lip. Irritated, she wiped them away with the back of her hand, hoisting her bundle across her shoulder to lessen its bulk as she trudged along. Since she had no idea in which direction to walk, she decided to follow the road, guided by the sun at her back, close enough to see it but far enough away not to be discovered should someone happen to travel along it. Time and time again she switched her bundle from one shoulder to the other, finding its weight troublesome every time she climbed a hill or crossed a hollow filled with stones. She cursed it and yet never once entertained the thought of leaving it behind.

Looking back once again to calm her fears of pursual, she noticed the sky burned a vivid hue of orange, reminding her of the day's end and of a problem she would soon face. What sort of creatures roamed the night? Would she dare risk starting a fire for warmth, knowing its light would act as a beacon, guiding the way to her hiding place? She spotted an assemblage of rocks that formed its own kind of sheltered ledge, deciding it would have to do for the night, and had started toward it when thundering hoofbeats filled the air. She spun around, recognizing the stocky shape of the man closing in on her.

"Cain," she breathed.

With little thought to its importance, she dropped her bundle and ran as fast and as hard as she could. In and out between the willow trees she ran, dodging first left then right, hoping to keep them between her and Cain. How long could she possibly keep it up? Her legs were already tiring and the pain in her side was unbearable. Then, before she knew what had happened, she felt the biting sting of the bullwhip tightening around her knees. She went crashing to the ground.

"You didn't really think you could escape, did you?" Cain asked, looking down at her. "It was foolish of you to try. I thought you knew that."

"I won't go back," she screamed.

38

"Oh, but you will. Either riding up here in front of me or walking at the end of a rope. The choice is yours," he grinned sarcastically, watching Alanna unwind the black leather whip from her legs and struggle to her feet. "You're an awfully tiny woman to be treated roughly, but one way or another you will return."

"I should never have been made to stay in the first place. Had you given me the chance to explain at the ship, I could have saved us both a lot of grief," she snapped.

"Have you any idea how many times I've heard what a mistake I've made?" he sighed impatiently. "Now, are you walking or shall I help you up?"

"I'll ride, only if you promise I may talk with Master Remington."

"Oh, you'll talk with him all right. But only to hear the punishment he finds suitable for a runaway."

The hair on the back of her neck rose, imagining the cruel sting of the whip tearing into her flesh. Surely Beau Remington wouldn't close his ears to her pleas. Or would he? Deciding she could not afford the risk, she turned and began to run again. The crack of the whip exploded in the quiet calm of late afternoon as it whistled through the air and burned the flesh of her arm, once more pulling her to the ground.

The gray light of dusk guided their way across the field and onto the road leading to the main house, surprising Alanna once she realized what a short time it took for their return. Then it came to her. All the while she had thought she walked due east, she had, in fact, followed the lay of the road, wandering about the rolling countryside, costing her precious time.

Word of Alanna's arrival spread quickly. As the foreboding house on the hill came into view, so did many of the people living on the plantation. She eyed them tearfully, wishing they would not watch the degrading fashion in which she was returning for Cain had tightly bound her hands with one end of the rope, the other held securely in his own. He paid little attention to her and many times along the way she stumbled and fell. But determined to keep what dignity she had left, she refused to call out, being dragged in the dirt, the rocks tearing into her hands and knees, and it was the sudden pull on the rope in Cain's hand that forced him to look at her. He stopped only long enough for her to stagger to her feet again.

The crowd, lined up on either side of the pair making their way forward, buzzed in expectation of the sentence the young woman would receive. A few placed wagers on the shed, others on the whip, while some were certain she would be sold. Beau Remington would not tolerate her defiance. For the most part, they found it a game, calling out jeers whenever she fell and cheering the man who held her rope. Those who disagreed with the more brazen and heartless ones shrank back within the group, unable to watch and thankful they were not in her place. Cinnamon was one of them, quietly sobbing and unable to do anything to help her friend.

Alanna's own fears manifested when the large white-pillared house appeared before her, knowing that somewhere within stood the man to whom she would answer for her open and foolish rebellion. Her mind reeled with sordid punishments: chains, a beating, solitude in a dark, rat-infested root cellar, or worse, death. She closed her eyes, listening to the rocks crush beneath her step, and wondered if this man was capable of putting someone to death for merely wanting to go home. Her lip trembled.

Cain tied his horse to a hitching rail at the foot of the veranda steps before removing the rope from her hands. With a nod over his shoulder toward the house, he silently instructed her to come with him, but she fell back, too afraid to move. He took a step toward her. She could feel her heart pounding, her body quaking, but knowing everyone watched, she courageously consented, denying them a chance to amuse themselves further. With her shoulders squared, her chin held high, and forcing down the fear that threatened to overrule her, she bravely ascended the stairs as Cain opened the front door of Raven Oaks. It was as if the gates of hell were beckoning her to enter.

Her fears momentarily forgotten, Alanna paused inside the door staring at the magnificent crystal chandelier hanging overhead. Thousands of minute teardrops adorned every inch, reflecting the light from the candles brightly about the room in tiny spotlights of blues, greens, and reds. At her feet lay a marble floor mirroring its rich elegance in the soft lights of the candles, spreading out in all directions to stop abruptly at the base of a long winding staircase. It circled high above her to a long balcony, its walls covered with richly framed oil paintings. Against one wall stood a small, delicately carved table, a mirror framed in gold hanging above it. Alanna stood in awe at the sight, suddenly aware of her own worth when she realized everything she owned was on her back. Absently, she touched a hand against her soiled and torn skirts.

A young black maid in a black gown and white apron

suddenly appeared. She took the hat that Cain had removed and, with a polite curtsy, informed them that Master Remington was in his study. Alanna waited in the hall while her companion went inside, knowing the only things that kept her from fleeing were the fear that had frozen her feet to the floor and the fact that Cain returned almost immediately.

"Come," he said quietly with a nod of his head toward the study. She mutely obeyed.

Shelf after shelf of books and maps and other paraphernalia essential in managing a great plantation lined the massive room. Opposite the door, a many-paned window overlooked the mill and most of the cabins. Before it sat a huge mahogany desk, nearly the color of a darkened sky before a storm. Alanna's mouth hung open. She had never seen anything quite so exquisite. Then her gaze traveled across its surface and up. Staring back at her was a pair of deep, dark, unreadable eyes, those eyes of which she had heard two men speak many weeks ago. She quickly snapped her mouth closed again and braced herself for what was to come.

He sat forward in the leather chair, one arm stretched out across the desk while the other crossed in front of him on the edge to support his upper torso. He studied her for quite a while until at last he leaned back and crossed an ankle to his knee. Still he remained silent, looking her up and down, and Alanna began to squirm under his piercing glare, the reason for Cinnamon's eagerness to join the staff at the main house becoming apparent. He was indeed handsome, with dark brows that arched softly above his hooded eyes, a thin, straight nose, and a firm set to his jaw. He frowned, and his nostrils flared just the slightest bit, holding his anger in tether.

Then, much to her relief, his gaze fell away from her, to the man at her side. "Leave us," he snapped, and no other sound than that of a slowly closing door was heard. Nervously, Alanna looked back to see if Cain had really left her alone with this man. For some reason, she felt a little safer with someone else at her side, even though he was not a friend.

"What did you hope to prove by running?" he quietly asked of her.

She turned back, deciding he obviously had no idea where she had intended to go. Hiding her smile, she vowed never to tell him. If her chance should come again, she would take it and not spoil it by having given a hint which way to look. She swallowed hard and refused to answer.

"Come now, surely you have a tongue," he said, the muscle of his jaw flexing with each word. "I have yet to meet a woman who didn't."

Alanna only stared, holding fast to her secret.

Irritated, he rested his foot upon the floor again, deliberately smoothing the wrinkles from the knee of his breeches before taking a slow, calming breath to continue again. "I see you have quite a bit to learn, young woman," he promised. "Do you know what indentured means?" He glanced up at her, found her staring back in defiance, and resigned himself to leaning forward against the desk again, his fingers interlocked beneath his chin while his elbows rested on the surface. "It means a contract has been met between two parties. Your passage here was paid for by me and in return you are to work for me for a period of five years. After that ti—"

"My father paid for my passage," Alanna stormed, cutting him off. "The man at the docks lied. My father sold everything we had to pay for it."

The Hawk considered her a moment in silence, knowing there was no sense in trying to convince her without proof. Pulling open the top drawer of his desk, he withdrew a paper, unfolded it, and then set his gaze upon her once more. "This document is signed by your father and dated over one year ago. If you will read—I assume you can—" he paused, waiting for her to acknowledge the skill before continuing, "you will see it is a contract legal and binding."

Alanna glared at him a moment thinking how much she'd like to dispute his honesty, and then realized it was her only chance to prove the misdeed against her. Cautiously, she stepped forward, keeping the desk between them, and took the paper he offered.

The undersigned has met and agreed upon a contract with one Beau Remington of Raven Oaks, Williamsburg, Virginia. In exchange for one passage on board an English ship bound for Virginia, he will in turn indenture the services of his daughter, Alanna Bainbridge, for a period of five years, to Mister Remington, that time to be serviced upon her arrival to Raven Oaks.

William Bainbridge

Alanna's eyes burned with unshed tears. The signature at the bottom of the page was unmistakably her father's. How could he have done this to her? Why hadn't he told her? What had he planned? She swallowed the lump in her throat, knowing it was something she would never learn.

"This makes no difference," she informed him. "This

agreement was made without my consent, and you shall not hold me to it."

"I shall and I will," he assured her, leaning forward on the desk. "If I have to keep you in chains to do it. You will not defy me in front of all the others. It would create trouble for me."

"Do you think I care what happens to you? I wish you were dead. Then I would truly be free," she snapped.

Beau fell back against the chair exhausted. With all the other problems he had, why must he be saddled with this slip of a girl? And now what was he to do? Keep his word and put her in chains? He pressed a thumb to his brow. If Cain had kept a better eye on her, he wouldn't have this problem. Well, something had to be done, and he had better make up his mind soon. He closed his eyes, trying desperately to think of a solution, and when he looked up again, a reflected flash of light hit his face. There before him stood a young woman half his size with a knife held challengingly in her hand. He looked directly to the desk top where he discovered the empty scabbard that had held his pearl-handled knife.

"Don't try to stop me," she warned. "I wouldn't hesitate to use it."

Beau couldn't stop the chuckle that escaped him. Did she really think a knife would scare him? Annoyed, he rose to his feet.

"I—I mean it," she stuttered, taking a step backward as he circled the desk.

"Give it to me before someone gets hurt."

"No," she half-screamed, taking a swing at him.

Beau merely retreated a step to avoid the edge of the blade when it threatened to sever the buttons from his coat. He waited a moment longer until she drew back to try again. When she lashed out the second time, he grabbed her wrist with one hand and a fistful of black mane with the other. Never before had he felt such a mass of thick, silken hair, and for a moment he forgot the reason he held her, wondering why he had never noticed her before the incident at the mill. He relaxed slightly, contemplating an answer to his problem that he found rather pleasing, since it had been his purpose for being there in the first place that morning. The possibility, however, was quickly abolished when the young woman seized her chance to break away.

She spun around to face him, the knife clutched in one hand, and began inching her way backward toward the door. With each step she took, he followed.

"Get away. I'll use this if you force me."

Beau tilted his head to one side and smiled.

She fumbled behind her for the latch, praying she could open it and run from him before he had a chance to grab her again. Free of the confines of the house, she was certain she could get away. But when her hand struck the knob, she carelessly glanced toward it, and, before she knew what had happened, he hit the knife from her hand. Stunned, she looked up to find a pair of deep brown eyes staring into hers, a hand on either side of her shoulders, pinning her against the door.

"Don't ever pull a knife on me again," he warned. "Next time I won't be so gentle."

"Then kill me now. I'll never give in."

"Kill you?" he questioned in honest surprise. "Do you really think I would kill you? You're only a woman. And a small one at that."

"I may be small, Mr. Remington, but you had better never turn your back on me," she spat.

46

"Oh?" he smiled, amused by her courage. "And just what might you do if I should?"

Alanna doubled up her fist and landed a blow to his rib cage, knocking the wind from him. He straightened, dropping his hold on her, and she instantly fled the room, hearing his hurried footsteps behind her. Reaching the front door only a few steps ahead of him, she awkwardly tried to open it, failing in her attempt when a hand came from behind her and slammed it shut again. Quickly, she backed away, Beau shadowing her every step.

It was impossible to keep an eye on him and where she was going at the same time, and she backed into a small table at the foot of the stairs and knocked over a vase. A quick hand kept it from falling, but she suddenly decided it wasn't worth saving. Hopefully, she hurled it at him, spun around and raced up the long staircase, hearing it shatter as it hit the wall and knowing that The Hawk had escaped unharmed. His muttered words had tones of anger, and she wasn't sure if it was the loss of the vase that disturbed him or the fact that she had tried to hit him with it. Whatever reason, she didn't care and she wasn't about to ask.

She had just reached the top of the stairs believing that in a few seconds she would be able to lock herself safely within one of the bedrooms when she felt his arms reach around her knees and pull her to the floor with him. She couldn't suppress her frightened scream as he pressed his full weight upon her, and she would have screamed again if his hand hadn't securely covered her mouth.

"Enough!" he roared.

He was on his feet in a second, dragging her with him, his fingers cutting into her wrist, and she had no other choice but to go with him as he stormed down the

47

hallway. When they reached a door at the far end, he threw it open, whirled her inside, and then slammed it closed behind her. The sound of the lock turning brought tears to her eyes.

"Please, Master Remington, all I want is to go home," she called, listening to the thudding of his footsteps fading as he left the hallway and went downstairs. She sank to her knees. "Oh, Papa. Why did you do this to me? I loved you. I thought you knew that. I thought you loved me." With the burden of all that had happened closing in on her, Alanna wept in the darkness of the room.

Four

Beau stalked back to his study rubbing his rib cage where the girl had struck him. "The little harlot," he growled between his teeth. "How dare she lift a hand against me!"

He went to his desk and poured a glass of wine, downing it all without a breath. It relaxed him a little, but still he poured another before settling in his chair. As he reached for a cheroot from the box on his desk, his eyes caught sight of the document he had given the servant. Slowly, he picked it up to read again, thinking of the first time he had seen the handwriting of William Bainbridge in a letter the man had written explaining his need for enough money to buy his daughter's passage on the English ship. Most of the sum he had received for the sale of his belongings had gone to pay back the debts he owed and had left him with barely enough to pay his and his wife's way to America, and he would not go without his daughter. A friend had given him Beau's name and explained how the child could work off the loan within a few years and then join her family. He had written to verify the fact and ask for the loan as soon as an

49

agreement was made. He hadn't liked the length of time it would take his daughter to repay the loan, but, finding no other solution, he had agreed. None of this, of course, was revealed in the paper Beau held in his hand, and he suddenly realized how awful the situation must appear to the young girl locked away upstairs. Especially if what Cain had told him was true and her father was dead.

That's not my concern, he thought, frowning, swallowing his glassful of wine and pouring another. I could spend the entire day playing nanny to these people if that was the case. The lines in his brow grew deeper, realizing that even if he tried to explain to the girl that her father had meant well, she wouldn't accept it. All she wanted was to be free.

He left his desk and strolled to the hearth, there to rest a foot against its marble base while he swirled the wine in his glass. He'd had trouble with servants before, but usually Cain had straightened them out. This one was different and gut feeling warned him that even Cain would have no affect on her. Maybe he should try to reason with her. Maybe if he explained the events leading up to the signed document, she would understand. He'd tell her that once she worked off the debt she could continue on as a paid servant and save the amount to return home if she wanted.

"Ah, hell, why should I tell her anything?" he snarled and returned to his desk and his wine. Let Cain deal with her. He downed another drink and leaned back in his chair to puff on his cigar.

Total blackness greeted him as he stared out the window, and the more he concentrated on it, the more its richness reminded him of the girl upstairs. Her hair was nearly the same color, highlighted with rays of gold as it glistened in the candlelight. He shook his head. He'd had too much to drink. Jamming the stub of his cigar in the ashtray on his desk, he rose and headed for his room.

A quiet stillness surrounded him as he listened to the sounds of his footsteps climbing the stairs, thinking of the last time he had done it. When he reached the top, he paused, staring at the locked door. The hall clock struck midnight and he waited until the last chord had died away before he took another step. Then he heard a strange sound coming from inside the room that held the young woman. Fumbling in the muted light of the hallway, his hand found the candle sitting on the small table beside him and he reached up to touch it to the flame of the sconce hanging on the wall. He unlocked the door.

Light spilled into the room and he immediately saw the open window. He frowned. Surely she hadn't jumped. Placing the candle on the dressing table, he started toward the window. But before he reached it, a noise behind him brought him around in time to see a small form lift a porcelain water pitcher high above her head, ready to strike.

"You crazy wench. Put that down—" he commanded hotly, his knotted brow smoothed in surprise when she threw her weapon at him.

He easily sidestepped the attack, hearing his beautiful water pitcher crash to the floor. His ire grew. He stepped in, intent on teaching her the lesson so foolish an act demanded, when she suddenly kicked out, planting her instep against his shin. He howled in pain, his dark eyes mirroring shock. No one had ever dared to strike him before. And she had done so three times now. He was master here and she would learn that fact in no uncertain terms. He straightened, lowered his head and drew a breath to voice his disapproval. But before a single word passed his lips, he witnessed the damning glare she presented him before she spun around to flee the room. With lightning speed he spoiled her departure by an unrelenting grip to her wrist.

"I don't know where in God's creation you think you're going, but you'll not leave this room." The heel of his boot kicked the door shut with a loud, thundering bang. His fingers bruised the flesh of her arm as he towered over her, a fleeting moment of admiration dashing through his mind when she seemed unaffected by his size or strength. But it pricked his ego all the more. "I'm going to tell you something and I want you to listen—" he began, confused by the faint smile parting her lips.

His chin sagged as he watched her double up a fist. Before he could react, she landed a blow to his stomach. His breath left him in a painful *whoof*. He released her to clutch his belly, thinking to declare surrender and suggest a truce for a moment to state the terms a compromise required, when all of a sudden she lashed out again, stomping her heel to his toes, rendering such words pointless. In an effort to defend himself against the onslaught, he raised his arms to shield himself, trapped between the wildcat and the door at his back, leaving him little space to escape.

"Stop it! Stop! Do you hear?" he half-demanded, half-begged, wincing when a fist found his ear, another threatening to blacken his eye. He must halt the barrage of right and left hooks before one found its target and left its mark for all to see. He raised up suddenly, striking the back of his hand to her cheek, and sent her tumbling to the floor. Maybe now she would hear him out.

His patience to see a quiet termination to their battle worn thin, he sighed heavily and extended a hand to help her to her feet, startled by the slap she presented his knuckles. He stood in muted awe, watching her scramble up and race past him toward the door. Determined to be the victor, he shook off his bewilderment and caught her elbow in a steely hold long before she reached her destination and twirled her back to the center of the room.

"Now listen to me, young woman—"

"May someone strike you dead in the road and leave the buzzards to pick your bones clean," she hissed, crouched as if to launch a second assault.

Oddly, he found her declaration amusing, that such a small woman could nurture a hatred twice her size. He reached up to rub the tired muscles of his neck. "Are you going to listen to me—"

"No!" she barked.

His shoulders drooped resignedly. "All right, have it your way. Until you agree to behave in a civil manner, you'll remain in this room. It matters little to me. But one way or another, you'll break. I'll see to that." He turned, his hand on the latch of the door.

"Never!" he heard her declare loudly, only an instant before the washbowl crashed against the wall near his shoulder, rifling tiny fragments of porcelain against his face and arm. The late hour, his consumption of wine and pressing business matters, mixed with the tirade of a woman half his size, drained his reserve, leaving his fiery temper ruling him. He spun around.

"I ought to beat this rebellious nature from you. Apparently your father never did."

He stepped in, determined to see his promise carried

through, not the least affected by the clenched fist raised to hit him. He quickly seized her wrist in a firm yet painless grip, the attack igniting his wrath, and before she could scratch his face with the nails of her other hand, he claimed it too. His clutch tightened, biting into the flesh of her arms.

"Must I hurt you?" he ground out through clenched teeth.

With the shake of her head and the appearance of tears lining her eyes, he lessened his hold, discovering too late the error of his move, for in a fleeting instant, she brought up her knee, determined to free herself.

"You little hellcat," he roared, hurling her to the bed and rubbing the thigh that had deflected her blow. She scrambled to her knees ready to flee, stopping abruptly when he pointed a warning finger at her. "Don't move or so help me God, I'll forget you're a woman."

His mind raced with thoughts of how to control her, knowing that given half a chance she would run again. Yet if he left her locked away in this room, she would see to its total destruction. He also realized what little value she would be bound and gagged. After all, he had spent good money to bring her here and expected something in return. His heated glare fell upon the tiny form staring back at him. Though dirt smudged her cheeks and the tip of her nose, the deep brown eyes trimmed with black lashes sparked a strange stirring in him. He appraised the flowing ebony mane cascading in disarray over her shoulders to shimmer in contrast with the smooth white flesh of her bosom heaving with each angry breath she drew. Such a tiny shape, smaller than any woman he had known before. He found himself wondering what it would be like to sample the beauty hidden beneath the tattered gown she wore. And why not? After all, she was his property. His pulse quickened with the thought. It just might be the thing he needed to subdue this vixen. His fingers quickly found the buttons of his waistcoat and popped them loose.

"W—what are you doing?" Alanna asked, her fear choking off the words.

He smiled evilly. "It's quite obvious, don't you think? You belong to me and I intend to sample what I bought." He slid the jacket from his shoulders and carelessly tossed it to the floor. "I will break your spirit, to have you obey. I see no other way." The silk shirt found its place beside the waistcoat.

Alanna scurried to the far side of the bed when he moved to sit down next to her to remove his shoes and stockings.

"You—can't—" she sobbed.

He stood, his fingers reaching for the buttons of his breeches. "Oh? And why not? I own you. For the next five years. You'll do whatever I tell you."

Panic ruling, Alanna slid off the bed and raced for the door, stopped short by the painful entrapment of her long, thick hair in his fingers. Pulling her back against his chest, his strong arms encircling her in a none too gentle fashion, he all but lifted her from the floor. Fear gripping her, she screamed, kicking wildly, her efforts spoiled by the numerous folds of her skirts entangled about her legs. He slid an arm beneath her knees, lifting her, and carried her to the bed.

"No!" she screamed when he threw her upon it. "Dear God, you can't!" She pushed herself up.

"If this is what it takes to tame you and bend you to my will, I must and I shall," he hissed, unfastening

55

his breeches.

"Oh, God, please," she cried. "I've never known a man before."

Laughter rumbled in his chest. "You think me a fool?" he asked softly, his mirth vanishing. "A beauty such as you could not have come this far untouched. You play the game well but I will not be tricked by you." He slid the breeches from his hips.

The yellow glow of candlelight flickered over his muscular frame and Alanna stared in horror at her first sight of a naked man. Her body trembled as she sat transfixed in the center of the wide bed until he moved to join her. She began inching her way back across the bed wanting desperately to keep her distance, but he swiftly reached out to capture her wrist. She squeezed her eyes shut, praying it was all a bad dream and once she opened them again he would be gone.

"Now you will learn what it truly means to be my servant. Remove the gown."

Her eyes flew open to stare in shocked disbelief.

He raised a brow. "The choice is yours. Save the gown for later use or have it torn from you," he replied smoothly.

"You—you expect me to submit?" she choked, bringing a smile to his lips.

"In truth? No." He pulled her closer. "Not at first. But in time—" he added, his voice husky.

His lust burned brightly in his dark eyes and Alanna knew her battle drew near an end, for her foe had proved more cunning and stronger, and a show of physical contest would award her nothing. But to passively allow him to take what was hers alone to give left a bitter taste in her mouth. She courageously sucked in a breath to plead her case.

"What must I do to sway your intentions? A promise of loyalty and silence?"

Beau laughed. "Make not so foolish a vow, young woman, for it is one you would find difficult to keep."

"I am not one to go back against my word, Master Remington. You know me not well enough to assume such."

"The truth be spoken," he agreed. "But you forget. You were brought to me because you ran away, you broke a rule, and I am the one to sentence you." He reached up to touch a strand of dark hair. "This is the punishment I have chosen. It speaks none too highly of my charms, but since you obviously would have it another way, it shall be a torture for you, not a pleasure. Now, will you disrobe or shall I help you?"

Alanna blinked several times trying to keep the tears from streaming down her cheeks. "Please, sir. You cannot do this," she wept.

"But I shall," he whispered, slipping his hand behind her head, eager to sample the sweetness of her kiss.

Filled with terror, Alanna fought to push him away, his strong embrace pulling her to her knees to crush her to his chest as his lips found hers, the masculine scent of him, his nearness, his nakedness threatening to rob her of her sanity. A warm and tender kiss. Alanna's mind whirled with the wave of a new sensation washing over her, then was suddenly repulsed when his tongue parted her lips and darted inside. She fought with renewed strength, twisting her head away from his demanding passion only to have him nibble at her earlobe, the slim white column of her neck, her throat, while his fingers agilely unfastened the buttons of her gown. The garment

57

fell from her shoulders, bringing a whimper from the young girl, a moan of desire from her captor, his kisses lightly trailing over her flesh. She pushed at him again, a shiver running through her when her fingers pressed against the hard muscles of his chest and dark mass of curls covering them. Her gentle nature demanded an end to so intimate an act, but she knew the plea, if voiced, would fall on deaf ears.

His ardor grew and with practiced hands he slid the dress down over her hips, enveloping her in his embrace once more to bring them down to the softness of the featherbed. She shrieked, feeling his manly boldness throbbing against her thigh when he rolled her beneath him, pinning her arms between them as he reached to toss the gown away. Again he covered her, his hands exploring the curves of her body, as a choked sob trailed from Alanna's lips. He did not hear. Instead he claimed the strings of her camisole, pulling them free. Before she could deter his course of defilement, he stripped away the garment, and a scream of protest tore from her throat. She reached out to rake her nails across his face, her wrist caught in a grip of steel only inches from her goal. In the muted glow of candlelight she saw him smile, his lust and passion intensifying the ebony depths of his eyes as he twisted her arm above her head, her other trapped beneath him when he slid to one side to view her beauty and explore the vision at his leisure. Slowly, he lowered his head to capture a full, round breast, his tongue teasing its peak while his free hand traced the slim outline of her waist, her hip, her thigh. She wiggled then stiffened when the caress of his kiss moved lower, to the smooth silkiness of her stomach. Certain no words, no pleas of any kind would stop the abuse, the humiliation of his deed, she vowed his victory would not come easily. A throaty growl exploded from her as she thought to bring up a knee to his chest to knock the breath from him. As though sensing her plan, and with little effort, his free hand caught her thigh, pushing her back as he raised himself above her.

"You would fight me to the end, wouldn't you?" he asked, a light smile softening his features.

"I only wish it were yours," she hissed.

His amusement faded slowly, a lusty gleam mirrored in his eyes. "Not a chance," he whispered.

His mouth came down hard on hers, bruising her lips, the entire length of him touching intimately against her. The muscles of her throat constricted, her tears choking her. Her flesh burned with the contact and the male hardness of him pressed to her thigh made her shudder. Then, in a new wave of terror, his knee forcibly parted hers. His hands moved to her hips, pulling them up to meet him. Innocent of his ways, she failed to react, her strength to fight gone, her will to have it end quickly making her accept her fate. He moaned as if in agony and she fleetingly wondered why until he thrust his manhood deeply inside her. She screamed, her body withering, pain bolting through every inch of her, certain he had torn her apart. Consumed by her own torture, Alanna only briefly felt him withdraw and his body tense before he seemed filled with the desire to hurt her again and again and again. He moved faster, deeper, until at last he called her name in muffled passion and fell quiet, his body wet with perspiration. A moment passed before he moved away.

Beau knew, once it was too late, that the young and innocent beauty had spoken the truth. He was the first.

59

As he lay at her side, his passion spent, listening to her mournful weeping against the pillow, he grew angry. How dare she act as if he hadn't the right to do with her whatever he wished? *He* was master of Raven Oaks and the sooner she accepted her plight, the better off she'd be. Unable to listen to her cry any longer, he rose, dressed, and left the room.

Five

Standing by the door of the bedchamber, Alanna listened for his footsteps, hearing only the ticking of the hall clock filter in, and the muffled sobs she fought to control. She had no idea where he had gone, but prayed he would not return, not until she had time to think, time to decide what she would do. With both hands pressed against the closed door, she leaned in, placing her brow to its coolness, her limbs trembling and pain surging through her veins. He had hurt her, violated her, degraded her, and she knew she would not stay in his house a moment longer, fearing he would use her time and time again. How could Cinnamon feel anything or him other than hate? Cinnamon! Yes, Cinnamon would help her. Spinning around, she retrieved her gown from the floor where it had fallen, shimmied into it, and froze when her gaze fell upon the disorder of the bed, burning memories of a lustful interlude surfacing sharply. She squeezed her eyes closed, blocking out the vision, and fought the knot that formed in her stomach, and quickly rose to her throat. She wouldn't be sick. She wouldn't! She would never let him have that victory. Straightening courageously, she took a deep breath, turned, and moved to the door.

The light of the sconce overhead flickered encouragingly against the stairs, flowing down them in a defused orange glow that spilled out onto the floor and met with the light coming from the study. Slowly, taking one step at a time, she listened to the rustling of papers and tinkling of glass as someone poured a drink. The blood pounded against her temples and she held her breath, certain it would be heard even in a whisper. She paused, closing her eyes and praying God would help her. The last tread moaned with her weight upon it, its eery squeal mushrooming in the stillness and filling her with panic, positive he had heard. She listened, hearing the thud of a book snapping closed, her quaking body startled by the sound, and smelling the odor of a cheroot drifting out across the hallway. Bravely, she took another step.

A few feet from her goal, she followed the stream of light coming from his study with her eyes, seeing it flow across the floor and spread about the threshold of her exit, knowing all he had to do was glance up to discover her escape. Oh, please, she begged, let him be too drunk to notice.

The latch clicked as it moved in her hand, but, knowing she had been extremely fortunate so far, she was driven beyond all caution as she pulled the door wide open and ran outside, not bothering to close it nor looking back as she raced toward the cabin and Cinnamon. She never once gave thought to the fact that Cain might be somewhere outside. She simply flew across the yard, down the path and along the road that led to the cabin that held her only hope for survival.

Darting across the weathered planks of the wooden porch outside Cinnamon's cabin, she bolted through the door and fell to her knees, too breathless to call out to her friend. Her tears renewed, she rocked back and forth, summoning from her reserve the strength to calm herself.

In the shadowed darkness, she heard Cinnamon call out her name before touching a flame to the candle sitting on the small bedside table, flooding the room with a golden light and revealing the agony the delicate figure endured.

"My God, Alanna, are you all right?" Cinnamon set the wooden candle-holder on the floor beside her and knelt before Alanna. Gently reaching out, she took Alanna's wrists and slowly pulled her hands away from her face. "Alanna, what's happened?"

"I must—get away," she sobbed.

Briskly, Cinnamon examined Alanna's face, arms and gown, not finding any obvious damage. "Why must you leave?" she pressed.

Alanna's small frame trembled. "I can't stay—in his house. He—"

"Who? Master Remington?"

Alanna hid her face again, nodding.

"What did he do?"

The back of her hand pressed against her lips, tears streaming down her red and swollen face, Alanna begged, "Please don't make me say it."

Cinnamon stiffened in rage. "Why that despicable son of a trollop," she hissed. "You mean he—" Staggering to her feet, Cinnamon stumbled to the window, grabbing for its frame to support her, a knot rising in her throat. She swallowed hard. "Why? Dear God, why?"

Cinnamon Cockrin had been only twelve years old the day she arrived on Raven Oaks. She remembered the incident as well as if it had been yesterday. Her parents had died of fever shortly before the ship docked in the port of Williamsburg, leaving her alone and very frightened. Cain and Jeremiah had met the ship, and upon learning of her heartache, Joshua Cain had taken special care of the child, allowing her to ride in the wagon seat next to him all the way to the plantation. When they reached the yard in front of the main house, he had told her to stay where she was until he returned, sliding off the wagon and disappearing into the house. He had reappeared a few minutes later, Beau Remington at his side, and the two men had talked comfortingly to her for nearly half an hour, assuring her that no harm would ever come to her. And none ever had. In the nine years she lived at Raven Oaks, she had never once been abused or mistreated. She had loved Beau Remington from the very first moment he smiled down on her, vowing her loyalty to him until the day she died. Now this.

"What can I do?" she asked quietly.

"You must hide me. Please, don't let him take me back. I'm afraid."

Cinnamon ran a fingertip across the sill of the window in thought. There must have been a strong reason for him to do what he had. She couldn't be that wrong about him. She looked back to Alanna. "There's a cave near the edge of the tobacco field. You can hide there until I can think of something else."

"Oh, thank you. I'll be eternally grateful." A vague smile flitted across her features, accompanying a quivering chin and new rush of tears. Then she noticed the girl stiffen suddenly. "What is it?" she choked.

Without answering, Cinnamon looked outside. "Dear God, they're coming. Run, Alanna, run!"

"But what of you? He'll know you tried to help me." Her voice came in ragged heaves as she scrambled to her feet.

"Don't worry about me. Just go!"

Alanna barely had time to flee the cabin before the men spotted her, shouting commands for her to stop. Ignoring their calls of protest, she raced off down the road, running with all the strength she had left. The drumming of their footsteps echoed in her ears and she knew it would not be long before they would overtake her. Frightened, she glanced back over her shoulder in time to see Cain lift his long black bullwhip high over his head, snap it down and send it whizzing toward her. She screamed for only a second before its long leather finger wrapped around her waist and dragged her to the ground. She lay there, weeping, until someone reached down and took her by the hair.

"Get up," The Hawk growled, pulling her to her feet.

Alanna's tear-filled eyes stared into his.

"It is through my carelessness that you find yourself here now. But it is through your stupidity that you shall come to know the punishment for running away." He turned to Cain. "Bind her hands and bring her to the yard. Jeremiah, ring the alarm. I want everyone present."

Hardly aware of the leather strip Cain tied about her wrists, Alanna tearfully watched the tall, dark figure stalk away, knowing that nothing or no one could help her now.

Joshua led her to a tree in the yard outside the mill. How ironic to be punished in the same spot where she first encountered the man who had ordered her here. Thinking of him again, she scanned the rapidly growing crowd for his presence as Cain tied a rope to the strap and then threw it over the branch of the tree, pulling her arms high above her. Satisfied that he had done an adequate job, he stepped back to wait.

Dangling on the end of the rope, Alanna twisted around to see why the buzzing of the crowd had stilled. Standing before them, she saw the towering muscular shape of their master, his arms folded across his chest, his feet spread apart and his chin held high in the air.

"Strip her," the dark shadow commanded and Alanna felt Cain's hands grab the back of her gown.

The cold night air touched her bare skin and she could not choke back the small cry of fear that tore at her throat or the shiver that raced through her, imagining the feel of the leather searing into her flesh. She closed her eyes, hoping it had all been a bad dream and when she opened them again she would be back home in England.

"The punishment you are about to witness is done because a rule has been broken," The Hawk thundered. "Remember what you see here tonight. No one disobeys my laws." He nodded toward Cain and waited until he had come to his side. With one last glance toward the girl bound to the tree, he signaled his overseer to begin and stepped away to stare into the darkness.

The long black snake whistled in the air, cutting its way to its victim, lashing against the white, unmarred flesh of her back. She cried out in pain as still another blow landed, and another, until she hung limp at the end of the rope that held her.

Dressed in their nightclothes or with breeches pulled hastily over them, the servants of Raven Oaks watched in silent revelation, never having suspected that such a punishment would ever be dealt, especially on one so small and fragile. Many of them hung their heads, regretting their games of a few hours past when they had taunted and teased the young woman dragged back to the plantation at the end of a rope. Now they could no longer forced themselves to watch the merciless beating of another, and they turned their faces to their master, with a silent plea for it to stop, and noted how he gazed out across the fields, a hard, stern expression on his face and not a single muscle of his body moving.

Then the horrible crack of the whip fell quiet as Cain turned to him. "Mr. Remington?"

The dark, motionless form appeared to relax with the summons, his arms falling to his sides as he turned to view the girl, knowing her to be unconscious by the way her knees buckled under her, her head drooping to one side.

"Cut her down and take her to her cabin."

"Yes, sir," Cain replied, his own stocky frame relaxing as he watched Beau march away. He motioned for Jeremiah's help and together they went to the limp form hanging from the tree to do as they had been ordered.

Jeremiah fumbled with the rope tightly bound to the tree, his dark, waxy brows knotting. He paused to examine the girl. "Masta Cain?"

"What?"

"Masta Cain, how many times you swing that whip?"

Cain grunted, lifting the unconscious body to ease the tension on the rope. "What difference does it make? It did the job."

"I held up a finger each time. I's more fingers than marks this here girl got on her back."

67

Cain looked sharply at his companion, glanced back over his shoulder to see if they were alone and then muttered, "Help me get her down."

"You miss, Masta Cain?"

He glared at the black man. "No!"

"Well, I's sure I didn't hold up too many fingers," Jeremiah said more to himself as he untwisted the knot of rope. "Musta missed."

"I'm telling you I didn't," Cain barked. "I only made it seem as if I struck her that many times." His weathered, lined face stiffened with his confession and he quickly looked about, fearing discovery of his deed. Satisfied of his safety, he turned back to the black man who stood in silent surprise. "You're not to tell a soul. You understand?"

Jeremiah nodded. "Yessur," he said, the hint of a smile reflected in his dark eyes.

"And wipe that smile off your face or I'll use this whip on you!"

Jeremiah hastily returned to his task, but all the while he eyed Cain studying the silent, unmoving form in his arms. His hard, troubled expression softened, and with it Jeremiah drew up the courage to ask, "Why yo' do it?"

Cain sighed. "Because I knew Mr. Remington didn't want her to die. It was as if he was blinded by his rage. There had to be more to it than we knew and I couldn't just question him in front of everyone."

Free of the bonds, the still body fell heavily into Cain's arms. Together, the men started off toward her cabin.

"How long yo' know Master Beau?" Jeremiah asked, easily keeping up with Cain in the long stride of his gait.

"All his life. I was there the night he was born." In the darkness, Jeremiah missed the pained look on Cain's face. "Nearly killed his mother."

"Yo' know his pa, too?" Jeremiah asked quietly, sensing Cain's mood.

An odd smile touched the older man's lips. "Better than anyone realizes," he muttered, bringing a confused look to Jeremiah's face. "Come on. We gotta get this little girl taken care of."

After seeing Alanna in the capable hands of Cinnamon Cockrin, Cain headed back toward the house. The wounds on the girl's back would heal in time, but right now he was more concerned with the ones from which Beau suffered. He went into the house and directly to the study, pausing only briefly before opening the door and going in.

Sitting behind his desk, Beau angrily glanced up. "Don't you ever knock?"

Cain didn't answer as he went to the desk, poured two glasses of wine, and held one out for Beau. "Never have and don't intend to start now."

Snatching the glass from him, Beau sent him a dark scowl the man ignored, then downed the contents in one swallow. Bolting from his chair, he turned his back on Cain to stare out the window.

"Feel better?"

Whirling on him, Beau slapped the empty wine goblet on the desk top, cast him a black glare, and stared outside again.

"It would help if you talked about it."

"What makes you think I have anything to discuss?"

Cain chuckled, but did not voice his opinion.

"All right, then," Beau concurred, looking back over his shoulder, "maybe I don't want to discuss it."

"You haven't changed a bit. Even as a boy you were as

stubborn as a jackass."

Beau gritted his teeth. "Cain, you seem to forget your place."

With a slight smile crinkling the corners of his eyes, Cain deliberately went to the chair by the fireplace and sat down. "And you seem to have forgotten our sessions in back of the house. It didn't take me long to remind you of yours and if you're not careful, I'll do it now."

Cain eyed the man fearlessly and before long, Beau could not restrain his laughter. "And I'm sure you'd win. That bullwhip of yours has a way of winning any argument." He looked back outside. "I only hope it won this one."

"The girl?"

"Uh-huh. I didn't like what I had to do."

"None of us did. But something had to be done."

"Was I wrong, Cain?"

He rubbed the stubble on his chin. "No. It's a rule. But what bothers me more is why you reacted the way you did."

Beau sighed. "That's why I'm staring out the window. I don't honestly know."

"And what will you do now?"

A lazy grin spread across his face. "I was wishing you'd decide. Like when I was a boy."

"I didn't always make your decisions."

"Yea. You always saved the rough ones for me. Will you at least give me your opinion?"

Cain smiled. "Of course."

"Don't move, Alanna," she heard a familiar voice implore. "It will only make the pain that much worse."

70

She struggled to lift her head and survey her surroundings, wondering where she had been taken, only to fall back in burning agony. It felt as if a thousand needles were piercing her back and with each beat of her heart they seemed to drive themselves in deeper.

"Please lie still," Cinnamon begged, kneeling beside her. "If you want anything, I'll get it for you."

Alanna managed a weak smile. "Where am I?"

"In our cabin. How are you feeling?"

"Awful," Alanna moaned. "How long have I been asleep?"

"Unconscious is the word and all night. Are you hungry?"

"No. Just thirsty."

"I'll get you a cup of water," her friend smiled, lightly patting Alanna's hand.

Alanna closed her eyes, listening to Cinnamon hurry about the room while she relived the terrifying night past behind the darkness of her lowered lids. What had she done that was so horrible to warrant such a punishment? She was guiltless from the very beginning, ignorant of her father's deed until it was done, irreversible in its doing, and she to pay the price. Had he truly hated her all these years, and sought to find revenge by placing her in the hands of this man called The Hawk? Had her father known what lay ahead for her, wishing it, wanting it, and approving of it? Her throat constricted. Somehow she could never believe he did. Her father was too soft-spoken, too kind, too understanding to allow anything of this sort to happen with his knowledge. He was nothing at all like the man who had stolen her innocence. And was this the way it was to be with any man? To be taken by force? Never granted the opportunity to voice her own

71

desires? Is this what she could expect when she came to the marriage bed? If so, she vowed never to wed, never to let herself be used in that manner again. Tears sprang to her eyes to steal between her lashes and run down her cheeks. If it was the death of her, she must get away from this nightmare.

"Don't cry, Alanna," she heard Cinnamon plead, her voice heavy with sympathy.

She opened her eyes. "I'm sorry you are forced to endure my problems, Cinnamon."

"I'm not forced to endure them, Alanna. I want to, because you're my friend."

Alanna forced a soft, trembling smile to her lips. "I'm very lucky to have one like you."

Kneeling on the floor beside the bed, Cinnamon stared at the cup cradled in her hands. "If I had been a true friend, I would have stopped Cain."

"How? By throwing yourself between us?" Alanna awkwardly wiped away the moisture from her cheeks. "I never would have expected you to do that, Cinnamon, no matter how strong our friendship. You must believe that."

A moment passed before Cinnamon lifted her eyes to meet Alanna's. "I do," she whispered.

Alanna rested quietly the remainder of the morning, as comfortably as possible considering she could only lie on her stomach the entire time. She had only been asleep a few hours when the sound of someone coming into the cabin woke her. She opened her eyes to see Beau's dark-faced maid.

"I'm sorry I woke yo'," the tiny girl said, feeling Alanna's eyes on her. "Masta Beau sent me."

"Why?" Alanna asked sarcastically. "To gloat over

72

my misery?"

"Oh, no. He told me I was to see yo' have everything yo' need to heal. I is to come here everyday until yo' feel better."

"How nice," Alanna sneered, closing her eyes again.

Confused by the embittered tone of her words, the maid looked to Cinnamon who shrugged and looked away.

"Well, I can't stay. But I'll be back later. We can talk then." She moved for the door and paused when she reached it, glancing back to Alanna. "I's real sorry this happened to you. Some day yo' 'll understand. Masta Beau is a fair man and did only what he had to." She waited for a moment, but when Alanna chose not to answer or even open her eyes, she smiled weakly at Cinnamon and left the cabin.

"You shouldn't be so hard on her, Alanna. Tilly is a sweet girl."

Her eyes still closed, Alanna sighed bitterly. "It's hard to be nice to someone who thinks 'Masta Beau' is fair."

"But Tilly doesn't know what happened to you or she probably wouldn't feel quite the same about the man. Believe it or not, it's never been told that Beau Remington ever took a female servant of his by force. Or any woman for that matter. You must understand Tilly's side in this."

"Are we going to argue again?"

Cinnamon bit back her retort. No, she'd given up arguing with Alanna Bainbridge.

If Tilly came later that day, Alanna wasn't aware of it. She slept most of the afternoon and then, after eating only a few spoonfuls of broth, dozed off again until the following morning. It was nearly noon before someone knocked on the door of their cabin and the dark-skinned girl appeared.

"Hello, Alanna," Tilly said sheepishly. "How yo' feelin'?"

Alanna didn't answer. Then remembering what Cinnamon had said the day before, she forced a smile to her lips. "Better, thank you."

"Masta Beau wants to know if yo' have another gown to wear. If yo' don't, I can get yo' one."

Alanna's nostrils flared. Even if she hadn't another gown, she certainly wouldn't accept one from him. "Yes, thank you, I do," she replied instead, masking her hatred.

"He also wants to know if yo' have enough ta eat."

Sensing Alanna's growing anger, Cinnamon quickly reached out and took Tilly's arm to draw her away. "I think we better let her rest. Tell Master Beau she's being well cared for. If we should need anything, I'll let you know."

Alanna watched the two women leave the cabin and step out onto the porch, chattering quietly to each other. Why did he keep sending her? Confused and resentful, Alanna closed her eyes and fell into a restless slumber.

The next morning, just as she had promised, Tilly appeared on their doorstep, and every day after that as regularly as the changing of seasons. Each time she would ask Alanna how she felt, and it didn't take Alanna long to realize the young woman asked because she was truly concerned, not because she was ordered to inquire. By the fourth day, all three women laughed and talked about things they each enjoyed, learning each other's

74

innermost secrets and desires, sharing them as only friends could do. Tilly explained how she relished working at Raven Oaks, as her master had never been anything but kind to her. Of course, she had never tried to run away, as she reminded Alanna, telling her that it could be the same for her if she would only allow it.

A week had passed since Alanna's flogging, and, although the cloth of her gown burned against the healing but tender scars, she forced herself to dress and move about, having grown bored with lying in bed. As best she could, she helped Cinnamon wash their breakfast dishes, thankful for the knock at the door that allowed her to stop for the moment.

"Hello, Tilly," she smiled from her retreat on the edge of the bed. "How are you today?"

"Fine," the girl replied with downcast eyes.

With a lift of her brows, Alanna glanced at Cinnamon, who could only shake her head and shrug one shoulder. She looked back at Tilly. "What's wrong?"

"Masta Beau wants ta see yo'."

Alanna felt the muscles of her stomach tighten. "Why?"

"Didn't say. Yo' will come with me, won't yo'?" Tilly pleaded.

"Do I really have a choice?"

Tilly looked to her hands folded in front of her.

"Yes, I'll come," Alanna sighed, laying aside her towel and starting for the door.

"Alanna," Cinnamon called, stopping her just as she had reached it. "Please don't say anything to make him angry. There's nothing you can do to change things, and if he finds favor in what you do, things could go easier on you."

Alanna stared at her a moment, then smiled. "I'll try."

Cinnamon watched the two women from the doorway of the cabin until they disappeared behind the house, praying her new friend had somehow decided his way was the only way. Little did she know, Alanna already had something else in mind.

"He's in the study," Tilly told her once they reached the hall.

"Won't you come with me?" Alanna asked hopefully when she noticed Tilly had stopped at the foot of the stairs.

"He only asked for yo'. I's sorry."

Alanna listened to the padding of bare feet across the marble floor as Tilly walked away, suddenly feeling quite alone and frightened. Drawing in a deep breath, she gently rapped on the study door.

A moment passed before she heard him give permission for her to enter, and, sullenly, she stepped into the room. Seated at the desk, he read a book held in one hand while the other toyed with an unlit cheroot, quietly absorbed in his task and failing to look up once she entered. It gave her time to study him. She judged him in his early thirties, terribly young, she thought, to be so rich and so powerful. His slate-black hair gently curled over the collar of his shirt and lightly touched the bronze complexion of his cheek, the obvious sign of a man who spent a great deal of time outside the confines of his study. Cocking her head to one side, she could see the pinkened lines of a wound just below his eye and wondered if it had been one she had inflicted upon him. She smiled. If only she had had the chance to stab him with his knife. The slap of his book snapping closed startled her and she jumped, wondering if he had been able to read her thoughts, relaxing only after she discovered that he had still to look at her.

"Tilly tells me your wounds have healed properly," he stated coldly before lighting up his cigar.

She remained silent, watching him take a long puff and let the smoke curl above his head, never once meeting her eyes. Then he looked at her with a hard, insensitive glare.

"The first thing you must learn is that when I speak to you, you will answer me and not stand there like some mute. Have your wounds healed or not?"

"Yes, sir," she apologized hastily. "I was merely—"

"And you shall speak only when spoken to," he continued, cutting her off. "Sit down." He pointed to a chair next to his desk with the end of his cigar and waited until she had done as he instructed. "I've given you some serious thought in the past week, since it's obvious you will continue to keep running unless some sort of compromise can be met between us. Tilly tells me that the two of you have become friends. Is that true?"

She nodded.

"Then you should know that she is my housekeeper. I have no intention of changing that, but with a house the size of this one, I sometimes wonder if the job is too much for one woman. Therefore, I want you to assist her. You will do whatever she wishes you to do without question. You shall also help plan any dinner parties I might have, see that there is enough help, that sort of thing. I might even call on you to be a hostess at such events. I don't mean you'll be invited to dine with us, but you may be requested to meet the guests at the door and see them out again." He studied her a moment, then leaned back in his chair. "You will be given a room in this house. One of

77

your own. And don't go thinking you'll have the run of the place, for you won't. At night you will be locked in it and it shall remain that way until you prove your trustworthiness. Any questions?"

The last thing in the world Alanna wanted was to be in his house under foot. It was bad enough to be assigned there during the day, but to be locked in one of its rooms all night, and he with a key—she swallowed the fear that had tightened her throat. "I am honored you have chosen me to help with the management of your house," she replied falsely, "but it would be too much to have you house me, too. The cabin I share with Cinnamon is more than enough."

"And more to your liking?" he asked with a raised brow and slight smile.

Alanna looked to her hands folded in her lap.

"As I said, it will only be temporary. I am no fonder of having you here than you are to be here. Now go and gather your things from the cabin and find Tilly. She will show you to your room and instruct you on today's work. You're dismissed."

With a heaviness to her step, she left the house and headed back toward the cabin, feeling the thick curtain of doom closing in around her.

Six

"Here, let me take yo' things," Tilly said, meeting Alanna at the door of the kitchen and guiding her further into the room. "I'll show yo' where yo' stay in a bit, but first I want yo' to meet my friends. Alanna, this here is Bessy. She's Masta Beau's cook."

A plump, smiling woman greeted her, and Alanna felt at east almost immediately. "How do you do," she smiled in return.

"I's fine, child," the black woman said. "I's hope yo' be happy here."

Alanna's smile disappeared.

"And this here is Horace," Tilly continued with the point of a finger.

An equally dark-complected man with shining silver hair rose from the table and bowed. "Glad to meet yo', girl," he said. "I's Masta Beau's butler. Won't yo' sit with us a while? We was just gonna have some of Bessy's sweetrolls and buttermilk."

"Sounds delicious, but I'm really not hungry. Besides, I don't think Master Remington would like it if he found me neglecting my new duties."

"Pooh," Bessy snorted. "He won't mind. He's gone, anyway. Come on, child. Yo' look like yo' could use a little fattenin' up."

Unable to stop the smile that tugged at the corners of her mouth as she slid into the chair next to Horace, Alanna said, "Yes, I guess I am a little thin."

"Are yo' feelin' all right now?" Bessy asked, filling a plate with rolls and setting them on the table in front of Alanna. "Did that Cinnamon take good care of yo'?"

"Oh, yes, I'm fine. And Cinnamon was a great help. Are you sure Master Remington wouldn't get angry finding us here like this?"

"Yo' have a lot to learn about the man," Horace said, pouring a glass full of buttermilk. "Most of the time he joins us."

"That's if'n he ain't too busy," Tilly added. "Like this mornin'."

Bessy watched the young Englishwoman look from Horace to Tilly with a surprised expression distorting her face. "It's true, child. Masta Beau treats us like family. 'Course we's been with him since the day he was born. Me and Horace that is. And Tilly, she practically growed up here."

Nibbling on a roll, Alanna dared to ask, "What's he really like?"

"Masta Beau?" Bessy questioned, easing her weighty frame into a chair. "He's a hard man to know, but I guess I knows him better'n most. I practically raised him. He's a moody sort and I guess it's 'cause he never had a chance to be a boy."

"What do you mean?"

"Masta Beau's pappy died when the boy weren't hardly

a man and the poor child was forced to take over runnin' this here plantation. Did a good job for such a young 'un."

"Sure did," Horace piped in. "This here place was near ruin, I hear tell, till he took over. Scared us all. We thought we'd all be split up and sent somewhere else to work."

Alanna sipped the warm buttermilk, thinking that if they weren't slaves they would have the choice to go anywhere anytime they wanted. Even if the plantation prospered or not. Well, if she ever owned a place like Raven Oaks, she would never own a slave. "Doesn't Master Remington have any other family?" she asked, changing the subject.

"No, Mistress Remington liked it—" Bessy began, her voice bitter. Then she spotted Horace, his expression full of warning, and Bessy suddenly decided to drink her buttermilk.

"Masta Beau's mother weren't able to have no more children after he was born," Horace explained, but Alanna knew from Bessy's silence that there was more to the story. "Masta Radford was the closest thing he had to a brother."

"Oh, yo' surely would like him," Tilly chirped, her dark eyes sparkling. "He's the nicest man I ever did meet."

"Tilly, hush yo'r mouth," Bessy scolded. "Sometimes yo' act like all those other crazy women with their eye on him."

"I do not," Tilly rebuked. "I like Masta Beau, too, and yo' don't say that about him."

Horace chuckled. "Yo'll have to pay them no mind, child," he said to Alanna. "They fight like two cocks in the chicken coop, but they never mean any of it."

"Oh, be quiet, you crazy ol' man," Bessy snapped. "Yo' know she has to be reminded of her place."

"I knows my place," Tilly pouted. "But I can like someone if'n I want."

"But yo's to keep it to yo'rself."

"I don't see any harm in telling her friends," Horace comforted. "She knows where she belongs."

Bessy shot the man a scowl and rose from the table. "Well, I have work to do. Maybe the rest of yo' all can sit around, but I can't."

"Oh, Bess, don't go actin' like that," Horace cooed.

"Like what?" she demanded and Alanna felt Tilly touch her arm.

"Come on. We better go," she warned.

Quietly, the two girls slipped from the kitchen as the sound of Bessy's angered voice grew more intense.

"Do they always talk like that?" Alanna asked, with a glance back over her shoulder toward the kitchen.

"Yes, but they never mean any of it. They'll be friends again before yo' know it. Come on," she said, pulling on Alanna's arm, "I show yo' where yo' stay."

Tilly led Alanna to a small passageway just off the kitchen and together they climbed the narrow stairs. At the top, Alanna noticed the hallway went off in both directions, a single door at the end of one while the other passed by several rooms.

"Where does this go?" she asked.

Tilly smiled playfully. "I show yo'."

With Alanna close on her heels, Tilly led the way down the hall and stopped at the end, where they met another set of stairs leading to the main door of the house.

"This place is full of surprises," Alanna mused.

"And more rooms than yo' can guess."

"Who does all the cleaning?"

"Me, mostly. But if there's walls to scrub or floors to shine, I bring in help. Wanta see yo' room?"

They turned around and headed back in the direction from which they had come, passing by a room Alanna already knew quite well. It had been over a week since the night she spent forcibly in Beau's arms, but in her mind it had happened only moments before. Keeping her eyes fixed on the floor ahead of her, she passed by without comment.

Tilly stopped outside the last door at the end of the hallway and Alanna came to a sudden halt. "Here?" she asked, looking back over her shoulder toward the room that had stirred her burning hatred.

"Oh, I knows it ain't much, seein' as how it's right over the kitchen and all, but it's comfortable. And besides, if'n yo' get hungry in the middle of the night, yo' can slip downstairs for somethin' to eat without anyone knowin'."

Obviously, Tilly hadn't been informed of her master's plan to lock Alanna in each night. She smiled weakly. "Yes, I'm sure I'll do just that."

Small but adequate, the room contained a bed, a dressing-table night stand, and a huge wardrobe that seemed to overpower the tiny area. She tossed her bundle on the bed and crossed to it. Expecting to find it empty, she discovered, instead, more beautiful gowns hanging inside than she had ever seen before.

"Oh, Tilly, there must be some mistake. Someone already occupies this room."

Tilly looked to the bare toes sticking out from beneath her skirt. "No. It's not used."

83

"But this is full of dresses."

"Yes, I know."

"I don't understand," Alanna said, turning back to her.

"I guess yo' could say they come with the room. And the job."

The fine arch of her brow knotted, searching for Tilly's meaning until she suddenly realized the conversation she and Cinnamon had had about Raven Oaks' new housemaid and the real purpose of the job. Her chin fell. "But I'm not going— He doesn't think I—"

"Oh, no, Alanna. I mean that this here room is used by—well—a—just because yo' here, don't mean he expects—"

"You're damn right," Alanna stormed. "He's addle-headed if he thinks I would ever permit such a thing." With an angry shove, she closed the wardrobe doors and went to the window.

"Don't worry, Alanna. I's sure it weren't what he meant when he told yo' to move in," Tilly said.

Alanna sent her a skeptical frown, then studied the yard below the window again.

"I know yo' don't believe it, but he's not like that. He's a good man. He cares about his people."

"Ha!" Alanna grunted.

Knowing it useless even to discuss the matter, since Cinnamon had already told her how many times she had tried without success, Tilly shook her head and moved for the door. "We'd better get to work."

It took Alanna the remainder of the day to learn the house: what rooms were used regularly, those that sel-

84

dom were, the ones that got special attention and those that didn't. Tilly stayed with her most of the time, but toward evening, when the young girl had to see to setting a place at the table for Master Beau, she left Alanna alone upstairs to settle herself in her new quarters. With the intense heat of the day added to that from the kitchen below, her small room seemed to close in on her. She hurriedly unpacked her things, deciding to join Tilly in the dining hall.

As she started for the narrow stairway, she discovered a room she had yet to explore. Cautiously, she went to its door, wondering why Tilly had omitted it. After a quick glance over her shoulder to affirm that no one would see if she entered, she lifted the latch and went inside.

Finding it nothing more than another bedroom, she turned to leave when she noticed a huge oil painting hanging over the fireplace. Inquisitive, she went to it. The poised figure of a beautiful woman dressed solely in black, her equally dark, stunning hair cascading across her shoulders, radiated her stateliness and grace to her observer. A gold locket dangled from her neck to rest invitingly against the soft swell of her bosom. Her dark, sultry eyes seemed to smile at Alanna, and she felt a strange curiosity about her identity.

"Her name was Monica."

Alanna jumped at the sound of a voice behind her. She turned to find Beau lounging in the doorway.

"My mother," he added, his eyes locked on her image.

Looking back to the portrait, Alanna suddenly saw the resemblance. "She's very beautiful."

"Yes, she was. But she was as cold as she was beautiful."

Alanna frowned.

85

"She loved my father very much, but for everyone else she had little affection."

"Even for you?" Alanna blurted out.

He smiled strangely. "Yes. I guess having a child reminded her of her age. And the older I got the more she resented me."

"How awful for a young boy to grow up thinking that," Alanna said, suddenly full of compassion for a boy she had never known.

"Oh, my father made up for it," he said, leaning a shoulder against the door frame, his fingers entwined together as his hands rested before him. "I think you would have liked him."

Alanna looked at him in surprise. Whatever made him say something like that to her?

"My father was the sort everyone liked," he continued, almost as if in a daydream, "and that was part of his problem. He did everything he could to make up for Monica's callousness, to the point of nearly causing his own ruin."

"Mr. Remington, I don't feel this is any of my business," Alanna said, wondering if he even knew she was there.

"Oh, but it is," he said with a wry grin and lift to one brow. "If, perhaps, you understand my upbringing, you will understand why I do what I do. You might say I've developed the stronger traits of both parents. My mother's indifference and my father's business sense— for at one time he was the richest man in Virginia. After he died, I took over the management of this plantation and brought it back on its feet, shall we say. I could only do that because I didn't care who I hurt to do it."

"I see," Alanna said with a nod, "just as you don't care

86

about me."

"Oh, I care. But only to the point that you understand I will not be cheated out of a single coin owed me."

"It's a shame," Alanna mocked, and he raised a questioning brow, "that you did not develop the weaker traits of your parents. At least then you might have been a likable man."

Beau laughed. "You remind me of her," he smiled with a nod toward the portrait. "Her beauty and wit. Not both are often found in a woman."

"You think because we wear skirts we have no brains?" she scoffed.

"If that was true in your case, madam, then why have you not put it to better use than wasting your time on these senseless escapes?"

"They are not senseless. Not to me," she argued, and then seeing the playful smile on his lips, started for the door. "I will see if your dinner is ready."

"It is also a shame," he said softly, blocking her way with an outstretched arm, "that you and I could not have met under different circumstances. I must admit, I find you quite appealing."

"Not really a shame, Master Remington, a blessing. It would only be a one-sided relationship, for I find you anything but appealing. Now, if I may be excused, I'll see your dinner is served right away."

She met his eyes with all the bravado any girl her age could, and they stared at each other for several moments, neither wanting to be the first to look away. Then, at last, Beau nodded.

"But see it's brought to my study. I have some work to do there and cannot afford to waste the time elsewhere." He lowered his arm and let her pass without another word, watching the graceful sway of her hips as she descended the stairs. He smiled softly. At first he hadn't liked the idea of having to keep her under foot to make sure she wouldn't try to run again, but noticing her now, he decided it might not be that bad, after all. It had been a pleasant experience to find a beautiful young woman wandering about his house. Even if she was there under protest.

Hastily, Alanna returned to the kitchen looking for Tilly, only to have Bessy inform her that Tilly had gone to the mill and that it would be her responsibility for the evening to see to the serving of Master Beau's dinner. Curling her lip at the thought of being forced to endure his presence again, she dutifully told the cook that he would be eating in his study and a tray would have to be made up.

As she carried the plates of steaming hot food from the kitchen, she found herself wishing she had a handful of salt to dump in his teacup, thinking how pompous and self-centered he was. Did he really think that had circumstances been different, she would find him any more appealing? Did he think every woman swooned when she met him? With a disgusted twitch to her upper lip, she stopped outside the study, balancing the tray in one hand while she gently knocked on the door and waited for his permission to enter. Seated behind the desk, he did not bother to look up when she stepped inside and crossed to him. She set the tray on the edge of the desk without asking and turned to leave.

"Where do you think you're going?" he asked, his eyes still trained on the papers before him.

"I was going to return to the kitchen. I have not eaten," she said with a frown. "Is that not all right?"

"Certainly," he said, but before she had taken a step, he added, "just as soon as I've finished my meal."

Her shoulders dropped. He certainly had a cold way of reminding her where she belonged. Oh, well, she thought, I guess I can tolerate it for a while longer. Just as soon as I can figure out a way, I will leave this place and never have to see his face again. Folding her hands in front of her, she waited for him to look up. "May I be seated while I wait?"

He nodded and watched as she calmly took a seat, wondering what had brought about the change. He rather enjoyed the way he could anger her with only a few words or mocking smile and felt disappointed that he hadn't managed it this time. With a mental shrug, he lifted the pot of hot water and added it to the tea leaves.

Nearly half an hour passed before Beau finished eating, all the while Alanna sat quietly observing. He would take a cut of meat and chew on it while he studied his books or wrote on the papers. It was only when he looked up in thought that he would notice the meal and take another bite. Time and time again he repeated the act, until Alanna was sure the food had grown cold.

I wonder if he always eats this way, she frowned. He doesn't even take time to enjoy a meal. She grunted. He probably doesn't enjoy anything. I guess it's a good thing that he isn't married. He'd bore his wife to death. With a wrinkle to the fine, straight line of her nose, she rested her chin on the back of her hand, her fingers fanning out like icicles dangling from a porch roof as she gazed out the window.

Beau closed the last book, placed the quill in the inkwell, and stretched back in his chair, catching sight of Alanna. The bright gold streams of dying sunlight spilled in through the window and caressed her face in a warm, alluring manner, and he found it quite difficult to look away. Soft, delicate, and only in the light that touched her at that moment, could he see how truly vulnerable she really was. What a shame, he thought. A woman such as this should not be made to work for others. She should be showered with silks and jewels and—he shook his head. Whatever made him think of that?

"I am finished now," he stated as he reached for a cheroot. "You are excused." The white smoke curled upward but Beau wasn't watching it. Instead, his gaze followed the gentle swish of petticoats as they left the room.

Seven

"Tilly! Someone's at the door."

"Can yo' see who it is, Alanna? I just got these here heavy curtains in the wash tub. My hands are all wet," replied the faint voice from the kitchen.

Alanna hesitated, not ready to play hostess, and opened her mouth to plead with the girl when the knock rang out again. Wiping a smudge from the tip of her nose, and with a slowness to her step, she went to the door and paused. I hope it's only Cain, she thought, and lifted the latch.

"Well, well, well. What do we have here?"

Alanna felt her cheeks tingle hotly with the stranger's appraisal. "Alanna Bainbridge, sir," she answered nervously. "Do you wish to speak with Master Remington?"

"It was the reason I came, but seeing you, I think I'd much prefer your company. I'm Radford Chamberlain," he smiled warmly.

Her mind whirled, trying to recall just where she had heard his name before. Then, remembering Tilly's

91

comments about the man that morning in the kitchen with Bessy and Horace, she relaxed with a sigh. "Oh."

Radford chuckled. "You sound disappointed."

She straightened immediately. "I'm sorry. I didn't mean it that way. It's just that Tilly has told me about you and—well, I've never done anything like this before. I guess I didn't really know who to expect."

"Surely you didn't think you'd find the king of England standing at Beau's doorstep, did you?" he grinned impishly.

Alanna laughed. "No."

"Then relax, you did just fine. Now where is he, anyway?"

Realizing she had no idea, she shook her head. "I don't know," she said, feeling quite inept.

"All right," he said, stepping in, "we'll find out. Beau? Beau Remington?" he called in a loud, thunderous voice.

Alanna instinctively touched his arm. "Oh, please. I'll see if he's in the study." Without giving him a chance to object, she quickly went to the door and rapped softly. When there was no response, she looked back. "Maybe he's in the dining hall. Would you care to wait in the parlor while I find him?"

"Only if you promise to return with him," he stated.

Alanna stared, a slight frown darkening her eyes until she noticed the vague smile reflected in his. She relaxed, knowing he was only teasing and matched his smile with equal zest before turning sharply and nearly colliding with Beau coming from the kitchen. "Oh, excuse me," she said, perplexed. "We didn't know where you were."

Beau scowled down at her. He had heard only the tail-end of their conversation and had assumed his new housekeeper openly flirted with Radford. "Obviously,"

92

he said coldly.

"Oops," Radford chuckled. "I think our friend has gotten the wrong idea. Honestly, Beau, aren't you ever in a good mood?"

"Return to your chores," he said to Alanna, purposely ignoring Radford's pleasantry. Then, without looking at him, he asked Radford, "Would you care for a drink in the study?"

Radford took a deep bow as he swept his arm outward, silently instructing Beau to lead the way. After he passed, Radford stood up, winking at Alanna and bringing a new rush of fever to her cheeks. She instantly looked to her toes, yet watched the man from the corner of her eye until he turned away. She glanced up and studied him covertly before he disappeared into the study. He stood nearly as tall as Beau, but was of a slighter build. His blond hair combed straight back seemed to blend with his pale complexion. Apparently he preferred the lighter chores of a true gentleman, and Alanna found herself intrigued by him. He was rather handsome. It must be his blue eyes, she thought coyly. Or is it just the way he looks at me? Absently biting the tip of one nail, she turned around and left the hallway.

"Well, who is she?"

"A servant, nothing more," Beau snapped as he poured them both a glass of wine.

"I figured that much. How long has she been here?"

"A month, maybe."

"Maybe?" Radford reflected. "You mean a beauty like that has been under your roof and you have no idea how long? Good God, man. What's wrong with you?"

"She hasn't been under my roof more than a few days. What I meant was, she's only been on Raven Oaks that long."

"And now she's your new housemaid," Radford grinned with a raised brow.

"No, she isn't," Beau said emphatically.

"She isn't?" Radford echoed, truly surprised.

"No."

"Then why is she here?"

"It's a long story," Beau said impatiently, watching Radford settle himself more comfortably in his chair.

"I have all day," he smiled.

Beau's shoulders dropped. "And I suppose if I ignored you, you wouldn't go away?"

Radford grinned all the more. "No."

Holding the crystal goblets by the rim, Beau stared at the man for several moments before moving in to hand one to him. He went back to the chair behind his desk and sat down, idly swirling the contents in his glass and knowing that no matter how long he refused to discuss the girl's presence, Radford would sit glued to his chair until he did.

"All right," he sighed, taking a swallow of wine. He leaned back, crossed an ankle to a knee and relived the events leading up to her arrival at Raven Oaks, how she'd lost her parents and how her father had sold her services without telling her. "No matter what I say, she won't believe me. She's tried to run away twice and I figured if I made her life a little more tolerable than before, she might settle down."

"What did you have her doing?"

"Nothing out of the ordinary."

"Then why did she run? I know how you treat your people. It doesn't make sense."

Beau stretched back in his chair. "The first time I saw

94

her was at the mill. She had just stepped outside when I turned around and ran into her. I knocked the bowl of flour she was carrying from her hands and it spilled on the ground." He smiled. "Was she angry. Anyway, after I tried to wipe the flour from my clothes—"

"Wait a minute. You mean she spilled it on you?" Radford asked, the corner of his mouth twitching in a smile.

"Yes," he said slowly, "accidentally."

Radford pressed a knuckle to his lips. "Go on."

"I'm not so sure I should," he said, noting his friend's glee.

Radford straightened in his chair. "I'm sorry, Beau. But I imagined such a funny picture. You must admit, it had to be."

"At the time, no."

"Yes, I suppose not. Something like that usually isn't, especially for you."

"What's that supposed to mean?"

"Well," Radford continued, leaning back in his chair, "you haven't been known to have much of a sense of humor."

Beau glared at him a moment. "Do you want to know about her or not?"

"Sure, sure. Go on."

Beau quietly leaned in on the desk and began to toy with the pearl handle of the knife Alanna had tried to use on him, and, without realizing it, smiled.

Radford frowned, puzzled. "Now you're smiling. What the hell goes on inside that head of yours, anyway?"

Beau glanced up with a start, knowing his thoughts drifted. "I guess you're right. I didn't have much of a sense of humor. But thinking about it now, I see how funny it all really was." He leaned back in the chair and removed the knife from the scabbard to run a thumb along its sharp edge. "Do you know that tiny creature hit me? Not once, but twice? She tried to run away because she didn't know what I'd do to her because of it. Of course, I didn't really know either. Anyway, after Cain caught her and brought her back, she pulled this knife on me. I think she really thought she could hurt me with it."

Radford laughed gaily. "She's a lady after my own heart. How many times I've wanted to stick a blade into your ribs just to see if you really have a heart. So then what happened?"

Beau's eyes darkened, remembering the incident in his bedchamber. For some reason, he didn't want to admit it had ever happened. Even to his one and only true friend. "Well" he continued, carefully avoiding the subject, "she tried to run again. So she was flogged."

"My God, Beau. You haven't dealt out that kind of punishment in a long time. Especially on a woman."

Beau grunted. "Don't let her size fool you. She's a lot tougher than you think."

"Well, I certainly hope it changed her mind about running."

"Wouldn't surprise me if it didn't."

"Maybe you should consider selling her papers."

Beau grinned. "To you, perhaps?"

"It's a thought. After all, you must admit I have a way with the women," Radford smiled, his pale blue eyes sparkling.

"Rad, my friend, someday some woman will take you for everything you own. I only hope I'm around to laugh about it."

"Can I help it if I adore women? Besides, I'm thinking

of settling down."

"Not with Melissa, I pray," Beau scowled.

"Well, her father does own the property adjoining mine. Someday I could be richer than you." Radford grinned mischievously.

"Being more wealthy than I cannot mean that much to you."

"No, of course not. But I'm not getting any younger and I'd like to live long enough to enjoy the heir to Briarwood Manor. And what of you, my brother? Shall you marry soon?"

"Ha!" Beau roared. "And give up my freedom? No, I shall rather enjoy growing old alone."

Radford shook his head. "The day will come when even you shall pledge your love, I'm afraid. Although you play the part of a man made of stone, I truly know you are no different than I."

"Do you?" Beau smiled.

"Ah, yes. Somewhere out there," Radford recited with a sweep of his hand, "is a woman, a beautiful woman, soft, alluring, and able to blind you to all else with a single word or a touch of her hand against your cheek. Mark my words, Beau Remington. Your castle made of stone will crumble."

Beau leaned back in his chair, placed an elbow on its arm and rested his chin against his knuckles, a wide, lopsided grin brightening his dark eyes. "You were born too late, Radford. You'd have made a great court jester."

"Mock me if you will, but I'm afraid I've said the truth," Radford returned in earnest. "And I'm afraid I've said too much. I must be going. I only came to see if you were still alive. It's been a long time since we've seen each other." He rose and Beau immediately joined him.

Standing at the top of the veranda steps, Beau watched Radford board his carriage. Reins in hand, the young man leaned back out. "If you decide to sell her papers, let me know. I'd rather enjoy having someone like her around." He flashed a smile and took off down the drive.

Beau remained on the porch long after Radford had gone, staring off at the horizon. For some reason, he hoped it would never come to that. Thoughtfully, he turned around and went inside.

"I see what you mean, Tilly," he heard Alanna say as he approached the kitchen. "Master Chamberlain is quite handsome. And quite a flirt. I think that if I had met him back home in England, I never would have left."

He paused with a hand pressed against the kitchen door, listening.

"Well, don't think just 'cause yo' a servant that he might not be interested in yo'. After yo' paid yo'r time to Masta Beau, yo's be free to go wherever yo' want."

"Oh, Tilly, don't be foolish. I'd still be below his station." Alanna absently swirled the water in the wash tub with her finger, a soft smile touching her lips.

"Then why yo' smilin'?"

"I can smile if I want. Besides, a girl can daydream, can't she?" She glanced playfully to her confidant, surprised to see the somewhat panic-stricken look on her face. Following her gaze, she turned around to find Beau standing in the doorway, and the gaiety of the moment was destroyed.

"Just remember that's all it is," he said, his voice full of warning.

"And if I don't, I'm sure you'll be there to remind me," Alanna muttered and heard Tilly gasp in fear. Alanna knew she would never have any more feeling for

98

Radford Chamberlain than that of a friend, should the possibility ever occur, but seeing the affect the idea had on Beau aroused the devil in her. "Wouldn't it just mortify you to think you might have to meet me on even ground?" she bravely added.

"That's enough," he hissed.

"Does it bother you?" she smiled.

Beau gave Tilly a fleeting glance before he reached out, locked hold of Alanna's arm and pulled her from the room. Without a word, he led her to the study and closed the door.

"I want you to know something," he said, shoving her into a chair by his desk so that he could rest a hip on the corner of it and stare into her eyes. "Radford Chamberlain is my friend. Has been for years, and I think of him more as a brother. I'll not have some trollop throwing herself at him. Do you hear?"

Lines between her brows formed as Alanna scowled angrily up at him. "I am not a trollop. And I don't have to sit here and be called one." Haughtily, she started to rise, only to have him hit her shoulder and push her back into the chair. "How dare you," she growled.

"I dare anything," he said. "Remember?"

Blood rushed to her cheeks. "You are a rogue. A gentleman would never speak of it."

"I have never claimed to be a gentleman. But until the day you set foot on my plantation, I never had cause to act the contrary. You do push me to the limits."

"Then why not rid yourself of me?"

"How? Toss you down the well? I'm sure your ghost would haunt me every waking hour and steal into my sleep," he scoffed.

"A much simpler way, m'lord," she told him. "Send

me back to England."

"Ha!" he roared. "And do you wish a new wardrobe for the journey?"

"I wish nothing from you, only that you set me free."

"No," he stormed, rising from the desk to go to the window and stare outside.

"If you will set a price for my freedom, I will see that it's met."

Beau spun around to glare at her, a dark frown shadowing his eyes. "How?"

"If you will allow me the use of your quill and a piece of paper, I will send a letter to England."

"England?"

"Yes. I have an aunt there, my mother's sister, and if I write to explain my dilemma, I'm sure she'll forward the coin I need."

"How can you be so sure? If this aunt of yours could afford to give away her silver, why didn't she give it to your father? You wouldn't have need to write her now, if she had."

She smiled when she realized Beau didn't believe her story. "As I said, she is my mother's sister. She truly hated my father and would not have lifted a finger to help him even if he had asked."

Alanna couldn't understand the look she saw in the man's eyes. If she hadn't known better, she would have sworn it was one of panic and loss. But loss of what? It reminded her of Aaron and the way he had looked when she had been forced to tell him that she was leaving England for good. Aaron loved her, as she truly felt she loved him, and sailing across the sea surely meant they would never be together again. He had cried that day, and although she doubted Beau Remington had ever cried in his life, she almost expected it as the startled, somewhat helpless expression he wore reminded her of Aaron's. Confused by this new side of Master Remington, she frowned. "It really doesn't matter how you are paid, does it? Service or coin?"

"No, of course not," he snapped, coming to attention. "You'll find what you need on the desk." He started for the door. "I must go to the fields. When you are finished, leave the letter there. I'll see that Cain takes it to the ship the next time he is in Williamsburg."

She watched the door close with a thud and wondered why he should be angry with her. If anything, he should be glad she had come up with a way to terminate their relationship. With a slight shrug of her shoulders, she rose and went to the desk.

There was no unused parchment lying on its surface and without a second thought, she pulled open a drawer and secured the needed item. Settling herself in the chair, she leaned forward to take the quill from its well when her eyes fell upon another paper partially hidden from view by his big leather-bound ledger. Ordinarily, she would not have given it a second look, but something peculiar about it captured her attention. Instead of the figures or the neatly written letter she expected to find, there were several heavily lined squares and circles and other such markings, the kind one might draw absent-mindedly. However, in the center of all his idle scratches, he had penned *Alanna*. And not once, but several times!

"Oh, dear," she moaned painfully.

Glancing up to make certain she was alone, she folded the paper and tucked it into the bodice of her gown. Just as soon as she could, she would talk with Cinnamon about it.

"You're taking an awful chance coming here," Cinnamon scolded. "What if he should find out?"

"I don't care. What I have to show you is important." Quickly, she pulled her booty from within her gown and handed it to her friend. "What do you think?"

Cinnamon began to fidget.

"What's wrong?" Alanna asked.

"I can't read."

"Well, there really isn't much to read," she said, easing the girl's embarrassment. "It's just a lot of scribbling. But look here," she added, pointing to the center, "that's my name."

Cinnamon studied it a moment. "Where did you get this?"

"From Master Remington's desk."

"Did he write it?"

"I know of no other who uses his desk. Do you?"

"No," Cinnamon said quietly. "What do you suppose it means?"

"That's why I brought it to you. I want you to tell me. What I suspect is the worst possible end."

Cinnamon paced the floor while she studied the paper, a fingertip stroking her chin. "If it belonged to any other, I could guess. But this seems unlike The Hawk."

"Then pretend that it does and tell me what you think," Alanna said, anxiously.

"It would appear to mean that you were in his thoughts even though you were not in his presence." The realization of her words struck home, the mental conflict she had endured since he had forcibly taken Alanna suddenly resolved. She smiled. Beau Remington had hit out at something that threatened his normal way of life. "I think he cares more for you than he would ever admit."

"You've lost your mind," Alanna said, snatching the parchment from her hand.

"Well, if you don't like what I've told you, then why did you ask?"

"I don't know," Alanna said, crumpling up the paper and tossing it into the fireplace. "Oh, how could things have turned out like this? Trying to hide from him only made matters worse."

"No, it hasn't."

Alanna turned on her, an incredulous stare on her face.

"Well, it hasn't," Cinnamon reaffirmed. "Look. If the man has fallen for you, it is to your advantage. You could probably get anything you want from him if—"

"If I pay the price," Alanna finished.

Cinnamon shrugged a shoulder. "A small price, I think."

"Well, I don't," Alanna exploded, moving toward the door. "I hate him, and just being in the same room with him is distasteful. No, I see this to mean that I must be very careful whenever he's around. All he truly feels for me is lust and he would not hesitate to sate that hunger whenever the mood strikes him."

"You're throwing away a beautiful opportunity, Alanna," Cinnamon said. "I would act differently."

"And you are not me," Alanna stormed, turning abruptly to depart the cabin.

Cinnamon stood in the doorway, watching Alanna

hurriedly scamper back to the house, wishing it had been her name Beau Remington had penned. Her freckled nose wrinkled with her smile. Obviously, Alanna had no idea what had happened, or if she did, she chose to ignore it. She shook her head. Of all the people in her life she had never met two more stubborn individuals, and if a union ever occurred between them, it would be a long time coming.

Eight

Alanna took deliberate pains to avoid seeing Beau the rest of the day. That night she excused herself early after eating dinner, pleading a headache so she could return to her room. Once there, she slid the bedside table against the door just in case he should decide to pay her a visit later that night while she slept. She stood back, examined her work and smiled, feeling secure, then she slipped from her gown and went to bed.

The next morning dawned hot and sticky. Even the gentle breeze from the window did little good. She forced herself from bed, donned a layer of clothing and washed her face with cool water from the washbowl before going to the door. As quietly as she could, she moved the night stand and tested the lock. The door opened slowly to her touch.

Cautiously sticking her head outside the room and finding the hallway bare, she heard Bessy's merry voice drifting up from the kitchen, singing a slightly off-key tune. Deciding that if Beau should be around she would be safer in the presence of others, she quickly fled her room and skipped down the back stairway.

"Good mornin', child," Bessy greeted her. "Sleep well?"

"Yes, thank you. I did until a short time ago. I think it will be very hot today."

"Might as well get used to it," Bessy said, spooning a plateful of fluffy scrambled eggs, "it's just the start. Does it get hot where yo's come from?"

Alanna poured herself a glass of buttermilk and sat down at the table. "Yes, but I don't think it could match this." Eagerly, she took the plate of fresh-baked sweet rolls Bessy held out to her, more hungry than she had first imagined. "Where's Tilly?"

"Oh, the young 'un feels poorly. I told her to stay in bed."

"What's wrong?"

"She was up half the night with her head in the washbowl. She had the notion she'd feel better if she was up and around," Bessy added with a click of her tongue. "Foolish child. Yo' never find a harder worker than that one."

"Is there something I can do for her?" Alanna asked, feeling a twinge of guilt about her own good health.

"Not now. She's asleep. If'n it don't get too hot in her room, I s'pose she will sleep most of the mornin'. We's can check on her after a while," Bessy added, pointing a wooden spoon at Alanna's plate. "Now eat. I don't need two sicklin's on my hands."

Alanna ate obediently, watching Bessy pour hot, steaming water into a wash pan. With Tilly in bed all day, she realized she would be left without an ally should she meet Master Remington alone somewhere.

"Has Master Remington eaten?" she asked casually,

casting a sideways glance at the cook. She didn't want to seem too eager with her question, but she had to know where he could be found, giving her the chance to avoid the area if at all possible.

"Oh, yes. Long time ago. He and Masta Cain had to go to the livery early. Now would be a good time to see to his room," Bessy said, adding a stack of dirty dishes to the sudsy water, obviously unaware of Alanna's predicament.

"His room?" Alanna echoed, her appetite gone.

"Why, sure. With Tilly sick, yo' have to do her chore, too."

"Oh," Alanna mumbled, "I guess I never thought of that."

"Well, yo' run along. Yo's got lots to do and I can finish up here."

Numbly Alanna pushed aside her plate and stood up, pausing several times to look at Bessy, seeking some sort of reprieve, but finding none. The very last room in the house Alanna ever wanted to see was his. Grudgingly, she climbed the stairs, thinking how her cleaning time there would be the fastest on record. Her waist-length, thick hair acted as a blanket, holding in the heat of the day against her neck and shoulders, and she stopped by her room only long enough to find a strip of cloth with which to bind it up before proceeding.

His enormous room overwhelmed her, and she decided that if he should pay a sudden visit she could get lost in it quite easily. Although the bed needed dressing, she still had trouble pulling her eyes away from it. Its high posters nearly reached the ceiling, and fastened from each corner hung a velvet canopy that matched the crumpled spread. What a grand place to sleep, she thought, spreading out the covers. Near the window stood a small writing desk covered with books and papers, a brass paperweight, quill and inkwell made of silver, and a crystal candelabrum. Running a great plantation must require a lot of paperwork, she concluded, remembering the similar disorder on his desk in the study.

A large wing chair before the fireplace had become the haven for yesterday's soiled clothes and she began picking them off as she thought how messy men were. Sweat ran down the back of her neck and she reached up to block its path, her eyes catching sight of the closed window. Laying the clothes aside, she went to it and let in the gentle breeze. The high collar of her dress, buttoned all the way to her throat, quickly absorbed the perspiration, and feeling the cool air drift in made her want to shed it for something cooler. But knowing she owned no other that would expose any more flesh, she unfastened the gown to the valley between her breasts, and with the tip of her hemline wiped her glistening skin dry. She stood there a moment before turning back to her chores and gasped when she saw Beau standing in the doorway.

"Where's Tilly?" he scowled.

"She's i-ill," Alanna stammered, her eyes drawn to the way he was attired. His ivory-colored silk shirt, opened to his breastbone, revealed the heavy mass of dark fur beneath it. His breeches hugged the muscular shape of his thighs and disappeared beneath the tall black boots that reached his knees. But what bothered her was the way the cloth stretched tightly across his manhood, leaving little to the imagination.

"Is there something wrong with the way I'm dressed," he asked, noting where her eyes had rested, "or do you

108

find the view to your liking?"

Every muscle of her tiny frame tightened, cutting off her breath, and she immediately looked away, unable to bring herself to look at him or dignify his crude remark with an answer. "I-I'm finished here," she managed to say, and picking up the discarded bundle of clothes, headed for the door. "If you'll excuse me, I have other things to do."

He stepped aside to watch her go, a smile of pure delight surfacing where only an instant before an irritated scowl had played with his handsome features.

"Damn him," she muttered to herself, hurrying down the stairs. "He traps me so easily with his outrageous insinuations. I must be more careful." As her foot touched the marble floor of the foyer, she heard him call her name and she stopped, an unwilling acknowledgment. She turned back to look up and found him leaning a hip against the banister.

"I had to leave the house in rather a hurry this morning and hadn't the time for a bath. Would you see that water is brought to my room?"

"Me?" she contested.

"Isn't Tilly in bed?"

"Yes, but—"

"Then I know of no one else for the chore." Before she could open her mouth to object, he turned and disappeared into his room again.

"He should have a servant for this kind of thing," Alanna growled as she added several more logs to the already blazing fire. "He does this to humiliate me."

"What does he do, child?"

Alanna glanced up to find Bessy coming into the kitchen, her dark arms wrapped securely around a large bowl full of flour.

"And why yo' stokin' the fire?"

"Masta Beau wants a bath!" Alanna said with a stomp of her foot.

"Again? Land sake's alive, that man is the cleanest thing I ever did meet."

"Again? You mean he already had a bath this morning?"

"Sure 'nough. Ain't never missed one in the mornin' fo' as long as I 'member."

"I knew it!"

"Knew what, child?"

"He only does this to embarrass me."

"Don't be foolish, girl. He sometimes takes another one, 'specially after workin' with them smelly ol' horses. Now hush up and get them feet a-movin'."

Alanna's tiny chin dropped angrily with her rebuttal then her mouth snapped shut with second thoughts. She couldn't very well tell Bessy why she disagreed. She'd never tell anyone what had happened between Beau and her, and she truly doubted Bessy would believe her anyway. No, she'd just have to bite her tongue this time and stay alert during her visit to Beau's room.

Sitting on the edge of his bed a few minutes later, Beau casually watched Alanna lug each bucket of water into the room without making the slightest move to help. When she finished and turned to go, he cleared his throat and motioned her to wait.

"A moment longer, if you please. I have need of your help," he said, lifting a booted foot in the air. "I managed with one alone but this one seems to be stuck."

Alanna felt certain that if she opened her mouth to speak, she would spout steam. I'll just bet it's stuck, she silently fumed, setting down her bucket and walking to the side of the bed. She paused, glaring down at him.

"Well, don't just stand there," he barked irritably, "grab hold."

She reached out to take the heel in one hand, the toe in the other and straightened sharply when he dropped his foot to the floor almost angrily.

"Not like that. Straddle it."

"Strad—"

Beau made a circling motion with one hand, indicating that she should turn around. It was bad enough that she had to touch him. Now he expected her to hold his foot between her knees. Oh, what she wouldn't give for another bucket full of water. Defiantly, she turned her back on him, missing the twinkle that suddenly surfaced in his dark eyes and the curl at the corner of his mouth as she bent down to take hold of his boot.

It proved impossible to budge. She switched hands and tugged harder. Nothing. She changed positions again, ready to declare defeat, when all of a sudden she felt him brace his stocking foot against her backside and give her a hearty shove. The boot pulled free and Alanna found herself on the floor, boot in hand. Angrily, she tossed it down, scrambled to her feet and stood before him, a fist knotted on each hip, ready to tell him exactly what she thought of him, when she discovered he had risen from the bed and proceeded to disrobe.

"Unless you care to watch," he mused, dropping his shirt to the floor and unfastening his breeches, "I suggest you close the door on your way out."

Alanna's cheeks burned. Without a moment's hesitation—certain he would continue no matter who watched —she whirled about, latched onto the bucket and ran

111

from the room, hearing the door slam closed behind her. Safely outside, she stopped, leaning a shoulder against the doorframe to catch her breath until the muffled sounds of his laughter reached her ears. Outraged by his sordid prank, she growled an oath at him and ran for the kitchen, tumbling into a chair near the table, her bucket falling noisily to the floor.

"Yo' always come in like that?" Bessy scolded. "Yo' scared the life outa me."

"Only when I flee the devil," Alanna snarled, gasping for air.

"Whoever do yo' mean?"

"Never mind," she mumbled, avoiding an obvious quarrel of right versus wrong should she mention his identity. "I think it's time I got the curtains off the line."

Without another word she left, a large wicker basket snatched off the floor dangling from her fingertips.

She had thought to find rescue from the torment she endured inside the house by venturing to the backyard and the clothesline. She found, instead, a different sort of torture under the sun's blistering rays. Within minutes her gown was clinging damply to her, and she hurriedly set about to gather the freshly laundered curtains from the line. A trail of sweat ran down the back of her neck, from temple to chin, from earlobe to neckline, and, without thinking, she paused in her task, reached down, grabbed the hemline of her gown and mopped her brow and face with it. Unveiling her ankles cooled her even more, and, paying little heed to the possibility that someone might watch, she fanned herself with the edge of her skirt before reluctantly letting it fall back into place. Had she not been so indifferent, she would have, in fact, sensed the vigil someone had undertaken and looked back at the house to discover the curtains of Beau's window carefully and only slightly parted apart to better the view. As it was, she innocently finished her chores and returned to the house and the task of hanging draperies.

Standing before the enormous parlor window, newly pressed draperies in her arms, Alanna wondered if she could manage the job alone. The top of the framework appeared twice her height, and she knew of no way to reach it without standing on something. Having borrowed a spindle-back side chair from the kitchen, she stood on tiptoes, still failing to reach her goal. Irritated but not defeated, she climbed back down in search of something else to aid her in rectifying her dilemma, thinking of the water bucket in the kitchen. A moment later, the bucket settled on the chair seat, she carefully climbed up once more. This time she easily reached the rod, but now she experienced a new difficulty. Each time she stretched to hang up a section of the drapery, she could feel the bucket wobble and her heart skip a beat. Latching onto the framework for security, she leaned out again, caught the first loop of cloth and proceeded to finish the job. Just as she was about to hook the last of it, the chair somehow got shifted away from the wall. Her breath caught in her throat, she clutched both hands full of velvet material and hung on, trying frantically to relocate the chair beneath her. But the more she worked at it, the worse it became, the chair legs squealing their discord with each move she made, until the angle in which she stood caused the chair, bucket, and Alanna to topple over, the heavy folds of draperies tearing free of the rod to bellow out and cover them all. From beneath her tent she could hear racing footsteps in the hall, and

113

she knew at any moment Bessy would come to her aid. Tears burned in her eyes and she lifted the hem of her skirt to examine her injured limb.

"Oh, Bessy," she sniffled, "I've hurt my ankle."

"Let me see it."

Alanna stiffened at the sound of his voice, wishing somehow she could hide beneath the fallen draperies until he went away, feeling the cloth lifted from her instead. She wiped away a stray tear before he could see and flipped her skirts back into place.

"It's fine," she mumbled.

"But you just said it hurt," he sighed impatiently. "Now let me look at it. You might have broken it."

Alanna felt every muscle in her tighten when he reached down and cupped her foot in his hand.

"How did you manage such a silly fall anyway?" he barked, obviously annoyed by the interruption she had caused. "Wasn't someone helping you?"

She shook her head dispassionately.

"Well, I can't be sure—I'm not a doctor—but I'd say you've only twisted it. Either way, you should stay off of it for the rest of the day."

The knot of her brow barely had time to form before he slipped an arm under her knees and his other around her waist without any warning and easily lifted her in the air.

"What are you doing?" she shrieked.

"I'm taking you to your room where you can lie down and be comfortable," he said, somewhat aggravated. "I can't very well leave you lying here in the middle of the floor."

"But I can walk," she argued.

He stopped abruptly at the doorway, his face only inches from hers. "I don't plan to seduce you in the

114

center of the foyer for everyone to see if that's what's worrying you."

Alanna could feel a different form of perspiration bead over her. She looked away. "I didn't really think you would," she whispered.

"Very well," he stated, gently shifting the weight of his load. "Now do be good and hang on. You don't weigh all that much, but you are making it difficult for me."

A bit apprehensively, Alanna locked her arms about his neck, hearing his hum of gratitude and feeling the muscles of his shoulders and chest flex with each step he took toward her room. The scent of him filled her nostrils, an aroma of soap from his recent bath and faint lingerings of cigar smoke upon his coat. Neither of them spoke all the way across the foyer and up the stairs, and, without realizing it, she stared quietly at his profile and marveled at the ease with which he carried her. His strength and lordliness intrigued her, and she found herself almost wishing they could be friends. There was a mysterious air about him, one which piqued her curiosity, and she longed for the opportunity to know him better, know him the way no other did.

When they reached her room, he placed the toe of his boot against the partially open door, nudging it wide and allowing them to enter easily. He strode to the bed, gently laid her upon it and then reached out to retrieve a pillow.

"Rest your foot on this," he said, carefully positioning it beneath her ankle. "It will help ease the throbbing."

He stood erect, a frown darkening his eyes, and glanced about the room to the open window. Without a word, he turned and left her. She barely had time to wonder at his sudden departure before he reappeared at the side of her bed, reaching down to scoop her into his

115

arms once more.

"It's too hot in here," he told her. "My room will be more comfortable."

"Oh, but I can't," she objected.

"And why not?"

A shrug of her shoulders started him on his way again. How could she possibly tell him why it would disturb her to be found in his bed, even with his permission. It obviously did not concern him, and she knew if she voiced her objections, he would only laugh and remind her of who ruled the manor.

Laying beneath the canopy, she stared up at it in wide-eyed appraisal. The mammoth quantity of cloth seemed to engulf her, and, although she would have preferred her own room, she decided to enjoy the luxury it afforded if only for one day.

"Is something wrong?"

She glanced up at him. "Oh, no. It's just that I've never—well—I feel out of place."

A faint smile glimmered in his eyes a moment then disappeared. "Just don't get used to it," he growled, turning on his heels and moving toward the door. "I'll have Bessy look in on you."

"Thank you," she whispered, watching him disappear into the hallway.

Nine

Having seen to the comfort of his new housekeeper, Beau returned to his work in the study only to find that the heat of the day had reached even his usually cool retreat. Before long he was perspiring heavily. Deciding a cool glass of water would refresh him, he rose to venture to the kitchen, spotting Bessy coming down the stairs as he entered the hallway.

"How is she?" he asked with a nod toward his room.

"Restin' good. Must have been some fall that young 'un took. Her ankle's swole pretty bad."

"Do you think a doctor should look at it?"

"Why, Masta Beau. Yo' know I's as good as any doctor," Bessy scolded playfully.

Beau chuckled, reaching up to scratch his brow. "Yes'm," he concurred, bringing a loud rumble of laughter from the woman at his side.

"Where yo' goin'?" she asked, falling into step with his long, easy gait.

"It's awfully hot in the study and I thought I might get a drink of water unless you can think of anything better."

"Well, I knows what yo' used to do whenever the heat got too much for yo'."

"And what was that?"

"Why, yo' always went for a swim in the river. It seems like I was always lookin' for yo' and sure 'nough, yo' be swimmin' in that there river."

Beau smiled fondly. "Yes," he agreed. "But that was a long time ago. I haven't a moment to spare on childhood pleasures now."

"Pooh," Bessy rallied. "Yo' could if'n yo' wanted and yo' know it."

"Yes, I could. But swimming in the river was meant to be enjoyed with someone else." He chuckled. "I used to go with Rad. You suppose that if I sent a message for him to meet me at the river for a swim he would?"

"Masta Beau, yo' know that man ain't growed up one bit since the last time yo' all went swimming. Of course, he'd meet yo' there."

Beau laughed heartily, knowing Bessy was right. "Those were good times. Too bad he wasn't really my brother."

Bessy noticed a bitterness in his tone and glanced up at him to find a hardened look on his face. "Yo' thinkin' 'bout yo'r mammy?"

Shaking off his thoughts, he reached out to envelop her shoulders within his arm, the smile returning to his lips. "There's one thing about you, Aunt Bess. I never could fool you."

"And why would yo' try? I always tell yo' true."

"I know, Bess. I was very fortunate to have you around when I was growing up." He straightened, gave her a gentle squeeze, and opened the door leading to the

118

kitchen to allow her to enter first.

Beau had worked in his study for only a few minutes when he discovered that the paper he needed to complete his figures was on his desk in his room. Without any thought of his visitor, he quickly set off in that direction, totally absorbed in obtaining the paper that would enable him to finish his work and visit the mill. Only after he had nearly crossed the room to his desk did he feel someone's eyes on him. He stopped short and looked back, finding Alanna staring at him.

"Oh, forgive me," he apologized. "I had forgotten you were here. I hope I didn't disturb you."

"On the contrary, sir, it is I who should be asking."

He straightened in surprise. "Why, no. I only came to get this," he said, lifting a paper from the desk. "I won't be staying, if that's what you mean."

Alanna smiled weakly.

"How is the ankle?" he asked, pausing at the bedside.

"Much better, thank you. But I really think I should be getting back to work."

"Nonsense. You stay where you are. The work can wait until you and Tilly are better."

"But I feel wretched just lying about not doing anything."

Struck with an idea, he glanced about the room until he found Tilly's mending basket lying on the floor near the fireplace. He went to the wardrobe, pulled out a shirt and picked up the basket. With both items in hand, he went back to Alanna.

"Here, this will give you something to do. I tore a

119

button from it and forgot to inform Tilly. You can sew it back on if you wish."

With an almost friendly smile, she took the proffered articles from him and settled herself more comfortably in his bed. "Thank you. But are you sure there are not more that you forgot?"

He thought for a moment, glancing about the room again, and then shrugged. "I can't think of any," he said, noticing a disappointed look wrinkle her face with his answer. Then, concluding her discontentment stemmed from the fact that this task would only take a few minutes, he turned around and walked from the room. A moment later he materialized again, with a similar basket in tow. "Have you any talents with the needle other than mending?"

"Well, yes. My stepmother taught me how to do embroidery."

"Good. This belonged to Monica. Maybe you can find something in it to occupy your time." He laid the basket on the edge of the bed and without looking back left her to return to his study.

A satisfied smile lightened his eyes as he walked down the stairs. For some reason he felt good, something he hadn't felt for a long time. Or maybe it was just because it had been the first time he was able to talk with the girl in a friendly manner rather than exchanging heated words. Well, it wasn't always his fault. He had only punished her because she had disobeyed the rules. He frowned. And if I hadn't raped her, she probably wouldn't have run, he let himself think. His mood changed.

He sat down behind his desk and picked up his quill, ready to begin where he had left off. For several moments he stared at the paper unable to write a thing. His thoughts had escaped him and in their place new ones began to surface, thoughts of a woman, soft, beautiful, and tempting, and his eyes wandered to the banister that led upstairs. He blinked, trying to force himself to work. Again he stared at the paper, recalling the moment when he looked outside his room and found Alanna at the clothesline. The hem of her skirt, lifted to wipe the perspiration from her brow, had exposed shapely limbs for him to admire. He leaned back in his chair. God, how he had wanted to go to her, to take her in his arms and place a gentle kiss upon her lips. He smiled as he rested his elbow on the arm of the chair and rubbed a finger against his brow in short, meaningful strokes. She certainly wouldn't have liked that. He shook off his memories, trying once more to concentrate on the work before him, but, finding no end to his turmoil, rose and went to the window to look out. Why couldn't she have been a homely old woman? Then he could have sold her papers as Radford had suggested and been done with her. Things could return to normal instead of his spending every waking hour thinking of her; while he ate or bathed or worked with Cain. Even while he lay awake at night, before total exhaustion overtook him, the young woman would steal into his thoughts. She was a curse, and he couldn't understand what grave injustice he had committed to warrant such an endless torture. His eyes sparkled as he thought how easily he could bring color to her cheeks. It was part of her captivating beauty. He sighed, knowing it was useless to try any longer to force his mind onto the figures on the paper, and he decided instead to go to the mill.

Walking away from the house, Alanna still on his mind, he looked back over his shoulder at the window of his room and stumbled over his own feet. Shooting a glance in all directions to see if anyone had noticed and finding he had been spared the embarrassment, he quickly headed for his destination, vowing never to let it happen again.

The air inside the mill closed in around him and he silently prayed rain would come soon to ease the distress it caused. He spoke with several of the workers, spying Cain a short distance away, and quickly walked toward him, hoping to return his thoughts to business.

"Morning, Mr. Remington," the man said.

"Cain," Beau nodded.

"I didn't expect to see you so early. Something wrong?"

Beau could feel a tingling to the flesh of his cheeks, something he had never experienced before. He reached up to stroke the line of his jaw and cleared his throat. "No. Just got too warm to work in the house."

"You won't find it any cooler here, I'm afraid," Cain said, wiping his brow with the back of his hand. "How's the girl working out for you?"

Wondering if Cain had sensed his dismay, he turned away to send a fleeting glance about his surroundings. "Fine. How's the mill running?" he asked, changing the subject.

Cain looked up at him and studied his rather uneasy expression. "As well as could be expected in this heat," he answered with a raised brow. "Something bothering you?"

Beau couldn't bring himself to look at the man. Joshua Cain had lived on Raven Oaks longer than anyone else. He had started working for Beau's father when the plantation was nothing more than a farm. He had been present at Andrew and Monica's wedding. He had been there when Beau was born and had helped raise him when Andrew was away on business trips. He, more than anyone else, knew Beau's every mood, and chances were he knew what bothered him now.

"It's the girl, isn't it?" he pressed.

Beau swallowed hard. "What makes you think anything is bothering me?"

Cain chuckled. "How long I know you? You really think I can't tell when you're troubled?"

"It's just the mill. You know how this time of year we always have trouble with it."

"It's runnin' fine. A few sticky parts, but nothing out of the ordinary. So why is it more important to you now?"

"Because it's my coin that is lost should it fail to function," Beau snapped before turning away. "I'm going to the livery."

"You were just there this morning," Cain added, failing to hide his smile.

"Well, I'm going again. Is that all right with you?"

"Surely," Cain said, fighting down a broad grin as he watched the master of Raven Oaks, the man called The Hawk, so labeled for his toughness, stride away. I wondered how long it would take for that little lady to get under your skin, he thought. You're coming apart at the seams, my young friend, and if you're not careful, she'll be your downfall. He smiled openly. And it's about time.

Beau passed several workers in the yard as he marched toward the stable. But, quite at variance with his usual concern for their happiness and well-being, he pointedly ignored them, keeping his eyes trained on the ground ahead of him and muttering to himself with each step he took. When he reached the stable doors, he paused to take a deep breath and gather his composure again. He would not let Cain's suspicions get the better of him. It was bad enough that he himself had discovered the spell this small woman had cast on him without letting someone else know of it. Especially Cain. There would be no rest for him if Joshua knew. Long ago Beau had vowed no woman would ever steal into his heart, making that pledge to Cain. The man had laughed at him, telling him that there wasn't a man alive strong enough to fend off the love of a woman and stating that a day in his life would come when he would discover it for himself. If nothing else, Beau never wanted to admit to Cain or to himself that he might be wrong.

The light from the opened stable doors flooded in and drew Jeremiah's attention away from his task of shoeing the hoof held tightly between his knees. He frowned when he recognized Beau's silhouette in the doorway.

"Something wrong, Masta Beau?" he asked, releasing the mare.

Beau sighed. "Why is it everyone thinks something is wrong just because I make an unexpected visit? Are you, in fact, guilty of something you fear I will discover by being here?"

Jeremiah took a breath to deny any wrongdoing, but before he could speak, Beau left him to untether a buckskin in the stall next to him and irritably throw a blanket over its back.

"If anyone is looking for me, tell them I've gone for a ride to cool off," he growled, tossing on a saddle and tightening the cinch.

Jeremiah stood in the shadows watching Beau lead the horse outside, skillfully mount the animal, and race off toward the river. He reached up to rub the back of his neck, shook his head and turned back to finish his work.

The wind against Beau's face and the strong animal beneath him felt good. A wild ride across his plantation always seemed to relax him. He needed to get away, to clear his thoughts, to bring some order to his life. There were some bank dealings he needed to clear up and he decided now would be the best time. He could solve two problems in one trip. Feeling a little better, he let the horse slow to a canter as the river came into view.

He led the horse upstream along its muddy edge until they came to a place where he had spent a great deal of time as a young boy. He dropped the reins as the animal eagerly stepped in for a drink and easily slid from the saddle. Although the river flowed at a rapid pace to the sea, this was one of the few spots where it flooded its banks and formed a pool of quiet, unmoving water. Beau studied it for quite a while until, feeling the heat of the day, he began to strip himself of his clothes. Bessy was right. A dip in the river was what he needed.

Ten

The injury from Alanna's fall healed quickly and she returned to work with an added zeal. Beau hadn't returned to his room that day until nearly bedtime, and when he had, it was only to tell her that she would sleep more comfortably where she was. She had argued the point, telling him how guilty she would feel knowing she had put him out, but he had only smiled, gathered a change of clothes, and left without a word. The following morning she had risen with the hopes of thanking him for his kindness, only to have Bessy tell her that the master of Raven Oaks had left the plantation for a few days on business.

Lying in his bed with little to occupy her mind had given her a lot of time to think. She had seen a new side of Beau, one of which Bessy, Tilly, and Horace had tried to tell her about. He *was* considerate, caring, concerned about others. Even about her. And in his own clumsy way he was trying to make up for all the hurt he had caused her.

Alone in his room as she had been, she had thought

back to all that had happened since she first arrived at Raven Oaks, her father's letter, the way Beau Remington had tried to explain it, and the disobedient, headstrong servant who had run away refusing to listen. Although she hated to admit it, she had been wrong. Her punishment had been a little extreme, she thought, but had she been in his place, she doubted she would have acted differently. Even her dislike for the man who had carried out the sentence softened. He had only done as ordered. And as Cinnamon had pointed out, if Beau Remington liked her, life here could be as pleasant as she wanted it. With this thought in mind, Alanna had to confess she found the master of this huge plantation intriguing. In fact, after he had unselfishly allowed her the use of his room, she discovered she actually liked him.

"My, yo's in a cheerful way this mornin'," Tilly said a day later when she caught Alanna humming a brisk, light-hearted tune.

She smiled.

"Ain't 'cause he's gone, is it?"

Alanna folded the linen tablecloth, the light smile still curling the corners of her mouth. "No," she said. "In fact, I sort of miss him."

"Yo' all land on yo'r head?" Tilly asked. "Or yo' funnin' me?"

The dark maid watched in silence as Alanna put away the richly made cloth and straightened it. "I noticed a flower bed out back that's in dire need of a woman's hand. Would you suppose I could tend to it? I do so love flowers."

Tilly eyed the girl suspiciously, knowing Alanna had avoided her question. "Well, I guess it would be all right. We's nearly finished here."

128

"Thank you, Tilly," Alanna replied excitedly as she headed for the door.

"Yo' can find the tools yo' need in a small shed near the garden," Tilly called after the quickly departing figure. "If'n yo' need anythin' else, ask Horace." Certain Alanna hadn't heard a word she said until she was rewarded by a distant "thank you," the young housekeeper could only stand there and shake her head. "Land sake's alive," she muttered. "That surely ain't the same girl who walked in here a couple weeks ago." With a shrug of dismissal, Tilly went back to her work.

Alanna had always enjoyed working with flowers, even when she was told to do so by her stepmother. It was always peaceful in the garden. Of course, the flower beds they had back home in England weren't nearly the size of the one before her now, but she still felt the same serenity she had then. Resting on her knees, she began to pluck the weeds, remembering a day not so long ago when she had been doing just the same. It had been warm that day, too, and she had tied up her long black hair in a yellow ribbon that matched the color of her gown. Her stepmother had told her to tend the flower bed, a job that was always hers while the elder Bainbridge women cleaned the old widow Nelson's house together, to earn what extra money they could to supplement her father's meager income. She hated it. Not the duty itself, but what it represented. She was tired of being poor. She had vowed years before, once her father had casually, but cunningly, pointed out Alanna's approaching marriageable age, that she would not marry for love as her stepmother had done, but for the wealth the man could offer. Then Aaron appeared at her side. He had seemed the answer to her unspoken prayers.

He was the son of a wealthy shop owner and his family was never in need of much. He had declared his love for her almost immediately and Alanna felt that in time she would marry him. But his parents hadn't agreed. She was the daughter of a common worker with no class or station in life. Both she and Aaron were only fifteen at the time, and, although his parents forbade the union, they would meet in secret places to discuss their future.

With each year that passed, Alanna found herself with many new male admirers, all of whom were amusing, but dull compared to Aaron. Then her father announced their plans to leave for America. Visions of that awful day when she had been forced to tell Aaron of her departure came rushing back in her memory.

"Poor Aaron," she whispered as she pulled another weed. "I do miss him."

"Miss who?"

Startled by the intruding voice of another, Alanna dropped the small spade she held and glanced up. Standing beside her in the bright sunlight towered the well-groomed, lean figure of Radford Chamberlain.

"I—I didn't hear you approach," she stammered, struggling to her feet. Radford reached out an aiding hand and took her elbow.

"I beg your forgiveness. I didn't mean to frighten you," he smiled with a deep courtly bow. "Sometimes I forget my manners."

Alanna couldn't suppress an equally warm but somewhat embarrassed smile. "It's quite all right. I'm afraid I was daydreaming and probably wouldn't have heard you call out anyway. Have you come to see Master Remington?"

Radford stared at her a moment before reaching up to

pick a stray tendril of hair from her brow. She blushed but he didn't seem to notice. "Yes, I have," he spoke softly, "but Tilly tells me he is away."

"On business," Alanna added. "But we expect him home soon. I'm sorry you wasted the trip."

"On the contrary. It was hardly a waste since it gave me the opportunity to see you." He smiled again and Alanna looked at her hands. "Tell me about yourself, Alanna. I may call you that, may I not?"

"I'd be honored," she replied, "but I'm afraid there isn't much to tell. I came here from England with my parents. They died on board the ship and I found myself here. If things go as I've planned, I will return to my homeland very soon."

Radford's brow knotted. "I thought you were an indentured servant. How could you leave before you have fulfilled your time?"

"Master Remington was kind enough to allow me to send a letter to my aunt in England requesting the pounds sterling that are needed to pay off my debt. When it arrives, I shall be on my way."

Radford continued to frown.

"Is something wrong?" Alanna asked, noting his expression.

"Er-no. I guess I was just thinking how it would be a great loss to Raven Oaks if you were to go away." He bent down and plucked a red flower, idly tearing its petals from the stem.

Alanna laughed. "I hardly think it would be that. But thank you for saying it."

"My pleasure," he nodded, "but whether you believe it or not, it is true. I'm certain many hearts will feel the loss."

Alanna had the feeling he wanted to say more, but instead, dropped the flower and raised an arm for her to take.

"Shall we stroll about the gardens?"

A flood of color darkened her cheeks. She was hesitant to touch him, but after a moment she consented, brushing the dirt from her hands against her skirt and entwining her arm within his. The moment her hand rested against the velvet softness of his sleeve, she felt a strangeness overtake her. Was this man trying to court her? Or just being polite? Whatever his motive, she decided she would enjoy his company while she could.

They wandered about the yard for several minutes, talking about anything that came to mind. They laughed and joked and never once did Radford try to pull his arm away nor did Alanna. They came to a willow tree whose branches formed a shady retreat and they stopped in the coolness of it. Alanna leaned back against its trunk and Radford pressed a hand to it just above her head while he studied her.

"You're very beautiful, Alanna."

She laughed. "You mustn't fill my head with such thoughts, Master Chamberlain."

"But you are," he exclaimed, as if hurt by her denial.

"And you are a flatterer, sir," she laughed again.

"Maybe so," he grinned. "But I am never tempted to be unless the need arises. And you, fair lady, must tempt even the hardest of hearts."

"I'm afraid that I have had little chance to practice the art," she said, remembering Aaron and their first clumsy kiss.

"Come now," he spoke persuasively. "Would you lead me to believe that you never had a man throw himself at your feet? Surely, there have been hundreds."

Alanna laughed in genuine amusement, her disavowel parting her lips. "Maybe a few, m'lord, but never hundreds as you say."

"And how many have tried to kiss you, only to be denied?" he teased lightheartedly. "I'll wager England has many a lad with broken heart that you have turned away."

Alanna lowered her eyes. "A few, perhaps."

"A few?" he cajoled. "You are too modest." Then his smile disappeared. "Would you deny me the chance, Alanna?"

Stunned by his request, she stared openmouthed.

"I assure you I want nothing else," he whispered earnestly.

"Oh, forgive me if I led you to believe I thought otherwise. It's only that you surprised me," she said, shaking off her bewilderment.

"Yes, sometimes I surprise myself. I shouldn't have asked," he apologized before turning away.

"Oh, no," she cried out, touching nervous fingertips to his arm, "I'm honored. After all, what am I? A mere servant being wooed by the master of a plantation, a man of wealth, one of high standing in this colony, I'm sure. It is I who should apologize for denying you."

The carefree look of abandonment returned to his eyes. "If only everyone thought of me as you do." He moved to face her and place a fingertip beneath her chin. "You are refreshing, my dear. Your honesty and sweetness brighten my usually dull life." He leaned in and would have kissed her, if a voice from behind them hadn't stopped him.

"I hope I'm not disturbing anything."

Alanna stiffened at the sound of the voice, knowing full well who had spoken. She looked past Radford to find Beau standing only a few feet away with his arms folded in front of him, a dark, angry scowl distorting his handsome features. She swallowed fearfully and stood paralyzed, too frightened to speak. Finally, Radford broke the silence.

"We weren't expecting you," he grinned, returning to his playful self.

"Obviously," Beau replied with just a hint of sarcasm.

"That's not what I meant," Radford lighted warned. "I came on business, and when I was told that you were away, I decided not to waste my trip. Besides, Mistress Bainbridge is much more pleasant to talk with," he added, sending a smile her way.

Beau chose to ignore his remark. "It didn't appear to be conversation that you found pleasant."

"Why, Beau Remington. If I didn't know you as well as I do, I'd swear you're jealous."

Beau stiffened immediately, his dark eyes growing stormy as he dropped his arms, silently cursing the man's impertinence. "See to some bath water, Alanna. I'm dirty and tired from the long ride," he growled, never taking his eyes from Radford.

She quickly left Radford's side, thankful for the chance to depart the scene, but as she passed Beau, he reached out and caught her elbow. "And wait for me in my room when it's done."

She looked up at him in surprise and then glanced back at Radford. He started to speak but obviously changed his mind, kicking at the pebbles beneath his feet with a toe. "Yes, sir," she answered weakly and set off in the direction of the house.

"Listen, Beau—" Radford began when she was out of sight, but stopped short when Beau raised a hand.

"No, you listen. You're to leave her alone. Do you understand?"

A fist resting on each hip, Radford shook his head. "Damned if you aren't jealous."

Beau's nostrils flared. "This conversation is at an end. Good day," he seethed, turning on his heels to stalk off toward the house.

"This conversation may be," he called after him, "but my visits here aren't. I intend to call on Miss Bainbridge whether you like it or not."

Radford stood alone in the shade of the willow with a smile of pure devilment sparkling in his blue eyes. He had never seen his friend react the way he had today and he was certain it wasn't just because of him. Beau Remington was fond of the girl and his presence had been a threat. He would continue to needle him as he had just done, careful not to push too far. But he had waited a long time for a chance like this, and he wasn't about to let it pass.

The slamming of a door resounded throughout the house, marking the return of Master Remington in an extremely black mood, and Tilly scurried out of his way as he stormed through the kitchen. This wasn't the first time she had seen him in such a foul temper, and she knew from past experience that it was best handled by staying out from underfoot. She stood in his wake, wondering what it was that had upset him.

Beau climbed the stairs two at a time and went straight to his room where he found Alanna struggling to position the brass tub for his bath. She stopped when she heard him enter.

"I thought I told you to stay away from Radford," he snarled.

"Yes, sir, you did. But it wasn't I who summoned him here. He came to see you."

"And found you instead," he added with a dark frown. "And I suppose it was his idea to kiss you, too."

"Yes," she answered quietly, "but I don't suppose you'd believe it."

"Oh, but I do," he said. "There isn't a man alive that wouldn't think of it after looking at you."

"What do you mean?" she asked, her own anger piqued slightly by his words.

"Well, look at the way you're dressed. The cloth of your gown is so thin I can nearly see through it. And your hair, bound up so invitingly, with just one strand resting against your brow, begging for someone to put it back in place. And whoever heard of a lady wandering about in the gardens without any shoes?"

"But I always dress in this manner," she argued with a sweep of her hand to her hair. "I only have one pair of shoes and I wish to save them for the cold winter months. And the dress is one Tilly gave me. It was one of hers. Would you have me clothe myself in a dark wool with long sleeves and high collar?"

"I would have you remove yourself from Master Chamberlain's presence the next time he comes!"

Tears welled up in Alanna's eyes. "May I be excused, sir?"

"No," he shouted, slamming the door closed behind him with the heel of his boot. "I have not finished with you. If it is a man you want, then that is what you shall have."

Alanna gasped when Beau stepped in and grabbed both

136

of her arms, pulling her against his chest as he pressed his mouth to hers, stifling any chance she might have to deny his assumption. He released her arms only to pull her wrists in back of her with one hand while the other roughly fondled her breast. She broke free of his kiss and screamed. Rage boiled up in him, and without a second thought he brought up the back of his hand to strike her cheek. She fell back, hiding her face with her hands, tears flowing freely.

"Damn you, woman! You force me to do things I shouldn't and regret them every waking hour. I *should* sell your papers and be free of you, but God knows even that would not end my torment."

Having heard his words, Alanna stilled her tears, but her mind began to spin in confused thoughts. Why, if he put her from him, would his torment not cease? And why did he not wish for her to speak with Radford Chamberlain? Was it because she was only a servant, someone below his station and not worthy of his company? Or because he was jealous, as she had heard Radford say as she walked away? No, she told herself. It was foolish even to consider it. Suddenly, Alanna felt his arms encircle her and knew he did not intend to apologize, but to fulfill a desire that frightened her. She pushed away from him.

"Please, sir," she begged, her throat tight, "I have work to do and it is the middle of the day." She started past him and he stepped in front of her. She looked into his eyes beseechingly. "What do you want?" she moaned resignedly.

Beau did not respond. He did not have to, for his answer shone clearly in his eyes. His anger had vanished, and Alanna thought, for only an instant, that she saw tenderness in them. Then a dark shadow hooded his true feelings.

"You, Alanna. I want you."

When he touched her shoulders to draw her close, a gentleness in the long, lean fingers, a flood of warmth poured over her, no desire to resist him commanding her moves. Weak and trembling, she closed her eyes when his lips brushed hers then softly rested on the red mark of her cheek before he hungrily kissed her once more. His scent intoxicating, Alanna's heart fluttered and, without thought, her hands came up to pull him nearer. Stirred by her response, he found the buttons of her gown as he covered her cheek, chin, and neck in a flurry of kisses, his teeth nibbling at the tender flesh. Impatient to have what he craved so lustfully, the few remaining buttons posing the only opposition, he tore at the cloth, ripping it from her in one swift movement to pool at her feet.

A vision of curves and beauty standing before him, Beau retreated a step to drink in the splendor with his eyes and noticed how she trembled beneath his regard. Reaching out, he trailed a fingertip along the lace trim of her camisole to pluck at the strings that held it in place. His breath quickened with each loop he unfastened until it too lay at her feet. His passion soaring, he cupped her delicate chin in his huge hands, pulling her face to his to sample the sweetness of her kiss once more. She groaned, a soft, tender sound that urged him on, certain now that she shared his all-consuming desire. His mouth covering hers, one hand entangled with the dark mass of hair at the nape of her neck, while he kicked off his shoes and slid from his clothes.

This is madness, Alanna's mind reeled. Have I no shame?

His naked body pressed to hers, locking her in a warm, passionate embrace, Alanna's flesh burned with his touch as his hands searched, explored, conquered, pulling her hips against him, his manhood hard and throbbing.

How can this be? she cried out inwardly. He thought of her only as a possession, nothing more, yet the overpowering desire to urge him on, to guide his hands, his kiss, denied her gentle upbringing. "Oh, please, Beau, don't do this to me," she half-sobbed, half-begged when he slowly fell to his knees, his lips and tongue tasting the softness of her flesh beneath her chin, her throat, the valley between her breasts, the silkiness of her stomach, his hands against her buttocks to pull her close. Her pulse raced, her mind screamed to bring an end, her heart begging him to continue, to consume her in his fiery passion.

Rising to his feet, he swept her in his arms and carried her to the bed, gently laying her upon it. His gaze raked over her, his eyes burning with his lust, before he rested one knee on the feather mattress and reached down to lift a dark curl from her shoulder. His body quivered with the breath he took. He fell to her almost brutally parting her thighs with his knee, pressing himself full upon her. He teased her, tempted her, and, before long, she heard herself begging him to take her, a sound very foreign to her ears.

"Oh, Alanna, Alanna," he breathed as his passion reached its pinnacle.

They lay trembling in each other's arms, having sated a hunger neither had ever felt before. For Beau, it was a mountain he had conquered, the summit he had reached. For the first time in his life, he had felt something other than contempt or lust for a woman. But to Alanna it brought a different reward. In fact, it was a failure. Although she felt no shame for what she had done, she experienced a yearning, a need for him to hold her closely, to kiss her, to say the words she had longed to hear a man say, a man who loved her. Tears filled her eyes. She knew he didn't love her, that he had only used her to satisfy his needs as he had done with so many before her. What made her think that he would feel any differently toward her? Her heart ached as she lay there nestled in the crook of his arm, his fingertips brushing away the hair from her brow. A gesture made from love? she thought. Or from lust? She knew the answer without having to be told. Beau Remington could never love a woman, and she began to hate herself for ever thinking that he could, that even if some miracle happened and he let his heart be touched, it would never be she who would bring about his change. She pulled away from him, pledging an oath to herself that she would never find herself weakened by his words or his touch again, and to return home to England as soon as possible.

"Must the little dove fly away so soon?" he whispered. "I promise you this hawk will not harm you."

Alanna felt as if her very heart was being torn from her as she forced herself to walk away. In a wild frenzy, she felt compelled to cover herself and, looking about, she spied his shirt on the chair next to her. With a secret loving tenderness, she reached out, took it, and quickly put it on. She turned back to him.

"Is that how you acquired the name?" she asked, knowing that what she was about to say would erect a barrier between them so great that nothing she could ever say again would ever tear it down. "It's quite fitting.

You are the hawk and the wench you have bedded is your dove. I have heard you play the game often." She began to fasten the buttons of his shirt as she walked toward the door. "However, sir, beware. Should we ever play at this sport again, you will find I am not one of your doves, for unlike those before me, I find your touch distasteful." She quickly looked away to hide the tears in her eyes. Silently, she opened the door and left the room.

Alanna hurried down the hall to her bedchamber, hoping no one would see her coming from Beau's clad only in his shirt, and hastily closed the door behind her. She had managed to keep her wits about her all the while she confronted him, but now that she was alone in her room, her tears boiled up inside her, and before she knew it they had broken free. She wept, hard and long, not only for the grief she felt but for the prison in which she found herself. Beau Remington had an insatiable desire for her, to own her, to possess her, and, until she was free of him, he would use her time and time again to fulfill that need, never feeling anything else but lust. If the pain she felt now was because she had fallen in love with him, she would do everything in her power to hide that love from him, for she knew he would only use it against her. Squaring her shoulders in a near fruitless attempt to swallow her agony, she wiped the tears from her face with the back of her hands and heard the sound of her door opening. She turned around to face her intruder. Standing in the archway was The Hawk, clothed only in his breeches, a dark, ominous shadow hiding the color of his eyes.

"Since you feel what we shared was nothing more than a game and wish that no one else should know of it, I have come for what is mine," he said with a nod toward his shirt. "It would not do for Tilly to find such an item in your room." He stepped closer and Alanna noticed her gown clutched in his fist. "Consider this a trade," he said, flinging the dress in her face, "my silence for yours. I wouldn't want it known that I lower myself to make love to just anyone."

Alanna's chin trembled and she quickly looked away so that he might not see. She crossed to her wardrobe, pulled a robe from it, and hurriedly exchanged it for the shirt. Timidly, she held it out for him.

Beau stared at her, unmoving and silent. Then he reached out, took the garment, and walked out.

Eleven

From behind her teacup, Melissa Bensen eyed the girl sitting across the room from her.

"Well, I think it's shameful," Blythe Robbins sniffed.

"You never have before," Melissa reminded her. "What makes it any different now?"

Blythe added a teaspoon of sugar to her tea. "You know well and good he intends to make her his mistress. Referring to her as a housekeeper is absurd, and a ridiculous way to cover up the fact."

"Oh, Blythe, don't be such a prude. It happens all the time," Melissa half-smiled, taking a sip of her tea.

"Well, of course, it does. But a *gentleman* would be more discreet."

"A gentleman?" Melissa laughed temptingly. "Are you saying that Beau Remington isn't?"

"Oh, no," Blythe shrieked, her face paling. "I didn't mean that. I just meant—"

"Perhaps you're jealous," Melissa cut in, baiting her friend.

"I am not!" Blythe retorted sharply.

Melissa grinned to herself. Let the woman say whatever she pleased, she thought otherwise. Blythe Robbins was a homely girl no matter how one looked at it. She was dreadfully thin, with no bosom to speak of, and it made her richly fashioned gowns appear to just hang from her shoulders. Her mousy brown hair, although styled in an abundance of ringlets, did little to offset the sharp, pointed features of her face. Her eyes, Melissa thought, were her only good feature. They were dark blue oval circles accented by heavy, thick lashes. But even that did not hide the fact that she had no color to her cheeks or her straight-lined lips. It was no wonder she was past marrying age. Even Radford had implied as much.

Radford, Melissa thought with a raised brow. Now there was a man who had her completely fooled. For years she had tried to trick Beau into marrying her, since he was the wealthiest bachelor in all of Virginia. She had decided a union between them would be perfect, but Beau, obviously, had thought otherwise, preferring the companionship of many women rather than just one. However, Melissa was not about to believe he didn't feel something for her and in an effort to make him jealous—or so she thought—she landed her hooks in his best friend, positive Beau would see his error and come running after her. But that had failed. In fact, she saw even less of Beau Remington. And as time went on, she realized she would have to settle for second best. With practiced grace and cunning, she trapped Radford into courting her.

They had been seeing each other for a over a year, and Melissa frowned when she realized how long it had been. She couldn't understand why he hadn't asked for her hand in marriage long before this. He lived alone on Briarwood Manor, the second-biggest plantation near Williamsburg, with only a handful of house servants and scores of Negro slaves. He was past thirty years of age and could well afford a wife. But for some reason he hadn't asked her. I really don't know why, she thought with a lift of her nose in the air. After all, my father is not poor, and my dowry will be quite large. And I'm far from homely.

"What are you thinking?"

She glanced up and saw Blythe. "I'm thinking how a buggy ride in the shade of the willows would be refreshing. Care to join me?"

"That's just an excuse to go to Raven Oaks, and you know it. Ever since Radford told you of her, you've thought of nothing else."

Melissa smiled coyly and took another sip of tea.

"There are other less obvious ways to see his new housekeeper, you know."

"Such as?"

"You could have a dinner party, invite Beau and suggest he bring the girl."

Melissa couldn't refrain from a chuckle. "He's quite brazen, my dear Blythe, but he'd never stoop to escorting one of his servants to *my* home."

"Oh, really?" Blythe sang disagreeingly. "What makes you think Beau Remington would be any more courteous to you than he is to everyone else?"

"Because, as you said, he is a gentleman. Now do you care to join me or swelter in this awful heat?"

Blythe was the only child of a dress shop owner whose husband had died when Blythe was a small girl. Her mother had recognized the lonesome plight of her shy daughter even then. When Melissa Bensen, the only heir to the Willow Glen plantation, showed an interest in her, Blythe's mother had pushed the relationship, feeling certain Melissa's influence and male admirers would affect Blythe. She had constantly drummed it into the girl to do everything Melissa suggested and never make her angry with her for fear of losing her friendship. Remembering the teachings of her mother, Blythe sighed in submission, for she really had no desire to go to Raven Oaks, but she knew she must.

"All right," she said. "Let's go."

Beau sat alone in his study, toying with the unlit cheroot he rolled between his fingers. He hadn't slept much the night before, lying awake thinking of what had transpired in that very bed only a few hours earlier. Why had he reacted the way he had when he had found Alanna and Radford together? And why had he forced himself on her? He stuck the cigar in his mouth. He hadn't forced himself on her. She had responded to his touch. He was sure of it. Then why did she say what she had? Damn her, he growled to himself, angrily rising from his chair to stare out the window, she's playing with me. She knows how she affects me and she's using it against me. How could I be so stupid? He returned to his desk and placed a hip to its edge as he once again rolled the cigar between his fingers.

His trip to Williamsburg had been what he had needed. He had taken care of his bank dealings in the morning and spent the rest of the time browsing the various shops along the main street. He had forgotten the young girl who lived in his house until he had passed a dress shop, spotting a bolt of dark blue velvet displayed in the window and thinking how beautiful a gown made of it would look on her. He had frowned, scolding himself for letting his mind wander, and stalked away. He took in a dinner theater that evening in the company of a beautiful brunette. It had been pleasant until he realized how very much the woman reminded him of someone else and knew he had chosen the woman's companionship for that reason. He sighed, knowing there would never be an escape from Alanna Bainbridge.

The following morning he had gone back to the dress shop, purchased the bolt of fabric and ordered a gown made of it. That evening, with an extra coin for having put it ahead of the rest, Beau took the brightly wrapped box containing the gown and returned to his room at the inn with the thought that upon his arrival at Raven Oaks he would present it to her. But things hadn't worked out that way. He had seen Radford's horse tied to the brass ring of the hitching post at the front of the house, and the untimely intrusion sparked his anger even before he walked in on the scene beneath the willow.

Beau poured himself a drink and, even though some of it remained in the glass, his ire had grown to such heights as he remembered the nearness of the couple that he viciously hurled it into the darkened fireplace, spraying fine droplets and shattered pieces of glass over the hearth. Feeling better, he went back to the window to stare outside again when a knock at the door interrupted his thoughts.

"What is it?" he growled.

The door opened slowly and Horace stuck his head in. "Excuse me, Masta Beau, but Mistress Bensen and Mistress Robbins is here to see yo'."

"Wonderful," he said with a roll of his eyes. "See

147

them to the parlor. I'll be there directly."

He listened to the door close quietly and replaced the somewhat tattered cigar in the box on the desk top before he straightened, tugged at his waistcoat, and took a deep breath. About the last people to whom he felt like being polite were Melissa and her simple little friend. But knowing there could be no avoiding it short of his sudden and unexpected death, he left the study and headed for the parlor.

As he crossed the foyer, he glanced up to the balcony that disappeared down the hallway, knowing Alanna was hidden away in her room. "You cause me more grief than you realize," he frowned. "I hope you have the good grace to stay where you are until my guests have gone." Sullenly, he advanced into the parlor.

Seated on the sofa, Melissa was surrounded by her bright yellow gown spread out around her. Trimmed in white lace around the sleeves and across the bosom, it failed to cover the full swell of her breasts, something Beau was sure she intended. Her long yellow curls dangled from beneath a wide-brimmed hat tied neatly with a white satin bow under one ear. She could present quite a striking figure when she wanted to, and this, obviously, was one of those times.

Blythe, on the other hand, could never manage to look more than plain. Such a thin girl, to the point of looking sickly. Beau wondered if Melissa didn't keep her around just for the effect.

"Beau, darling," he heard Melissa sing as she came to meet him. "How are you? You come by so rarely anymore, I never know what you're up to. You're not angry with little ol' me, are you?"

"I've been busy, Melissa," Beau answered flatly.

She had taken his arm and only out of politeness did he escort her back to the sofa, seat her and then stand to one side.

"You remember Blythe, don't you, Beau?" She smiled up at him with a flutter of her lashes.

He nodded toward the young woman and couldn't help noticing the sudden flush to her cheeks. If she felt uneasy, it was nothing compared to how he felt at the moment.

"Do sit down," Melissa said enticingly as she patted a spot next to her on the sofa. "We have so much to talk about."

"Thank you, but I'd prefer to stand. I've done nothing but work at my desk all morning and I find I need to stretch my legs," he replied with a twist to the truth. "Would either of you care for some tea?"

"That's very kind of you to offer," Melissa murmured coquettishly, "but I'm afraid Blythe and I have had our fill. Haven't we, Blythe, dear?"

Again, Beau looked at the woman and saw her nod her head, wondering if Melissa ever allowed her to speak for herself. He frowned, curious as to why they had come. Melissa never showed up unexpectedly without a reason. He set his gaze on her again.

"So," he began, forcing a casual tone to his voice, "what brings you to Raven Oaks?"

"Oh, it was so hot at Willow Glen that Blythe suggested we go for a cool ride," Melissa told him with a rather suggestive dab of her handkerchief to the valley between her breasts. "And before we knew it, we found ourselves here."

Beau smiled weakly. It was as good an excuse as any. "And how's your mother and father?"

"Oh, they're fine. Papa just said this morning how it's been such a long time since you've come to visit. Didn't he, Blythe?"

About to wipe the perspiration from her brow when addressed by her friend's foolish question, Blythe fidgeted nervously. She hadn't seen Mathew Bensen in days, much less talked with him. "Yes," she replied quietly, avoiding their host's eyes.

"Why don't you join us for dinner some night? You and Radford can ride over together," Melissa said. Then, as if she had had a second thought, added, "Of course, that is, unless you'd prefer to bring someone—" Her voice trailed off.

Beau hoped his reaction to the unveiling of her reason for their sudden visit didn't show on his face. Obviously, she had come to his home in hopes of seeing Alanna. Radford must have been quite busy at work, filling the woman's head with all sorts of jealous ideas. Well, she had wasted her trip. He wouldn't even mention his newest servant.

"Tell your father I'd be honored to come. Just send a message and let me know the evening."

Their conversation turned to the weather, the crops, and Melissa's newly ordered wardrobe from France. Beau politely listened, joining in where needed, but all the while he thought of how outraged Melissa would be if she came face to face with Alanna at her doorstep.

"Alanna, yo' can't stay in here all day."

The dark-haired girl continued to stare out the window of her room.

"Bessy says if'n yo' feel poorly, I is to give yo' some

150

cod liver oil. Yo' ever taste it? It's horrible and I sure yo' don't want it if'n there's nothin' wrong." Tilly waited for an answer with her fists resting on each hip. "Yo' hear me, Alanna Bainbridge?"

"Yes, Tilly. I hear you." Alanna shifted positions on the sill. "Has Master Remington left the house yet?"

"I ain't seen him all mornin'. Now are yo' gonna come downstairs or do I get the bottle?"

Alanna looked at the dark face angrily staring at her. Poor Tilly. She would never know why Alanna did not want to leave her room. It would hurt her to know, since she cared a great deal for her master. She just wouldn't be able to believe it. "Yes, I'll come," she replied softly.

"Good. The first thing I need yo' to do is to gather up the silver from the parlor and bring it to the kitchen so's we can clean it. Now get goin' or I'll send Bessy after yo'," she threw back over her shoulder as she walked from the room.

Slowly Alanna rose from her perch on the windowsill and went to her dressing table. No wonder everyone thinks I'm ill, she mused, looking at her reflection in the mirror. Dark circles beneath her eyes marred her pale complexion. If only she had something with which to hide them. She picked up a brush and worked her hair in long, listless strokes, studying the somber face staring back at her. Why couldn't she have been born a boy? She tied back her thick mane with a strip of cloth and started for the parlor.

As she descended the stairs, her thoughts elsewhere, she realized she had heard the soprano tones of a woman's laughter coming from the parlor. Maybe Tilly couldn't wait any longer for her and had decided to fetch the candlesticks and tea service herself, but who would have made her laugh? Curiously, she continued down the stairs and across the marble floor.

"Tilly?" she called, stepping into the archway, and stood paralyzed when she found three pairs of eyes staring at her. "Oh," she finally managed to say, "excuse me. I didn't know anyone was here."

"Oh, that's quite all right," Melissa said, her eyes narrowing as she appraised the newcomer.

Unable to look away from the woman who had spoken, Alanna stared shamelessly, knowing she had never seen a lady quite as beautiful before. Her yellow hair, arranged perfectly in long ringlets, haloed her face, only slightly hidden from view by the enormous bonnet she wore. Her cheeks were the color of a pink rose and contrasted remarkably well with her sea-green eyes. Her lace-trimmed gown clung tightly to her waist before billowing out around her. She had all the grace and beauty of a queen, and Alanna found herself wishing she was half as stunning.

"My name is Melissa Bensen," she said when no one chose to speak, "and this is my friend, Blythe Robbins. Who might you be?"

"Alanna Bainbridge," Alanna said, with a quick bend to one knee.

"How delightful," Melissa sang as if complimenting a child. "You do that so well. Did Tilly teach you?"

Her first impression of the woman shattered, Alanna stiffened, holding back her angry retort. "No, miss, my mother. I'm sorry I intruded, and if you'll excuse me, I'll be on my way," she rebuffed her, failing to disguise her irritation as she turned to leave.

"You must be Beau's new housekeeper," Melissa continued, stopping Alanna immediately. "Radford's told me all about you."

The implication in her words all too clear, Alanna decided not to grace her with an answer. She started for the door again.

"Do be a peach, child, and bring us some tea."

Alanna glanced back at Beau. The expression on his face told her nothing, but the nod of his head did. Inwardly seething, she left the room to do as she had been instructed.

Elbow deep in sudsy water when Alanna entered the kitchen, Tilly looked up to find her assistant empty-handed as she plopped down in a chair. "Where's yo' head this mornin', Alanna? I told yo' to bring me the silver from the parlor."

"That is what I started out to do, but when I reached the parlor I found Master Remington entertaining guests. Who is Mistress Bensen?"

"Lordy, is that who's in there?"

"Yes. And her friend, Blythe Robbins."

"What an awful pair for yo' to be walkin' in on without no warnin'. If I know'd, I wouldn't have sent yo'."

"Oh, that's all right. How were you to know? Who are they?" she asked, her own curiosity aroused by the other's obvious dislike for the women.

"Mistress Bensen's pappy owns the plantation next to Masta Chamberlain's. He and the mistress have been seeing each other for a long time. I guess they'll marry some day."

"Marry?" Alanna said with surprise.

"Yes. I's afraid I feel the same. Masta Radford is too fine a gentleman to be tied to her all of his life."

"Why do you say that?"

"Because she's a terrible nag. Whiney and all. She'd

153

make his life miserable. That's why I thought maybe—"

"Maybe what?"

"Well, the other day when Masta Radford came to see Masta Beau and found out he wasn't here, he seemed happy. 'Specially when I told him yo' were out in the gardens. Didn't waste no time lookin' for yo'."

"Oh, Tilly, you're making that up."

"I is not! I knows when a man is interested in a woman."

"He is not," Alanna exploded, leaving her chair to hang a kettle over the fire. "Besides, I'm not the lady Mistress Bensen is."

"Ha! Yo' twice the lady that one ever hope to be."

Alanna smiled. It probably wasn't true, but it certainly was nice to hear someone say it. She frowned. Too bad someone else didn't consider her a lady.

With the teapot and three cups and saucers sitting on a tray held securely in her hands, Alanna headed back to the parlor, pausing just outside the door to prepare herself for an unavoidably tense few minutes. Apparently, Mistress Bensen thought very little of Beau's new housekeeper, and if what Tilly thought was true, Melissa had even more reason to dislike her. With a gallant lift to her chin, she quietly entered the room.

Melissa laughed coyly at something Beau said but when she spotted Alanna, her mirth vanished. She unfolded the fan from her lap and began to flutter it beneath her chin, eyeing the girl down her nose.

"I do hope you brought cream, child," she said, as if annoyed. "I simply can't endure tea without cream."

Choosing not to speak, Alanna nodded politely, set the tray on the table near Melissa and headed off after the forgotten substance.

"Honestly, Beau," she heard Melissa say as she left the room, "you really should teach the girl how to perform. A servant in my house wouldn't last long if she was as incapable as that one."

Alanna couldn't hear his answer, but she was sure he had agreed. The two of them would make a better couple than Radford and Melissa, she deduced bitterly. They both are egotistical bores. With a hardness to her step, determined not to be beaten down by their cruelty, she obtained the cream pitcher from the kitchen and returned to her foe.

"Papa says Mr. Washington and several other representatives will be in Williamsburg soon," Melissa was saying when Alanna entered the room again. "I do so hope they'll come."

Beau smiled at her, but his attention had been drawn away as he watched the shapely, barefooted figure cross the room and place the cream pitcher on the tray next to the teapot. Without a word, she turned to depart.

"Where do you think you're going?" Melissa demanded tensely. "Pour me some tea."

Without comment or even a show of her irritation, Alanna turned back and proceeded to fulfill Melissa's request.

"Really, Beau," Melissa said sourly. "I do think you should teach this young thing respect for her betters."

Alanna bristled, but made no sound. "If that will be all, I wish to be excused. I have work in the kitchen," she said crisply.

"Yes, Alanna, that will do," Beau answered, his voice filling the hostile silence of the room while inwardly

155

applauding the calm way in which Alanna had handled the audacious treatment she was forced to endure. He stood back and watched the squared shoulders, the proud lift of her chin, and the dignified walk as she started for the door.

"She certainly is a pretty thing," Melissa said half-heartedly before Alanna had made her exit. "But then you always did choose beautiful mistresses."

Alanna spun around. She opened her mouth to speak, caught sight of Beau, and promptly snapped it closed. However, she did not hide the hateful, outraged feeling she had for Melissa as she glowered at her.

And Melissa did not miss it. She instantly straightened in her seat, and lifted her nose in the air, an equally outraged strain heaving the muscles across her chest.

"That will be all, Alanna," Beau warned, quickly coming to her side, for he too had seen the reaction of his ward.

"Are you going to allow her to look at me like that?" Melissa demanded hotly, coming to her feet. "It was an obvious show of defiance. Well?"

Beau ignored the woman long enough to usher Alanna from the room with instructions to go to the kitchen and wait there until he came for her. Once she was out of sight, he turned back to Melissa, who had angrily followed them to the door.

"You can't say you didn't have it coming, my dear," he said softly. "It was presumptuous on your part to assume the girl was my mistress. Not everyone who works here is, you know."

"But she is a servant. She had no right to look at me the way she did. I demand an apology."

"Let it rest, Melissa," Beau cautioned. "This is my house and I will say what is right or not. If you disapprove of the way I handle things, it is your choice not to come here."

The anger vanished from her face. "Oh, Beau, darling," she mewed, turning suddenly sweet. "I didn't mean to imply you weren't handling the girl correctly. It's just—well, no servant ever looked at me like that. You understand, don't you?" she said, batting her lashes at him and reaching up to place the palms of her hands against his chest.

It was quite apparent that she expected him to sweep her in his arms and kiss away the hurt, but little did she know that she only disgusted him. Firmly, yet politely, he put her hands from him and went to the table that held a decanter of brandy.

Melissa shot Blythe an angry pout. Damn, she thought, it always worked on Radford. But then, who could be romantic with Blythe sitting there, her mouth agape. With a swish of silk, she returned to her place on the sofa, daintily spread out her skirts, and politely folded her hands in her lap. "Anyway, as I was about to say, Papa told me I could have a huge ball this month. You will come, won't you?"

He finished the brandy before turning back to his guests. "Yes, of course," he sighed. Right then he'd have said anything to satisfy her. "Just let me know the date. But right now, I must beg my leave. I have some pressing matters to attend to."

"How thoughtless of me. Of course, you must." With a cultured grace and rustle of petticoats, she rose. "We really must be going now anyway. Come, Blythe."

Beau showed the two women to the door and managed to smile until it appeared that the dark carriage had swallowed them up. Well, my dear Melissa, he thought, how did you like your first encounter with my new servant? Wasn't what you expected, I'll wager. He laughed aloud and went back inside.

Twelve

Sitting at the long table in the kitchen, Alanna irritably tapped a wooden spoon upon it, unaware that Beau had joined her. Bessy, busily washing dishes, smiled when she looked up and saw him. However, he did not return the smile, venturing instead to the hearth, where he took a bucket sitting on the floor near it and handed it to the woman.

"Fill this with water from the well," he said.

"But—"

"Just do as I say, Bessy," he warned and the woman obligingly wiped her hands on her apron before taking the proffered item. He watched her until she had disappeared from view, then sat down at the table across from Alanna.

"I can't have you acting that way to Melissa Bensen," he said firmly.

"I'm sorry. I didn't know she meant so much to you," Alanna answered quietly as she continued to tap the spoon.

The mere thought of it made Beau gag and he raised a

knuckle to his lips as he cleared his throat. "She doesn't. But she was a guest in my house and you were rude."

The tapping continued.

"Do you understand?"

"Yes," Alanna answered, tapping a little louder.

"And you will see that it doesn't happen again?"

Only Alanna's eyes moved to him. "Yes," she said again before looking away.

He studied her, a soft smile parting his lips. She had every right to be angry. Melissa had a way of making anyone angry, only Alanna, as a servant, couldn't be voicing her displeasure at the woman's treatment of her. He tilted his head to one side. It had been rather refreshing to see another woman stand up to the spoiled, pampered blonde—only he couldn't tell her so. It wouldn't be right. The sound of the wooden spoon penetrated his thoughts.

"Alanna," he beckoned. When she chose not to respond or even look his way, he lost his patience. Angrily, he seized her spoon-tapping hand. "Stop!"

The wooden instrument fell to the table. "May I be excused? I have work to do."

More angry with himself at this point than with Alanna, he sighed, wishing for once they could talk in a civil manner rather than snapping at each other. "Yes," he half-whispered.

She didn't move, and his face reflected his amusement until she looked to the hand still held tightly in his. Slowly releasing her, he watched her briskly leave the kitchen, her suppressed anger evident in her walk by the way she clutched a fistful of her skirts in each hand and swished the hem from side to side with each step she took. He shook his head in defeat and started to rise when he heard Bessy return to the kitchen.

"Is there a problem I should know about?" she asked, seeing that they were alone. "I mean with the help?"

"Nothing I can't handle, Bessy," he said, and then smiled with the irony of it all. "Inform Tilly that I won't be back for lunch."

"Alanna, honey, do Bessy a favor."

"Surely. What is it?" Alanna asked, laying aside the freshly polished silver.

"Take this here flour tin to the mill and fill it. I's got to watch this chicken in the pot so's it won't burn."

"Be right back," Alanna called, running from the house with the bowl perched upon her hip and silently thanking Bessy for a chance to escape the intense heat of the kitchen. Although the sun shone brightly overhead, its penetrating rays beating down across her shoulders, the gentle breeze that played with the hemline of her skirt felt refreshing. She slowed, enjoying the fresh air.

Several of the men outside the huge stone building paused when she passed by. Many of them hadn't seen her since the night Cain had tied her to a tree in the yard. Rumors had spread among them that she had died or that their master had locked her away in one of the many rooms of his house to torture and beat her. But seeing her now, they realized it had been foolish to accuse Master Remington of any cruel or ill treatment of the young woman. She looked as healthy as any of them.

"Good afternoon, Alanna," one of them called.

"Good afternoon," she returned in surprise, not understanding why anyone would take the time to speak to her.

When she reached the huge doors of the mill, still another man quickly pulled them open for her. She smiled and went inside before half-turning to study him. That's odd, she thought. They act as if I were mistress of Raven Oaks rather than one of them. With a dismissing shrug of one shoulder, she set about to do as she had been instructed.

Although the deafening grind of the enormous wheels turning around to crush the corn into meal drummed in Alanna's ears, the sight of their progress never failed to entice her into watching, something she did nearly every time she came to the mill. She stood in silent admiration of the process.

"Quite impressive, isn't it?"

Looking up to find Cain walking toward her, her breath quickened as she thought to be reprimanded for dawdling. "Yes, sir," she answered politely, noting a smile on the man's lips that eased her tension a degree.

"Did you know that Mr. Remington built it with his own hands?"

"He did?" Alanna asked, surprised to learn that the man was capable of such a tremendous project.

"Yes'm. And designed it, too. That young man has quite a head on his shoulders."

Alanna looked back at the immense piece of machinery with a different respect. Indeed, it took a man of high skills to produce such a thing. "How does it work?"

Cain smiled proudly. "Water. And that's the ingenious part. When Mr. Remington's father decided to erect a mill but saw no way to achieve it, it was his son who devised a way. The plantation was too far from the river and no creek flowed nearby. Come. I'll show you how he managed it."

162

Cain gave her no chance to object as he took her hand and led her to the other side of the building. She willingly followed him, for she couldn't understand what he had meant about there not being a creek. She had seen one many times. In fact, she had often washed the heat of the day from her brow in it. When they had reached the door, Cain nodded her through it.

"I'm afraid I don't understand," she admitted as they watched the creek wind its way toward them.

"Fifteen years ago that creek wasn't there."

"What?"

"That's right. You see, Andrew Remington, that's Mr. Beau's father, started this place with only a house and a barn. He knew the nature of spring rains and built the house quite a distance from the river so he wouldn't get flooded out every spring. Then, as his place grew, he added buildings farther away, never once thinking about the benefits the river had to offer." Cain smiled broadly as he leaned a shoulder against the stone wall of the mill. "If he cursed himself for it once, he cursed himself a hundred times." He straightened, shaking off his memories. "Anyway, when Mr. Beau was about seventeen, he told his father how he planned to erect a flour mill. The man nearly split a gut laughin'. 'How ya gonna do that?' he said. And Mr. Beau only smiled. The next day, every man, woman, and child on this place had a spade in his hand and they started digging a trench."

"You're not serious," Alanna exclaimed.

"That's pretty much what his father said," Cain added with a grin. "But he was. And within a year that young man had designed and built it and had it operational. I'll never forget the look on Andrew's face the day his son handed him the first loaf of bread made from his

163

own mill."

"He must have been very proud of his son."

"Yes. He sure loved that boy." His eyes grew cloudy and Alanna suspected he was recalling fond memories of the past. Then he sighed with a smile. "Come—I'll show you how it works," he said, taking her hand as he pointed to the mammoth paddle wheel. "See how the axle turns with the water flow?"

She nodded.

"Inside, that axle rotates a gear that interlocks with another. At the base of that axle is the grinding stone. It's designed so that when a worker throws the grain against it, it crushes it against another stone."

"That much I knew," she added. "I've watched it many times. Seems simple enough."

"Ah, but it isn't," he said. "Let's go inside and I'll show you why."

They returned to the workings of the mill.

"That's where our problems arise," he shouted above the noise. "The barrings are made of wood. They have to be greased continually. Especially when the air is heavy with moisture, like it is now. If they swell or dry out, they won't move."

Just then one of the men began to climb up a narrow set of wooden stairs that led to the grindstone. In one hand he held a bucket and in the other a brush already blackened with grease. When he reached the top, he swirled the brush in the bucket then leaned out over the edge of the rail and wiped the wood with the lubricant.

"See how it's done?" Cain hollered.

Alanna nodded. "It looks rather dangerous."

"Only if you don't know what you're doing. Even then a few have lost a finger or two. Let's get out of here. I

164

don't know about you, but I'm hot."

Alanna smiled her agreement and quickly followed the man to the front doors.

"I could use a cool drink from the well. How about you?"

Alanna hoped her bewilderment at his offer did not register on her face as she accepted his proposal and stepped in stride with the man as he headed for the well.

"Sure is a hot one," he said casually as he handed her the dipper.

"Mmm," she agreed. "From what Bessy tells me, it always gets this hot." She watched him as he took a long drink, then poured the remainder of the water over his head and let it trickle down his face and neck. He pulled a large red handkerchief from his back pocket and wiped away the moisture, appearing to be somewhat refreshed.

"Why do you look at me like that?" he asked when he caught her staring at him.

"Just trying to figure you out, that's all."

Cain laughed. "That would take some doing. Why do you try?"

Alanna shrugged her shoulders as she rested a hip upon the stone well. "It just seems funny, you asking to show me the mill and all. Seems like I'd be the last person you'd want to be nice to."

"Now what makes you say that?"

"I've caused you nothing but trouble since I got here. If I were you, I'd stay as far away from me as I possibly could."

Cain laughed goodheartedly. "I don't hold any of that against you. In fact, if I had been in your place, I'd have done the same. You are the one who would be expected to run the minute I came around."

She watched her bare toes appear from beneath her skirt every time she swung her leg, realizing how she had misjudged the man, thinking him to be as cold and callous as his employer. "You were only doing your job. Not a nice one, I might add, but just the same, a job."

"That makes me feel better," he said. "I'd hate to think you'd spend all of your time here despising me." He bent down and picked up a twig from the ground, snapping it into little pieces before throwing it away. "How did you like Mistress Bensen?"

"Ohhh," Alanna growled. "I've never met a more rude, conceited—" She stopped and eyed the man at her side.

"Oh, don't quit," he chuckled, "you haven't hit all the words I use to describe her."

Alanna smiled. "How did you know that I'd met her?"

"Figured as much when I saw her carriage. I didn't think it would be very long before she came to call."

"I hope you don't think I'm a little thick-headed," she frowned, "but I don't see the connection."

"Maybe you wouldn't," he said, rubbing the stubble on his chin. "After all, this was the first time you met her. My guess would be that Master Chamberlain ran right over to tell her what a beautiful young woman Beau Remington has working for him. And Mistress Melissa, being the jealous type, had to see for herself. I sincerely believe she didn't come here with the sole purpose of visiting Mr. Remington."

"Thank you for the compliment, Master Cain, but I doubt that was truly her reason. Besides, why are you telling me all this?"

"Just wanted you to be warned. It will not be the last time you see Melissa Bensen. You can count on it."

"Does she come here quite frequently?"

"Not as much as she'd like."

"Meaning?"

"Meaning that if she could, she would much prefer to marry Mr. Remington."

Alanna's chin fell. "But Tilly told me she plans to marry Rad—er—Master Chamberlain. Doesn't she love him?"

Cain roared with laughter. "Love? She doesn't know the meaning of the word. Thank God, Mr. Remington saw through her the first time he escorted her to a ball. I've worked for him for a long time, but if he had married her, I'm afraid I would have moved on."

Toying with the hem of her apron, Alanna wondered if she dare go on. "Doesn't Master Remington have a girl?" she asked hesitantly.

"No," he said. "Never has, and sometimes he makes me wonder if he ever will. If only things had been different for him when—" He bent down and picked up another twig.

"When what, Mr. Cain?"

"None of my business, little lady," he said, putting an end to their conversation as he tossed the stick into the dust. "And I've got work to do, as I'm sure you do."

"Oh," Alanna gasped. "I forgot all about it. Bessy will be furious with me." She slipped from her perch on the edge of the well. "Thank you for showing me around. I really enjoyed it. And our conversation." She sent him a bright smile, turned, and started off toward the mill.

"My pleasure," Cain hummed, knowing she could not hear him. He stood there quite a while watching the spot where she had once been. She's a very forgiving sort, he thought. And very delightful. He smiled and turned to go when he looked up and saw Beau riding toward him, an angry frown knotting his brow. "Good afternoon, Mr. Remington," he called, but noting the expression on the man's face, knew the goodness of the day had ended.

Beau reined his horse to a halt at Cain's side. "Haven't you work to be doing?" he scowled down at him.

Cain only stared back at him. Then, "Haven't you a better tone to use on me, young man?"

Beau stiffened in the saddle. "Come to my study. I'd like a word with you, if you can spare me the time in your busy day," he said, glancing toward the mill and then back at Cain.

But Cain had not moved.

"Please," Beau added clumsily.

Cain smiled and swept an outstretched arm for him to lead the way.

By the time Cain reached the house, Beau had already gone inside. He entertained the thought of lingering outside a while longer, just enough time to irritate his young friend that much more, and then changed his mind. With a half-smile twisting the corners of his mouth, he climbed the veranda stairs and went inside.

"Close the door," Beau snapped after Cain had nearly reached the desk, and Cain stopped where he was to study him.

"What's ailing you, Beau? You come flying in here like the wrath of God, ordering me about like some bondsman, irritated over what I have or haven't done. Would it be asking too much to know why?"

Beau looked up at him and then sighed. "No. It's not too much, but would you please close the door so that everyone else won't know my problems too?"

Cain seated himself in the chair he pulled near the desk

after fulfilling Beau's wish, settled himself in, and crossed an ankle to one knee, waiting for Beau to begin. He already had an idea what the problem was, but until Beau voiced it, he would keep quiet. Of course, that was if he would admit to it. He sat patiently as Beau reached for the brandy decanter on the desk, offered him a drink, which he refused, poured his own, and settled back in his chair.

"I saw you talking with Alanna," he began.

Cain nodded, but said nothing.

"Well?"

"Well what?"

"Why were you talking to her?"

"Because I wanted to enjoy the company of a lovely young woman. Something you don't seem to have developed a taste for."

Beau downed his brandy in one gulp. "I mean, what were you talking about?"

"The mill. I showed her around. She's quite a young lady." He eyed Beau for a moment, and when he knew the man wasn't going to comment, he smiled to himself and added, "She'll make someone a very good wife."

Beau's handsome features marked a sudden change in his mood. "So that's what you're up to," he said, relaxing in his chair.

"What?" Cain asked, feigning ignorance.

"You're back to your old tricks. Trying to match me up with a wife."

"I simply said how she'd make someone a good wife. How do you know I didn't mean one of the servants? Or maybe even Master Radford?"

"Ha! That young idiot would take the first female that caught his eye." Beau reached out and took a cigar from the box on his desk.

"He's not so young. He's only two years younger than you, and even he is past marrying age."

The line between Beau's brows deepened as he touched a flame to the cigar tip. "And why should either of us marry?" he asked defensively. "Women are nothing but trouble. They weaken your mind so you can't think of anything else. They ruin your day by falling down and causing you to worry. You have to act as mediator between rivals, which is ridiculous when she's twice the lady with twice the beauty of Melissa—" Beau's face flushed, something Cain had not seen since he intruded upon his young friend behind the mill many years ago kissing a girl.

He smiled. "I'd say you have a problem."

"No, I don't," Beau argued, angrily rising from his chair to go to the window and stare outside.

"Don't lie to me, Beau. Or to yourself. There's nothing wrong with loving a woman."

"Yes, there is," Beau growled, returning to his desk. He began sorting the papers that lay upon it, stacking then restacking them until finally he angrily pulled open a drawer and stuffed them inside. "It awards you nothing. You dedicate your life to them, trust them, give them your heart, only to have them tear it apart."

"That was Monica. Not Alanna."

Beau felt a gentle hand upon his shoulder, knowing Cain had quietly come to his side. "What guarantee is there that any woman is different?"

"Take my word for it. I knew your mother for a long time. She was the one who was different. Her biggest fault was her vanity. And you, unfortunately, were a constant reminder that she was growing old. Alanna

170

Bainbridge hasn't a vain bone in her body."

"No, only hatred." He snuffed out his cigar and poured another drink.

"I don't believe that."

"You should. It's true. You don't know the whole story." He stood, swirling the contents of his glass. "I raped her." He swallowed his drink, slapped the glass on the desk, and started for the door.

"Beau, wait," Cain called.

"I have work to do," he said before disappearing from sight.

Cain didn't move as he stared at the empty doorway. So that was what was troubling him. If only there was some way he could help. A light smile touched the corners of his mouth.

Thirteen

Several days had passed since Alanna's encounter with
Cain at the mill. She had been quite certain that it had
been purely by accident, but after the third such meeting,
she was beginning to wonder if he hadn't planned it that
way. It seemed that every time she went to the mill for
flour for Bessy, Cain was somewhere waiting for her. She
enjoyed their visits and before long looked forward to
them.

She learned a great deal about the man, discovering
that flogging another human being was something he
detested but felt compelled to do, since he had dedicated
his life to the service of a man called The Hawk. Joshua
Cain had come to America when he was a young man,
hoping to find a rich life in the new country. Instead, he
had found poverty and sickness. It was at that time that
he had met Andrew Remington, a young farmer with high
hopes of some day owning a plantation. They teamed up,
struggled through the lean years, and before long turned
a small farm into a prospering one with boundless
possibilities. They acquired the help of indentured

servants—Andrew had forbidden the use of slaves—and soon began to show enough profit that he could add on more buildings and equipment. He purchased more land and utilized the river that ran adjacent to it to sail his cotton and tobacco to England. Within ten years Raven Oaks was the wealthiest planation in Virginia. Then he married Monica.

Alanna found herself totally absorbed in the tales of this strange and beautiful woman and how demanding she had been, respecting that trait and at the same time wondering why she had not been more compassionate. Especially with her young son. But whenever she would question Cain about it, he would suddenly change the subject, and she suspected that he had too much respect for his dead friend to say anything against someone Andrew had loved.

"Tell me more about Master Beau," she begged one morning as they strolled to the well for a drink.

"What do you want to know?" he asked, toying with the band on his big, floppy hat.

"What was he like as a boy?"

Cain smiled warmly. "Full of the devil. He and Master Radford used to get into all kinds of trouble."

"Like what?" she asked, settling herself on her usual perch of the well edge.

Cain chuckled loudly. "I remember one time when the two of them took this old black cat and whitewashed a strip down its back. Then they turned it loose in the kitchen. You should have heard old Bessy scream. Thought it was a skunk, she did."

"Oh, that's awful," Alanna said, trying not to smile.

"Not nearly as bad as when Bessy realized what it really was. She took a willow branch to both of them.

174

Then she made them clean up the cat. They had a heck of a time getting that paint off. They finally just shaved it. It was the funniest thing I ever saw. There was this cat with a three-inch-wide shaved spot runnin' down his backside." Cain smiled as he hit some imaginary dust from his pants with his hat. "Somehow I never really believed it was Beau's idea. That Radford was the damnedest scoundrel you'd ever want to meet. But even though Beau was blamed for it, he never denied it. He loved that boy as much as if he was his own brother. Still does. And Radford is the only one other than me that can say what he pleases to Beau."

"You love him, don't you, Mr. Cain," Alanna said, cocking her head to one side.

"Surely do. And it hurts me to see him troubled," he sighed, casting her a glance from the corner of his eye.

"Raven Oaks isn't in tro—"

"No, no," he quickly assured her. "His trouble isn't of the pocket but of the mind."

"How so?"

"It's none of my business. And I really shouldn't be talking about him like this. He wouldn't like it," Cain said with an added emphasis on the mystery that was sure to entice his beautiful companion.

"I won't tell anyone, Mr. Cain. I promise. Maybe if I knew what it was, I could help you figure out a way to end his torment." Alanna slipped from the edge of the well, glanced about them, and then touched his arm. "Please? No one will hear."

"Well, I don't know—" he began, feigning hesitation when all the while it was what he had wanted. "You really promise you won't breathe a word of this to anyone?"

Alanna nodded excitedly.

"All right, then. But it has to be our secret." Cain hooked his straw hat on the handle of the well and then ran his fingers through his hair, giving all the necessary impressions that he shouldn't say what he was about to disclose. "Beau hurt someone. Both physically and mentally, someone he cares a great deal for. He isn't the type to apologize and his guilt is tearing him apart." He stole a furtive glance to find her frowning and smiled to himself when he knew his plan was working so far.

"Doesn't this person know he didn't really mean to hurt them?" she asked.

"That's the tough part. This person doesn't know him well enough to realize it."

"Then it would probably be easier to make this person understand Master Remington than it would be to have him apologize," she said, placing a fingertip to her chin as she considered the problem. "Don't you agree?"

Cain shook his head. "No. This person has every reason to hate him."

"Oh," Alanna murmured. "That is a problem."

"And one I have no idea how to solve."

"Do they see each other regularly?"

"Nearly every day. Why?" he asked.

"Do they avoid each other?"

"It's rather hard. Their jobs force them together."

"Good. Then maybe we can do the apologizing for them," she smiled with a twinkle in her eye. "I love to play the Good Samaritan."

"Wait a minute," Cain warned, thinking he had overstepped his good intentions. "How can I possibly do that?"

"Not I, Joshua Cain, we," she grinned.

176

"What?" he gasped.

"Surely. Since you may talk so freely with Master Remington, you can work on him. I will take care of the other person if you will just tell me who it is." She stood expectantly before him, a smile of pure delight brightening her eyes.

"Oh, I couldn't," he said, shaking his head.

"Why not?"

"It just wouldn't work. You—I—I must be going. I have work to do," he stammered before reaching for his hat.

"Joshua," she called as she watched him hurriedly walk away. "Joshua, you said you wanted to help. Joshua!" But the man was already too far out of hearing range for her to waste her breath. "Now that's curious," she mused, and then a thought struck her. If he wouldn't tell who the other person was, she would just have to find out for herself. With a lightness to her step, Alanna headed off toward the kitchen and her chores.

During the rest of the day, Alanna watched Beau without his knowing it. She noted to whom he spoke or those whom she felt he was avoiding. But with each and every one of those she suspected, he seemed finally quite at ease. Only when he approached her did he seem to withdraw, cutting short his remarks so that he would not have to spend a great deal of time with her. And this irritated her. If she was to ever learn who it was that caused his unrest, she would have to remain in his presence for longer periods of time. Well, she thought, tonight will be my chance. I will serve him his dinner and see to his comfort.

"Are yo' sure yo' want to?" Bessy asked when Alanna took the tray of food from her hands.

"Yes, I'm sure," she answered. "If I'm to learn to be a hostess, I better start now." She sent the dark woman a smile and left the room.

Beau had decided to take his meal in the dining room, something he hadn't done in quite a while and, luckily for Alanna, her request to serve the man seemed only natural because of it. Pushing a hip against the heavy swinging door, she gracefully entered the room. Seated at the end of the table completely absorbed in the paper he held in his hand, he paid no attention to her as she crossed to him and placed the tray on the edge of the table. He continued to read, and Alanna contemplated clearing her throat to draw his attention to her, but decided against it. He always seemed short-tempered with her, and if she hoped to spend any time at all with him, she would have to do it under his conditions. She placed the bowls of steaming hot food near him, then picked up the teapot and waited for him to look up.

"Just leave it," he said, his eyes still on the paper. "I'll pour my own."

Alanna frowned. This wasn't working out at all as she had planned. "Yes, sir," she replied disgustedly, returning the teapot to its tray with a thud.

Startled by the noise, Beau immediately looked up, the irritation of her intrusion marked clearly in his eyes. "Try to be more careful," he snapped seeing whom it was.

178

"I'm sorry," she apologized sincerely when she noticed the annoyance in his expression. Now I've made him angry, she thought. He'll surely dismiss me from his presence. Quickly, she tried to make amends. "I didn't mean to disturb you. I was only trying to practice the art of serving dinner."

"You have a lot to learn," he growled and returned to his paper.

"Yes, sir," she agreed. "That's why I was hoping you would allow me to practice on you."

When he looked up again, she smiled sweetly.

"I haven't the time right now," he said drily and started to read once more.

"At least let me pour your tea. I promise to be very quiet."

Beau leaned back in his chair, laying the paper on the table next to his plate. "If it means you will leave once the task is done, then do so, by all means."

Alanna gave him a short curtsy, quickly retrieved the teapot and began to pour. She knew he was watching, and since he had made it rather clear that he did not wish for her to linger, her hand began to tremble, causing her to spill some of the tea over the edge of his cup. Much to her dismay, it splashed tiny droplets on his paper.

She gasped. "Oh, dear. I'm afraid I've made a mess of your work. Here, let me wipe it off." She reached out to pick up the paper, but before she could, he seized her wrist.

"Don't bother," he warned. "You've done enough."

"Yes, sir," she whispered with downcast eyes. "I'm sorry."

"You're always sorry," he replied, letting go of her

179

hand. Picking up a cloth napkin, he gently blotted up the spilled tea.

"There's nothing wrong with being sorry," she said, jumping at her chance. "If you've done something you regret doing, you should apologize."

"And what is that supposed to mean?" he said crossly.

"I mean it takes a bigger man to apologize than to keep it inside. You should try it sometime. I'd wager you'd feel better."

"And just what should I apologize for?" he asked, eyeing her angrily.

"Well, I really don't know. But if you've hurt someone you care a great deal for, you shouldn't let that person go on thinking you aren't sorry for what you've done."

"Alanna, you aren't making any sense at all," he sighed impatiently.

"Well, think about it. Isn't there someone you've hurt by your words or actions, and you really didn't mean to? Don't you think you should—" Alanna's breath caught in her throat. Dear God, she thought, Cain meant me! Without another word, she turned to leave.

"Now where are you going?" he asked.

"I've bothered you long enough," she said once she reached the door. "I'll clear away the dishes after you've gone. Will that be all?"

Beau smiled in amusement at her sudden change in manner. "Yes," he said with a nod. "You may go." He rested an elbow against the arm of his chair as he tapped a fingertip against his chin, listening to the door close behind her. I guess I will never understand that one, he smiled, and turned back to his meal.

When Beau had finished eating, he picked up his work and headed for the study, determined to find the peace

180

and quiet he had been looking for when Alanna had made her untimely entrance. He closed the door behind him and sat down at the desk, where he spread out his work before him. He had just picked up a quill when a knock at the door interfered.

"Yes," he called and waited, watching the door open.

"Excuse me, Masta Beau," Horace said after sticking his head in, "but Jeremiah asked if yo' couldn't come to the stable. One of yo'r mares is havin' trouble gettin' her young 'un born."

"Thanks, Horace," he said, rising from the chair. "Tell Jeremiah I'll be there directly. I better change out of these clothes first."

Beau climbed the stairs two at a time and quickly entered his room, stopping abruptly when he found Alanna turning back the covers of his bed. Her face reddened the moment she saw him.

"Excuse me, Master Remington," she said. "I didn't think you'd be coming to bed so soon. Otherwise I would have done this earlier."

"I'm not coming to bed. I simply came to change my clothes. It seems one of my mares is about to give birth." He went to the armoire, pulled open its doors and selected a shirt. Unbuttoning the one he wore, he turned back to her. "Have you ever seen a mare foal?"

"Only once. When I was very small," she said, looking at her toes.

"Would you like to come along? I'm sure Tilly and Bessy won't mind."

Suddenly filled with dozens of emotions—surprise that he had thought of her let alone extended the invitation, glee at the thought of experiencing the birth of a new creature, relief at the chance to break her

181

boredom, and dread at the prospect of being alone with him—she could only stare. She knew how he affected her. "Are you sure I won't be in the way?" she asked finally, watching him remove his shirt. She quickly looked back to the floor.

"Look," he smiled, "I'm sorry I snapped at you a while ago. I had some important matters on my mind—" He chuckled gaily.

"What's funny?" she asked, surprised by the foreign sound.

"Well, didn't you hear me? I just apologized. I guess your lecture did me some good, after all."

Alanna couldn't stop the smile that spread across her face. That proved it. Cain didn't mean her as she had thought he had, otherwise Beau wouldn't have apologized. After all, Cain said it was someone he cared a great deal for, and she was positive Beau felt nothing for her.

"Well, unless you're going to stand there and watch me undress, I suggest you wait for me downstairs."

A new rush of color darkened her cheeks, and Beau smiled broadly as he watched her hurriedly turn around and leave the room.

"You haven't seen much of Raven Oaks, have you?" he asked later as they walked to the stables.

"No, only that which I saw on my way here from the ship. Even then it was dark," she replied, quickening her step to keep up with his long, easy gait.

"I'm expecting a shipment of supplies from England at the docks in the morning. Would you care to come along? I could show you some of the plantation that way."

Grateful for the darkness that surrounded them, Alanna felt certain it masked her surprise at his offer. "I don't think you could get much work done with me

182

tagging along," she said.

"Don't be silly. As long as you stay in the wagon, you won't be in the way." He smiled down at her, and for the first time since Alanna had met the man, she felt at ease in his presence.

"I'd love to," she smiled in return.

Fourteen

The warmth of the sun stealing into the room between the slit in the curtains aroused Alanna from a peaceful slumber. She stretched and yawned, the corners of her mouth turning upward into a smile. Eagerly she left her bed, went to the washbowl sitting on the bedside table, and bathed the sleep from her eyes. After brushing the tangles from her hair, she tied it back with a strip of cloth and donned the only nice dress she owned. It didn't make sense to her that she was actually excited about being with Beau Remington, but whatever the reason, she decided not to think about it. She was going to thoroughly enjoy the morning.

"My, you're up early this mornin', child," Bessy said when Alanna came bouncing into the kitchen. "I figured I have ta come pull yo' out of bed as usual. Somethin' ailin' yo'?"

"I'm fine," Alanna grinned. "I just wanted to get my chores done early so that I'd be ready when Master Remington is."

"Masta Beau?" Bessy frowned.

"Yes'm. He's invited me to go with him when the supplies from England arrive at the docks," Alanna said as she made herself a cup of tea.

Bessy's frown deepened, watching Alanna settle herself at the long kitchen table before taking a sip of tea. Half-heartedly, she went through the motions of kneading her dough for the sweet rolls she would make later, eyeing Alanna suspiciously. It appeared to her that the young Englishwoman was rather pleased with the idea of spending the morning with Master Beau, and Bessy couldn't understand why. It hadn't been difficult to see how much Alanna had disliked the master of Raven Oaks—and now she actually seemed anxious to be with him. Bessy shrugged her thick shoulders. White folk, she mused. I guess I'll never understand them. "Well," she said aloud, "if'n yo' twos are leavin' early, I better hurry up with his breakfast. Run upstairs and see that he's awake."

"There's no need Bessy, my dear, I'm already up and about."

Alanna turned nervously in her chair at the sound of his voice and found him standing in the doorway smiling back at her. She nodded her own greeting, feeling somehow uneasy in his presence. Her stomach churned.

"Well," Bessy continued, her voice oddly biting, "it's a good thing I got up earlier'n usual. Otherwise the water wouldn't even be hot for tea. Nobody ever tells me nothin'."

A lopsided grin pursed his lips. "And are you always so cordial this time of morning? No wonder Horace stays away from the kitchen."

"Yo' watch yo'r tongue," Bessy warned, a flour-covered fist knotted on one hip. "Yo' still ain't too big for

186

me to take a willow branch to."

Alanna's eyes widened with their exchange of words, wondering if what she heard was sincere or only their usual form of morning conversation. Then she saw Beau take a short bow.

"Yes'm," he said with a mocking click of his heels. "But don't trouble yourself with breakfast. I'll just help myself to tea like Alanna." He smiled warmly at her and went to the hearth to gather what he needed. Mug in hand, he returned to the table and settled himself next to her. "Did you sleep well?" he asked, testing the tea.

She started to answer, discovering the muscles in her throat tight. She swallowed and said hoarsely, "Yes, thank you." She could feel the heat rise in her cheeks.

Setting down his mug, he studied her a moment. "Why are you blushing?"

Alanna's hand instantly went to her face. "Am I?" she lied. "I think it's only the heat of the room that makes it appear so." She couldn't bring herself to look at him.

He raised a noncommittal brow. "Then you should spend your time here. It flatters you," he added and took a sip of tea.

With his attention drawn away for the moment, Alanna quietly let out a long, slow breath, wondering if she would live through the day. "Will Cain be going with us?" she asked, changing the subject.

"If he doesn't, I expect no other excuse than his passing in the night," Beau smiled. He sat thoughtfully quiet for a moment, then added, "Once you get to know him, I'm sure you'll find him a likable man."

"Oh, I already do," Alanna blurted out.

"Oh?"

"Lordy yes, Masta Beau," Bessy cut in. "The two of

187

them spend more time together than a young couple courtin'."

"Oh, we do not," Alanna replied defensively. "We only talk for a few minutes at the mill each day."

"And then at the well," Bessy added. "I sees yo' all. One of these days my bread won't have time to rise waitin' on the flour like I do."

"Well, I can understand his reasons, but not yours," Beau said. "What could the two of you find to discuss?"

"Lots of things," Alanna replied excitedly. "He showed me how the mill runs and operates and said how you had made it. We talked of when he first came to America and his dreams." An amused smile spread across her face.

"And a few secrets?" Beau asked, resting his chin against his fist.

"I was only thinking of the cat you and Master Radford painted."

His face reflected no sign of amusement, but Alanna couldn't miss the gleam in his dark eyes. "I think he has too much time for idle talk."

"Oh, don't be angry with him," Alanna begged, and without thinking touched a hand against his sleeve. The warmth of his flesh penetrated the cloth, sending that warmth through Alanna in an instant. She quickly pulled away, hoping he had not noticed the effect this simple act had had on her.

"Did he also tell you of the time Rad and I found him swimming in the river?" he asked, a gentle smile on his face as he held the teacup with both hands, studying its contents. "And how we stole all his clothes so he couldn't get out? He must have looked like a prune by the time darkness fell. I just wish I could have seen him sneaking

188

back to his cabin hoping no one was about."

"Beauregard Travis Remington!" Bessy exploded. "You mean you and that good for nothin' Radford did that?"

"Oh, come now, Bessy. Surely there wasn't a person in miles that didn't suspect us," he smiled.

"Oh, of course," she mocked. "And why wouldn't we? Especially when yo'r father found yo' sleeping so soundly in yo'r room. I wish he were alive. He'd probably take a stick to yo' even now."

Beau sighed, leaning back in his chair. "Yes, I suppose he would. He'd have a lot of reasons to." The gleam in his eye and smile on his lips disappeared. "I caused him a lot of grief."

"And he loved every minute of it, Beau Remington," Bessy scolded. "And don't you forget it."

He smiled again. "Don't you ever open your mouth without chewin' on my ear, old woman?" he teased.

"What? And make yo'r life easier?" she growled. "Now get out of my kitchen. I have work to do and yo' all is in my way."

Beau suddenly grabbed Alanna's hand, pulling her to her feet. "I think we better leave before she throws something at us," he whispered playfully. It wasn't until they had left the house that he released her, but even then Alanna could still feel the warmth of his hand around hers.

While they walked to the stables in silence, Alanna noticed Beau's quick step and the vague smile on his lips. He was happy. Obviously so, and she wondered if maybe he didn't always start out his day this way, not just because she was there.

"Mornin', Masta Beau," Jeremiah called from the

semidarkness of the stable.

"Good morning, Jeremiah," Beau returned just as cheerfully. "I'm afraid we'll need a wagon today. As you can see, I've brought company."

The bed of scattered straw beneath his feet muffled the sound of his footsteps as Jeremiah approached. He touched a fingertip to his imaginary hat brim. "Good mornin', Miss Alanna. It's gonna be a beautiful day."

"So far," she smiled, with a quick look at Beau who had already turned away from them and gone to the stall where the newborn colt stood with its mother. She eyed him with new interest. He was dressed differently this day. Instead of the silks and velvets, he wore a cotton shirt with its sleeves rolled up past his elbows and dark breeches that were tucked deep into his black leather boots. It appeared to Alanna that he had every intention of lending a hand whenever and wherever he might be needed. She studied him unobserved and came to the conclusion that Raven Oaks prospered simply because this man would not be content to sit by and let others do the work for him. She cocked her head to one side in silent admiration. He was different from the few men of wealth she had known of in England. They had always been satisfied to let the burden of their responsibility lie with others.

"I want to show you something," he said once he had joined her again. "It's down here." He reached out, even before she consented, took her hand in his and gently led her through the darkened stable. Alanna could feel the heat rise in her cheeks again and a quickening of her pulse.

They passed many stalls, each occupied with a wide variety of horses, and paused in front of one near the end.

"Have you ever done much riding?" he asked, letting go of her hand.

"Yes, but it was only my father's old mare. She wasn't good for much except a ride into town for supplies."

"Well, then you should appreciate this." He reached out, opened the latch to the stall, and stepped back.

Alanna peeked inside. Standing tethered to one side a beautiful chestnut mare pranced nervously, whinnying softly at the intrusion.

"She's beautiful," Alanna breathed admiringly.

"I thought you'd like her. Cain just brought her home yesterday."

"May I touch her?"

He smiled a nod.

Slowly, Alanna went into the stall, softly cooing to the animal as she reached out a hand to stroke the velvet nose. "Does she have a name?"

"Well, she did, but I'm thinking of changing it. Have any ideas?"

"Oh," Alanna said, "the naming of this beautiful creature is something that should not be rushed. May I consider it and then offer my suggestion?"

"Then take your time," Beau answered softly, "for the name you select shall be the one she carries."

Alanna looked to him in surprise. "But she is your horse. You should be the one to decide. Not I."

"I have many horses for which I choose names. I will not feel cheated out of this one."

"Then I would be honored to have the pleasure," she smiled.

"Would you care to see the rest?" he asked, stepping from the stall in a sudden burst of discomfort. "It will be a moment before our wagon is ready."

They paused before each stall, and Beau told Alanna the animal's name, heritage, and how long he had owned the creature. Not once did he mention their value, but it wasn't difficult to figure out that they all had thinned his purse to some degree.

"May I be so forward as to ask why you own so many?" Alanna said when they had reached the last stall.

Laughter sounded deeply within his chest. "They do seem more than I need, don't they?" He bent down and picked up a piece of straw that he idly twisted around his finger while Alanna leaned back against the freshly painted gate of the stall. "Some men spend their money on women. I find the purchase of a good piece of horse flesh is never wasted. In fact, I make a profit when I find a man who would do anything to acquire one of my animals."

"Then you are a horse trader as well as a plantation owner."

Smiling, he flicked the rumpled piece of straw away. "Not really. I have usually found it hard to part with any of my animals." He straightened. "One of my faults, I guess, for there is always a profit to be made in the sale of a horse, but I seek other ways to obtain profits." He looked back over his shoulder. "Come. I'm sure the wagon is ready by now."

Alanna squinted in the bright sunlight as they stepped outside the stable, seeing the flatbed wagon standing ready for them, Jeremiah next to it.

"Has Cain shown his homely face yet, Jeremiah?" Beau asked once they had reached him.

"No, sir."

"Well, when he does, tell him we've gone on ahead," Beau replied before turning back to Alanna. "May I help you up?" he asked with a nod over his shoulder toward the wagon.

She would have rather he did not, simply because it meant he would touch her again, and the sensation his touch caused was one she wished she wouldn't feel. But knowing there was no way out of it without leaving him wondering, she reluctantly accepted his offer. With great ease, and the appearance that it didn't bother him in the slightest to find himself so close to her, he put his hands around her tiny waist, lifted her from the ground, and gently stood her on the edge of the wagon.

"We'll return around noon," he told Jeremiah as he slipped a toe between the spokes of the wagon wheel and climbed on next to Alanna. "Ready?" he smiled, and she nodded in return.

When Beau pulled the wagon around in the direction of the river, it surprised Alanna to see how the plantation had already come to life. Women hung freshly washed laundry on the endless lengths of clothesline, while children screamed and chased each other in and out about the white sheets dancing in the gentle breeze. The sounds of logs splintering beneath heartily swung axes announced preparation for the fires that would soon be started to cook breakfast, even though the smells of ham and sweet rolls already filled the air. What really surprised Alanna as they made their way along the rows of cabins was that each and every person who saw them stopped what they were doing to wave or voice a cheerful greeting to Beau. They showed no signs of unrest or displeasure at living on Raven Oaks, and something Cinnamon had said the first night Alanna had arrived there came rushing back to her.

"You'll learn to like living here," she had said.

Apparently everyone else had.

The wagon rattled down the narrow road jostling its passengers about as it hit the potholes of the well-traveled path. The beauty of the countryside captured Alanna's attention and she soon lost herself in the splendor of it, for in a way it reminded her of home and the serenity of a country existence. She felt a lump form in her throat as she thought of her father, and was thankful when Beau broke the silence by pointing to a white-tailed deer as it scurried into the thicket.

"Cain has told me that your father started out as a small farmer," she said.

"Strange you should mention that just now," he replied. "Look over there."

Alanna followed the direction in which he pointed. In the tall weeds stood the tattered, weatherbeaten remains of a building, its windows broken and a portion of its roof fallen in.

"That was his house," he said. "He and Cain shared it until my father married Monica. She refused to live in such a small place, and, of course, Cain wouldn't be allowed to join them. That's when my father moved further inland."

The wagon hit a rut, throwing Alanna against him. He quickly reached out to steady her.

"Are you all right?"

"Yes," she replied, looking at her knees. "I guess I should hang on."

Beau smiled, studying the delicate lines of her jaw and noticing her shyness as if for the first time. "My father would have liked you," he said suddenly and looked back to the road ahead, missing the surprised frown on her face.

"I really don't think so," she disagreed.

Beau pulled the wagon to a stop. "Why would you say that?" he asked, turning in the seat to face her, a foot resting on the wagon frame, an arm across the back of the seat.

"I'm nothing more than a servant," she said, glancing up at him and then back to her lap.

"My father was not a snob, Alanna. He knew everyone who worked for him and called them by name whenever he met them. Besides, my mother was nothing more than a dressmaker in Williamsburg when he met her."

"Really?" she gasped.

Beau laughed. "Did you think her the daughter of an earl?"

Alanna shrugged. "I guess I did."

He remained quiet for a moment before reaching for the reins again. "At times, so did she," he said flatly with a slap to the horse's rump.

A few yards further on they left the road, heading for a thick grove of willows. Alanna wondered why, but said nothing as she wrapped her fingers tightly around the edge of the wagon seat to keep herself from being thrown off, the wagon seeming to hit every hole. At last, when she felt that her tiny frame could take no more abuse, Beau pulled the wagon to a stop and climbed down.

"Come," he said, holding out his hands to help her, "I think you'll enjoy this."

They made their way through the denseness of the willow branches and finally reached a hidden body of water. At the pool's edge fallen trees encompassed it and formed a ledge to sit on. The gentle breeze teased the surface of the water, causing it to ripple as it danced against the darkened bark of the logs.

"It's beautiful here," Alanna whispered. "It reminds me of home."

Pressing the palm of one hand against a tree, he watched her venture nearer the water's edge, lifting her skirts only enough to keep them dry, but enough to reveal her bare feet. His suntanned brow wrinkled in displeasure.

"Do you really only have one pair of shoes?"

Lost in memories of home, Alanna settled herself on a fallen tree trunk and dangled her toes in the water before glancing back up at him. She shivered. The biting cold water numbed her, but she loved it.

"Yes," she finally answered. "However, I see no need for a second pair. I always went barefoot as a child." She smiled fondly. "My father was always trying to get me to wear them."

The snapping of a twig brought her around to see Beau walking toward her. He, too, settled on the tree trunk, his back to the water as he picked up a dried leaf from the ground.

"Your father was right," he said, stretching out his long legs before him.

"Why?" she laughed.

"You're not a child any longer. And working in my house is different from the things you did back home."

"I see no harm in it," she replied in earnest.

Beau swallowed the lump that had tightened his throat. How could he tell her that every time she lifted her skirts or bent over to make his bed or reached up to dust a cabinet, the very sight of her ankles stirred a desire in his loins. He shook his head. Why couldn't she have been twelve years old? "It's not proper attire for the housekeeper of Raven Oaks," he half-lied. "And tomorrow you and I shall go to Williamsburg."

"Whatever for?" she asked, pulling her feet from the water and wrapping them in her skirt to dry them.

"To buy you a pair of shoes," he said, rising. "And another dress or two."

"But you can't. I mean you mustn't," she pleaded, quickly freeing herself from her haven on the log. "What will the others think?"

"Why should they think anything?" he laughed, the line between his brows deepening.

Alanna quickly looked to the ground beneath her. "No reason," she whispered. "I don't know what made me say that."

She knew what *she* would think if Master Remington's new housekeeper suddenly acquired a new wardrobe. Maybe Tilly and Cinnamon wouldn't, but she was sure everyone else would. Of all things, she didn't want a single person to suspect what had happened between Beau and her, and the giving of gifts was the same as a public announcement in her mind.

"What are you thinking?"

Alanna glanced up with the sound of his voice. She half-smiled and turned away, letting the cool dampness of the tall grass against her bare feet soothe her jittery nerves. "Nothing," she said quietly.

He watched her awhile, recalling the conversation he had had with Joshua. Odd, how that man always knew what bothered Beau, especially when he wasn't even sure himself. Yes, if what he felt for this woman could be described as love, then he loved Alanna Bainbridge. He cocked his head to one side. And how did she feel about him? He couldn't explain why, but he almost sensed she didn't hate him anymore, possibly even liked him. But

197

how much? Could she ever forgive him for the way he had treated her? He nearly laughed out loud, realizing he had actually cared what a woman thought. Smiling, he looked down at the cluster of wild flowers growing near his feet. He bent and plucked a single bloom.

"Alanna, I'd—I'd like to apologize for—well—for all the things that have happened." He studied the soft pink shade of the petals.

Alanna's breath seemed to leave her. Had she heard him correctly? Did this man, her owner, humble himself to apologize to a mere servant? She turned to face him, a strange sensation washing over her when she found him standing beneath the shade of a willow, a delicate flower held gently in his hands. "There is no need, Master Remington. What happened was of my own doing."

Surprise crimping his brow, he looked up. "Not everything," he argued. "I shouldn't have forced myself on you." He laughed nervously. "Whether you'll believe me or not, I assure you I never did anything like that before." He looked back at the flower he twirled by the stem between his thumb and forefinger. "And I'd feel better knowing that I at least tried to make up for it."

Suddenly embarrassed at the feelings Beau was revealing, Alanna bowed her head, unable to look at him, and said, "Then rest well tonight knowing that I understand."

Her answer caught him unawares, and yet it had been as he expected, for this young woman was different from all others. Even Joshua had seen it. She had no vanity about herself, and now he realized she no longer nutured any hatred. A forgiving soul for so young a beauty. As if all worries had suddenly been lifted, he looked up to find her spotlighted in the single ray of sunshine that fought its way through the tangled mass of willow branches as though summoned by the angels. Indeed, he thought, a true angel. Compelled to go to her, he closed the distance between them in three easy strides, pausing before he reached up to place the pink blossom in her hair above her ear. Gently touching a fingertip to her chin, he raised her face to study it. She did not pull away or seem to find his gesture unwarranted, and, without a thought, he lowered his head to place a warm and tender kiss on the corner of her mouth.

Did he truly feel the words he spoke? Alanna's mind reeled, intoxicated by his nearness, his kiss, the gentle touch of his hand. But did it matter? He was here, now, pledging never to hurt her again. Although she had promised herself never to play his dove again, she found the yearning to have him hold her in his arms overpowering. Her eyes closed, she breathed the scent of him, and, turning her head to welcome his kiss, her arms raised to encircle his neck.

He kissed her softly, tracing her lips with his tongue before it darted inside. Her mind whirled, knowing now how she had longed for this. His hands entwined with her long dark curls, pulling her closer, the strong, hard muscles of his chest pressed against her heaving breasts. He kissed her hungrily, one hand slipping to the small of her back to pull her hips to his. She heard him moan and wondered if he shared the burning desire she had, desire that threatened to consume her, to spiral her to heights she had never before reached. Freeing her lips of his searing kiss, he brushed her cheek with his, hoarsely whispering her name over and over again.

Stepping back, he unfastened the buttons of his shirt and slid it from his shoulders, his eyes never leaving hers.

He stooped, spreading out the garment on a blanket of green foliage on the ground. Coming to her again, he cupped her delicate chin in his hands, his lips finding hers once more. Instinctively, Alanna slipped her arms around him, her hands caressing the taut muscles of his back, his shoulders, a silent invitation to continue.

Only the cool wisp of the gentle breeze sparked her awareness that he had undone the buttons of her gown and pulled it from her shoulders, his kisses finding the soft flesh of her neck and throat, moving lower, to the pulse racing there. Head back, eyes closed, lips slightly parted, Alanna savored his embrace, his quest to possess her, to sample once more the sweetness of her womanhood. Feeling no shame, she eagerly allowed him to pull the gown from her arms to glide earthward. She shuddered, but not from the crisp bite of the early morning air, rather from the bewitching desires he stirred in her, lost in the fog of emotions, oblivious to her surroundings. His stroking thumb against the thin cloth of her camisole set her blood pounding through her veins and made her nipples taut, a chill of passion penetrating to the core of her soul. He kissed her again, his fingers untwining the strings of the garment to let it fall with the other at her feet. Reaching out, he took her hand and gently pulled her down upon the bed of grass. Kneeling, his lips found hers, his touch exploring the curves of her breasts, her belly, her hips and thighs, before he half-lifted her in his arms and curled her beneath him to fall together with her onto their love-nest. Passions soaring, her breath caught in her throat when his mouth captured the rose-hued peak of her breast, nibbling gently, his hand caressing the soft flesh of her inner thigh. She moaned, reaching out to hold him closer, to guide him.

Fearing his change of mind when he pulled away, Alanna smiled softly as she watched him quickly shed the rest of his clothes instead, opening her arms to welcome him. The warmth of his naked flesh pressed full against the coolnes of her own. Her mind whirled with desire, with the need to unite their bodies as one. Without a care for the consequences, she wiggled beneath him to open her thighs and urge him to take what she offered and he so obviously longed to claim. The fiery hard flesh of him drove deeply, his impatience ruling as his mouth came down hard on hers. They moved in blissful harmony, each sharing in the rampant lust that consumed them until at last they fell exhausted in each other's arms, their passion spent.

Nestled in the crook of his arm, Alanna stared up at the umbrella of softly swaying willow branches overhead, oddly content never to leave their haven, yet knowing they must. She giggled when Beau reached over to lightly trace the tautness of her nipple, cool breezes bathing her bare flesh.

"I could stay here forever," he said softly.

Alanna smiled, wondering if he had read her thoughts.

"But we mustn't," he sighed. "In fact, if we don't show ourselves soon they'll come looking for us. And this would be a little difficult to explain, don't you think?" He grinned broadly at the slight blush that arose in her cheeks. "And if you don't clothe yourself in the next minute, I won't care who watches, I'll sample your sweetness again."

Wiggling free of him, her eyes wide, she hurried to do as bidden, for in the brightness of the day her modesty returned tenfold, and she feared the possible arrival of spying intruders.

"I shall rather enjoy spending some time alone with you in Williamsburg," he smiled, tugging on his boots and picking up his shirt. His brows furrowed as he stared at the green marks on it. "I believe I will have to set my imagination to work with this when Tilly asks how I managed to stain it." He shrugged into it. "Oh, well. A very small price for what I got in return." He stood and came to her side, brushing away her hands to fasten the buttons of her gown. He turned her to face him. "I plan to buy you many gowns, my sweet."

"Not many, sir, I beg you," Alanna pleaded.

"And why not? 'Tis my money." Pulling her close, he guided her toward the buggy. "Now I'll hear no more about it."

What they shared was theirs alone to know. A private matter. But if he insisted on showering her with gifts, not only would others suspect, but she would feel no better than a whore. Didn't he understand that what she had given him had no price? Suddenly filled with shame, her brow wrinkled, tears burning her eyes.

Fifteen

Alanna hoped Beau would forget about the purchase of her new wardrobe, but that hope vanished the following morning when she went to the kitchen for breakfast and found him already there having tea and one of Bessy's sweet rolls.

"It should be a pleasant ride into Williamsburg today," he smiled as he rose and pulled out a chair for her to sit down. "There isn't a cloud in the sky, and it's cool for a change."

"I wish I was goin'," Bessy sighed. "I love ta look in all those shop windows."

I would gladly exchange places, Alanna thought with a weak smile.

"Now don't look so scared, child. Masta Beau will take care of yo'. If'n he don't, he'll have me ta answer to," Bessy warned with a wrinkled brow in his direction.

"Rest assured, good woman. She is safe in my hands," Beau said, shaking a finger at her.

Alanna's cheeks burned with the irony of his comment and, rather than have either of them notice, she quickly rose from the table and went to the hearth to pour a cup of hot water into the tea leaves. She toyed with it for several minutes.

"I'd prefer you wear something other than that dress," Beau said when she finally had the courage to return to the table. "And shoes and stockings."

"But—but I have no other dress," she replied weakly, absently running the palm of her hand over her skirt in an effort to smooth out the wrinkles.

He smiled. "I'm well aware of that. There would be no need to travel to Williamsburg if you did. Tilly!" he called.

The hurried slap of bare feet against the floor sounded in the hallway and a moment later the young girl appeared in the doorway.

"Yes, Masta Beau?"

"Take Alanna upstairs to the guest bedchamber and find her something more suitable for travel. We'll be spending a couple of days in Williamsburg and I prefer she not look like a ragamuffin."

"Yes, sir," Tilly said with a short curtsy.

Glancing back at Alanna with a satisfied smile, he spotted the troubled expression marring her otherwise flawless face. "Something wrong?" he asked, sobering.

The silence of the room penetrated her thoughts with a start and, finding all eyes centered on her, Alanna fidgeted with the nail of one thumb.

"No, sir," she said with a quick shake of her head.

Doubting her, he watched her until she met his eyes. "Are you sure?"

"Oh, yes," she reaffirmed, forcing a smile to part her lips.

A twitch of one brow denoted the fact that he still

wasn't convinced, but rather than make an issue of it, he nodded, "All right, then run along. But don't waste any time. We have a long ride ahead of us." He turned in his chair to watch the shadows envelop both girls.

"Why ya goin' into town, Alanna?" Tilly asked as they climbed the stairs.

"He's decided I shouldn't run barefoot," she mumbled, hurrying to keep up with Tilly's quick steps.

"Oh," Tilly sang in an all too knowing tone, not breaking stride as she disappeared into the bedchamber.

"What's that supposed to mean?"

"It means he likes yo'," Tilly retorted, slightly piqued by Alanna's crisp words. "What did yo' think?"

Glancing both directions down the hallway to verify that no one followed, yet still worried someone might hear, Alanna pulled the door closed noiselessly behind her. "I'm sorry I snapped at you. I know you would never assume what everyone else will. It's just that I don't want him to buy me anything."

Tilly shrugged off the apology. "Why? And just what will everyone a-assume?"

Alanna studied the brightly colored Persian rug beneath her feet. "That I'm his mistress."

"Is that all?" Tilly sighed, turning about and crossing to the big wardrobe sitting against one wall. "So what if they do? What's wrong with that?"

"Tilly! I don't want anyone to think that. It isn't true."

"So why yo' care? As long as yo' know it ain't, no one else matter." She struggled with the wide doors of the chest.

"You don't understand," Alanna pouted.

"No, I don't," Tilly exclaimed, turning back with a

205

knotted fist perched on each hip. "If Masta Beau likes yo', he could make life nice for yo'. Why not let him?"

"Because he'll expect something in return," Alanna stormed. "I'm not a trollop and he won't turn me into one."

Tilly's arms slumped to her sides. "Yo' don't know him very well. He's never forced hisself on a woman in his life."

Alanna burst into laughter. "Oh, Tilly. If you only knew," she moaned. Then she noticed the confusion on the dark face staring back at her, and instantly regretted her thoughtless words.

"What do yo' mean?" Tilly asked with a pained frown.

Alanna's pulse quickened, knowing she had gone too far. "Nothing. I sometimes open my mouth when I shouldn't. Forget it." Coming to the girl's side to look past her into the wardrobe, she could feel the concentration of a pair of dark brown eyes fixed on her. "There certainly are a lot of gowns in here, aren't there?"

"What do yo' mean?" Tilly asked again.

Wishing somehow she could make Tilly forget her outburst, she pointedly ignored her and thumbed through the rainbow of colors hanging in the chest until the tenseness in the air and the awful silence of her friend forced her to glance back at Tilly, finding her with a full lower lip protruding.

"Don't yo' think I can keep a secret?"

"Oh, of course, I do," Alanna reassured her, reaching out to touch her arm. "It's not that."

"Then what is it?"

Tears sprang to her eyes, a mixture of wistfulness for not having held her tongue, and shame as she recalled the need. She broke away from Tilly and went to the bed to sit down, carefully avoiding Tilly's eyes. "It's just that I know how much you think of Master Beau, that's all. I wouldn't want to say anything to spoil that."

"What could yo' say to make me change my mind?"

Alanna blinked several times, moistened her lips with the tip of her tongue, and avoided any response at all.

"What?" Tilly demanded sharply.

Alanna could feel a tightening in her throat as she listened to the footsteps coming toward her, knowing that if she looked up she would cry. She bit her lip, hoping she would be able to contain her tears.

"What, Alanna? What?" Tilly shouted with a stomp of her foot.

Her lip trembled and she shrugged, praying Tilly wouldn't notice. "That he raped someone."

"Dear God in heaven," Tilly whispered, her small hands pressed against her face. "Who was it?"

Alanna raised one shoulder again.

"But yo' gotta know. How's else would yo' know it happened?" Suddenly Tilly gasped and fell to her knees. "It was yo', wasn't it? Bessy said somethin' was wrong, that Masta Beau ain't acted the same since yo' was beat. I never thought he would do that. Oh, Alanna, I's so sorry. Say yo' not angry 'cause I keep askin'."

Eyes glistening with tears, Alanna looked up. "You mean you believe me?"

"Why wouldn't I? Yo' wouldn't lie to me."

Alanna pressed shaky fingertips to her trembling mouth. "Only you and Cinnamon know of it. Just promise not to tell another soul. And please," she begged, taking Tilly's hands in hers, "don't hate him for it."

Tilly fell back against her heels, her mouth agape. "The man took yo' against yo'r will and listen to yo'. Yo'

207

ask *me* not to hate him."

"But you have no reason to hate him."

Tilly angrily stood up and went to the window. "I do now."

"No," Alanna moaned. "You mustn't. It's why I wanted to keep it from you. I couldn't bear the thought of having destroyed your friendship by the slip of a tongue. Please, Tilly, say you don't hate him."

A long moment passed before Tilly spoke again, her voice low and strained. "Yo' knows why it 's hard for me to agree, don't yo'?" 'Cause yo'r my friend and he hurt yo'. I can never forgive him for that. But I guess I don't hate him."

"Oh, thank you, Tilly," Alanna wept, coming to her side, her arms reaching out to enfold the slight form as she pressed a tear-moistened cheek to hers.

They stood at the window in silence, each with her own thoughts, and comforting each other with gentle pats of their hands.

Evening shadowed their arrival to Williamsburg the next day. They had spent the previous night in an inn some miles away from Raven Oaks. They had eaten and retired to their rooms with the thought of rising early to get a good start on their journey. Alanna had been apprehensive of traveling unchaperoned with Beau and even more worried when they had gone to their rooms, wondering if he might knock at her door later. But after she had fallen asleep, it was only the sunlight stealing through the curtains that woke her.

"It's too late to visit the dress shops, now," Beau said, pulling their carriage to a stop outside the Chesterfield

House. "We might as well have dinner and spend the night here."

Alanna didn't answer, praying this night would pass like the one before.

The extravagance of the inn overwhelmed Alanna as she stood just inside the front doors staring up at the immense chandelier hanging overhead. It measured three times the size of the one at Raven Oaks, its crystal teardrops sparkling in every color imaginable. Captivated by its splendor, she failed to notice that Beau left her to go to the large desk set off to one side of the large room until a stranger accidentally bumped into her. Discovering that she stood in the way of the entrance, she quickly apologized for her rudeness and stepped out of the way of the crowd of people bustling about to wait patiently for Beau to return.

"Good evening, Mr. Remington," the round little man behind the counter smiled. "It's always good to see you."

"Thank you, Thomas," Beau nodded, setting their bags on the floor beside him. "I'd like two rooms. We'll probably be here a couple of days."

"Certainly. The usual two?" the desk clerk asked.

Having reached for the ledger spread out on the desk top to sign his name, Beau hesitated only a second before answering. "Yes," he said quietly, and stole a glance at Alanna to see if she had heard the man's unthoughtful and badly timed question. She hadn't. Or at least she appeared not to have heard, for her attention was centered on the wide doorway leading to the dining hall. He smiled. Rich, warm aromas came from the room, and he knew how hungry she must be, since they had skipped their last meal in an effort to reach town before dark. But knowing Alanna, he was sure she would go to bed hungry before asking one thing of him.

"Smells delicious, doesn't it?" he asked a few minutes later as he stood beside her.

She nodded.

"I've ordered water heated for a bath. Once we've rested awhile, we can join the others in the dining hall."

"That would be wonderful. I'm afraid I shall faint if I don't have something to eat," she laughed, bringing a smile from him in return as he held out his arm for her.

As they passed the counter, Beau looked to the man behind it. "Have someone bring up our bags," he instructed without losing stride and vaguely hearing the man's reply as he turned to Alanna. "I hope Tilly packed a nice gown for you. We'll take in the theater if she did."

"Much against my protests, I must admit," she said, lifting her skirts to ascend the stairs. "I saw no need, but Tilly is much wiser than I."

Beau chuckled. "Yes. Sometimes I could swear that girl can read my thoughts."

"She's very loyal. You know that, don't you?"

"Yes. I realize it every time I think how long she's been with me. It must be close to ten years now."

"Did you—buy her?"

Beau fought down his smile, knowing how distasteful the idea must seem to an Englishwoman. "Yes. She had been badly abused by a distant neighbor of mine and Bessy had heard about it. She asked, no, she begged me to buy her so she could care for her. I must admit, it was the wisest money I ever spent."

"How many of your servants did you purchase?"

"Only the Negroes. All the others are indentured, like you. And someday they'll move on to start their lives here in the colonies, just as you shall do."

Alanna stopped abruptly in the center of the staircase and met his eyes. "Oh, but I won't. I have an aunt in England to whom I can return and with whom I can make my home. I could never afford to live comfortably in America. I would always have to work for another. Someday I hope to marry a man who can give me all I could ever want, and I certainly won't find him working on your or anyone else's plantation." She started up the stairs again. "No, *I* must return to England."

"Is there such a man in England?" he asked curiously.

She paused, looking at him, and stepping to one side to allow another guest to pass. "There was. But I'm not sure if he will wait for me. Or even want me now." She sighed, looked at the stairs and took another step. "Besides, his parents did not think me worthy of him."

"Ha," he growled. "Then they are fools."

Alanna's step faltered and she instantly felt his arm around her. She knew he thought she had stumbled. Could he truly mean what he had said? Did he honestly feel she was good enough for anyone other than a stable boy? Did it mean there might be a slight chance that he would see her in a different way? As a man looks at a woman rather than a master at a servant? No, she sighed. He had only expressed an opinion.

Alanna had never eaten so much or so well in her life as she did that night in the dining room of the inn. The petite blond waitress continually added bowls of candied yams, corn, rice, ham or sweet rolls to the table and only disappeared after Beau informed her that they had been well served. Even then, she presented herself one more time with two big slices of apple pie for them to sample.

Both Alanna and Beau could only stare at the delicacy, knowing full well they hadn't an inch of room left in their stomachs to hold another single bite. And when she had looked to him in desperation, he read her thoughts and laughed, eliciting an equally merry response from her.

They had just settled back in their chairs to let the fullness of their meal ease when Beau looked up and saw Radford Chamberlain enter the room, Melissa Bensen at his elbow. He immediately slouched down and looked the other way, hiding his eyes with a hand held against his brow. However, Radford had already seen him.

"Beau," Radford sang, coming toward their table. "I never would have expected to see you here tonight." He smiled warmly at his friend until his gaze fell on Alanna, his surprise at her presence marked clearly on his face. "Alanna?"

She nodded politely at him, trying unsuccessfully to keep her attention focused on him rather than on the fashionable woman at his side. A white powdered wig, sprinkled with pearl-tipped hairpins, completely hid Melissa's yellow curls. Holding her spine erect, her shoulders squared, she forcefully projected her bosom to strain against the seams of the dark velvet gown that clung tightly to her slender waist, causing Alanna to wonder how many corset strings she had broken to produce such a noticeable figure. Yards of fabric flowed about her, and Alanna experienced a twinge of envy that she could not dress as elegantly.

Noticing where her gaze rested, Radford straightened, slightly embarrassed by his own lack of manners, and gently took Melissa's elbow to pull her closer to the table. "I believe you know Melissa, but I doubt she will recognize you as the same woman. I know I didn't.

212

Melissa, this is—"

"I know who she is," Melissa snapped, twisting free of his hold. She turned to Beau, who had reluctantly come to his feet, and smiled. "Good evening, Beau. Will you be staying the night in Williamsburg?"

Having folded his arms over his chest, Beau studied the fingers resting on his sleeve before looking up. "Yes. We plan to stay two, in fact."

"That's great," Radford exclaimed. "So do we. Maybe we can spend them together."

A faint hint of a frown crossed Beau's brow. "I don't think so. We didn't come for pleasure."

"Now, I can't believe you'd take Alanna home without her seeing some of the sights in Williamsburg. We were planning to go to the theater after dinner. Surely you both have time to join us." As he extended the invitation, he smiled down at Alanna, missing the darkened scowl that hooded Beau's eyes. "You'd enjoy that, wouldn't you, Alanna?"

A weak smile parted Alanna's lips as she glanced up at Beau, knowing it was not her decision to make, and she elected to fold her napkin instead.

"Now I won't take no for an answer," Radford continued when neither of them spoke. "Curtain call isn't for another hour. It will give us time to eat and you time to relax. Come, Melissa. They probably have business to discuss and it would be rude of us to intrude. We'll take another table and meet later. See you then," he threw back over his shoulder as he led Melissa away.

"Would you care for a glass of wine?" Beau asked, returning to his chair and motioning for the waiter.

"Yes, thank you," she replied quietly, certain she would need its effects to steel herself for the evening. She

213

toyed with her napkin until the waiter had served a decanter of dark red wine and two goblets, unable to bring herself to look at Beau. "I'm sorry your evening has been spoiled," she said softly.

The decanter tipped in the air as he filled the second glass. Beau glanced up in surprise. "Is it that obvious?"

She nodded.

"Well, don't let it bother you. I want you to enjoy the theater. Not everyone has a chance to go, and it can be quite an experience." He downed the entire contents of his glass in one swallow and glanced at the couple sitting a few tables away from them. He poured another drink.

"Joshua has told me how much you think of Mr. Chamberlain. Why does his presence disturb you so?" Alanna asked, taking a sip of the wine.

He sighed, resting an elbow on the table, a thumb pressed to his temple. "For as long as I've known him, he has the uncanny knack of appearing at precisely the wrong time. However, it isn't his presence that disturbs me the most."

"Mistress Bensen?"

He leaned back in the chair and stretched. "Yes. Why I tolerate her, I will never know. I guess it's because I think so much of her father."

"What I do not understand is that if you think so little of the woman, and you and Mr. Chamberlain are as close as brothers, why would he find her appealing?"

He grinned. "That, my dear lady, is something I, too, do not understand."

"Something else I don't understand is why you have not married. Or at least have one lady you prefer more than others."

Beau laughed heartily. "The question is, who would

214

have me? I am intolerable, stubborn, moody, insensitive, and always put business ahead of everything else."

Alanna leaned forward against the edge of the table. "Oh, I don't agree. You're not all those things."

He smiled as he studied her a moment. "You of all people should see me that way."

"How can you say that? Here we are, sitting in this fine hotel about to see a play and on the morrow you plan to spend your money to buy clothes for me. I would hardly call that insensitive."

"What would you call it?" he asked, leaning back in his chair as he pulled a cheroot from his coat pocket.

"Generous."

"You are a strange woman, Alanna Bainbridge," he said, leaning forward, the tip of his cheroot touching the flame of the candle that sat upon the table. He watched the white smoke curl overhead. Then, obviously, an idea struck him, and his eyes took on a playful gleam. He motioned for the waiter, handed him enough money to pay for their meal, and turned to Alanna. "I don't know about you, but I grow weary of sitting here. Shall we take a walk along the streets of Williamsburg?"

"But—" she began, glancing back toward Radford and Melissa.

"But what?" he asked, mocking innocence, and she instantly knew his intent, bringing a smile to her lips.

As they headed for the door, Beau leaned down so only she could hear. "If we're fortunate, they will be too caught up in each other to notice our disappearance. I just might be able to enjoy the theater, after all." He winked and Alanna could not suppress a giggle.

The cool bite of night air had taken on the smell of jasmine when Beau and Alanna stepped outside the

Chesterfield House, losing themselves among the group of people crowding the wooden sidewalks. Beau's step slowed while he casually took Alanna's hand and draped it around his arm, covering it with his own hand. She could feel the slow, steady beating of his heart as he pressed her hand against his chest, causing her own to flutter and at the same time allowing her to relax just a little into a moment of pleasure. As they neared the end of the row of buildings, she could see in the distance the lights of the harbor and hear the gentle slapping of the waves as they rushed to shore. She longed to stand near them and feel the cool spray of mist against her cheek.

"Master Remington—" she began.

He stopped abruptly. "Please, Alanna," he smiled, "call me Beau. It would appear strange to anyone who might hear you address me so formally."

A nervous smile answered him. "I was wondering if we might stroll to the harbor. I do so love to watch the ships."

"It wouldn't be wise. Even I dare not venture there. There are ruffians who would not hesitate to take you from me and abuse you, and since they very rarely travel alone, I would be helpless to stop them. I'm sorry."

"I understand," she said. "I guess I shall just have to be content to enjoy them from afar."

He smiled in the darkness as they crossed the street and headed back toward the inn. "Your young man in England is very lucky," he said.

"Why?" she asked, wondering what made him think of Aaron.

"You are not like most women. Standing at the harbor to watch the ships would bore them. They would prefer something a little more exciting such as a theater or going to a ball." He chuckled. "Melissa would find it appalling."

"I think you're too hard on the woman. After all, she has known wealth all of her life. I haven't. Doing something as simple as watching the ships in the harbor is exciting to me only because I haven't known the things that interest someone like her. Had she never attended a ball or gone to the theater, she, too, might find the harbor exciting."

He looked down at her a moment. "Well put, my dear. However, I have known all of these things and would much prefer a quiet, private evening."

She smiled. "And you, sir, are a man. How could you possibly know what interests a woman?"

"A battle of wits against a man, perhaps?" he grinned.

Alanna lifted her brows. "Perhaps."

Alanna had never seen so many beautiful women dressed so richly than she did later that night at the theater. There were gowns in every shade of the rainbow, with high necklines and puffy sleeves or cut so daringly low that she feared the ladies would expose their bosoms should they move just the slightest. Fine jewels hung at the tips of their ears and adorned their throats, painfully reminding her of her bare ears and neck. And the white powdered wigs! But even had she been dressed as elegantly, she would have felt out of place among these ladies of wealth and their companions. As soon as she opened her mouth to speak they would know from where she had come. Beau must have sensed her discomfort, for he carefully avoided speaking with anyone and took them directly to their box overlooking the stage, pulling the curtain closed behind them for total privacy. Little did she know he had done so partly to avoid being seen by Radford.

The buzzing of voices stilled as the curtain began to rise, and Alanna sat breathless as she watched and listened to the play being performed for the crowded theater. No sounds other than the voices of the actors were heard, and when the curtain came down she felt disappointed that it had ended so soon.

"It will be a few minutes before the second act," Beau said. "Would you care to stretch your legs?"

Alanna blushed, hoping he wouldn't notice in the soft light of the candles that glittered in their sanctuary. "Yes," she murmured.

The lobby was full of people sipping glasses of wine and talking gaily among themselves. Beau and Alanna made their way toward the front doors. It had grown stuffy inside, and he decided a short walk in the cool night air would refresh them. But just as they reached the exit, someone called out his name. They turned to see Radford and Melissa elbowing their way toward them.

"Damn," Beau muttered. "We shouldn't have left the box."

Melissa, dressed in the most ravishing gown Alanna had ever seen—a different one than she had worn to dinner—purposely avoided looking at Alanna, rather centering her attention on Beau. Soft shades of pink accented the smoothness of her skin and highlighted the tall alabaster-hued wig adorned with diamond-studded combs, its delicate ringlets trickling down her neck. She presented herself beautifully, and Alanna suddenly could not understand why Beau would not be attracted to her.

"Where did you go?" Radford scolded once they had

218

reached them. "We looked everywhere for you."

"We decided to take a walk," Beau said flatly.

"Well, at least we found you now." He turned to Alanna. "Are you enjoying the play?"

"Really, Radford," Melissa cut in, "I doubt she understands a word of it. How could she possibly be enjoying it?"

"Oh, but I am," Alanna exclaimed, not having caught Melissa's sarcasm. "I find it very exciting. It's something I'll remember always."

"I'm sure you will, since you shall probably never attend another," Melissa sneered and turned to nod a greeting to someone she recognized.

Alanna retreated a step. "Yes, I'm afraid you're right. However, it is a memory I shall always recall with fondness, no matter what might be said in an effort to spoil it."

Melissa stiffened, her nose lifting just the slightest as she opened her mouth to retaliate. But Radford, quick to see the forthcoming exchange of heated words, reached over, took the woman's hand, and pulled her closer to him.

"You will join us in our box, won't you?" he asked of Beau.

"Thank you, no. We have our own."

"Then, perhaps, you will join us afterwards."

"I see no need," Beau snapped and Alanna quickly stepped in, placing her arm on his.

"But we have no other plans," she said softly, "and I fear you will grow bored with only me to share your company."

"Then that settles it," Radford beamed. "We'll meet you here after the play is over." He smiled as he bid them farewell and turned with Melissa held securely on his arm.

"Why did you do that?" Beau asked angrily.

"You are friends. I will not be the one to change that just because Mistress Bensen does not approve of me."

"To hell with Mistress Bensen," he retorted. "If she doesn't approve of who I keep company with, she can very well stay away."

"My point exactly, Mr. Remington," she smiled. "You must not let her decide your friends."

Alanna continued to smile up at him until his anger had obviously eased and he smiled back at her. Gently, he tapped the end of her nose with his fingertip. "If I keep you beside me always, I think some day I shall learn not to grow angry." He chucked. "Cain wouldn't know what to think of me if a single day passed without my heated words echoing in his ears. It should be fun, I think."

They both laughed and turned to make their way back to their box and the play.

The production ended in a frenzy of applause and excited cheers from the audience. The players returned to the stage three times before the final curtain dropped and the people began to leave the theater. Sorry to see it come to an end, Alanna wished but somehow it could go on forever. But knowing it would never be, she decided she would have to be content with her memories. Together, she and Beau slowly made their way to the door to await Radford's arrival. Only a few minutes passed before she recognized his smiling face among a sea of strangers.

"I've invited a few friends to my room for a glass of

wine," he shouted above the noise. "I hope you don't mind. I do so enjoy an after-theater party. Besides, it will give Alanna a chance to meet a few people."

She could feel the muscles in Beau's arm tighten beneath her hand and she quickly answered before Beau had a chance. "That will be lovely," she said, glancing up at Beau from the corner of her eye. She grinned, and in the same instance she felt him relax.

"Like I said before—" he whispered.

A few people turned out to be twenty, and although Beau found that he didn't have to endure Melissa's snide remarks toward Alanna as he would have had they been alone, he was irritated by the fact that he was forced to be pleasant when he felt far from it. He never enjoyed parties, always considering it a waste of good money and time he could well use in the running of his plantation, and idle talk bored him. Especially when it came to women and their feeble attempts at conversation regarding topics they knew nothing about but chose to pursue for the opportunity to flirt.

They had barely entered the room before Radford stole Alanna from him and left him alone to be entertained by Penelope Carter, a rather buxom woman nearly ten years his senior with the foolish idea that she appeared that much younger. Beau found himself drinking more wine than he had intended to do just so that he could withstand her constant chatter. The only thing that saved him was when her husband joined them and engaged his wife in a rather heated discussion of how she always managed to leave him alone. Thankful for the chance to slip away unnoticed, he went to the fireplace, rested an elbow against the mantel, and studied the portrait hanging above it while he finished his fifth glass of wine.

"Did you enjoy the play?" he heard someone ask and turned to find Melissa at his side.

He sighed inwardly, thinking how much he'd rather be listening to Penelope than spend even a moment with Melissa, and smiled when he realized how insulted Melissa would be if she knew his thoughts. "Yes," he said. "And you?"

"I found it rather tedious," she replied with a gentle lift to the curls resting against her neck. "Or maybe it was just the company."

Beau fought back his angry defense of his friend and offered to get her a glass of wine instead. She declined, stating that a lady should not overindulge in something meant for a man's enjoyment, and she cast a meaningful glance in Alanna's direction. He, too, looked over at the woman dressed in lavender and immediately saw the glass in her hand. His irritation began to grow.

"Whatever possessed you to bring her to Williamsburg anyway?" Melissa asked once she noticed how he openly studied Alanna.

"I don't think it's any of your business what I do, Melissa," he said coldly.

She shrugged. "Of course not. But I certainly think you would much prefer a lady at your side to one of your mere servants."

Beau sent her a tiresome glance. "So far tonight she is the only lady I've had at my side."

Melissa gasped in outrage. With her shoulders squared, her nose high in the air, she turned on her heel and stalked away.

Beau grunted, watching her. What did she expect? he mused. A kiss on the forehead? He sighed, and when he looked up again he could feel the attention someone was paying. He looked around, found Alanna smiling at him, and decided to join her party. After all, he was her escort for the evening.

"Beau," Radford sang when he looked up and spied him walking toward them. "You know Henry Wilkes and his wife, Agatha?"

"Of course," Beau said extending his hand to the man. "The editor of our noteworthy paper. Agatha?"

The gray-haired woman curtsied with a smile. "It's been a long time, Beauregard. How have you been?"

"Busy. But then again, aren't we all?"

"We were just enjoying the company of your lovely young lady. She's quite refreshing, you know. Especially to someone like me. I'm afraid I'll never get to travel to England, and she's probably about as close as I'll come." Agatha smiled fondly at Alanna. "How long have you been here, dear?"

"Only a few months," Alanna said.

"What brought you to the colonies?"

"My father. He wanted to settle here," Alanna answered quietly.

"You sound so sad. Didn't you wish to come?"

"Oh, yes," Alanna assured the woman. "It's just that he died before we reached America."

"How dreadful, my dear. It must be hard to adjust in a strange land all alone."

"Not really, Mrs. Wilkes. Beau takes quite good care of his servants." All eyes turned to Melissa as she haughtily slipped her arm into Radford's. "Isn't that so, Alanna?"

One by one, Alanna's gaze fell on the people who surrounded her. She couldn't find the words to explain how she had never meant to fool anyone and hoped that they would understand, but in that awful moment of silence, nothing that seemed fitting would come to mind. She lowered her head.

"A servant?" she heard Agatha Wilkes reply. "Now I don't know why that surprises me any. Beauregard Remington has never done anything that I wouldn't expect of a man of his caliber. I think it's delightful. Come, child," she added, reaching out for Alanna's hand, "let's refresh ourselves and you can tell me what it's really like living with a man like that." As the gray-haired woman passed him, she gave Beau a click of her tongue and shake of her head.

"It must have been awful for you, child," Agatha soothed Alanna when the two women had found the privacy of Radford's bedchamber, leaving the others behind in the sitting room. "I know how mean Melissa Bensen can be at times. I don't want you to think that Henry and I feel the same. I was nothing more than a servant when he asked me to marry him, and I don't think Melissa knows that or she wouldn't have been so free with her words."

"It isn't for myself that I feel shame. I just regret having embarrassed Master Beau that way," Alanna said, sitting down on the bed.

"Embarrass him?" Agatha laughed. "Honey, I doubt there is a thing in the world you could do to embarrass that man. In fact, it's usually the other way around. And if we had stayed a moment longer, I'm sure you would have witnessed that."

"What do you mean?"

"I mean that I'm certain he has by now properly put Melissa in her place. Lord knows she deserves it." Agatha went to the small dressing table and began to fiddle with her curls as she studied her reflection in the mirror. "I just pray Radford never marries her. He's too sweet a young man to be saddled to her for the rest of his life." She pinched color to her cheeks and turned around. "Feel better now?" she asked and seeing Alanna nod, she added, "Good. Now let's go back to the others and see how humble Melissa can be."

As they entered the sitting room, it was Radford who first reached Alanna. "I'm sorry for what happened. I should have warned you how nasty Melissa can be at times," he said as he wrapped her arm within his. "Would you care for another glass of wine?"

"No, thank you. I think I've had enough." Eagerly looking about the room, she found Beau still at Henry Wilkes' side. "If you don't mind, I think I should join Master Remington."

"Certainly," he said, but before he let go of her, he bent down so that only she could hear. "Alanna, I'd like to call on you sometime."

"I—I don't think that will be possible, Master Chamberlain," she stammered. "Master Beau wouldn't allow it."

"Then at least let me send a gift. Sort of an apology for what happened here tonight."

She looked up into his blue eyes. "I really don't see how I can stop you, but it isn't really necessary."

"Just grant me one small favor and I shall be content with that," he bowed dutifully, bringing a smile to her lips.

"Granted," she laughed, reluctantly freeing her hand of his hold as she crossed the room to join Beau and his companion.

"What was that all about?" Beau asked once she

reached him.

"What was what all about?"

"The two of you. It seemed you were sharing secrets."

"Oh, that," she sighed. "He was only apologizing for Mistress Bensen."

"And well he should. Only I think she should be the one to do the apologizing and not use a proxy."

"Please. It is over and forgotten and even *I* know she will never change. Don't let it spoil the rest of the evening," Alanna implored.

"Beau, what do you think?"

Startled by the sound of his name, Beau glanced up. "I'm sorry, Henry. What did you say?"

"I was just wondering if you had an opinion on this House of Burgesses that Washington and his friends have joined."

"I'm afraid I don't pay much attention to politics," Beau confessed.

Henry smiled. "Well, neither do I, really. But Washington, Patrick Henry, and a chap called Benjamin Franklin will be in Williamsburg very soon to attend one of its meetings. Agatha wants me to go. If for nothing else, just to write a story about them for the paper."

"Then do it," Beau agreed.

Henry swirled the contents of his glass. "Yes, I guess I will. Don't suppose I could get you to go."

Beau chuckled. "No. I've enough problems of my own without getting into someone else's."

Henry nodded agreement. "You're right, I suppose. But getting into someone else's problems comes with my job." He pulled the gold watch from his vest pocket, studied the time, and looked about the room for his wife as he clumsily returned it to its place. "It's getting late.

And since I have a newspaper to get out tomorrow, I think my wife and I had better be going."

"May we walk with you?" Beau asked, jumping at the opportunity to escape a rather trying evening. "I'm sure Alanna must be tired, too."

"We would enjoy the company. Even if it is for only a few minutes," Henry smiled warmly, looking at Alanna.

"The Wilkeses are a very nice couple," Alanna said later as she and Beau stood outside the door to her room.

"Yes, they are. I don't know why I don't see more of them. Too busy, I guess." Suddenly feeling quite awkward, he looked down at his feet. "I hope you managed to enjoy a small measure of this evening. It wasn't what I had planned at all."

Alanna smiled, studying the hem of her gown. "I did. Most of it, anyway. Thank you."

He looked up and considered the delicate lines of her profile for a moment. "Well, you better get some rest. We have a lot of things to do tomorrow. I'll see you at breakfast." He hesitated, turned, and walked away.

Alanna sighed as she leaned her head against the door frame, watching the steady, even gait of the man she had once hated. How things had changed. If only—

Sixteen

Beau and Alanna spent the following day visiting nearly every dress shop in Williamsburg, or so it seemed to Alanna's tired feet. The new shoes didn't help, even though she knew that in time they would be as comfortable as going barefoot. They stopped at a little store that sold nothing but bonnets and, even with Alanna's repeated protests, they left the shop with a brightly colored straw bonnet perched upon Alanna's head and tied tightly with a satin bow beneath her chin.

"It's for working in the sun," he had said. "I know how awful the heat can be without shade for your face."

How could she tell him that she didn't spend that much time outdoors?

Toward midafternoon they hired a buggy and driver and set out to tour the countryside. They rode through a meadow of tall grass dotted with wild flowers and Alanna excitedly begged for the chance to stop and pick a few to take back to her room. Beau stood beside the carriage, his arms folded across his chest as he leaned back against the carriage frame and watched her, a bright smile lighting the darkened depths of his eyes. For the first time in years, he was happy.

The carriage climbed the narrow road leading to a hill that overlooked the sea. The pungent smell of salt and fish filled their nostrils when they reached the top and ordered the driver to stop. They climbed from the carriage and strolled to a nearby rock, the wind tossing about Beau's curls and tugging at Alanna's bonnet.

"It's beautiful," Alanna sighed.

Spread out before her for as far as she could see the blue-green waters of the ocean, tipped with white waves, rolled inland, crashing to a showering death as they hit the rocks. The harbor, filled with vessels, took the brunt of the attack in stride, standing defiantly against the ever testing sea, while the huge merchant ships danced about in the waters. Off to one side lay Williamsburg, the long wooden docks stretched out from the city like gray, weathered fingers reaching for the warm, sun-baked shore. Marred only by an occasional sea gull as it soared inland, the pale blueness of an endless sky was speckled with white fluffy clouds.

"I could have a house built and live here forever," Alanna whispered. "Couldn't you?"

He laughed. "And who would keep the demon of poverty from your door?"

Her brows wrinkled. "Must you always think in terms of money? Can't you dream?"

"I told you before," he said, resting a boot against the rock on which she sat, "that I always put business ahead of all else. I cannot afford to dream."

"Then why did you bring me here? It obviously isn't the first time for you."

He smiled, joining her on the perch overlooking the

shoreline. "I thought you'd enjoy it."

"I do. But surely you did not always travel here to think out problems that concerned Raven Oaks."

"True. I came here to forget them for a while."

"You see," she said enthusiastically, "you can dream. Putting things from your mind that disturb you is sort of a way of dreaming."

Reaching up, he pulled a strand of hair free from the ribbon of her bonnet. "Is life always so simple to you, Alanna?"

"I do not think of life that way. I just do not let it trouble me overmuch. I find the more pleasant things to dwell on."

"And what pleasant thing has captured your thoughts today?"

"Being here," she answered honestly, looking back out across the sea. "The ocean, its waves, the trees and rocks about me are pleasant enough things on which to center my mind."

"How old are you, Alanna?" he asked suddenly.

"I have seen my twentieth spring. Why?"

"You have not lived long enough to know the hardships life can bring."

She laughed almost bitterly. "Haven't I? I was told repeatedly as a young girl that I should never expect anything more out of life than I already had, that no man of wealth would every marry someone like me." She turned her face toward the wind, letting it relax her. She sighed. "And when that man did come along, it was his parents who turned me out, reminding me of my earlier lessons. But we fought that destiny—only to wake up one morning to find that an ocean now separated us." She looked back at him, and Beau could see the pain

231

reflected in her eyes. "Then both my parents were taken from me, a slow, painful death, and I was hurled into a new existence. I had been bought and paid for. But that was only the beginning. I needn't say more, as you are a witness to the rest." Suddenly and unexplainably, Alanna's anger overtook her, and she left her perch and Beau to stare out to sea.

A playful smile flashed across his face as he leaned down to pluck a wild flower at his feet. "I had forgotten the temper you have," he said before rising. "And you are right, of course. From that point on, I am responsible." Slowly, he reached out and tucked the lavender flower in her hair above her ear. "An unpleasant start, I know. But things could change. It's up to you." Bringing her eyes to meet his, he cradled her face in his hands and kissed her.

A warm and gentle embrace. She relaxed, thinking how he had never held her in such a way before. In fact, he had never treated her more kindly than he had in the past few days. Could it be that he, too, as Aaron had, found her to be more than just a common girl of little wealth and simple upbringing? That here, simple though she might be, was a soft and willing soul ready for the love of a man, eager to return all that love and devotion of which she was capable? Slowly she reached up to place her arms around his neck, feeling him move to envelop her, one hand sliding down her spine until it rested against her buttock, pulling her closer. She stiffened. Had he mistaken her gesture? Suddenly, shame at her wanton desire, and confused ideas that maybe it was only desire motivating him, raced through her. Was that all he wanted? She had to know. Defensively, she pushed him away as his statement rang in her ears.

232

"Is that why you brought me to Williamsburg, spent your money on me, took me to the theater? You thought to show me what I could receive in trade?" Her small frame shook with pain. "Well, you were wrong," she choked. "I will not be your mistress. By choice or any other means." The sounds of the pebbles crushing beneath her feet as she stomped back toward the carriage carried in the wind and seemed to grow in volume tenfold, marking the distress she was experiencing.

"Wait just a minute, Alanna," he commanded, catching up to her in two easy strides. He grabbed her shoulder and spun her around. "I do not have to buy the attentions of a woman. If I had to, I would not want her. You are no exception, so do not flatter yourself so."

"Flatter?" she shrieked, her agony turning to rage. "To be bestowed with your attention, honorable or otherwise, would not be a form of flattery, sir. Contrary to what other women may think, you are no great prize."

The wind grew stronger with each heated word, whistling about the trees and stirring up the particles of sand that had sought a haven among the rocks, spitting them against the figures that stood silhouetted against the burning sky of the sunset and going unnoticed by them, immune as they were to all else but each other.

He glared at her for what seemed an endless amount of time, until the distant whinnying of a horse cooled his rage, and he realized they had not been alone. "We shall discuss this at another time," he said, taking her hand firmly in his and starting for the buggy. "I do not care to air our differences before others."

Alanna ate dinner that night alone in her room, having

sent word to Master Remington that she had developed a headache and would not join him in the dining hall. When darkness fell, she sat by the window, not a single candle lit and her door locked, staring outside at the flickering lights of the city, wishing she had anything of value to sell in exchange for passage back to England.

Be patient, she thought, shaking off the idea. It won't be long before I receive a letter from my aunt and I can walk on board like a lady instead of a begger. She sighed, listening to the chirping of the crickets. If only it would arrive soon.

In the distance, she heard the muffled sounds of a woman's laughter, distant, yet within the Chesterfield House, and she found herself envying her gaiety. It could have been her laughter had she willed it that way. Suddenly, she knew what Beau had tried to tell her. If she would curb her anger and her wicked thoughts, and choose to be his companion rather than his foe, they could enjoy each other's company. She lifted the window sash higher and settled herself on the sill, feeling the warm, gentle breeze against her face. Drinking in the aroma of the night smells, she thought back to how things had been between them before that moment on the hill. It had been exciting, and they had shared a feeling of friendship, not of master and servant. She had come to know him in a different light, as a man of compassion and giving, a man who needed and wanted a friend, no matter how he spoke the contrary. She smiled as she remembered his reaction to Melissa and admired the fact that he did not try to hide his feelings out of courtesy. The wind whipped her hair about her face, and she reached up to pull away a strand that had rested across her nose, smelling the salt of the sea in the air. America was

234

beautiful, and although it would never quite be England, she knew in time that she would come to love it as her father had dreamed he would. The laughter sounded again and, since the night was young, she scurried from the windowsill, having decided to make amends with Beau. She ran a brush through her hair, not bothering to bind it, and left the room.

She passed several people in the hall and smiled sweetly at them as she stopped in front of Beau's room. She watched the strangers disappear around the corner before tugging at the bodice of her gown and gently rapping upon the door. Silence drummed in her ears. Then she heard Beau's deep voice beckon her to enter. Her heart pounded, and she smiled softly with the thought that never before had anyone, including Aaron, affected her the way this man could. She lifted the latch and pushed the door open.

He stood near the darkened fireplace, a drink in his hand, and at first she could not understand the look on his face. Then she saw her. Lounging comfortably in the chair beside him was Melissa.

"O-oh, excuse me," Alanna whispered, unable to pull her eyes from the woman. "I didn't know you had company." She quickly glanced around expecting to see Radford and found they were alone. "I'm sorry to intrude," she apologized, her voice shaky. "I'll leave you." Without a protest from either of them to stop her, Alanna pulled the door quietly closed and stood there staring at it, her eyes filling with tears, her throat tight with despair. She turned and raced down the stairs and out into the night, not knowing where she ran, only that she must escape the scene that tore at her heart.

She started across the street, hearing the rattle of a

buggy thundering dangerously near, the sound of an angry voice cursing in the night air as she concentrated on the ground ahead of her, and only after she heard the hostile voice again did she look up to find herself directly in the man's path.

"You crazy woman. Ya trying to kill yourself?" he roared.

She ran from in front of the wagon and quickly stepped onto the sidewalk across the street from the Chesterfield House, her heart pounding from the near disaster. The air burned her lungs as she took several deep breaths to calm herself. She watched the buggy clatter away.

The sidewalk was full of people, mostly men crushed in all around her, and when they began to notice her with longer, more appraisingly curious glances, she quickly turned and started down the walk. She had no idea where she was going but thought it best to keep moving lest one of the men think she was something she was not. She passed several darkened storefronts, and at the end of the first row she discovered a well-lit building with a stream of people coming and going from within. The sign above the door, hung from two black metal bars, read McNally's Cove. She stood there a while watching the crowd and smelling the sweet aromas of pastries, wondering if she might enter alone since it appeared to be a place to dine, when the café doors swung open again and Radford Chamberlain stepped out.

"Alanna," he said, bewildered. "What are you doing here?" He glanced around in all directions. "Are you waiting for Beau?"

"Ah-no," she answered nervously. "I had merely gone for a walk and got lost."

"A foolish idea on the part of such a lovely young

236

woman, Alanna," he smiled, reaching out for her hand. "You shouldn't walk the streets alone at night."

"Yes, I know, but my room became stuffy and I thought to get a breath of fresh air," she lied.

"Then may I walk you back to your room?"

"I'd be grateful if you would. I didn't realize what I was getting myself into when I left." She let him wrap her arm around his and together they crossed the street and headed back toward the inn.

"I would have thought you and Beau would be spending the evening seeing the rest of Williamsburg by night. It can be rather romantic." He laughed. "Of course, not everyone would agree. I had much the same thought, but Melissa developed one of her headaches and returned to her room right after dinner."

Alanna squeezed her eyes tightly closed for an instant, fighting back the urge to tell Radford exactly where Melissa was at the moment. She had lied to Radford as Beau had lied to her. Obviously, he did not find Melissa as distasteful as he had led her to believe. For some odd reason she suspected he had planned the whole thing. Melissa would develop a headache to free herself from Radford. He would create an argument with her so that she would not want to spend the evening with him, and then, after a comfortable amount of time, they would meet in his room. Discreetly, of course. But she had spoiled that, and right now she was very glad.

"Alanna, what's wrong?" Radford asked when he felt her stiffen under his touch.

"Er-nothing," she said quickly and smiled up at him in her most convincing way. "Last night you asked if you would be able to call on me. Have you changed your mind?"

"Of course not," he exclaimed. "Have you?"

"Yes. I would be most honored if you would."

In the shadows, he missed the pained look in her eyes, for if he hadn't he would have known her sudden change of mind was not the result of a new affection she felt for him, but of something else. Something he would have questioned.

As they entered the Chesterfield House and started across the foyer, Radford patted her hand resting against his arm. "Shall we start with a glass of wine in the dining hall?"

She smiled her acceptance with a brief look toward the stairs that led upward, inwardly hoping Beau and his companion would choose this moment to leave his room and venture to the dining hall as she and Radford had elected to do. Seeing where her gaze rested, Radford gave her hand a gentle squeeze.

"Don't worry about him," he said. "Beau isn't going to like the attention I shall shower upon you, but I think I can handle him. Besides, if he is so blind that he would let a beauty like you slip through his fingers, he deserves to spend his nights alone."

Alanna smiled weakly with the irony of it.

The dining hall had only a sprinkling of people seated at the tables, and it seemed to Alanna that every one of them looked their way when they entered the room. It was only her imagination, she was sure, but somehow she couldn't stop the feeling that she was doing something she shouldn't have been doing. They took a table near one of the windows facing the street.

"So," Radford began as he poured them both a glass of wine, "tell me what you think of Williamsburg."

"It's quite beautiful and very exciting, but I fear I

enjoy the quietness of the plantation instead." She took a sip of the wine.

"I think you'd get used to it," he said leaning forward to cross his arms on the table. "I know I did. And sometimes we all need a little excitement. I grow bored at Briarwood Manor."

"Don't you have anyone there to keep you company?" she asked, finding it easy to relax in his presence.

He shook his head in mock sadness. "Only Maybelle, Lilly, and Amos."

"Brothers and sisters?" she asked with honest interest.

He laughed heartily. "I'm sorry," he apologized when he saw the hurt look on her face, "I didn't mean to laugh at what you asked, but you would not be able to refrain from a chuckle if you could see them. Maybelle is the housekeeper and maid, Lilly is my cook, and Amos is the butler. They're all Negro slaves."

"Oh," Alanna breathed with downcast eyes, feeling the heat of embarrassment staining her cheeks.

"No," he sighed, leaning back in his chair, "I'm afraid I live alone. Maybe that's why I come to Williamsburg as often as I do. And someday I hope to find a wife."

"Have you not already?" Alanna frowned.

"Melissa? Although she feels I have, I do not quite agree." He pushed his chair away from the table and crossed one ankle to his knee, relaxing in the muted light of the dining hall.

"But everyone thinks you will marry one day," Alanna argued.

"Maybe," Radford shrugged. "But at the moment I'm not ready to settle down. Not with her, anyway." He grinned. "You know, my mother always told me

239

the girl that I would marry wouldn't be from around here. She was guessing, of course, but I always wondered if she'd had a vision."

"How long ago did she die?" Alanna asked, glad to change the subject from one that was confusing.

Radford picked up his glass and studied its contents. "About five years ago. She knew Melissa rather well." He laughed. "Maybe that's why she kept telling me I would marry someone I hadn't met yet." He paused, looking about the room. "My father didn't like her, either."

"You sound almost bitter."

He glanced at her and then back to his glass. "Father and I didn't get along very well."

"Oh, I'm sorry," she whispered.

"Don't be," he said. "It was just one of those things. Father was all business. I, on the other hand, would rather play. I've always enjoyed a good time and running a plantation bores the devil out of me. I always told him he had the wrong son. Beau should have been his offspring. They are two of a kind."

"Didn't you ever have any brothers or sisters?"

"No," he said after taking a sip of the wine. "I don't think Father wanted any more after the way I turned out." He laughed, but Alanna had the feeling it wasn't from amusement.

"Tell me about your mother. Was she pretty?"

"She was beautiful," he said dreamily. "She had hair the color of the sunlight, and I remember how she used to sit for hours just brushing it. I miss her." He poured himself another drink and looked at Alanna. "But tell me about you. I'd much prefer to hear you talk."

"There really isn't much to tell," Alanna laughed. "I

240

never lived on a plantation or went to the theater."

"Surely you didn't just sit about all day. What did you do as a child?" he coaxed.

She ran a fingertip around the rim of her glass, a faint smile parting her lips. "Most of the time I read."

"Books?" he asked, amazed.

"Well, of course, books," she teased. "What else does one read?" Uncertain, she thought she saw a slight coloring to his cheeks just before he raised a knuckle to his lips.

"Yes, of course," he replied. "Forgive me if I sound like a prude, but I never imagined someone like you acquiring such a skill."

She smiled warmly. "I do forgive you. It isn't common for any woman of my station to know how, so I am not offended that you are surprised to find that I do." After setting her glass on the table, she cradled her chin in the palm of her hand. "It was a gift from my father and a very dear friend."

"Really?" he asked. "And just how did he manage it?"

"After my mother died, times were hard for us. Father couldn't work and watch me at the same time, so he left me in the care of Meldon and Beda Adams—the town printers. When I was old enough to be of some help, Mr. Adams would allow me to help him set up the presses." She laughed. "There were many times when he would have to reset the type because I had misspelled a word. And that's when he decided I should learn how to read if I was ever to be of any real help to him. He would spend every spare minute he had teaching me."

"And I'll wager you were an excellent student."

"Not always," she laughed. "There were many times I

241

would have preferred to be playing with the other children instead of reading the Bible or *Canterbury Tales*. But my father would always scold me and tell me how important it was that I learn to read and write. He had such dreams that someday I would become a governess." Her gaze drifted upward in thought and then she sighed. "Then my father married again."

"Were you an only child?"

"Yes. Giving birth to me made my mother's health fail. I was three years before she died. Papa took her death very hard—I guess that's why I was nearly eleven before he married Alica. She was a dear woman, but barren. I sometimes wondered if he blamed me for not being a son."

Radford smiled brightly. "Why would any man want more if he already had you?"

Alanna laughed gaily. "You are too kind, sir," she said, looking to him. Then her eyes caught sight of a movement from outside the window near them.

Someone stood there staring, and she had to squint to distinguish the figure in the darkness. She froze. The faint lights of Williamsburg silhouetted the shapes of a man and woman, the latter of which had hair the color of corn silk. They moved a step and the light from the dining hall spilled out onto them, staining the man's face with golden rays that seemed to be reflected in the black depths of his eyes as he glared at her.

"What's wrong?" Radford asked.

"Master Beau."

Radford turned to look outside, finding only darkness. "Are you sure?"

"Yes. I must return to my room." She came to her feet, followed courteously by her companion. "Thank you for being so kind, Mr. Chamberlain. I hope we'll see each other again soon."

"The honor was all mine. May I walk you to your door?"

"It won't be necessary. But thank you, anyway." She smiled weakly, glanced at the window again, and left him.

Seventeen

The summer storm had yet to break. No rain had fallen, but the threat of a downpour was inevitable as the impenetrably ominous clouds continually changed shapes, denseness, and size, all the while harboring flashes of lightning that seemed to chase each other from one hiding place to another. A rich, sweet aroma filled the air.

Beau viewed the intensity of the storm from the window of his study, one hand pressed against the window frame high above his head, the other shoved deep into his pocket. A scowl darkened his eyes. The tempest that shook his being raged from within him, rather than howling about the large plantation. An hour earlier, a groomsman from Briarwood Manor had knocked on the door with a package for Alanna. It had contained a black velvet choker with a cameo carved of ivory pinned in the center. With it came a note. Beau didn't have to read it to know what it said. He could tell by Alanna's soft smile, the faraway look in her eyes, and the way she clutched the package to her as she turned and retreated to her room.

He stood by the window for a long time wondering why it had upset him. It wasn't the first time one of his servants had received a gift from an admirer. After all, that's just what she was. A servant, nothing more. Why, then, did this small act, something that happened with regularity, affect him so? Was it because he felt Radford was insincere, that he was promised to another and Alanna would foolishly hope for a romance that could never be? No, of course, it wasn't. He knew Radford was free to court whomever he pleased. Only Melissa thought otherwise.

"Melissa," he growled, kicking at the chair leg that threatened to trip him as he moved toward the cabinet and a fresh bottle of brandy. If only she hadn't come to his room that night. If only Alanna hadn't seen her there, maybe none of this would have happened. He poured himself a drink, downed the entire contents, and looked outside again. He couldn't really blame for her for what she had thought. He knew what it must have looked like. Just as he had thought the worst when he found her with Radford. He rolled the empty glass in the palm of his hand awhile, then angrily spun about and threw it into the fireplace, the shattered remnants spraying out upon the floor. He stared at it a moment, then seized the bottle of brandy by the neck as if he wished to squeeze from it whatever form of life it might have, knowing nothing he could do not would change any of it. Instead, he decided to get pleasantly drunk and forget the matter.

Nearly a week had passed since the day Beau had spent alone in his study. Things had returned to normal, and because of his avoidance of Alanna he had been able to put his private hell from his mind. Then another grooms-man bearing gifts appeared at his doorstep. This time the box was larger and heavier than before. A squeal of delight escaped Alanna when she tore away the decorative wrappings, for in her hands she held a box of sweets with a label that told her it was made in England. It was something she had never tasted even while she lived there.

Chocolate, Beau sneered, his upper lip curling in silent observation. How original.

But even his black disapproval could not spoil Alanna's bliss at receiving such a fine gift. She instructed the young, finely dressed groomsman to express her gratitude to Mr. Chamberlain, and watched as he mounted his horse and rode off, a soft smile playing with the corners of her mouth. Ascending the stairs on her way to her room, her step did not falter, even though she could feel Beau's eyes upon her, the heat of his regard burning through her. Nothing he could say or do at that moment would ruin how she felt.

Beau was leaving the kitchen after issuing instructions for the evening's meal and quietly made his way to the study when the dull rapping of the brass knocker echoed in the foyer. Thinking it was another gift, he jerked open to door to glare at the small black boy dressed neatly in a gray suit.

"Now what? Flowers?" he roared.

The frightened youth retreated several steps, his eyes growing wide in apprehension of the menacing form before him, and not comprehending his meaning. When he continued to stare, Beau lost his patience.

247

"Well?"

The boy jumped with a start at the thunderous demand, looked down and fidgeted with the item he held in one hand. "I have a message from Willow Glen, sir."

"Willow Glen?" Beau rallied.

"Yes, sir."

Beau stared at him for a moment, not quite able to believe it wasn't some sort of trick to catch him off guard, that hidden behind the bushes at the foot of the stairs another such boy didn't wait with a fistful of flowers, ready to spring out and run inside in search of Alanna. He shook his head. This is ridiculous, he thought, sighing, extending his hand to the groomsman. "Well, then, give it to me."

The rolled yellow parchment seemed to burn his hand as he watched the youngster mount his horse and gallop away, leaving only a small cloud of dust to mark his presence. Beau stared after him for several minutes, trying to gather his wits and figure out what was happening to him. He had never acted like this before. The heavy door moaned on its hinges as it swung closed, and Beau walked to the study, listening to the click of the lock echoing in the stillness.

Leaning back against his leather chair, he laid the message aside and looked out the widow, discovering, as if for the first time that day, the brightness of the countryside and the serenity it never failed to instill in him. He had always enjoyed late afternoon and the quiet peacefulness it brought. But of late it seemed only to torment him in his loneliness. Hardly a moment passed that he wasn't tempted to find Alanna with any excuse he could think of, just so that he could enjoy the sound of her voice and gaze upon her beauty. Several times he had gone to the foot of the stairs, but no further, having second thoughts about disturbing her. She seemed content in her privacy, and he wasn't about to be turned away by a female only half his size. Thus he grew irritable, causing everyone in the household to shy away from him or find reasons not to be around. His being alone was of his own making, but that was something he had yet to discover.

One hour and nearly half a bottle of brandy vanished before he remembered the incident at the front door with the young boy. He began to unroll the parchment when a loud rapping at the door forced him to look up.

"Yes," he called, and waited while Horace entered the room.

"Yo' have a visitor, Masta Beau."

"Who is it?" he snapped, thinking how he never had a moment to himself.

"Masta Chamberlain, sir. He's waitin' in the parlor. Shall I tell him yo' be right there?"

Beau collapsed against the back of his chair with a heavy sigh. "Yes, I suppose you'll have to," he said, tapping his fingers on the edge of the desk as he watched the door slowly close again. Why did Radford have to choose this moment for a visit? He was anything but willing to have a conversation with him. Squaring his shoulders for the battle he was certain would take place, he rose from his chair and headed for the parlor.

"Good afternoon, Beau," Radford smiled. "It sure is a beauty."

"I doubt you came to discuss the weather, Radford," Beau hissed, settling himself in a chair, one foot crossed to his knee.

Radford's smile disappeared. "Right to the point, as

always," he said, taking a chair opposite Beau. "Then I guess I'll do the same. I'm here about Alanna."

Beau rested his chin against the knuckles of his hand, his dark eyes telegraphing his dislike of the subject. "What about her?" he asked in guarded calm.

"I would like to call on her," Radford said, then added, "with your approval."

"And what if I didn't give it? Would the two of you sneak around to see each other?"

"No. I'd offer you a deal instead."

"A deal? What kind of deal?"

"I'm willing to pay whatever she owes you and a little extra so you can make a profit. You name it."

"You make it sound like you're trying to buy a horse."

"Only to you, simply because that's how you think of her. I happen to think otherwise."

"Oh?" Beau said with a raised brow. "And just what might that be?"

"I'm fond of Alanna. And if she'll have me, I'll offer her marriage."

Beau's face reflected a mixture of surprise, anger, and fear. He knew Radford meant what he said, and that if he had to, he'd wait for her. He'd take her away without Beau's being able to do one thing about it. In desperation, Beau said the first thing which came to his mind.

"You'd marry her even if you knew it wasn't a virgin that came to your bed?"

A smile parted Radford's lips. "If that really mattered, why would I be seeing Melissa? Besides, I'm not stupid enough to think that any female living under your roof would still be a virgin."

"Then I hope you're prepared to wait, for she will not

leave here one minute before her time is up."

"Is that your last word on the subject?"

"It is."

A moment passed as Radford returned the intense stare of his friend before a long, pain-filled sigh escaped him. "Then there is no reason for me to stay any longer." Rising, he went to the door, turning back to look at Beau. "I only hope your feelings on the matter will not ruin our long friendship. I have always thought of you as my brother, and no matter what happens in the days to come I will still feel the same. Good afternoon, Beau."

Glaring at the empty doorway, Beau fought with all the pent-up emotions that he felt at that moment. He wanted to chase after his friend, call for him to return, to share a drink, to pretend that none of their conversation had been spoken. He wanted to erase everything that had happened in the last several weeks, to make things return to the way they had been before—his breath caught in his throat. Before Alanna had come to Raven Oaks.

He nearly knocked Horace to the floor as he sped by the man on his way to the study, and Horace could only hurry out of his way, wondering what it was this time that had made Master Beau so angry. He stood alone in the hallway shaking his head.

Stalking across the room and around the desk, he threw himself into his chair. He *should* sell her papers. Then he would be done with her and his life could return to normal. He reached out, poured himself another drink and settled back in his chair, his feet crossed at the ankles and resting against the edge of the desk. He took a long, slow drink, studying the bottom of the glass. His eyes began to focus on the disfigured yellow item on his desk. He set down his glass. The message from Willow Glen. He

251

had forgotten all about it. Picking up the rolled parchment, he untied the ribbon that bound it and began to read. A slow smile spread across his face, one that suggested revenge. He lay the paper aside and raced to his room.

Searching beneath his bed, he found the box he had hidden there many days ago. He laid it on the small writing desk, stood back, and studied it, deciding how to handle his idea most effectively. The smile returned.

"Do either of you know where I can find Alanna?" he asked, coming into the kitchen a moment later, his gaze traveling from Tilly to Bessy and back.

"In the dining hall, Masta Beau, polishing the silver," Tilly said, wiping her hands on her apron. "Is there somethin' I can do?"

He stopped at the doorway. "Yes. You can go to my room. You'll find a box sitting on the desk with a gown in it. It should have an iron pressed to it."

Tilly shot Bessy a confused frown, receiving only a lift of the older woman's shoulders in response. "Yes, sir," she said and watched him disappear from the doorway.

Finding Alanna where Tilly had said he would, he paused just inside the archway to watch her unobserved, noticing immediately that she still chose to go barefoot. His pulse quickened with the gentle sway of skirts that teased his view of her trim ankles. His gaze traveled up the slight form, lingering on the narrow waistline, so slender he felt certain he could span it easily with his hands. Her hair, twisted into a knot on top of her head, seemed to beg him to uncurl it, and when she moved as if to turn and discover him, he quickly gathered his senses, straightened, and walked further into the room.

"Alanna, may I speak with you a moment?"

252

She turned abruptly. "Yes, sir," she nodded, running a nervous hand up the back of her neck to catch a stray curl.

He motioned back over his shoulder indicating his desire for privacy in the study and held open the door until she had passed through. Silently they went into the study, and he waited for her to sit down before taking a seat in the leather chair behind his desk. For some reason, he felt as nervous as a young boy.

"I received a message from Willow Glen today," he said, managing to hide his feelings.

"No trouble, I pray."

He smiled secretly. "No, no. It's merely an invitation to a ball next week," he added, feeling his tension grow. Hoping to mask it, he leaned forward, took a cheroot from the box and touched a flame to it. He watched the smoke fade into the air before he continued. "It does, however, create a problem for me."

A flicker of confusion crossed Alanna's brow.

"On such short notice, I find it difficult to obtain the presence of a lady as my companion. I would like you to join me." He glanced up, saw the knot of Alanna's smooth features, and quickly added, "Or do you find that objectionable?" The moment the words spilled from his lips, he realized how it sounded. Damn it, he wasn't begging. He stuffed the cigar in his mouth, chewing irritably on the end.

"Oh, no sir. It just surprised—"

"Good," he cut in, feeling the need to draw their conversation to an end. "It will be one week from tomorrow. Have Tilly help you with your hair and such matters. Now if you'll excuse me, I have work to do." He leaned forward, pulled out a leather-bound book and

253

began to read as Alanna slowly came to her feet. Once she turned away he looked up, a mixture of pleasure and unrest enhancing his dark, handsome features. After the door closed behind her, he fell back in his chair and breathed easily again, studying the barred aperture. He hoped things would go more smoothly at the ball.

As Alanna walked away from the study, she repeatedly looked back over her shoulder at the door. If she could understand the reason he had requested her presence at the ball, it might have enabled her to enjoy the anticipation of the event. And was it her imagination, or did he appear nervous? She shook her head. Not hardly. Beau Remington was always in full command. Deciding she would ask Tilly about it later, she headed back to the dining hall.

For Alanna, the week before the social gathering of her life seemed to pass in a blur and, before she knew it, it was time to prepare herself both physically and mentally for the upcoming encounter with the mistres of Willow Glen. She knew it would take immense doing on her part, since she had never been educated in the proper social graces, which would probably become apparent within the first hour after her arrival. But nonetheless, she was determined to attend.

After a lavish, lavender-scented bath, Alanna sat before her dressing table while Tilly brushed the tangles and dampness from her hair. Once this was accomplished, the young girl set about with practiced hands to curl the thick, silkened mass in the most becoming and stylish manner befitting a young lady such as Alanna. Before long, Alanna viewed the work of art with gratitude. It had been pulled away from her face and knotted high on her head, with soft curls cascading down the back and sprinkled sparingly with twigs of baby's breath. Without dark curls about her brow, the deep brown intensity of her round eyes shone clearly under the soft arch of her brow. The high cheekbones were lightly blushed against the fair smooth skin, and her small, sensuous mouth was the color of strawberries ready for picking. She might not be as captivating as Melissa, she thought, but she certainly would cause the woman some unrest. Especially when she arrived on the arm of one of Virginia's most eligible and sought-after bachelors. Suddenly a line formed between her brows.

"Why yo' look like that?" Tilly questioned, noting the girl's troubled expression. "Don't yo' feel well?"

"I'm fine, Tilly. But I should be scolded for what I'm thinking."

A black brow lifted slightly as Tilly eyed Alanna in the reflection of the mirror.

"That I don't have a gown worthy of such an evening, and I just returned home but a few weeks ago with more than enough gowns from Williamsburg. I'm afraid I'm terribly ungrateful."

Tilly couldn't refrain a chuckle. "That's a woman's right, Alanna. But don't worry. Masta Beau already thought of that."

Alanna twisted in her chair to watch the maid's tiny figure as she left the room, a look of wonderment darkening her eyes. A moment later, Tilly returned with the most beautiful gown Alanna had ever seen draped over her arm.

"Oh, Tilly," Alanna moaned, "it's gorgeous."

The dark blue velvet of the gown shimmered to ebony

in each fold of its skirt. The neckline, cut low, accented the gathering of cloth across the bosom with tiny pearls at the waist. Each full sleeve also displayed a similar row of pearls at the wrist. When Tilly held the gown up before her for Alanna's further inspection, its massive skirts flowed about her.

"I hope I have no reason to faint tonight, else I'm afraid I shall have to lie where I fall. I will be too heavy in that gown for anyone to assist me to my feet again," Alanna laughed.

"Oh, I don't think so, Alanna. Lookin' like yo' will, every gentleman there will wanta help yo' any way he can," Tilly giggled.

"I think you've exaggerated a little, but I must admit I find the idea much to my liking," Alanna grinned as she helped the girl spread the dress upon the bed. "Where did Master Beau find such a treasure? Did it belong to his mother?"

"Oh, no, Alanna. I's never seen it before. He musta got it in Williamsburg his last time there."

"For whom?"

Tilly shrugged. "Don't know. But from the looks of it, I'd say it was made for you."

Standing back to appraise the gown's workmanship, Alanna shook her head. "This time I know you're wrong."

Impatiently, Tilly elbowed her friend. "So who cares? Aren't yo' gonna put it on?"

Alanna stared at it, a new smile spreading across her face. "I want to, but I'm afraid it will vanish before my eyes if I touch it again."

"Oh, it will not," Tilly laughed, bending down to capture the gown in her arms.

Wiggling the numerous folds over her shoulders and past her hips, Alanna was amazed at how well it clung to her form, as if a dressmaker had fitted her for it. Next came the multitude of pearl buttons that fastened up the back and, once they had all been hooked, she stood before the mirror to appraise the finished product of an afternoon's work.

"Why, yo' don't look the same, Alanna," Tilly said, looking over Alanna's shoulder into the reflection, a twinge of envy flashing through her and disappearing just as rapidly.

"Better, I hope," Alanna smiled back.

"Better? Why I's declare yo' is the most beautiful thing I ever did see."

"Thank you, Tilly," she said, turning around to give the girl a gentle squeeze. "I couldn't have done it without you."

"Oh, go on," Tilly laughed in embarrassment. "Yo' got ta have good stuff to work with before ya can do anything. And yo'll knock 'em off their feet."

"Well," Alanna sighed, running a hand along the velvety softness of her skirt, "do you suppose Master Beau is ready?"

"One way to find out," Tilly answered, picking up the discarded towels from the floor. "I'll go ask him."

Beau, too, had bathed and washed his hair, whistling or humming a merry tune the entire time, for nothing could spoil his mood. Even when he snagged his stocking, it didn't upset him as it would have any other time. He had always hated going to a ball, no matter who gave it. He had thought it a waste of time and good money. But

257

tonight was different. He had a very good reason for going to Willow Glen.

He had elected to wear his dark blue velvet coat and breeches much the same shade as the gown he knew Alanna would be wearing, and he smiled at his own cunning, pulling the garments from the armoire. Everyone would know at a glance that she belonged to him, in more ways than one. After donning the breeches and the black shoes, he lifted the white ruffled shirt to his shoulders, slowly fastening each button and hiding the dark mass of curls that covered the strong, lean muscles of his chest. Next came the ascot, a simple form thing, but one that never failed to prick his patience. Maybe it was the delicate knot he had to tie, or possibly the slickness of the cloth, but for whatever reason he found himself folding and unfolding the piece several times before it hung at his neck in perfect order. A useless form of fashion, he thought, as he noticed the crooked way it looked in the mirror, but rather than ask anyone's help he quickly put on his coat to hide what he could of it. A knock sounded at the door.

"What is it?" he called.

"Your carriage is waiting, Masta Beau," he heard Horace reply.

"Thank you. I'll be right down." He turned back to the mirror, picked a stray tendril of hair from his brow only to have it fall back, and shrugged off its defiance before leaving the room.

"Is Alanna ready?" he asked of Tilly as he walked down the long staircase, pulling on his gloves as he did.

"Yes, sir," she answered with a short curtsy. "Shall I go fetch her?"

"Yes, please. I'll wait here for her."

258

Tilly dashed by him hurriedly, darting up the stairs toward Alanna's room. Once she had disappeared from sight, Beau turned to Horace, who politely waited by the front door.

"Well, what do you think?" he asked with a sweep of his hand.

The old man smiled. "I think yo' look mighty grand, Masta Beau. Miss Alanna will sure be honored when yo' take her on your arm."

Beau chuckled to himself. Not if she knew the reason, he thought, and turned to examine his appearance in the small mirror hanging above the table in the hallway. Noting the strand of hair against his brow again, he reached up to try once more to remove it when a movement from behind him caught his eye in the mirror. He froze, his gaze fixed on the figure descending the stairs, his reserve suddenly shattered. Slowly, he turned to face her.

Beau had never imagined Alanna could look as beautiful as she did at that moment. The gown fit her perfectly, a secret compliment to his judgment of her form, and he watched in awe as she gracefully descended the stairs, not a single trace of the English country girl she really was. She was quite alluring in the soft light of the fading afternoon, and he found himself swallowing the lump that had suddenly formed in his throat. Without a word, he picked up the tricorn from the table and forced himself to go to the end of the stairs to meet her. Holding out a gloved hand to assist her, he gently enfolded her arm within his, and they left the house in silence.

*　　　*　　　*

From within the growing shadows of the day, Cain stood beneath the branches of a willow tree in the yard beside the house watching the couple as they climbed into the carriage. He smiled to himself. It had been a long time coming, but he had never doubted it would. The young master of Raven Oaks had finally met someone he could not so easily forget.

Eighteen

The orange glow of the lantern danced flitteringly about the carriage, casting warm shadows over the plush leather seats and the rich mahogany graining of the walls. Alanna smiled softly, a flood of contentment racing through her as she studied the odd shapes and figures. The evening air smelled of jasmine, a fragrance sweet and comforting. She closed her eyes, lost in the magic of the moment and suddenly thinking of her father. He would have been proud of her, for this had been his dream, to see his daughter clothed in the finest of cloth and riding in an expensively built carriage on her way to a ball. And what of the man who escorted her? Would her father have been pleased with Beau Remington as her chaperone rather than himself? She felt certain he would have, for Beau possessed all the qualities her father had admired in a man: wealth, power, a good business sense, and the respect of his peers. She looked furtively at the man at her side. He gazed out the small window of the carriage, staring off into space and allowing Alanna a moment to study him.

His black hair curled gently over the collar of his coat, and Alanna thought it a little shorter than fashion allowed. But then again it was, as usual, a small measure of his defiance against the way things were expected to be. A vague smile flitted across her face. In many ways they were alike—headstrong, rebellious, determined, anything contrary to the accepted way of life. They both demanded more than what they had and would not settle for anything else, not if there was a way to achieve it.

Her fingertips stroked the velvet cloth outlining her thigh. "I think I should tell you how much your asking me to accompany you tonight means to me," she said quietly.

More startled by the soft tones of her voice than the words she spoke, he glanced at her, opened his mouth to respond, then changed his mind. He looked back outside. "It shouldn't," he said drily.

The fine arch of her brow wrinkled briefly. What did he mean? How could he possibly think she wouldn't be grateful for such a noble evening as he intended to give her? She drew in a breath to question his remark then thought better of it. He had his reasons, she supposed.

The golden rays of sunlight, stained with orange, fought to stay above the rapidly engulfing horizon that had already seemingly swallowed up the last hope of day. Before it lay Willow Glen, its host of timber set ablaze in the last few minutes of the day's finale. Its stately mansion, not nearly as large as Raven Oaks, still presented a magnificent spectacle as it stood there, set aglow with a light in every window, haloed in the burning embers of dusk. It silently received the large number of guests descending their carriages as if this was a common occurrence.

Alanna could not suppress the excited tremor that shook her as their carriage waited its turn to draw up before the wide pathway leading to the house. Viewing the height of the massive white colonnades adorning the veranda, she unknowingly hugged her arms to herself in an effort to calm the restlessness that stirred within her until her attention casually centered on the style of dress each guest wore. Men and women alike each wore an exquisitely fashioned periwig. She gasped.

"Is something wrong?"

Alanna shot him a look of outrage. "Yes, Mr. Remington, there is." A sweep of her hand invited him to discover their faux pas for himself, and she pressed back in the leather seat to allow him full view. His wide shoulders shook with his amusement at the sight.

"I see nothing funny," she hissed, "or did you plan to embarrass me?"

His mirth suddenly gone, his gaze lingered on her face. "You misjudge me, madam," he said quietly. "I laugh because I find the custom amusing. While they suffer beneath the English fashion, I will be quite comfortable. As will you, I might add." He moved past her to descend from the carriage when a well-dressed butler opened the door to allow them to exit. Standing beside the carriage, his hand extended to assist Alanna down, he waited until she stood next to him before he added, "Besides, your hair is much too beautiful to hide beneath a powdered wig."

"But no other woman wears her hair as I do," she grated out.

He folded her hand within the crook of his arm,

nodded at the butler, and started up the path. "Nor is any half as beautiful," he said, quite matter-of-factly.

Alanna's discomfiture dissolved instantly as she digested his unexpected compliment, yet she was uncertain of his sincerity. For the past week, she had seen little of him. Business seemed to draw him out of the house before breakfast and late into the night, and he took his meals alone in his study. One morning as she had stepped from the kitchen, she had looked up in time to see Beau deliberately turn around and walk in the other direction. He pointedly ignored her, casting her off as if she was a stick of furniture. Alanna speculated that he was trying very hard to portray a man who had no attachment to anyone. Especially her. She frowned, the awful feeling that he was up to something pricking her security.

As they stepped into the archway of the ballroom, they paused when another well-dressed, white-haired butler approached them. She looked to Beau, since she had no idea why he had singled them out, and jumped when she heard the tinkling of the bell that suddenly appeared in his hand. The music stopped instantly, and, much to her discomfort, Alanna found that all eyes centered on them while Beau whispered in the man's ear. Straightening to face the curious audience, the butler cleared his throat.

"Hear ye, hear ye," he began in an authoritive tone, "Master Remington and the Lady Bainbridge."

Alanna's heart seemed to stop beating. She had known that there would probably be some very difficult and uncomfortable times for her before the evening was over, but she had never dreamed she wouldn't even get through the door before it started. It might have been different if she were back home in England making her debut on her father's arm, but somehow she felt as if this was an announcement of her true position at Raven Oaks, or, worse yet, an admission that she was now The Hawk's newest mistress. But if that was what everyone thought, they hid it rather well, for as quickly as the music had stopped it began again, and for the most part nearly everyone continued on with what they had been doing. Everyone except for the trio that stood across the room from them.

"And just who is *Lady* Bainbridge?" Beatrice Bensen sniffed with an unmistakable emphasis on the title and an arrogant flutter of her fan.

"Oh, Beatrice, you know perfectly well who she is," Mathew Bensen barked. "Melissa's told us all about her—and you've obviously believed every word," he finished in muttered tones beneath his breath.

His gaze traveled across the room again, resting pleasantly on the slight figure at Beau Remington's side. Yes, Melissa had told them all about the young woman, but she had carefully avoided mentioning her beauty. The dark velvet of her gown shimmered softly in the lamp's glow, enticing his eyes to linger on its folds, then guiding his curiosity to the gentle swell of her breasts before he forced himself to study the face that reflected a mixture of shyness, innocence, and apprehension. If Beau Remington had searched the entire colonies, he would never have found a more stunning and fitting companion. She complimented his taste and at the first opportunity, he would tell Beau of the excellence of his choice.

"Mathew!"

White fluffy brows arched in surprise, he realized he had stared unforgivably and failed to hear his wife's curt remarks. He masked his embarrassment with a tug of his ascot and a repositioning of his white powdered wig.

"I'm sorry, my dear. I missed what you said."

"And no wonder with the way you're gawking. You're a little old to be thinking you stand a chance with that strumpet."

"Oh, I don't know Mama," Melissa chimed in, "I imagine just about anyone could have her if they paid the price."

How like her mother, Mathew observed. All the silks and jewels in the world would not cover up the fact that they both were snobs. His wife he could understand. Beatrice was nothing more than the daughter of a dressmaker whose father had run out on them when she was hardly more than an infant. She had grown up knowing what hunger felt like and the bite of the cold winter winds against a sparsely clad body. Her dark yellow hair never glistened with luster, her cheeks were never pink with color, her eyes were dull pools of insensitive moods. When he thought of it now he wondered how he had ever managed to fall in love with her or why, after all this time, he still loved her.

As for Melissa, he knew she spoke out of jealousy. She was their only child, and they had pampered her, loved her, and spoiled her. Anything she wanted, they laid at her feet. Then along came Beau Remington, the first obstacle they couldn't maneuver. Outraged by his open indifference to her, she had tried at every turn to even the score, failing miserably and being forced to strike back in any way she could. Rumor had it that Lady Bainbridge was Beau's newest mistress, and attacking the young woman as she had was Melissa's way of revenge against him.

"Must I remind you two that they are guests in our house and I expect nothing but politeness to pour from your mouths again?"

"But Papa, she's a servant. She's mingling with people above her station."

A knowing smile played at the corner of his mouth and he reached up to cover it with a noncommittal gesture of one fingertip. "Are you going to be the one to tell Beau that she is not welcome? I certainly am not."

Silently fuming, Melissa turned to her mother for help and was rewarded by a surrendering shrug of one shoulder, the acknowledgment that there wasn't a soul within miles with the courage to confront Beau Remington. Containing her irritation and displeasure, she fell into step behind her parents as they crossed the room to welcome their newest guests.

Mathew extended his hand in a warm greeting long before he had reached the couple, fondly calling Beau's name and thanking them for coming. Then, almost instantly, his gaze fell on Alanna.

"Please. Introduce us."

Beau chuckled. "Somehow I feel you wouldn't have been nearly as cordial had I come alone," he grinned watching Mathew take Alanna's hands in his. "Alanna, may I introduce our host, Mathew Bensen. Mathew, Alanna Bainbridge."

"It's an honor, my dear," he smiled. "And so refreshing to find a rose among the thorns."

Alanna gave him one of her most practiced curtsies, sensing his words as heartfelt sincerity. What a surprise to find Melissa's father actually welcomed her openly when all the while she had dreaded this moment, certain that he, too, would find fault with her presence. She smiled warmly at him for a moment before her eyes looked to the women standing behind him.

"Oh, forgive me," Mathew apologized when he realized he no longer held Alanna's attention and what it was that drew her eyes away. He took his wife's elbow and presented her to their guests. "Beatrice, you remember Beau Remington."

Even dressed in all her finery and lavishly styled wig, the woman failed to hide her contempt for Beau as she raised one brow just the slightest with a nod of her head, one Beau returned with a quick nod of his own. She turned to Alanna.

"My dear, I'd like you to meet Alanna Bainbridge. Mistress Bainbridge, my wife, Beatrice."

Again Alanna curtsied her finest, stealing a peak at the woman from lowered lashes to discover she hadn't moved an inch. Feeling the heat rise to her cheeks and hoping no one would notice, she stood up slowly, her eyes downcast, and failed to see Mathew's own look of embarrassment. He turned to his daughter.

"Melissa, I'd like for you to meet—"

"We already have," she snapped.

Alanna humbly stood by as Melissa entwined her arm with Beau's and casually led him away into the crowd of dancing figures, wishing somehow she could disappear. She knew she didn't belong here, whether Beau had brought her or not. And yet, at the same time, had she known what her reception would be and the choice was again hers to make, she still would have come.

The enormous ballroom was filled with tens of people, all dressed in rich silks and velvets, all different, although from a distance they all looked the same in their white powdered wigs. She reached up to gently stroke the back of her hair.

"Well, at last they've left us alone," a tired voice said at her side.

Glancing up, she watched Beatrice amble away, her huge frame swaying with each step. Surely she must crush Mathew beneath her whenever they made love. Surprised at herself that she would think such a thought, and praying Mathew could not read her mind, she cleared her throat furtively and smiled weakly at her host.

"I hope you'll forgive them, my dear," he was saying, "but your presence seems to cause a threat." He smiled half to himself.

"It is I who should ask forgiveness of you."

Mathew's short round figure straightened in disagreement. "Oh, I wouldn't have it any other way. Although I love them both dearly, I realize at times like these how unkind they can be. It does them good once in a while to be reminded they are no different than any other. But in Melissa's case, she is experiencing a different kind of justice. Until you, her beauty was unequalled. Now, enough of them. May I get you a glass of wine?"

Alanna smiled graciously allowing him to lead her toward one of several servants carrying trays filled with goblets of wine, thinking how it had sounded to her as if Mathew was only making excuses for his daughter's rudeness. But then again, who else would better know a person's nature than her own father? She felt sorry for him. In just the few short minutes they had spent together, she had already decided how much she liked him, and having a daughter like Melissa must certainly be a trial.

"So," Mathew began after handing her a glass of dark

wine, "tell me a little about yourself."

"Well, I won't lie to you. I'm Beau Remington's housekeeper."

"Oh, I already know that," Mathew said, shrugging it off as if it didn't really matter. "What I'd like to know is where you're from."

How unlike Melissa, Alanna thought with a shake of her head. "England."

"England, is it?" he sang. "My mother was from England. Always missed her homeland, she did."

"I know the feeling," Alanna admitted.

"Oh, you'll get used to it. You are planning to make your home here, aren't you?"

"No, I don't think so. This was my father's choice for a home, not mine. And since he and my stepmother are both dead, I plan to return to England just as soon as I can."

Mathew shook his head sadly. "England's gain is our loss."

Alanna smiled back at him and had just lifted her glass to her lips when the ringing of the bell filled the air and stilled the music again. Her gaze slowly drifted across the room before it fell upon the newest arrival. Beside the butler stood Radford Chamberlain, dressed in a dark brown velvet suit and gold brocade waistcoat, ivory-colored stockings and dark shoes with bright gold buckles. He, like every other gentleman there but Beau, wore a white powdered wig, perfectly combed and tied in back with a ribbon. He presented quite a dashing figure, and her eyes took on a special gleam the instant she saw him.

"Do you know Radford?" Mathew questioned once he saw her reaction.

"Oh, yes," she half-whispered with a smile. "He's been to Raven Oaks several times."

"Good," Mathew said, "then you shall play the hostess for a moment and help me welcome our new guest." Playfully, he held out his arm and waited for her to take it before they started off toward Radford.

"Good evening, my young friend," Mathew smiled as he and Alanna approached Radford. "I believe you know my companion."

"Alanna?" he asked as his gaze traversed her slight form. "I never dreamed you'd be here. You look beautiful."

"Thank you," she said, "and you look very handsome." She smiled up at him, feeling her heart flutter when he took her hand from Mathew.

"I'm sure you have other guests to attend to, don't you, Mathew?" he asked, his eyes never leaving Alanna. "I can take care of Miss Bainbridge."

"I don't see where I have a choice," Mathew laughed, watching the couple walk away.

"Oh, Alanna," Radford whispered once they were alone. "You don't know how close I came to not being here tonight. I thought it would be just a boring evening listening to Melissa talk. Thank God, I changed my mind."

Blushing, she glanced down at the folds of her skirt and back up again, catching sight of Beau across the room from them. He seemed too preoccupied in conversation with the men surrounding him to notice that she watched, but what bothered her more was that Melissa no longer clung to his arm. "I'm glad, too," she said, forcing her attention back to Radford. "I fear I will need an ally before this night is through."

271

"Is he making things difficult for you?"

"No. On the contrary, I hardly see much of him. That's why I was so shocked when he told me I would be attending the ball."

"Now that you mention it, I'm not surprised at all," Radford said, taking a glass of wine from one of the servants and lifting it to his lips.

"Why?"

He smiled. "Well, I know if you belonged to me and another man started to shower you with gifts, I would do anything possible to remind him just to whom you belong."

"Do you really think so?"

Radford nodded as he glanced about the room to find Beau. "Just wait until he discovers you're with me right now. You'll see what I mean."

Warmed by the hope that Beau might show even a small measure of emotion toward her, favorable or not, a vague smile parted her lips as they quietly studied him. Then Melissa suddenly appeared before them.

"Hello, Radford," she said through clenched teeth.

"Hello, Melissa," he returned politely. "You look lovely, as always."

"You're late," she continued.

"Am I?" he asked with a raised brow. "Considering that up to an hour ago I had no intention of coming at all, I'd say I'm right on time."

"Not coming?" she echoed.

"That's right. Somehow this evening didn't appeal to me. However," he said with a look at Alanna, "that idea was quite foolish."

"Really?" Melissa hissed. "Well, now that you're here, I suggest you spend the time with me. After all, she is with someone else. Apparently you both seem to have forgotten."

"Not exactly," he frowned. "When I arrived you were already sharing *your* company with someone else. Let the blame lie where it should, my dear."

Melissa straightened and sent an icy glare Alanna's way. "Then forgive my rudeness. Shall we start again?" she said, slipping her hand into the crook of his arm to lead him away.

Finding herself alone, Alanna sipped her wine, hoping no one had seen what had transpired. She hated being the cause of anyone's argument, but she knew that, in Melissa's case, she could never deter it. One of the servants drew near, and she eagerly followed him to substitute her empty glass for a filled one. Right now, the only thing that seemed to relax her was the wine.

The quartet of instruments began to play a minuet, and Alanna's attention fell on the numerous couples before her taking their places to begin the dance. She stood there watching them with a slight tap of her toe, longing to be a part of the dance. Suddenly a soft voice distracted her.

"May I have the honor, madam?"

She looked up expecting to find Beau, or maybe Mathew, but instead, to her surprise, a stranger smiled down at her. A rather tall man. She found herself craning to look up at him. He too was wearing a periwig with small ringlets of white curls above each ear and pulled back with a ribbon. His broad shoulders seemed to fill her vision, and, although she had no idea as to his identity, it was clear that he was a true gentleman. However, having been caught completely off guard, she found the moment awkward, and said the first words that came to her mind.

"Ah—I'm with someone."

"Yes, I know," he replied with a nod over his shoulder toward the men. "But they seem busy at present, and I hate to see a beautiful young woman just standing about when she could be dancing. Allow me to introduce myself. My name is George Washington," he said with a sweeping bow. "And you are Lady Bainbridge. That much I heard."

"Alanna Bainbridge," she quickly volunteered.

"A lovely name, my dear. Now, are we going to let this waltz slip away, or will you grant me a few moments of pleasure?"

When the song ended and another began, Alanna found herself still held in the young man's embrace and captivated by his stories of the battles he had fought in a place called the Ohio Valley. He told her of his plantation in Mount Vernon and the young woman called Martha Custis that he planned to marry. Alanna knew very little about the form of goverment the colonists had, but when he told her that he was a member of the House of Burgesses that had met in Williamsburg, his reason for being so far from home, she began to have a true sense of the caliber of the guests at Willow Glen.

As the couple swept about the floor, Washington caught sight of a pair of brown eyes glaring down on them. "It would appear, Lady Bainbridge, that your escort has finally come to his senses," he whispered in her ear, aware of the puzzled look on her face. "Your young man seems to disapprove of my attentions to you."

As they twirled again, placing Alanna in Beau's direction, she instantly understood. "Yes, so it seems," she replied with a satisfied grin.

The music ended, and, expecting to find Beau at her side to claim her, she found instead another stranger.

"You never cease to surprise me, George," he bantered. "Out of all the beautiful women here, you manage to get a dance with the loveliest."

"Lady Bainbridge, let me warn you about this man. He's a connoisseur of the forms of flattery." He laughed, taking the man's elbow to make an introduction. "Patrick, this is Lady Alanna Bainbridge. Alanna, may I introduce a friend and fellow legislator, Patrick Henry."

Henry took her hand and pressed a gentle kiss upon it. "I'm honored. And since Colonel Washington has bored you beyond distraction, I'm sure, may I sweep you away and fill you with the words a beauty such as you should hear?"

"Now it is I who would be honored, Master Henry," she nodded happily as she accepted his arm.

During the next hour Alanna found herself being twirled about the floor by several new partners, each as exciting as the one before. Her last was a middle-aged, slightly bald man with graying hair and a round belly, who wore thin wire-rimmed glasses perched on the end of his nose. If Henry had a way with words, Benjamin Franklin was a real scholar. Each time he spoke, Alanna felt as if no other woman in the world was as important as she.

He was about to plead exhaustion and offer a glass of wine when another strong hand took hers in his and politely stole her away from the consenting statesman.

"I was beginning to think I would never have a chance to talk with you again. I told Beau you would be the center of all eyes tonight," Radford smiled, holding her close. "One thing is for certain, a rather hostile pair of blue ones has been boring holes in you all evening."

She glanced about until she spotted Melissa glaring at

her from within a group of women. No doubt she had apprised them of the true identity of the mysterious young woman who had won the hearts of all the men, married or single, for all the women stared haughtily down their noses at her. Perplexed, she looked away. "Yes, I see what you mean."

"Oh, don't let it bother you. Melissa can be quite a prude when she wants," he assured her. "Besides, you're having fun, aren't you?"

Alanna nodded weakly.

"Then why should it matter? I only wish I could cause her as much discomfort." A smile flashed across his face. "And I know just how to do it. I've been wanting to talk with you in private, anyway."

The surprised look on her face barely had time to form before Radford pulled her through the crowd of guests toward the French doors that led to the gardens. He paused only briefly to gather two glasses of wine and then nodded his companion outside.

"Here," he said, handing her a glass as they stepped into the gallery. "This way if anyone follows we can explain that we came here to refresh ourselves and have a drink."

"Radford, why are you really doing this?" she asked, confused by his sudden desire to be alone with her.

He wiped a droplet of wine from his lip with one finger, looked back over his shoulder toward the house, then gently took her elbow and led her deeper into the profuse thickness of willow branches dangling about them. When he felt they had gone far enough for safety from eavesdroppers, he turned to face her in the soft, flickering lights of the torches that lined their pathway.

"I've had a talk with Beau," he said.

"What about?"

"About you."

"Me?" she gasped.

"Yes. I told him that I wanted to marry you and, if necessary, I would wait however long it would take."

The shadow of a frown darkened her eyes as she touched shaky fingertips to her brow. "Marry?"

"Yes, Alanna, marry. I fear I have fallen hopelessly in love with you," he smiled warmly.

"But Radford, you hardly know me."

"I know enough to know I love you," he said, gently taking her elbow to force her to look at him. "Oh, I don't expect you to love me. Not now, anyway. But I can give you everything you could possibly want. Please, Alanna, say yes."

Spotting a small wooden bench built around the trunk of an oak tree a few feet away, she pulled free of his hold and went to it. Slowly, she sat down, listening to his footsteps bring him to her side. Her mind whirled with confused thoughts, draining her of the right words to say. Had she unthinkingly led him on, teased him into believing there would ever be a special feeling for him? Should she have not accepted his gifts, returning them with a cordial note of appreciation but a firm reminder of the folly such a venture afforded? And what of Beau? Would she find herself a spinster waiting for words of love to come from his lips? The answer to that, she suspected, was yes. She studied the wine goblet in her hands. And if she agreed to marry Radford, what then? Surely it would end a lifelong friendship between the two men. No, she couldn't do that to them. She knew where she belonged.

"The only thing I really want is to return home to

England," she said, wondering if he noticed how shallow her words sounded.

"To what?" he argued, taking her glass of wine to set next to his on the bench. He crouched down before her, softly covering her hands with his. "You've already told me that your parents are dead. Don't you see, you can make your home here. With someone who loves you." A smile broke the serious lines of his face. "And who knows? In time you may even learn to love me."

He leaned forward hoping to draw her attention, but when she refused to look at him, he placed a fingertip beneath her chin, lifting her gaze to meet his, grinning all the more when he found her smiling back at him.

"I never thought that I would ever find someone as kind as you in this Godforsaken country, Radford. And I thank you for it. But I sincerely doubt Master Remington will ever allow it."

"Don't worry about him. A few coins added to those you owe will satisfy him."

Her smile disappeared. Moving away from him, she stood up and walked a few steps, idly playing with the tip of a willow branch that dangled in her way. He had no idea how much effect his words had on her. He made it sound as if she were nothing more than a plot of land being sold off to the highest bidder. But then again, wasn't that how Beau really thought of her? A possession, an unreasoning object he owned and could do with whatever he pleased? If what Radford spoke was truth then the simple act of exchanging a few coins would free her from Beau and give her a comfortable life with a man who would lay the world at her feet. Her choice was easy. But something inside her begged her not to answer in haste, rather to satisfy her doubts before making such a commitment.

"I need time, Radford," she announced quietly.

"I can understand that. But, please, not too much time," he begged, coming to her side. He pulled her around to face him. "May I ask one thing more?"

Cocking her head to one side, she smiled her approval.

"A kiss to help me make it through my time of torture."

She laughed. "A small request. You have my permission."

His pale blue eyes warmed at her consent and she knew without question that Radford Chamberlain was indeed in love with her.

Beau had watched Alanna's every movement since Melissa had dragged him away. He had seen her in the arms of nearly every man there including their host and it never really bothered him. Alanna's presence added spark to a party that would otherwise have been dull and that Melissa would have managed to dominate. He wasn't even upset when he saw Radford take his turn, not until he witnessed his handsome opponent lure his young woman to the gardens. Now he was outraged. Excusing himself from the group of men around him, he headed off in their direction.

Reaching the doors leading to the gardens, he heard Melissa call out his name and knowing it would be rude to ignore her, and quite obvious, he regretfully put aside his plans until he could graciously excuse himself. He drew a deep breath before turning back to her, in hopes of masking his anger.

"Were you on your way to the gardens?" she asked

with a flutter of lashes.

"I thought to get a breath of fresh air," he said, disregarding the open display of flirtation. Coming from Melissa, it always sickened him.

"Good, then I'll join you." Capturing the bend of his arm with her hand, she started to lead him outside. "It's rather stuffy in here and I'm afraid I've lost sight of Radford."

The muscle in his jaw twitched. I haven't, he seethed inwardly.

Stepping onto the torchlit patio, he felt Melissa pull him closer to her, pressing his arm to a full round breast. A knot formed in his throat but his step did not falter. He had come to expect nothing less from her. She had tried for years to win his affection, a goal not motivated by love, but rather by a desire to share his wealth at any cost. He remembered a similar evening many years ago when she had lured him to these same gardens hoping to entice him into coming to her room later. But he had had no desire to make love to her, already knowing the purpose. She had hoped to become heavy with his child, a way to force him into marriage, and that was something he did not want. With any woman.

They strolled about the gardens in silence, nodding politely to the other couples they met while Beau secretively glanced about them searching the shadows for any sign of Radford and Alanna. Melissa, however, had other plans. A short distance ahead was a small wooden bench where she would ask Beau to sit with her, intending discreetly to steal a kiss from him, and possibly something more. But as they reached the spot, she stopped suddenly, her eyes affixed to the scene before her. Standing beneath the gentle sway of willow

280

branches, she found Radford and Alanna entwined in a much too familiar embrace. Rage boiled within her.

"Radford!" she screamed. "What is the meaning of this?"

Reluctant to bring their kiss to an end, Radford slowly released Alanna, knowing anything Melissa could say or do would never affect the joy and love he had experienced at this moment. "It means I have asked Alanna to become the mistress of Briarwood Manor," he said softly, his gaze drinking in the beauty of the woman he held in his arms.

"W-what?" The question caught in her throat, choking her and bringing a wave of anger coursing through her veins. She took a step forward intent on pulling them apart, but feeling a strong hand grab her wrist to stop her instead. She looked up, seeing the hooded glare of her companion glowering down on the couple.

"And what was her answer? Or need I ask? What did you promise her, Rad? The necessary silver it will take to free herself from me? Surely your wealth is all that would interest her."

Having expected such a reaction from his friend, Radford dropped his hold on Alanna and turned to face Beau. "At present, I'm sure what you say is true. But given time, I think I can make her fall in love with me. Any woman would if she could be taken away from the existence I'm sure she experiences with you."

"And what is that supposed to mean?"

"Other than the trip to Williamsburg, have you ever shown her one ounce of kindness?"

"She lives in my house!"

"And so does Tilly. But Tilly is not Alanna."

Angrily, Beau stepped forward and cruelly seized Alanna's wrist. "They are both servants. Obviously you both have forgotten that. She belongs to me. I had hoped your seeing her here tonight would have confirmed that fact. You'll see me dead before I allow you to pay off her debt to me." Jerking Alanna forward, he turned away and started back with her toward the house.

"Take your hand from her, Beau," Radford warned, standing his ground.

Frozen in his tracks, Beau's frame stiffened, his eyes as dark as a menacing thunderstorm. Slowly, he cast a threatening glare on his friend. "Or what?" he seethed.

Radford straightened and took a deep breath. "Or you'll force me to take her from you."

Feeling Beau tense with the challenge, Alanna knew that if she didn't do something, one of them would get hurt because of her. After a useless attempt to pull herself free of the painful hold to her wrist, she threw herself in front of Beau, separating the two men.

"He's right, Radford. I am his servant. I must go back."

"No. I won't let you."

Painfully, Alanna found herself thrown upon the ground, looking up in time to see Beau land a huge fist to Radford's jaw that sent him reeling backward, unconscious before he hit the ground.

"Radford," Alanna cried, her tears blurring her vision. Scrambling to her feet, she threw herself at Beau, beating her fists against his chest. "I hate you," she screamed.

Effortlessly, he took her wrists, stilling the attack, and turned to the silent woman at their side. "I'm sorry for this, Melissa. It won't happen again."

She didn't respond. She couldn't. Her last hope of a richly beneficial marriage lay in a crumpled heap at her feet. Her eyes blazed murderously. But they didn't fall on the unconscious man. They threateningly followed the tiny form being dragged away in the rapidly engulfing darkness.

Nineteen

Alanna sat on the far side of the carriage, her shoulder, arm, hip, and thigh molded against the wall, wishing to be as far as possible from Beau. They had traveled nearly all the way back to Raven Oaks in silence, during which time Alanna stared at the lantern swaying with the pitch of the carriage, trying desperately to concentrate on anything that would block out the sight of the dear, sweet man she had left lying unconscious on the ground. But she failed, and it seemed that nothing would rid her memory of the awful scene. At last, when she could no longer endure the pain in her heart, she cast a damning glare at her companion.

"You're cruel."

She watched him turn a slow, penetrating glance her way before looking back outside again and, drawing courage from his silence, she twisted in the seat to face him.

"How could you do that to a friend?"

Again he turned to look at her, the yellow beams of lamplight touching his face, giving him an almost sinister appearance. "He isn't a friend."

"Not anymore," she rallied bitterly. "I doubt you have any."

Resting an elbow on the window frame, his jaw to the back of his hand, he spoke almost inaudibly. "I don't need any."

Throwing herself back against the leather seat, she stared straight ahead, her body rigid, hands folded tightly in her lap. Tears sprang to her eyes and she fought to hold them back. "Why don't you let me go?" she choked. "I've caused nothing but trouble. And now I've caused two friends to fight each other. Please, just let me go home to England where I belong."

"No," he said flatly, studying the darkness that loomed down on them.

The lantern's glow danced in the moisture lining her lower lashes. She blinked, sending a flow of tears down her cheek. She looked to him again, beseechingly. "Why?" Waiting, the moments seemed endless, pricking her anger and forcing her to thoughtlessly double up a fist and land a painless blow to his shoulder. "Answer me, damn you."

His elbow fell to his side as he turned on her, his ire reflected in the depths of his eyes. "I'll tell you this. If you say one more word, I'll gag you. I'm not in the mood. And lay one more hand on me and I'll return the favor." He looked outside again.

Deciding he would not grace her with an answer should she voice her question again, and certain he would see his threat fulfilled if she did, she wiped the tears from her cheek with the back of her hand and stared out the window in the same manner as her angry companion. It seemed as if everything was closing in on her. She had been highly honored when Radford proposed marriage and for a fleeting moment she had thought it would be just what it would take to reveal Beau's true feelings for her. She laughed to herself. And it had. But they were not the feelings she had wanted to learn. He truly did think of her as a possession, something that angered him when he thought he would lose it. She clamped her teeth together, hoping to stop the quiver of her chin.

As the carriage pulled up in front of Raven Oaks, it hadn't come to a complete stop before Alanna had thrown open its door and quickly jumped down.

"You little fool! Do you want to get hurt?" Beau called after her.

She paid him no heed, and before he realized what she was doing she had stomped off away from the house. He hurriedly left the carriage to grab her elbow before she had traveled very far.

"Where do you think you're going?" he demanded.

Angrily, she jerked away from him and started off again as she threw back over her shoulder, "I will *not* spend another night under the same roof with you. Good night, *Master* Remington."

"And just where do you intend to spend it?" he asked loudly, ignoring the pointed insinuation of the title.

"In my cabin with Cinnamon. It's where I belong. Remember? I'm your servant. As all the others here are," she added with a sweep of her hand.

"Oh, no, you're not," he growled, taking a step toward her, and Alanna suddenly twirled around, her arms stiff, hands clenched and a slight flare to her nostrils.

"If you lay one hand on me, I'll scream my bloody lungs out."

"Then go ahead and scream. I could care less who hears," he said, thinking it an idle threat. But before he had even lifted a foot toward her again, she burst forth with an ear-piercing scream.

Out of desperation, he lunged for her, circling her waist with one arm and clamping a hand over her mouth to silence the alarm. Instantly he knew the foolishness of his venture, for in the distance he heard Cain calling out for him.

"It's all right, Cain," he called back. "It's only me."

"But I heard a woman scream."

"I said it's all right. Go back to bed."

A moment of quiet passed before Cain acknowledged the order and silence fell about them once more.

"You are a trial," Beau sighed against the silkiness of her hair. "Now will you behave and come inside of your own accord or do I have to drag you?" Unable to understand her mumbled words, he cautiously pulled his hand away.

"No, I will not," she spit at him and took a breath to resume her protest.

"All right," he avowed, covering her scream before it could do any damage, "have it your way."

He discovered, too late, that his job would be greater than he had imagined, for with every step they took, she tried to pull away, tearing at his hands to break his hold and kicking out at him whenever she could. More than once her feet became entangled with his, nearly causing them both to stumble. His anger began to grow. Tightening his grip only seemed to provoke her and before long he lost all patience. Spinning her around, he placed a shoulder against her belly and stood erect once more. Let her scream, he thought. The coachman has

288

seen everything anyway, and by morning the entire plantation will know of this.

The great door of the mansion came crashing open as Beau kicked it in, sending its thunderous roar echoing throughout the house. He took the stairs two at a time, the weight on his shoulder a small burden. In a hurried state, he entered his room and threw her across his bed, leaving her to light a candle.

The breath knocked out of her, she lay still a moment until the frightening realization of where she lay bolted her upright. Scooting off the bed, she ran for the door, instantly halted when Beau cut her off, his outstretched arms blocking her way. She retreated several steps.

"The very first time you defied my authority, I should have had you bound in chains to serve out the rest of your time. But no, I was stupid enough to bring you into my house. You weren't punished. You were rewarded! Then I was even foolish enough to take you to a ball and introduce you to all of Virginia. And now one of the wealthiest men in the state offers you marriage and the chance to free yourself from the debt you owe. I have every right to be angry with you."

"Why? You should be happy to be rid of me. I—"

"Because you've made a fool of me since the day you raised a hand to me in front of my men. You've planned all of this from the very beginning, haven't you? And to think," he raved, looking upward as if seeking a higher understanding, "I nearly fell in love with you."

Alanna's breath caught in her throat, the blood pounding in her ears. Had he actually said the words she had longed to hear him say? Or was it an idle fantasy? Her lip trembled and she fought to voice her question loud enough for him to hear. "Love?"

"Yes. You planned that, too, didn't you? You've managed to fool Radford, but not me. Not anymore. I shall have what is mine," he growled, putting an end to any other ideas she might have had, "right now."

Too stunned to react, and blinded by her tears, she stood unmoving, an easy target for the merciless revenge he felt justified in having. Reaching out, he seized the neckline of her gown, and in one swift wrench tore the beautifully fashioned velvet garment from her to lie in ruins at her feet.

A chill overtook her, and Alanna knew the night air was not its source. How could he believe all that he had accused her of? It simply wasn't true. Not any of it. And now this. He had destroyed in one moment's fit of rage one of the few things he had given her. It was as if he had torn out her heart.

"I hate you." The words trailed from her lips belying the truth that ached inside.

"Then if you hate me so much, it won't matter anymore what I do with you, will it?"

"And if I said it did, would you let me pass and seek the privacy of my room? I am no fool, Master Remington. You will do whatever pleases you without considering me." She reached up to catch a tear before it reached her chin. "Tell me, do you think by doing this that Radford will not want me because I am no longer innocent? You forget. You took that from me several months past. You do this only to degrade me."

The muscle of his jaw twitched. "I do this because I want to. Since that night I have spent the rest as a monk. And in torture. You managed in a few short moments to infect my mind with your beauty and arouse in me a desire that drives all sense from me. I am crazed with longing. Whether given freely or by force, I will possess you one last time and by the grace of God put you from my mind forever!''

The shadows of the room danced across his face as they stood there staring at each other. Time seemed to stand still. Then, without a word, he lifted her in his arms, carried her to his bed and gently placed her upon it.

Exhausted of any strength to fight him and knowing it was useless to try, Alanna lay unmoving in the center of his huge bed, oddly finding no desire to sway his intentions, satisfied to watch him slip from the velvet coat and breeches, silk shirt, shoes and stockings. Could it be that the yearnings he ignited in her came only from lust, as they so obviously did for him? If so, then why did her heart ache? Why couldn't she fill her thoughts with other things in the early morning hours, at midday, or late at night when sleep would not come and she stood at the window of her room staring out at the star-filled heavens?

She watched him come to her, silhouetted in the candle's glow, appraising the taut muscles of his lean thighs, flat belly, wide, strong shoulders, certain he could crush her in one embrace, one fit of rage. Yet, his touch was gentle, and she trembled in its power, wanting to turn him away, deny him his pleasure and knowing she couldn't. She sighed when his lips softly found hers, drinking in the scent of him, a flood of warmth pouring over her. She reached up, pulling him to her, feeling his naked flesh against hers, and returned his kiss twofold. Lifting up, he studied her face in silence, his lips parted as if wishing to speak the words he felt, masked suddenly by the lustful rage engulfing him. He kissed her hungrily, his tongue darting, teasing, his breath growing rapid, his hands seaching. She parted her thighs to welcome him. Their passion soared, bodies meeting in equal ecstasy until at last they lay weary in each other's arms.

Though wrapped in the comfort of his embrace, Alanna had never felt so alone, her grief, her loss tightening the muscles in her throat, testing her strength to hide her tears, her love for this man. She knew in that moment all he would have to say was one word to stop her from going and she would have stayed by his side forever. But that word was never spoken, and because it wasn't, she decided to accept Radford's proposal. Life with a man who loved her was better than a life made from lust, for obviously Beau no longer cared.

Twenty

Bright morning sunlight filtered in through the partially drawn curtains and filled every corner of the room with its cheerfulness. From the vastness of the four poster bed, weary, muffled sobs pierced the stillness of early dawn and went unheard by the ears of one who could with a single word bring an end to the pain. To cry would bring a final peace when all the grief was spent. She would rise again, the defiant, strong-willed woman she had once been, with the courage to face the world and all the trials it would place before her, for she had vowed that nothing, and no one, would ever hurt her again.

Alanna dragged herself from the warm softness of his bed to cover her nakedness with a discarded shirt from the floor, her legs and arms heavy from a night spent without rest. When his passion had ceased and he had fallen into a fitful slumber, she lay awake staring at the misshapen shadows on the ceiling, unable to find any peace of mind or body. And when he had risen and gone, she had discovered that the emptiness of the bed was not nearly as great as the emptiness she felt within. Finally, not able to hold back her grief, she wept until she had no more tears. In their wake came a strength, a courage, and confidence that she could face the days to come without the help of anyone.

Crossing to the window of his room, she pulled the curtains aside and perched herself on the sill to study the empty yard below, relaxing in the solitude of early morning and wondering where Beau could have gone. Not that she cared. He certainly wasn't troubled with what he had done and there would be no need to feel pity for him in his time of unrest. She leaned her head back against the window frame and let the cool breeze hit her face, watching the minute outline of an eagle soaring gracefully into the air, longing to be just as free. How long had it been since she had written the letter to her aunt? Long enough for her to answer it? She stiffened with the thought. What if her aunt decided to ignore her pleas for help? Or maybe she would not be able to find the amount it would take to bring her home to England again. A single tear formed in the corner of her eye.

A sudden gust of wind whipped about the branches of the tree just outside her refuge, breaking free a leaf to swirl in the air and flutter haphazardly into the window to land on her knee. Picking it up by the stem, she twirled it slowly in her fingers as she thought of the only other alternative she had. Radford Chamberlain. It seemed the simple answer. He had pledged his love for her, and if he truly spoke the feelings of his heart, she could live the rest of her days in comfort. Something she felt certain would never be at Raven Oaks. She frowned. Why couldn't Beau have told her sooner of his love for her?

Maybe things would have been different. Maybe—

"Jeremiah," Alanna called as she stepped into the stable. "Jeremiah, are you here?"

From the far end of the building she heard a noise, and in the shadows strained to see what had caused it.

"Yes'm. I'm here," he called back. "What can I do for yo'?"

Alanna waited for his dark figure to take shape as he came to meet her, rubbing his eyes with one hand and trying unsuccessfully to hide his yawn with the other.

"I'm sorry I woke you," she apologized.

"That's all right, Alanna. Time I was gettin' to work anyhow."

"Would you saddle a horse for me?" she asked, and quickly added when she saw his hesitant look, "it's all right. Master Beau gave me permission."

Running his fingers through his frizzy black hair, he shrugged one shoulder. "Well, I suppose I could. But are yo' sure yo' should be ridin' alone?"

"I won't go far and I promise not to be gone too long. Please? It means a lot to me."

After studying her a moment, he turned away with a shake of his dark head. "I give yo' the gentlest mare we got. And don't go runnin' her. She's pretty old."

Alanna nodded respectfully, feeling her pulse quicken, knowing that within the hour she would be at Briarwood Manor.

Slouching in the chair before the cold hearth of his

study, a half-empty glass of whiskey dangled from Radford's fingertips, thoughts of the events of the night past running through his mind time and time again. From the very first, he had handled it all wrong. He should never have told Beau that he wanted to marry Alanna. He should have found another way. Silently, he cursed his lack of foresight and downed the remainder of his drink in one swallow.

Radford had a long way to go to be comfortably drunk and when he first thought he heard the hoofbeats of a horse galloping in, he ignored them, believing himself to be more intoxicated than he realized. Then Amos appeared at his side. Lazily, Radford looked past his shoulder, following the butler's form with his eyes until he saw the troubled frown on his dark face.

"What is it, Amos?" he asked, disheartened.

"Miss Alanna, sir. She's in the parlor."

Straightening sharply in his chair, Radford ran shaky fingertips across his brow, wondering if he had heard correctly. "Here?" he asked, more to himself. He rose nervously, handing his glass to Amos and, tugging at his waistcoat, he took a step forward, then stopped. "How do I look?"

But before Amos could answer, Radford waved him off and left the room.

Seeing the slight figure standing at the window gazing out, Radford stopped, wondering if she was only a dream, something his mind had conjured up to fill the void his life had taken on. Then she turned and smiled at him, her voice barely above a whisper.

"I hope I'm not disturbing you."

Radford could hear the pounding of his heart in his

ears, and he felt the warmth of blood rising to his cheeks. He reached up to smooth his tousled hair.

"Disturb me?" he spoke softly. "Alanna, you have done nothing else since the first time I saw you. You haunt my dreams and my every waking hour. And I love every minute of it because I love you. Please tell me you're here to accept my offer of marriage and let Beau Remington live the rest of his life missing something he could have had."

"Then you haven't changed your mind?"

"Changed my mind?" he moaned, coming to stand by her side. "Never. My love for you is endless."

The darkness of her eyes softened with his pledge, but then appeared troubled when she looked away.

"What is it?" he implored reaching for her hand. She pulled away.

"Before I say anything, you must know something." Rubbing the palms of her hands together before clasping them as if in prayer, a fingertip lightly touching her trembling lip, she looked upward, taking a deep breath before continuing. "I don't love you. Maybe I never will. I rather doubt I will ever love any man."

"It doesn't matter."

"It could," she groaned, turning back to him. "Maybe not for a while. But in a few years, or months, you may grow tired of a wife in name only. I wouldn't blame you."

A slow smile wrinkled his cheek. "Maybe you think I was playing with you when I said my love for you is endless. I wasn't. I meant it. I do love you. And I want you at my side at any price, Alanna."

The pale blueness of his eyes reminded Alanna of an early morning sky, revealing the kindness and the gentle soul within him. His ruffled blond hair, signs of a night spent restlessly, lightly touched his fair complexion, bringing to mind the innocence of a child. Suddenly compelled to hold him to her, she smiled her acceptance, knowing a life with him could never bring unhappiness.

Feeling as though all the troubles of the world had been resolved by a few simple words, she sighed happily and went to the sofa to sit down. "Although I am as eager to be free of him as you are to have me here, there is still one problem. Beau made it very clear last night that he would not set me free even if you paid my debt."

"*Especially* if I paid your debt," he corrected, his voice sounding tired.

"Well, I have an idea that might solve that. Several weeks ago, I was given permission to send a letter to my aunt in England. In it I asked for the money to pay Beau what I owe him. Maybe he won't accept your money, but if he thinks it's mine, from my aunt, he'll have no choice."

Radford's eyes lit up instantly, heartfelt laughter breaking free. "Alanna, you're brilliant."

Radford did not try to see Alanna for the next several weeks, having agreed it would be best. They couldn't take the chance of having Beau grow suspicious. It must seem to him that his warnings to Radford had been understood and he might possibly be deceived into believing that his friend had lost interest in her. Thus, in a few months when the letter from England—the one Radford had forged—arrived with enough money to pay Alanna's debt, Beau would be none the wiser.

298

Summer turned to a beautiful early fall. The hilltops glowed with color, oranges, golds, and reds, the kind of richness one felt inclined to reach out and grasp only to discover it was not meant to hold in one's hands. It brought with it a mixture of peace and yearning. For Alanna, it brought unrest. It had been nearly two months since that evening of the Bensens' ball and the night she had spent in Beau's arms. Maybe it was just the tension of her deceit that caused her to be late, but soon it would be the third month that she had missed her womanly curse. Maybe Radford loved her. But did he love her that much?

"Are you sure?" Radford asked one late afternoon when they met in a meadow adjoining the two plantations.

Alanna looked away, too ashamed to face him. She nodded, but would not utter a sound as she pulled the heavy cloak around her to protect herself against the crisp bite of the wind.

Slowly, he walked away from her as he led his horse to a cluster of rocks, resting his foot against the largest. He crossed his wrists upon his knee and studied the erratic movement of the tall grass swaying in the breeze. The gentle nudging of his horse's nose against his shoulder made him straighten, aware of the heavy silence surrounding them. He looked back to Alanna.

"I will understand if you've changed your mind," she said.

Radford's brows knotted as he shook his head. "No, no," he assured her, "that is not why I hesitate. It is only a shock, that's all."

"But you must understand that if you marry me, the heir to Briarwood Manor would not be of your blood but rather that of your friend," she reminded him. "And all of Virginia will laugh behind your back."

"How will they know the father?" he cried out. "I will not be the one to spread the rumor."

"But they may suspect it," she whispered. "I will not be the cause of your shame."

"Alanna," he moaned as he quickly went to her and pulled her tightly into the circle of his arms. "You will never cause me shame. I love you too much. And besides, if it's true, I will love the child as my own. I have always, and still do think of Beau as my own brother. I love him as one, even now. And I will love his child as greatly. Even more, since I love its mother." Tenderly lifting her face to his with a knuckle beneath her chin, he smiled down at her. "It's all right, Alanna," he whispered.

"Oh, Radford," she cried, throwing her arms around his neck. A tear raced down her cheek and tasted salty in the corner of her mouth. "Thank you. Thank you, Radford." Without any urging, she stood on tiptoes to place a gentle kiss upon his lips.

Alanna didn't have the usual signs of pregnancy, only occasional fatigue, making it easy for her to hide her condition from Beau. Not that he would have noticed. He spent his days away from the house and his nights after dinner alone in his study doing paperwork. Business seemed to call him away from Raven Oaks more frequently for longer periods of time and it didn't take Alanna long to realize that he did everything possible to avoid her. Then during one of his rare stays at home one afternoon, Cain appeared at the front door with a parcel tucked under his arm looking for Beau.

"He's in the study," Alanna told him when she let him in. "Is something wrong? You look—so funny."

"No, no," he hurriedly replied. "Just business."

There *was* something wrong. She could tell it by the way he kept looking back at her as he went to the study door and, once he disappeared inside, she decided to wait on the stairs until he returned. She wasn't one to let curiosity get the better of her, but this time she couldn't help it.

Not having expected to see Cain for the remainder of the day, Beau looked up in surprise. Cain had been told to go back to the fields to supervise the harvest of cotton that had begun several days before. His blatant disregard for orders could only mean a matter of utmost urgency. "Trouble, Cain?"

Joshua's brows lifted slightly. "A parcel just arrived for Alanna. It's from England."

Slowly, Beau laid down his quill. "England?"

"Ah-huh. From a woman by the name of Martha Westbrook. Have any idea who it might be?"

Staring at the item tucked in the crook of Cain's arm, Beau's eyes slowly lifted to meet Joshua's questioning gaze. He shook his head. "Bring it here and then go fetch Alanna."

The brown wrapped package sat on the far edge of his desk. Beau could only stare at it, afraid that if he touched it it would be consumed by the fires of hell and take him with it to a fiery grave. Somehow it represented all the evil wrongdoings he had forced on his young and guiltless housekeeper. Fearfully, he pressed back into his leather chair, praying the distance between them would be enough.

"You sent for me, sir?" a soft voice asked, penetrating his private world of guilt. He looked up to find the source of his torment staring down at him.

Quickly gathering his composure, he straightened in his chair. "This came for you," he said, nodding toward the edge of his desk.

Hoping the relief of those many weeks of apprehension and waiting didn't show on her face, Alanna eagerly took the box from its resting place. Had it really been from England, she would have sought the privacy of her room to open it. But since it had all been done for Beau's benefit, she went to the chair by the hearth and sat down, pulling at the twine that held its wrappings.

Fighting the smile that threatened to capture the soft line of her mouth, Alanna concentrated on the items in her hands, along with a letter sealed with wax, Radford had sent a box of chocolate. To all appearances, it seemed innocent enough, even though she knew its real purpose and the one who had actually sent it. Studying the letter of credit made out from the Bank of England, she masked her surprise at the amount it represented, certain it was more than her aunt could possibly afford. But realizing Beau had no way of knowing how rich or poor Martha Westbrook might be, she folded the document and stood.

"It's from my Aunt Martha," she proudly announced. "She has sent the money I requested to pay off my debt. If you would be so kind, Master Remington, as to advise me on the sum I currently owe, I will transfer that amount to your charge and leave your hospitality as soon as possible."

Alanna noticed the darkening of his eyes as he stared at her and the sharpened, suspicious tone to his voice when he agreed, feeling the triumph of her victory tugging at the corners of her mouth, yet oddly experiencing a heaviness in her heart. But when she turned to leave, she failed to see the flare of his nostrils and the way he ground his teeth in suppressed anger. Little did she know, but Beau had figured out exactly from where the money had come. Only after she had closed the door behind her did he pull out from the desk drawer the letter that she had written many months before; the one he had never given to Cain.

Twenty-One

"What a fool I've been," Beau growled, staring out the window of his study at the lengthening shadows of evening. "All this time I thought Rad had forgotten his silly notion of marriage. Now this. They must have had a gay time planning out every minute." He turned away from the darkness. Rocking slightly on his heels, he spotted the empty wine bottle resting on the edge of his desk. He went to it, picked it up as if to examine the workmanship of the glassblower, then slammed it back down with such force that it shattered in his hand. "Damn them!" he cried.

With an ear pressed to the study door, Tilly jumped with a start at the rantings she heard coming from inside. A worried expression wrinkled the smooth skin of her brow and, although she normally did not interfere with her master's affairs, she turned sharply for the kitchen and the back entrance of the house. Maybe Cain should know what was going on.

"I tell yo', I never see'd him like this 'fore, Masta Cain," she exclaimed as the two of them started back

305

toward the house. "Ever since yo' brought Alanna that package, he's been actin' like a crazy man."

Cain only grunted.

"I is afraid he hurt hisself if'n someone don't stop him," she said, hurrying her step to keep up with him. "What are yo' gonna do?"

"I don't know. But I want you and everyone else to go to bed. I'll stay with him." He heard Tilly sigh.

"Thank goodness. I really worry for him."

"Don't. He's a grown man and he's gotten himself into this mess. If he wants, he'll get himself out."

"What mess, Masta Cain?" she asked as they hurried up the front steps.

"Never mind, child. Just do as I told you."

He waited in the foyer until Tilly disappeared from view, listening to her excited chatter in the kitchen before it faded into silence. Then a muffled crash came from inside the study, drawing his attention to the matter at hand. He knocked loudly.

"Who is it?" an angry voice demanded.

"It's Joshua, Beau. May I come in?" He waited, tilting an ear toward the door to hear his reply, but when none came he straightened in alarm. "Beau?"

"If I said no, you would anyway."

A smile deepened the lines in his cheeks.

Sitting in the desk chair turned at an angle toward the window, his arms draped over its sides, a glass dangling from his fingertips and his long legs stretched out before him, Beau stared blankly out at the shadows. The room had no light save the small stream that flooded in from the foyer when Cain opened the door and looked in, casting an eerie gloom on the dark figure sitting alone.

"A little chilly in here, don't you think?" Joshua

asked, noticing the darkened fireplace as he walked further in and closed the door behind him.

Beau remained silent, unmoving.

"Mind if I start a fire?"

"Like I said before—" he mumbled, renewing Cain's smile.

He went to the hearth where he placed logs in a stack, and within minutes a ruddy glow warmed the room. He stood up and faced Beau, a frown coming to his brow almost immediately when he noticed the unkempt manner in which Beau was dressed. The tail of his wrinkled shirt, opened nearly to the waist, failed to remain tucked into his breeches. The lean line of his jaw darkened with the stubble of beard he had neglected to shave, and his eyes showed the unrest he was experiencing.

"Are you going to tell me about it?"

"Tell you about what?" Beau grumbled into his drink as he pressed the glass to his lips.

"Why it is you're sitting here in the dark, all alone, and drinking yourself into a stupor."

Only Beau's eyes moved in Cain's direction. "I don't think I have to explain my actions to you. You only work here."

A slight shrug lifted Cain's shoulders as he leaned back to rest an arm along the mantel, feeling the warmth of the fire chase away the chill the darkness had caused. "That's true. But before Andrew died he made me promise him something." He cocked a brow, waiting for Beau's interest to arouse the question to form on his lips, realizing his task was to be greater than he had assumed when Beau uncaringly looked away. The muscle of his jaw twitched. "He asked me to look after you, but he

307

didn't have to. I would have done it anyway. You mean as much to me as my own son would have had I been blessed with one." He looked down, watching the firelight dance against the floor. "It pains me to see you like this."

Unexpectantly, Beau spun around in his chair, an outstretched arm sweeping the contents of the desk to the floor in a loud crash. "Then why not spare yourself and leave me be?" he stormed, tightness in his throat choking off his words.

The suddenness of the act failed to surprise Joshua or even startle him. He remained statuesque, his voice firm and soothing. "Everyone needs a friend now and then, someone to confide in. I reckon you're in dire need right now."

"I don't need anyone! Not you—or Tilly—or Jeremiah—or Radford—" he drew a deep breath, the growing fury crackling the deep tones of his voice, "or some trollop," he roared, slamming his fist down against the desk.

"Alanna?" Cain asked in quiet calm.

"Yes, Alanna!" He threw himself back against the chair, and turned away, his elbow placed to the arm of it while he pressed his fist to his mouth.

Casually strolling to the desk, Joshua took a cheroot from the cigar box and walked back to the fireplace. Placing the end of a taper into the fire to light the cheroot, he watched the white smoke curl above his head before continuing. "Has this to do with the parcel that came for her?"

"No," Beau snapped.

Joshua took a puff on the cigar again, hearing a tired sigh fill the room.

"That's only part of it," Beau said, dropping his hand

308

to his lap. "They lied to me. They tried to trick me. Alanna, I can understand. But not Radford."

Joshua looked back at him. "Tell me about it," he said softly.

In the dancing flickers of light, Cain noticed how hard it was for Beau to swallow before he took a breath to speak. "I don't know where to begin," he said, shaking his head. "I guess I don't really know where this all started."

"Start with the parcel," Cain suggested, sitting down in a chair before the fire. Having placed himself in the shadows, he could watch Beau without fear of revealing his own feelings until the proper time, if that time should come. He remembered another time when Beau had leaned on his friendship. It had been the day Andrew died.

Placing his elbows on the desk, Beau rubbed the moisture from his eyes in a slow, tired movement, then leaned back in his chair, the glow of the fire softening his troubled expression. "The parcel contained a letter, supposedly from Alanna's aunt, and a letter of credit, enough to pay her debt to me. It was to appear to be in answer to the letter Alanna sent her many months ago."

Cain frowned in the darkness. "What letter? I don't remember taking such a letter to Williamsburg."

A half smile curled the corner of Beau's mouth. "You didn't. I never gave it to you."

"Then how—"

"Radford," Beau volunteered. "It was really from Radford, as was the letter of credit."

"But why? What was the purpose?"

Beau crossed an ankle to one knee, his hand draped across it. "Radford came to me a few months ago, just before the Bensens' ball and asked to buy Alanna. He said he loved her and that he wanted to marry her. I refused. So—they found another way."

"You mean Alanna has agreed to the marriage?" Cain asked, sitting upright in the chair.

"It would appear so."

Cain shook his head, the palms of his hands turned upward. "But I don't understand. I thought Alanna—"

"Oh, I think I do. She hates me enough to do anything to get away from me." Picking up the pearl-handled letter opener from his desk, he rolled it in his hand to absently study its ivory beauty.

"You're wrong, Beau. I think she loves you."

Beau grunted. "Sure is a funny way to show it."

"Maybe it's because she always felt it was one-sided," Joshua pointed out with a lift to one brow.

"It's too late now if she did. The damage has been done." Smiling softly at Cain, he rose and went to the window to stare outside. "If you don't mind, I'd like to be alone now."

Where had it all gone wrong? Joshua wondered, studying the dark profile at the window, his heart aching with the pain he was sure Beau fought to hide, but couldn't. Wasn't there something he could do, something he could say to change things around? Knowing the hurt had gone too far, too deep, he sadly left the chair and crossed to the door, looking back at Beau one more time before making a quiet, reluctant exit.

Tilly stood trembling in the doorway of Alanna's room the next morning watching her stuff what few belongings she had into a satchel. "But where will yo' stay?"

310

"I'll find a room in Williamsburg. I have enough money now to live comfortably for several weeks until the wedding." She looked up to find Tilly crying, and, laying aside her task, went to her. "Don't cry, Tilly."

"I can't help it. I never see yo' again."

"That's not true. We'll be neighbors. I'll never let our friendship die, believe me." Pulling Tilly into the circle of her arms, she embraced her comfortingly until the maid's weeping ebbed. "Now go and see if Jeremiah has the wagon ready."

"Yes'm," Tilly whispered, her tears renewing, but rather than let Alanna know, she kept her head down and quickly left the room.

Dressed in the only gown left her after her long journey by sea, Alanna picked up her small bundle and started for the door. When she reached it, she paused to look back. It was as if a part of her life had come to an end. A sad one. Surely what lay ahead would bring some joy. She turned and walked out.

As she descended the stairs, she heard a woman's laughter coming from the study, a laughter she had heard before but could not immediately recognize. Knowing the wagon waited outside the kitchen door, she intended to pause briefly to gaze across the foyer at the study, wishing somehow she had the courage to say good-bye to him, secretly wanting him to stop her, no, praying that he would. Although she suspected being Mistress of Briarwood Manor would provide some glorious times for her, they would never fill the emptiness that ached in her heart at this moment, never substitute the need for Beau's love. Pressing shaky fingertips to her mouth to hide her trembling lip, she swallowed the lump in her throat and turned away, hearing the door to the study

311

open suddenly. She took a hurried step, stopping short when she heard him call out her name.

"Does this mean you'll be on your way?" The callous tone of his words burned in her ears.

She straightened. "Yes," she answered, hoping to sound just as cold, and forcing herself not to look at him.

"Then why not say good-bye to your friend here. I don't imagine the Mistress of Briarwood Manor will ever pay us a social visit, and this will be the last time you may ever see her."

Her? A startling realization of whom the laughter belonged to flooded Alanna's mind, bringing with it so much pain she thought she could not endure one moment longer. She knew without looking who waited to greet her. Fighting back a whimper, she forced a smile to her lips. After all, this had been what Cinnamon had wanted for years, and she would not spoil it for her. What truly brought about the renewal of her agony was knowing the reason he had chosen this girl above all the others. He had done it to hurt her, to add one more stab to her heart. But vowing he would never witness the satisfaction his act had created, she turned back to face them, her tears gone, her shoulders squared, and a bright smile lighting her face. He tested that smile when he reached out to drape his arm about Cinnamon's shoulders.

"She'll be taking your place. In fact, I've given her your room. So you see, everything has worked out fine," he said, his own smile matching hers.

Alanna nodded graciously. "So it has. I only hope Cinnamon will not have any regrets."

"As I do you," he smiled.

She opened her mouth to retaliate, but noticing how

Cinnamon had yet to lift her gaze to meet hers and nervously bit at her lower lip, Alanna decided against it. Moistening her lips with the tip of her tongue, for they had suddenly gone very dry, she looked down at her hands, wishing she could say what she truly felt for Cinnamon. But knowing how shallow the words would seem at this minute, she elected to remain quiet, bidding her farewell instead.

"Alanna," Cinnamon called, stopping her just outside the kitchen door, "I'm sorry."

Turning back, her satchel held in both hands, she asked, "For what? We both finally have what we want." She smiled warmly at her, glanced up at Beau, then to the floor before turning around and disappearing into the darkened archway of the kitchen.

The bright sunlight overhead and the crystal clearness of the pale blue sky failed to cheer Alanna as she walked out onto the back porch. But finding Tilly, Bessy, and Horace waiting in line at the side of the wagon, she forced her steps to lighten, appearing as if she hadn't a care in the world. She smiled at them, but only Horace returned it, reaching out to take her bundle and toss it in the back of the wagon, drawing her attention to the dark figure sitting on its seat, the reins hanging limply in his hands.

"It just won't be the same without yo' here," Bessy declared with a shake of her head.

Moving closer, Alanna enveloped the woman's bulk in her arms and placed a kiss on her cheek. "And I'll miss you, Bessy. All of you," she added, sending each one a smile.

"Are yo' sure this is what yo' want?" Tilly asked, her dark eyes filling with tears.

"Yes. It is," Alanna lied.

"Yo' all come to visit, won't yo'?" Bessy asked, her throat thick with sadness.

Alanna nodded reassuringly and reached out her hand to Horace. He eagerly took hold of it. "Take care of Master Remington for me," she whispered.

"Yes'm, I will," he answered quietly, guiding her to the front of the wagon where he helped her climb on next to Jeremiah. "And yo' take care of yo'self, hear?"

Placing a kiss to her fingertips, she waved it their way as Jeremiah heartily slapped the reins against the horse's rump, starting them off down the road. Twisting in the seat, she waved good-bye one more time, blinking back a tear and stealing a glance at the house, wondering if he cared enough to watch. Certain that he didn't, she studied the horizon ahead of her, listening to the rocks crush beneath the wheels.

"Is something wrong?"

Standing by the window in the shades of his study, Beau strained to see the wagon as it pulled away, trying not be be seen by its passenger. When it vanished from sight, he turned, a dark, unreadable expression hooding his eyes.

"No, not anymore," he said quietly, studying the girl who had spoken, and wondering why he had never noticed her before. Dark auburn hair touched with the colors of fire flowed about her shoulders and rested invitingly against her full, round breasts. "Wait for me in your room," he instructed, watching the gentle sway of skirts as she left the study.

After pouring himself a glass of wine, he rested a hip against the edge of his desk and looked outside at the road

314

again. Maybe now things could return to normal. Maybe now he could go to the girl waiting upstairs for him and take her in his arms and make love to her. Could he? Would Alanna's leaving make a difference? Could he put her from his mind so easily? Of course, he could. He finished off the glass of wine, set the stemware on the desk, and headed for the room where an eager and willing woman waited.

By the time he reached the top of the stairs, some of his courage faded. When he touched the latch of the door, it vanished. He stood there, closed his eyes, and took a slow, deep breath. Well, maybe tomorrow. Right now he wasn't in the mood.

Twenty-Two

Sea-green eyes, moistened by tears, stared pleadingly at him. "But Radford, darling," Melissa whined, "you promised to marry me."

Cringing at the sound, he turned his back on her. How he hated it when she used that tone on him, knowing that at any other time it would have softened him to her needs. But not this time. This time he would not sit idly by and let her have her way. He poured himself another drink and braced himself for the quarrel he was sure would follow.

"I never promised to marry you," he reminded her quietly, returning to stand by her side at the sofa.

A sob escaped her, accompanied by a delicate, well-executed dab of her handkerchief to the end of her nose. "But—but we talked of marriage many times and you know it."

"You talked of it. I usually listened." He took a sip of wine and stared straight ahead.

Twisting in the sofa to look at him, she allowed a single tear to trickle down her cheek. "But you led me to believe we would get married. You took advantage of me." She looked away, a pained expression drawing her brows together, her hands clutched to her bosom. "Whatever will I do if I'm—carrying your child?"

He sighed and closed his eyes. God, how he wished he didn't have to listen to this. "If you were meant to have a child, you would have found yourself carrying one long ago." He finished his drink, set the glass on the end table, and went to the window to stare outside, the fingers of one hand tucked into his waistcoat pocket, the others grasping the folds of drapery. "It won't do any good to argue. I've made up my mind. I'm going to marry Alanna."

Outraged by his calm dismissal of her, she bolted from the sofa, her tears gone. "She's not good enough for you. She's only a servant."

"She won't be after I marry her," he corrected softly.

"But she can't love you. Not as much as I. Doesn't that matter?" she demanded, watching him run his fingers through his hair in a slow, tired movement.

"No."

"You're a fool, Radford," she hissed, rounding the end of the sofa to stand at his side. Angrily, she hooked her fingers in the crook of his arm, hoping to force him to look at her as she continued, "She's tricked you. She fashioned herself a lady and you were fooled by it. She's nothing but a slut. Beau took her and God knows how many others. She's probably lying in his arms this very minute!"

"Stop it! Stop it," he thundered, knocking her hand away. "You will not say another word against her. Do you hear? Not another word."

Surprised by his unusual display of anger, she shrank

318

back in momentary fear, allowing him to brush past her and stalk back to the table that held the wine and a fresh drink. The soft arch of her brow lifted slightly. She had never known Radford to let his temper get the better of him. Many times she had thought it a game to try any way she could to arouse such an emotion, but she had always failed. Obviously this woman meant enough to him for him to defend her honor no matter who spoke against her. If she was to win him away from Alanna, she would have to be very careful in choosing the right words.

Taking a deep breath, she began again. "Let's be sensible about this. Miss Bainbridge has nothing to offer. I would bring you a large dowry. You know you've always had an eye on Papa's land. Someday it would all be yours. But only if you marry me."

She watched him consider the glass he held in one hand for several moments before glancing over his shoulder at her, the anger gone from his eyes. "I can live without it."

A tremor of rage overtook her as she fought down the urge to strike him. The fool! How could he be so blind? In a whirlwind of skirts and and petticoats, she swept her wide-brimmed straw hat trimmed with a yellow satin ribbon from the sofa and started for the door. "You've not heard the last from me, Radford Chamberlain. You'll regret the day you rejected me for the likes of that woman." Her small frame rigid with fury, she cast him an icy glare before stomping from the room and his house.

His eyes closed, he rubbed the heel of his palm across his brow. He had known that someday he would be sorry for ever having courted Melissa, and now that time had come. Exhausted, he wearily walked to the window to watch her climb into her carriage and wave the driver on.

He really couldn't blame her for her anger. He had led her on. But she knew he had never loved her. She knew and it had never mattered before. He sighed. For some reason, he suddenly felt dirty. Placing his empty glass on the table as he passed, he set off for his room and a bath to hopefully wash away his memories of a bad affair.

With the coming of October, Radford found himself bound to the plantation, supervising the harvest of his crops and seeing to their loading at the docks. Morning turned to night, days into weeks, and nearly a month had passed since Alanna had moved into a boardinghouse in Williamsburg. Each night, alone in his room, he sat at the small desk and penned a letter to her, declaring his love and his loneliness, praying the time they were apart would end. With the letter, he sent a gift, its worth each time exceeding that of the one before it, and once he had seen the parcel safely into the messenger's hands with instructions to hurry, he returned to his room to get quietly drunk, hoping to fall asleep quickly and bring an end to his torture.

An orange light stole in across the room and pressed heavily against his eyelids. He stirred, the throbbing of his wine-sodden slumber hammering in his temples. He rolled onto his stomach, dragging the quilt over his head and bringing darkness upon him once more. If only the sun would go away. Excited cries sounded below his window and he buried his head beneath the pillow hoping to block out the voices. Again they sounded, only louder and in chorus. Didn't they know he wanted to sleep? Dragging his tired body from the bed, he rose to call out to them from his window, coughing when his lungs filled with smoke. Stumbling backward, he tried to clear his mind. Where was he? His eyes burned and he shoved his knuckles into them to wipe away the tears. Once again he went to the window.

The searing flames reached upward, licking their orange tongues against the blackness and lighting up the sky in a blaze of heat and destruction. Dark figures raced about screaming instructions and carrying buckets of water that splashed out upon them before they could hurl what was left on the fire.

Radford coughed again, not finding an escape from the smoke the wind had carried into his room. "The barn," he choked, squinting his eyes. "Dear God, the bales of cotton are in there!" Turning away, he pulled on a pair of breeches and ran from the room.

"Alanna, there's someone at the door for you."

"Thank you, Elvira," Alanna called from her room, recognizing the voice of the old woman who rented the room next to hers. "I'll be right down. Please tell him to wait."

Hurriedly, she put aside her needlework and ran a brush through her hair, frowning at the pale reflection that stared back at her in the mirror and wondering if he would notice. A smile replaced the frown, knowing it would not matter, and she excitedly lifted her skirts and headed for the stairs, seeing Mrs. Allison and Elvira Brooks waiting for her.

"It's not your young man, Alanna," Elvira said with a skeptical lift to one brow. "I'm beginning to wonder if there is such a person."

"Hush, Elvira," Mrs. Allison warned, taking Alanna's

hand once she reached the pair. "Pay no attention to her idle talk, child. She's just jealous no man sends her gifts."

"I am not," the old woman shrieked. "In my day, scores of men chased after me. Why I remember one time—"

"Elvira, why don't you go to the kitchen?" Mrs. Allison smiled. "I just finished baking some tarts. You may have one if you wish."

"Tarts?" Elvira sang. "Oh, I so love tarts."

Her past momentarily was forgotten, and Alanna and Mrs. Allison watched the tired wobble of the round little woman as she ambled toward the kitchen, her inaudible mumbles hardly reaching their ears.

"She's such a sweet, meddlesome old woman," Mrs. Allison smiled, "that I find it hard to stay mad at her." She glanced back at Alanna, the pleasant look on her face changing to one of concern when she noticed Alanna's attention on the door leading to the parlor. "Don't look so sad. You know times are busy with the harvest. He'll come to see you just as soon as he can."

"I know," Alanna agreed. "I guess I just worry that he'll have a change of heart."

"Silly girl," Mrs. Allison scolded, reaching up to pinch Alanna's cheek. "A man would have to be crazy not to marry you."

Absently, Alanna touched a hand to her rounding belly.

"Even with a family not far behind," Mrs. Allison added, having noted the dubious gesture.

A smile stole across Alanna's face. "I don't know what I would have done without your friendship these past weeks," she said, thinking how very much the owner of the boardinghouse reminded her of her Aunt Martha. "Thank you."

Shaking off the compliment, Mrs. Allison gave Alanna a gentle shove in the direction of the parlor. "You see what he wants and I'll bring him a fresh-baked tart. From the looks of it, I'd say he could use it."

A frown wrinkled the smooth line of Alanna's brow as she walked across the hallway, failing to understand Mrs. Allison's concern for the messenger. All of Radford's servants were well fed and exquisitely dressed no matter what time of day or night, and Mrs. Allison's thinking this boy needed extra food in his belly worried her. She stepped into the parlor and stopped. Idly running a fingertip along the deep wood carvings on the cigar box Mrs. Allison kept there for her male visitors, stood the ragged form of a very young boy, thin and sickly looking. His coat hung from his narrow shoulders, obviously never having been ironed, and the tattered sleeves were rolled up several times to free his hands from within an overabundance of cloth. Mrs. Allison was right. He looked as if he needed a good meal, but even more so a hot bath.

"Hello," she said walking further into the room. "Did you wish to see me?"

The boy came to attention, blushing beneath the smudges of dirt. "Yes'm, if you're Mistress Bainbridge."

"I am," she smiled, sitting down on the sofa. "Won't you have a seat?"

Running a hand over his backside, he eyed the red velvet of the sofa. "I don't think I better," he said. "'Sides, I gotta be goin. Can't make no money lollygagging in some parlor." He shoved his small hand in the deep folds of his coat pocket and pulled out a sealed

323

letter. "A man on the ship said to give this to ya."

Her heart skipped a beat, wondering who could possibly have written to her. Then, remembering the letter she had sent to her aunt months before, she sighed, vowing to return any money the woman might have sent with a note of explanation on her upcoming wedding plans and why she no longer needed the funds to return home. She began to tear apart the seal, feeling the boy's eyes still upon her and, sensing an air of uneasiness about him, she looked up to find him dancing from one foot to the other.

"I'm afraid I haven't a coin to give you, but if you'd prefer, I'm sure Mrs. Allison won't mind paying you for your thoughtfulness with one of her tarts."

A wide smile flashed across his face. "Thank you, ma'am. I'd really like that!"

"Then go to the kitchen and tell her what I've said. She might even give you a glass of warm milk to go with it." Alanna smiled with a shake of her head, watching the boy skip from the room. "The poor child," she murmured, "I wonder where he sleeps." Suddenly her thoughts returned to the reason he had appeared in the parlor and she anxiously finished tearing apart the seal of her letter and started to read.

Tears filled her eyes, for the letter was not from her aunt, but rather from a man by the name of Benjamin Potter, an English lawyer. Martha Westbrook had died of pneumonia nearly three months prior to the arrival of the letter, and in it he explained the matter of Alanna's inheritance, in cold, precise, to-the-point formal wording. Teardrops dotted the yellow parchment resting against Alanna's knee. "Oh, Aunt Martha," she wept.

"And all I could think of was myself. Please forgive me."

The next morning, Alanna left the boardinghouse with the lawyer's letter tucked safely in her purse. As Mr. Potter had written, her inheritance had already been forwarded to an account set up in her name at the bank in Williamsburg. All she had to do was sign for it.

After talking with one of the tellers behind the cold metal bars that divided them, she was instructed to go through the small wooden gate that separted one desk from all the others, and speak with a man by the name of Samuel Honeywell. Nervously, she approached the gentleman sitting behind the desk, his head down reading some sort of document he held in his hand, and cleared her throat to gain his attention.

"Mr. Honeywell?" she asked, once he looked up.

Instantly he came to his feet and she noticed how young he appeared, too young, she thought, to be in charge of such matters.

"My name is Alanna Bainbridge," she said. "I'm here about my inheritance."

Mr. Honeywell guided her to a chair beside the desk, waited for her to sit down and resumed his place, smiling warmly all the while. "I was expecting you," he said, leafing through the stacks of papers on the desk top. "I'm sure you'll be pleased when you see how substantially wealthy you've become." He stopped abruptly and looked at her. "I don't mean I assume you'll be pleased for the manner in which you've acquired it" he apologized, relaxing a little with Alanna's half-smile. "Now, if you'll just put your X at the bottom—"

"I can read, Mr. Honeywell. And write," Alanna offered, followed by the man's embarrassed cough.

"Yes, miss," he mumbled, handing over the document.

For the most part, the paper read in legal terms, very little of which Alanna understood, but her eyes widened when they fell on the figure listed at the bottom of the page. Twenty-one hundred pounds. "Oh, my," she breathed, "are you sure of the amount?"

Honeywell's thin nose went up. "Of course. I pride myself on being accurate."

"Oh, I didn't mean that," she corrected, looking from him to the paper again. "I just didn't realize my aunt could possibly have that much."

"Well, it most certainly will come in handy," he scoffed.

Lost as she was in concentration mixed with feelings of grief, a moment passed before his statement penetrated her thoughts. She looked up sharply. "How do you mean?"

"Well, you are marrying Radford Chamberlain, aren't you?" he said, straightening his cravat and running his long, narrow fingers across the side of his head to slick down his hair. "Lord knows you'll need it."

"What are you saying, Mr. Honeywell?"

"I'm not at liberty to discuss the financial situation of one of this bank's members," he said, eyeing her most challengingly.

"Well, you brought it up," she declared, glaring back in the same manner. "If there's something you find unfavorable about Mr. Chamberlain, I suggest you spit it out." She leaned forward, her dark eyes flashing. "Or should I speak with your superior?"

326

He straightened abruptly, his adam's apple bobbing up and down as he glanced about them as if looking for the man in question. Then he inched himself closer to her. "Well," he whispered, "you mustn't tell anyone where you heard this."

Alanna let out a long, impatient sigh, wondering where she could find a bigger gossip than Samuel Honeywell.

"Briarwood Manor is near ruin." Hearing her rapid intake of breath, a satisfied grin parted his lips, but he quickly discarded his amusement when she cast him a suspicious glare.

"How do you know?" she demanded crisply.

"I handle all his bank notes," he answered with an indignant lift to his shoulders. Sorting through the papers on his desk again, he shoved one beneath her nose. "It's all right there. He spends more than he earns."

Alanna quietly studied the markings on the page, painfully aware that what Honeywell had implied was true. Slowly, she returned the paper to the desk top. "If I read correctly, Mr. Chamberlain is short nearly two thousand pounds. Is that correct?"

Honeywell nodded.

"Then see that he gets it."

"Ma'am?"

"Transfer enough money from my account to pay his debts," she said, clutching the strings of her purse as she stood and moved for the gate, pausing to look back once she reached it. "And I'll need a receipt. I'll be back later to get it."

"You know, Miss Bainbridge," he said coldly and not bothering to rise, "you may be throwing good money after bad."

"How so, Mr. Honeywell?" she asked in guarded calm.

"If he receives a good price for his crops this year, wisely spends what he earns, he just might do all right. Otherwise—"

"Good day, Mr. Honeywell," she hissed, turning on her heel to depart his company. Reaching the main door to the bank, she paused to glare back at him one more time, flung the door open, and slammed it loudly closed behind her, marveling at the way its glass managed not to break and almost wishing it had. She would have made Honeywell pay for its repair.

She set off in a brisk walk angry with the little man, and at the same time grateful that he had been so bold as to tell her of Radford's problem. Her step slowed, feeling sure she had done the right thing. After all, Radford had used his money to free her from a life of unhappiness and it seemed only right that she pay him back some way. She smiled. This would be her wedding gift to him even though he would never know of it.

A crisp, cold wind stirred up, striking Alanna's face as she walked along the wooden sidewalk, stinging her cheeks and bringing the smell of salt water to her nostrils. She looked up, letting the cool air refresh her and noticed the ships anchored offshore. Slowing her step even more to enjoy the view, she realized how her inheritance would have enabled her to return to England, something she had longed to do. She sighed, knowing there would never be a need to go home anymore. All of her family was dead now, and the only person who might be waiting for her was Aaron. And even he would quickly abandon her once he learned she was heavy with child. Sadly, she rested her fingertips against the fullness beneath her breast. It wouldn't be long before everyone knew of the child.

Crossing the street on her way back to the boarding-house, she noticed a carriage waiting outside the general store. Although she doubted she knew its owner, something familiar about it aroused her curiosity. As she drew closer, she saw a man standing near its horses and knew instantly why she had been unable to look the other way.

"Joshua," she called happily, quickening her step to reach him.

He looked up, a smile brightening his tired expression. "Well, I'll be—I never thought to see you here today. How are you?"

"Just fine," she beamed, carefully studying his stocky figure from head to toe. "And you look the same. How's Tilly? And Bessy?"

"Good," he nodded, pushing his hat further onto his head when the wind threatened to whip it from him. He paused, noticing the rosy glow of her cheeks, the sparkle in her eyes, and wondering if it had been the wind that brought the color to her face, talking with an old friend that made her happy, or if marrying Radford was truly what she wanted. He looked down and cleared his throat. "Alanna. I hope you have forgiven me for not seeing you off that day you left Raven Oaks. I—"

A small hand rested against his, bringing his gaze to meet hers. "There's no need to explain. I understand," she smiled, grabbing for her cape when the wind caught its edge and whipped it in back of her. Quickly she pulled it around her, but not before Cain's eyes had seen what she had tried to hide. She turned away to readjust the strings of her purse and mask her uneasiness. "Have you come here alone?"

"No," he answered painfully. "I'm waiting for Mr.

329

Remington. Alanna—"

Her heart quickened at the sound of his name on Cain's lips, and she glanced back at the storefront, longing to see him, but knowing she mustn't. Everything she had worked so hard to overcome would shatter with the mere sight of him, and everyone would know in an instant what she had tried so carefully to conceal. She turned back to Joshua.

"Then I mustn't stay. Give my love to everyone," she said, placing her fingertips against Joshua's cheek.

Reaching up to take her hand from his face, he asked, "Alanna, you're not—"

"Hush, Joshua. He's not to know. Not until after the wedding when it will be too late."

"Know what?" a voice from behind her asked.

Without turning, she knew who had spoken and forced herself not to look at him, fighting with the tears that seemed to choke her.

"And from whom are you keeping secrets? Surely not your betrothed," he continued, the callousness of his words burning in her ears.

Her chin quivering, her eyes filling with tears, she bravely looked up at Joshua. "It was wonderful seeing you again, Joshua," she whispered, "but I fear I must be on my way. Good-bye."

Cain touched the brim of his hat in return, allowed her to pass, and watched as she walked away, the brisk wind rippling her cape and skirts.

And Beau watched, too, in silence, until she stepped from the sidewalk ready to cross the street again. It was then that he noticed the fullness of her profile. Stunned, he looked to Cain and opened his mouth to confirm his discovery, only to have Cain look away, the sadness he felt reflected in his movement.

"Alanna, wait," Beau called, starting off after her.

She stopped in the middle of the street when she heard her name, but seeing who had summoned her she quickly grabbed the heavy bulk of her skirts and started to hurriedly walk away. He called again, and this time she ran. With the street and sidewalks full of people, she carefully darted around them, never once looking back. She had to get away. Suddenly a hand seized her arm.

"Alanna, please," Beau begged. "I must talk with you."

"We have nothing to say to each other," she said, jerking free of him.

"And I think we do. Now either we discuss it here in front of everyone, or you'll come with me to McNally's Cove."

She glared defiantly up at him.

"If you think it a bluff, let me assure you I am not ashamed to claim what is mine," he added firmly.

Fearing others had heard his bold remark, she worriedly glanced about them, finding several people had stopped to stare. "All right, then," she whispered. "But only because you've forced me." Irritably pulling her cape over her betraying figure, she allowed him to lead her back across the street and into the dining hall.

They took a place in the far corner of the large room. The table had been partitioned off with a wooden lattice surrounding it and was partly hidden from view by the heavy curtains adorning it. They ordered tea and remained silent until after they had been served.

"Why didn't you tell me?" he asked, once they were alone.

"Tell you what?" she mocked, not surprised by her

own courage, for it seemed that every moment they spent together was spent bantering words.

"Alanna—"

"And what would you have done if I had? Offered to pay for the child's upbringing?"

Having crossed his arms to the edge of the table, he straightened in surprise. "What else would you have expected?"

"There are enough bastards in the world already, Mr. Remington. I don't need to add another." She pressed back in her chair, angrily toying with the tip of one finger.

"You wanted marriage?"

A spiteful smile twisted the corners of her mouth. "Yes. Would you have offered?" she asked, watching the dark frown flash across his brow.

"You thought not, and that was why you accepted Radford's offer, wasn't it?"

"I knew not of the child when I accepted," she scoffed.

"But had you, you would have come to me first?"

She stared at him a moment, thinking him an arrogant rogue to make such a statement. "No. I wouldn't have," she said flatly and looked away.

"But it is my child, isn't it?"

"Of course," she gasped, outraged. "I have known no other." Tears threatened to spoil her brave facade, and she forced herself to concentrate on the teacup sitting before her.

Noticing the moisture that glistened in her eyes, he fought down the temptation to reach out and touch her, pull her into his arms, hold her. When he spoke, his voice softened. "Do you think me a cruel man, Alanna? Did you really believe I wouldn't have cared?"

She could feel her lip tremble as she opened her mouth to speak. "How can you sit there and ask such a question when only a few weeks ago you allowed me to leave Raven Oaks without a word. And before I had gone, you had selected another to replace me. How else could I feel? Or are you telling me you would love your child and not the woman you forced to bear it? If that is so, then you will have to suffer the loss, for I will marry Radford, and there's nothing you can do about it." Angrily, she pulled her cloak across her shoulders and started to rise. "I believe we've said all we need to say. If you'll excuse me—"

"Does Radford know of the child?"

"Why should that matter?" she asked, one brow lifted hesitantly as she watched him run a thumb along the calluses of one hand, slowly interlace his fingers, then place his elbows against the table and rest his chin on his fist.

He shrugged apathetically. "Because if he doesn't, you just might find yourself on my doorstep again, begging to be taken in."

Alanna clenched her teeth. "Don't count on it," she said, leaving her chair. He caught her wrist, not painfully, but enough to halt her departure. She glared down at him.

"I think there is something else you should know." He nodded toward the empty chair. "Please," he added, when she made no move to do as he instructed.

When she had sat down again, he carefully looked about them to make certain no one would hear. "Through various business dealings, I've discovered that Briarwood Manor is in serious trouble. There is a great chance everything Rad owns will be taken from him by

333

creditors. Since I care a great deal about him, and now with the child, I simply want to offer my financial help. He doesn't have to know."

Alanna stared at him quietly, a smile slowly spreading across her face. "How kind of you, sir, but your sources have failed you or they would have told you of my gift to Radford."

"Gift?"

"Yes. I transferred enough funds to him to keep those creditors away," she told him with a lift to her chin. "So you see, Mr. Remington, we don't need your help, nor do we want it."

"And where would you get enough money to do that?"

"An inheritance, sir. I only wish I had received it long ago. Then I wouldn't find myself sitting here talking with you now. I would have returned home to England and everyone would be happy."

He nodded. "Maybe. But what's stopping you from doing it now?"

"There's nothing left for me in England."

Leaning back in his chair, he folded his arms across his chest, eyeing her doubtfully. "But what of the boy you spoke of once? Surely he would be most anxious to have you, if what you said was true."

Alanna's eyes narrowed. "If you were he, would you be eager to open your arms and accept a woman who carries another man's child? I think not, Mr. Remington."

He straightened sharply. "And that's the whole point, Alanna. It is *my* child, *my* flesh and blood, and I will not be cheated of it."

She rose haughtily. "Then you should have contemplated the possibility before you planted your seed. It is too late now and you shall pay the price. We don't need you any longer and I would appreciate it if you will take great care in staying away. Good-bye, Mr. Remington," she said, tossing her cape about her before moving away.

Beau sat in silence, staring at the chair that had only moments before held her. All of a sudden he felt empty, as if the world was closing in on him. He was alone and he knew what she had said was true. He had done this to himself. He turned in his chair for one last look at her, but she denied him that as well. He sighed, a long, unexpected sigh that shook his whole body. Dejectedly, he rose and left the dining hall.

Twenty-Three

The icy winds of December bellowed the sails of the ships anchored off the docks of Williamsburg, tossing the smaller crafts about as if they were leaves pressed against the ocean's watery face. A single rowboat challengingly trudged through the white-capped water haphazardly zigzagging toward shore, its two dark figures struggling with the oars. The blackened sky hissed small droplets of rain that stung the faces of those seeking shelter, their heads down for protection against the assault and unaware of the pair about to join them.

Stepping from the boat, they started off toward a nearby pub, their coats clutched tightly beneath their chins to keep the biting cold wind from cutting through them like the blade of a knife. Their step quickened as the door of the pub came within reach and one of them had just lifted a hand to the latch when a shrill whistle behind them pierced the night. They turned wary, suspecting gazes upon the black man who motioned for them to wait.

"What is it, boy?" one of them demanded, his hand resting on the butt of his pistol stuck in his breeches.

"A moment of yo' time, sir. And for a profit."

"Where would ya be gettin' silver for me pocket?" the other laughed.

"Not me, sir. My mistress. Over there." He pointed.

Inside the carriage, Blythe shook in fear as she watched the black man and the two strangers look her way. "Oh, Melissa, this is crazy."

"Hush. They won't hurt us. Not when they find out what's in it for them."

Blythe sank down in the seat. "Why did I ever let you talk me into this?" she muttered.

"Oh, stop your whining. You thought it was a good idea when we talked of it last week. It's no different now," Melissa reminded her, peering outside at the trio again.

"But I never dreamed they'd be so—so—"

"Evil looking?"

Blythe nodded.

"Well, what did you expect? They're pirates."

"And how do you know they won't just run off with your money? Or maybe kill her?" Blythe said with a brave lift to her chin. "Did you think of that?"

Melissa sighed impatiently. "Yes, Blythe, I have. That's why I've decided to only pay them half the amount I offer now. The rest when the job is completed. Besides," she said with an evil grin, "I don't really care if they do kill her."

Blythe's face paled. "I never agreed to be party to murder."

"Shush. It's too late now, anyway. Here they come."

The carriage groaned with the weight of the two seamen as they climbed in, having had Melissa's consent, and took the seat opposite the women. The orange light

338

from the lantern that hung above the door of the carriage danced across the men's faces, and for a moment terror surged through Melissa's veins. Although dressed cleanly enough, not at all what she had expected, the size and nearness of them reminded her that this was not a game she was playing. The smaller of the two wore a beard that nearly covered his entire face, while the dull brown hair on his head fell in disarray about his brow, leaving only a small opening for his eyes. He stared at her without blinking. Then she looked at the other man and gasped.

He wore a tricorn with a large plume stuck beneath the band, which did little to shadow his face and the grotesque scar that ran from his temple to below his chin. Nor did it hide the thick mass of red hair covering his ears. His brows, just as thick and red, failed to disguise the furrowing beneath them as he studied her in a quiet mood of suspicion. His thin lips, set in a straight line, masked any emotion, and his nostrils, the only thing that moved, boldly warned Melissa that this was not a figment of her imagination.

"May I assume that one of you two gentlemen is the captain of the ship which recently anchored off shore?" she asked, managing to find her voice. Even to her it sounded shaky.

Neither of them replied.

Melissa drew a breath again and could feel her chin quiver as she cleared her throat to go on. "It is important that I speak with him."

Still they only stared.

She shot Blythe a glance and found her cringing in the corner, her knuckles pressed against her lips, her eyes wide with fear and, knowing she would be of no help,

Melissa turned back, absently running her tongue across her lips, for they had suddenly gone dry. "I assure you, this is not some sort of trap the British soldiers have devised to catch you. No one knows we are here."

She watched the bigger man purposely pull back his cape, revealing the huge, many-jeweled handle of his dagger resting in the scabbard that hung from his belt. The carriage light seemed to spotlight its way to it, reflecting a multitude of colors, which danced intimidatingly across his face. He smiled when he saw her eyes widen. "I be havin' no such fear, lass," he said in a thick Irish brogue. "In fact, I can't be thinkin' of anythin' that frightens me." A smile flashed across his face again. "My name is Dillon Gallagher. And to whom do I owe this pleasure?"

Melissa could feel her heart pounding in her chest. "My name is of no importance," she said, stumbling over her words. "The bargain I propose is."

"A bargain, is it? And what could a grand lady like yourself be wantin' ta make a bargain with the likes of me?" he asked, relaxing in the soft lights of the carriage.

"To have someone disposed of," she said, feeling her knees shake.

"Then 'tis a hired assassin you be seekin'?"

"No, no! I do not mean killed. Merely that the person be removed from the area. To New Orleans, perhaps."

"Then I'm afraid I can't be helpin' ya. We won't be settin' sail in that direction."

"But you will be well paid for your inconveniences, captain. Do not think me a fool," she retorted.

"And how else would I be thinkin'?" he asked, calmly looking about the small cubical they shared. "I see no man here to protect you."

Melissa's heart pounded in her throat, certain an ill fate awaited her when she saw Gallagher smile impishly.

"But, of course, I could change me mind if what you say strikes me fancy. Suppose you explain what it is ya be wantin'." He settled back against the thick leather seat, crossed his arms, and waited.

Again, Melissa looked at Blythe. She hadn't moved, but Melissa noticed the paleness of her face, and was certain that at any moment the young girl would faint. Drawing in a deep breath to calm her own nerves, she found it difficult to swallow before voicing her proposal. Straightening courageously, she said, "I am here at the urging of a very close—shall we say—friend. We are willing to pay you a thousand pounds as soon as you have the woman on board—"

"A thousand pounds for a woman?" Gallagher cut in.

"Yes, a woman. Does that make a difference?"

Thoughtful a moment, he idly ran a fingertip along the length of his scar, making it appear to be uglier than before. "I guess not. Whether I be paid in full, that does."

"And you shall be," she assured him. "You are to take her to New Orleans and sell her to a brothel by the name of Entre Nous. I know of the proprietor, and once the money has changed hands, he will contact me. Then you shall return here the last of next month and receive another thousand pounds. Agreed?"

"An easy enough way to make a livin'. I wonder what surprises might await me, though."

"Surprises?"

"Aye, lass. Ya not mention how difficult it be to find the lass or if someone else might not be agreein' with her hasty departure."

341

"Leave that to me," Melissa said, pulling open the strings of her purse. "I will send a message to her to meet someone here in two days."

"And how will I be knowin' her?"

"She'll be wearing a red bonnet. Now do you agree?" Melissa asked.

Gallagher tapped a fingertip against his lower lip, silently contemplating the deal. "Aye, lass. Agreed."

"Good." Melissa smiled for the first time. "And give this to her once you are out to sea. It's very important."

Gallagher took the paper she held out to him, stuffed it into his shirt and nodded to his companion. Once they climbed from the carriage, he stopped and looked back at her. "I shall be gettin' down on me knees this night and pray to all that's holy that a poor Irish boy like meself will never have cause to anger you so. It would surely be the death of me," he said, touching a fingertip to the edge of his tricorn before he threw back his head and laughed wildly, a sound that renewed Melissa's fear.

The morning sky grew dark with gray, threatening clouds and the promise of sleet before the day was out. But it failed to dull Alanna's enthusiasm. Standing before the mirror in her room, she smiled at her reflection, knowing that within the hour she would be with Radford. The crimson velvet gown clung tightly against her breasts, shimmering with each breath she took, its bodice falling in generous folds over her thickening waistline. It flattered her, she thought, reaching up to pick away a piece of lint from her shoulder, and wondered hopefully if Radford would agree.

She looked at the small clock sitting on top of the

mantel and knew she must hurry. His note had said eleven o'clock, and for a fleeting instant she wondered again why he had chosen the docks as a place to meet. Shrugging it off, she went to the hat box laying on the bed and removed the lid. Lovingly, she lifted the red bonnet from it and returned to the mirror to appraise its beauty as she tied the satin ribbon in a bow just below her ear. Of all the gifts Radford had sent to her, she was sure she loved the bonnet most.

With an added zeal to her step, Alanna skipped down the staircase and out the front door, heading for the livery stable and a buggy she might hire.

The wind had picked up by the time her rented carriage pulled onto the main thoroughfare to the docks, stinging her cheeks and bringing moisture to her eyes. She huddled deeper into her lap blanket, tucking its edges beneath her thighs, and scanned the horizon for any sign of Radford. Ahead of her, she could see the harbor and its docks filled with ships; recognizing the flag of England flapping in the breeze atop the mainmast, her heart ached in a momentary twinge of sadness as she recalled the weeks she had spent on a very similar ship.

Suddenly her carriage screeched to a halt, nearly throwing her from the seat. Readjusting her bonnet, she glanced up to discover the cause of such an unwarranted mishap, finding the narrow road crowded with numerous freight wagons, all of which seemed destined for the docks, and blocking her path. Moving closer to claim the lead, two of the wagons nearly collided, and she watched, wide-eyed, as their drivers irately climbed down to discuss the ineptitude of the other's skills. A display of fisticuffs ensued only a yard or two away from her and she sat terrified, observing the men roll about on the

343

ground, kicking and hitting and screaming vile words at one another. Paralyzed by the open demonstration of brutality and helpless to curtail it, her attention rested solely on the scene before her, failing to notice two burly seamen approach her buggy from either side until one of them pressed a foot to the carriage step.

"What do you want?" she demanded, her voice lacking authority.

Shifting his weight, the second ruffian made to climb in.

"Stay out!"

Panic-stricken and knowing no good could come of this, Beau's warning not to venture near the docks even with him ringing in her ears, she twisted out of the lap blanket binding her legs, hoping to knock one of them out of the way and allow her the chance to run. But as she reached up to strike the first, a meaty fist came from behind her to seize her arm, throwing her off balance and easily allowing the other seaman to encircle her knees in his arms. Kicking and screaming wildly, she was carried from the buggy.

"Radford," she squalled. "Please, someone help me!"

Tears streaked down her face and blurred her vision of the assailants, a death-fearing pain cramping the muscles across her chest. She opened her mouth for another desperate plea, her jaw forced open further by the foul-smelling rag terminating the alarm. Its rancid odor gagged her.

With both arms held cruelly behind her, the pain the seaman inflicted stilled any desire she had to kick out again when the other barbarian released his hold on her legs. Her eyes widened in fear, watching him raise a fist high above his shoulder and bring it down with a stinging

344

blow to her temple.

The men easily covered the limp form with a burlap bag, securing the end of it with a rope about her knees. Without a single glance in any direction to indicate any concern about their misdeed, one of them lifted the small weight in his arms, threw it over his shoulder in a none too gentle fashion, and started off down the street, his partner close behind.

From within the darkened recesses of her carriage, a pair of sea-green eyes watched intently as the bundle wrapped in burlap was carried away. A smile flitted across Melissa's face.

Twenty-Four

Darkness pressed in around her. Not a single light could penetrate the heavy weave of the burlap. She sat very still, listening to the scratchings of something at her feet, fearfully aware of the rodent that brazenly snuck closer to her. She retreated further to her corner of the room. Her side ached. She wanted to cry. The pounding in her temples was unbearable. A whimper filled the room and she dug her nails into the palms of her hands, realizing it had been her own voice that had cried out. She was alone. Where, she didn't know, but she heard them bolt the door after they threw her down. God, help me, her mind screamed.

Alanna jumped at the sudden grinding of a chain only inches from her. Chains? she questioned. What could it mean? It sounded again. She concentrated on it, remembering another time she had heard a similar noise. She shook off her thoughts. It couldn't be. That had been the anchor of the *Sea Wind* just before they set sail for England. A ship? Dear God! It couldn't mean she had been put on board a ship. But why? Who would kidnap a woman and put her on a ship? Even in the blackness of the foul-smelling cloth, the reason came to light.

Muffled voices and hurried foosteps filtered through and she could only assume they had dropped the sails. Soon they would put out to sea, and she knew if she didn't free herself quickly she would be their unwilling passenger. Frantically, she tore at the rope binding her knees, her fingers growing numb in their attempt, when of a sudden she heard a rendering tear of cloth as the rotted seams of the bag gave away. Desperately, she stripped it from her.

A thin stream of muted light from under the door acted as a beacon guiding her way to it. Praying against all hope, she seized the knob, imploring it to open with her touch. But the lock held firm. The ship listed a gentle reminder that it was underway, bringing panic to the small woman held prisoner in its belly.

"No," she screamed, beating her fists against the uncompromising barrier, pain shooting through her body until, at last, she crumpled into a heap before the door, sobs racking her small frame.

Impossible to judge the time. Alanna could only guess that several hours had passed since her capture and the ship's having set sail, giving her time to think. If it was gold they sought, she would offer as much as it would take to free herself. Surely one of the men on board had heard of Radford Chamberlain.

"More likely they know of Beau Remington. These are the kind who strike me as his friends," she hissed in the darkness. "Excuse me, captain, but I was once a slave of your best friend. Would you mind telling him that I'm

348

here?" She laughed sarcastically. Then her laughter turned to tears, filling her with despair. "Please, God. Don't let them use me. I am with child and it would surely take his life from me!"

The sound of something heavy being dragged across the deck overhead reverberated in her prison, startling her, and she wrapped her arms about her for what comfort it might bring. Silence came again. A scratching noise beside her made her jump, and she crawled across the darkened space to seek safety in another corner. The ship moaned with the current of the sea, and the awful darkness around her began to take its toll. Was this the way it was to be? Would she be held prisoner in this black cavity until the men had need of her, then returned to it to suffer her abuse in private?

Distant footsteps clicked against the wooden deck. She wiped the tears from her cheeks, listening to them grow louder, and she knew full well they were coming for her. Should she hide? For what good? They knew she couldn't have escaped. It would only be unrewarding to try. Should she attempt to overcome the man at the door and run from him? Where would she go? To an icy, watery grave? Feeling total defeat, she struggled to her feet to meet her destiny with what dignity she had left.

The door groaned open, flooding light in and instantly blinding her until the figure of a man crossed it and put her in the shadow of his body. He seemed three times her size, and Alanna felt a momentary shudder of fear standing before him.

"Capt'n wants to see ya," his gruff voice told her. "Says not to hurt ya, but if ya refuse, I'm ta bring ya any way I can."

"I'll come," she replied, stepping past him into the

narrow passageway leading to the ladder and topside.

Once they reached the main deck, she paused, breathing in the clear, fresh air and ridding her nostrils of the musty, wretched odor of the hold. It felt good to have the sun warm her face again. She bit her lower lip, knowing it would be a strain for her to return to the confines of her prison.

"He said straight away," the voice behind her warned, the palm of his hand giving her a shove.

She stumbled and nearly fell, only the railing of the ship keeping her on her feet. Fearfully, she glanced back at the man, but first noticed the multitude of eyes upon her. Every mate on board stared quietly at her, a few without expression, some with an unmistakable lustful gleam in their eye. She cringed, wondering which one would be the first.

"Get to work," someone shouted and she quickly looked away, listening to their disgruntled voices as they returned to their tasks. How long would a simple word keep them in place?

"Wait here," the man at her side instructed before knocking on a door and disappearing inside.

Alone, she leaned back against the bulkhead to study her surroundings and gather what composure she could. Her gaze traveled up the length of the mainmast, its base thicker than her arms could encompass and seeming to narrow to a fine black line in the cloudless blue sky. She watched in amazement as one of the men climbed the riggings, his agile bare feet skipping from one rope to another on his way to the mainsail and to secure it in place with the lanyards. His task completed, he descended the riggings in much the same manner, the tensed, hardened muscles of his shoulders and back straining the seams of his shirt. She looked away, hoping he had not noticed how she stared.

A gravel-throated chant drifted up, drawing her attention to the men on the half deck, crouched on hands and knees as they sang an unfamiliar song in rhythm to each stroke of the brush with which they scrubbed the deck. None of them wore pistols stuck in their breeches, and she frowned, wondering why. Surely pirates never walked about without some sort of weapon. Then she spied a great number of wooden barrels stacked neatly in a row and she cautiously inched her way back to the railing to look over the side and confirm her suspicions. Protruding from every gunport, she could see the black muzzle of a cannon, poised and ready. Her spirits sank to even lower depths as she realized that when Radford came to rescue her he wouldn't stand a chance against a ship as ready and armed as this.

"Look alive! I'm talkin' to ya!"

Alanna jumped at the sharp sound of his voice. "I'm sorry. I was only—"

"The capt'n 'ill see ya now," he snarled.

"Yes, sir," she mumbled, and wearily followed him inside the cabin.

Alanna could hardly believe her eyes. The captain's quarters were bigger than anything she could have imagined, with a huge mahogany desk sitting boldly in the center, an ornately carved high-back chair behind it, and a bunk nestled in one wall that she was certain would sleep the whole crew. But what captured her attention was the aft of the ship filled with hundreds of small paned windows, each of' which allowed the streams of sunlight to penetrate the room and flood it with a bright yellow glow. She stood in awe until her eyes fell upon the man standing off to one side staring out at the ever changing surface of the sea, a mug held tightly in one hand, a cigar in the other. He had yet to look at her, and she found the moment both awkward and frightening. His short, round figure proclaimed the fact that he lacked for nothing. The breeches and shirt he wore indicated wealth, the rings upon one hand were priceless and the minutely carved, many-jeweled pistol was stuck beneath the sash he wore at his waist. His hair, combed neatly and pulled in back to knot above his collar, shimmered red then gold then red again, and Alanna could only stare. Suddenly, he belched, and she jumped at the sound, bumping into the man at her side.

"Stand still, wench," he growled, and she instantly moved away, feeling the palms of her hands grow moist with perspiration.

"Yes, sir," she mumbled in hardly a whisper, casting him a respectful glance before looking at the captain again. Her eyes widened in fear, and before the scream could escape her, she pressed her knuckles to her mouth to stifle the sound. Only a small gasp cut through the silence. She swallowed hard, her eyes trained on the purplish scar that trailed down the man's face, never moving as she watched him nod to her companion. A moment later she heard the door swing closed and she could feel her body tremble, beginning at her knees and working upward until even her teeth chattered.

"Must ya be gawkin' so, lass? I know I am an ugly sort, but I figured ya to be a lady."

Alanna swallowed the knot in her throat and pulled her gaze from him.

"That's better," he said, taking a drink from the mug

352

and belching again. "T'isn't Irish whiskey, but it will have ta be doin'. Care for a drink, lass?"

Fearfully, she shook her head.

"Ah, ya don't drink, now, do ya? Forgive me. I should have known better."

Horrified, Alanna glanced about the room, carefully avoiding the captain. He frowned.

"What is it ya be lookin' for?" he asked. "A pistol to blow out me brains?" He laughed loudly. "Would be senseless. I think ya be outnumbered."

"Please, sir," she begged, finding her voice. "Tell me why you've brought me here? Is it ransom you seek?"

"Ransom," he mused, contemplating the idea as he eased his bulk into a chair. "And are ya worth a great deal of money?"

"No. But my betrothed would pay whatever you ask."

"Your betrothed?" he questioned.

"Yes," Alanna eagerly volunteered. "Maybe you've heard of him. His name is Radford Chamberlain."

"Radford—" Gallagher began. "Aye, that I have. But I don't think he'll be helpin' ya none."

"Oh, but he will. Just send word to him," she pleaded, and Gallagher raised a hand to quiet her.

"T'isn't that I wouldn't do as ya ask. I simply don't think he be carin'."

A frown knotted her brow. "I don't understand."

"Here," he said, pulling the paper Melissa had given him from the drawer of his desk and sliding it across the surface at her, "read this. I think then you'll be knowin' what I mean."

Cautiously, and full of mistrust, Alanna slowly walked to the edge of the desk and picked up the paper that lay upon it.

My dear,
    I know you will probably never understand why
I've done this horrible thing to you, but, given time,
you will see it was for the best. I have found that I
really love her and you would only be in the way.

                                                    Radford

The blood drained from her face. Everything in the
room began to spin, and before Captain Gallagher could
reach her, Alanna fell limp to the floor, Radford's note
clutched tightly in her hand.

"Ya gave me a start, lass," she heard a strange voice
say.

Alanna's eyes fluttered opened then closed again.

"Now don't ya go swoonin' on me again. I know ya had
a fright, but t'isn't as bad as ya think."

Alanna turned her head away from his voice. Even
with her eyes squeezed tightly closed, a tear managed to
steal down her cheek. How could he possibly understand
that her world had crumbled, that she was alone again,
only this time she had an unborn child to think of.
Instinctively she pressed her hand against the growing
life within her.

"Now don't be worryin' about the babe, lass. The two
of you will be makin' out just fine. 'Tis better off without
him, anyway."

Alanna's chin quivered as she fought to control the
flood of tears threatening to break free. He had no idea
what Radford meant to her. How could he? And how

could he assume life without him would be better? When she had agreed to marry Radford, she had thought to free herself from the hold Beau had on her, to make a new life with a man whom she thought loved her, and to give her unborn child a father who would love and take care of it. Now all of that was gone. There was nothing left for her.

"Did ya hear me, lass?"

Alanna opened her eyes and looked at him, cringing when she saw the scar.

"Now don't be lookin' at me like that," he scolded lightheartedly. "I won't be hurtin' ya. I had no idea ya was carryin' a babe or no amount of silver would have brought ya on me ship." He rose and returned to his desk.

"You mean you'll let me go?" she asked, suddenly filled with hope.

Gallagher chuckled as he eased himself into the chair. "No, child. Ya mean money to me."

"Money?" Alanna frowned, pushing herself up on her elbows. "But I have none. How could you think that I'm worth money to you?"

Resting an elbow against the desk top with a thumb pressed against his cheek, his finger slowly trailed along the outline of his upper lip. He watched her out of the corner of his eye. "The deal was half a sum for kidnapping ya, the other once I'd sold ya to a brothel in New Orleans."

"A—a brothel?" Alanna choked, her tears renewing and clouding her vision of him. "You mean he instructed you to sell me to a place like that?"

"Aye, would appear so."

She sat up, feeling the painful beat of her heart against her chest. "But he didn't have to do that. If he had changed his mind about marrying me all he would have had to do was say so. I would not have held him to it."

Gallagher's brows shadowed his eyes. "Are ya forgettin' about the babe?"

Alanna shook her head. "It isn't his."

"Would ya have married its father then?" he asked, straightening in his chair, the furrowing of his brows noting his confusion.

Again, Alanna shook her head. "He wouldn't have married me."

"The scum," Gallagher roared. "And who might the blackheart be?"

Surprised by his anger, she stared wide-eyed. "Why do you ask?"

"Ya might be thinkin' me nothin' but a pirate and one without principles, but I ain't one for likin' to see a woman wrongly used. What's his name, lass?" he demanded.

"Remington," Alanna whispered, shrinking back into the haven of his bunk.

"Beau Remington, The Hawk?"

She nodded slowly. "You've heard of him?" she asked.

Leaning back in his chair, he smiled broadly. "Aye, that I have. Before me alliance with England, I sailed their seas and pirated their vessels. It was me bad luck that one of them be belongin' to Beau Remington. He sent an army of men ta find me. That's how I got this," he said running his thumb along the purplish scar. "Cost me me ship and nearly me life." He sat up and laughed. "I've never met the man, lass, but I don't mind tellin' ya, I wouldn't be likin' ta meet up with one as determined as him."

"Don't worry," she sighed. "You won't be meeting him on account of me. He doesn't care what happens to

356

me." She reached up to catch a tear before it could run down her face. "No one cares anymore."

Dillon cocked his head to one side, raising a brow. "Feelin' sorry for yourself, are ya?" he asked with a smile.

Alanna glanced up at him and looked away.

"Ya should be afraid," he reminded her.

She smiled wearily. "Afraid. Afraid of what? There isn't much left for me to be afraid of."

"Then ya be wantin' to live in a whorehouse?" he asked. "Ya be wantin' men to touch ya, ta kiss ya, to squeeze your tits and run their hands up your skirts? Come now, surely ya can't be meanin' that?"

Alanna fought down the bile that rose in her throat. "It will never happen."

"Oh?" he sang. "And how will ya be stoppin' it?"

"I'd kill myself first," she said quietly.

Dillon's breath caught in his throat, his mind instantly filled with memories, recalling the day his mother died giving birth to his younger sister. Shortly after that his father had deserted them, and he had been left to raise a young child on his own, not much more than a child himself. In many ways the young girl he now found himself with reminded him of Bevin. Her hair was just as black, her eyes just as pleading, and what she had just admitted reminded him of something he had tried for years to forget.

Bevin had only been in her fourteenth summer, blossoming into full womanhood. She was gentle and kind and in a flattering way so shy she would many times hide behind her brother whenever a boy would speak to her. Dillon had loved her. More than he loved life, and he would have done anything to protect her.

He had gone to work at the docks unloading the ships that constantly anchored there, leaving Bevin alone in their small room over the pub near the waterfront. He had worked late that night, coming home in the early hours of morning to find a wild crowd of men in the street in front of the pub. Hanging from a tree in the yard dangled the lifeless form of a man.

"'Tis what he deserved," someone shouted.

"I say we should have cut it off and let him bleed to death. Hangin' is too good for him," another cried out.

Puzzled by the scene and suddenly worried about Bevin, Dillon pushed his way into the crowded pub. More angry voices greeted him and soon Dillon learned that the dead man had abused a young girl. Fear flooded over him and he shoved his way through the men, heading for the stairs and Bevin. When he reached the top, John O'Mally, proprietor of the pub, stepped out in front of him and blocked his way to the room he shared with his sister.

"Don't go in, lad," O'Mally warned.

Dillon stepped back, his body rigid with fear. "What's happened?"

"'Tis Bevin," he said sadly. "She's been hurt."

"Oh, God," Dillon screamed, pushing his way past the man.

A woman sat by the side of the bed, holding Bevin's whimpering form in her arms. When the woman looked up, he could see that she, too, cried. She immediately let go of the girl, and Dillon could then see the ugly bruises covering Bevin's pretty face. Her eyes found him and she started to cry hysterically.

"Oh, Bevin," he whispered holding her tightly in his embrace, "please forgive me. I never should have been

358

leavin' ya alone." They sat, cradled in each other's arms, until the morning light came stealing into the room.

Two days later, Bevin Gallagher put a knife to her throat.

"I'll not be listenin' to talk like that," Dillon bellowed, shaking off his memories. "And I won't be sellin' ya to a damned brothel, either." He rose angrily from the chair, crossed to the door of the cabin, and threw it open. "Parker," he screamed, "fetch me a bottle of whiskey."

Alanna watched him, wide-eyed, wondering what had brought about his sudden and angry change of mind. Surely she meant nothing to him, but it was as if her threat of death had sparked a compassionate side of him, one she had never expected. He was a man who looted and killed for a living, and one more death on his head certainly couldn't cause him such guilt as it now appeared it would. She huddled in the far corner of his bunk afraid to breathe much less voice her questions.

"I'll not be leadin' ya ta think I'd put a pretty face ahead of money," he said, strolling back to the desk. "I be havin' need of it more. But I won't be leavin' a woman in the motherly way to the hands of anyone with the price." He sat down in his chair again, one elbow resting on the desk top to support his chin against the knuckles of his hand, the other pressed against the arm of his chair, the elbow cocked and in the air. A dark scowl shadowed his face, adding to the already menacing lines of his brow as he pondered an idea. "Ah," he grinned suddenly, "I think I have it. We'll find a worthy street wench, loan her the use of your name, and that way I have me money and you your freedom." He sat smiling at her until another thought crossed his mind. "What's your name, lass?"

"Bainbridge. Alanna Bainbridge, sir," she said hastily.

"Alanna," he hummed, pursing his lips as a finger slowly scratched his thick neck. "Sounds Irish ta me. Ya wouldn't be from me homeland, now would ya?"

"No, sir," she hesitated, wondering if it would be the right answer. "England."

"England?" he scoffed with a raised brow. "Ha! Ah, well, everyone has a cross to bear, so ta speak," he grinned playfully, leaning back in his chair to study her. She was such a tiny thing, so frail and innocent, so much like—he frowned. Radford Chamberlain ought to be hung from the yardarm.

Twenty Five

Beau frowned, staring out the window of his room at the
Chesterfield House. Where is she? he wondered, looking
at the people on the sidewalk below him, their heads
down to brace themselves against the cold. All that
seemed important to them at the moment was keeping
warm. His expression softened. And why not? Who was
Alanna to them anyway? His gaze wandered to the
horizon dotted with what seemed hundreds of masts,
their yardarms blanketed with rolled-up sails while they
anchored off shore, recalling the previous morning,
when Radford had raced his buggy up the drive of Raven
Oaks. Alanna had disappeared without a trace or a word
left behind. Had she had a change of heart and returned
to England, too afraid to face Radford with the truth, that
she would rather return home than marry him? To what?
he frowned. Her parents were dead and there was
nothing, no one there. It didn't make sense. Something
had to have happened to her. From what Radford said he
had learned from the old woman who owned the
boardinghouse where Alanna stayed, Alanna had been

happy and content, looking forward to her wedding. When she had not returned for supper that evening, Mrs. Allison had, in fact, thought she was with her betrothed. But when the second evening had passed without any word from Alanna, Mrs. Allison grew very concerned, sending a message to Briarwood Manor in hopes of finding Alanna there.

A knocking at his door brought him around to stare at it a moment. Then, before answering it, he went to the small table in the room and poured a glass of wine. Radford could probably use it.

"Good morning, Rad," he said drily, closing the door behind him and handing him the glass. "Did you sleep well?"

Radford shrugged, downing the entire contents of his drink. "Not much." He eased himself onto the sofa of the sitting room, knees apart and leaning his elbows against them as he studied the empty glass. "What's happened to her?" he asked for what seemed the thousandth time.

Beau returned to the window in silence. He looked outside again.

"I knew it was too good to be true," Radford muttered.

Beau didn't answer, already knowing what Radford was thinking since they had held the same conversation over and over again for the past three days. Strangely enough, it had yet to grate on Beau's nerves.

"I loved her the very first time I saw her. Didn't you, Beau?" Radford asked, looking up, his eyes glistening with tears.

"Rad," Beau replied softly, looking back over his shoulder at him, "you make it sound like the end. You of all people mustn't give up hope. We'll find her."

"You really believe that?" Radford asked forlornly.

Beau smiled gently. "Of course, I do. That's why I'm here, isn't it? We agreed the best place to start would be here in town where she was last seen."

Leaving the sofa, Radford crossed to the hearth where he pressed the palm of his hand to the mantel. Staring into the fire, he said softly, "You don't suppose she changed her mind about me and went home to England, do you?"

"I asked myself those same questions just before you came. The answer is no."

"How can you be so sure?" Radford asked, continuing to watch the flames dance brightly at his feet.

"Just think about it. First off, she doesn't have any money. So how could she have afforded passage? Secondly, what did she have to return to? No," Beau added with a shake of his head and looking back outside again, "there's no logical reason for her to have left of her own accord. Unfortunately, I think someone else had a hand in it."

"Then why hasn't someone come forth with the truth? It's been two days since you sent word of a reward for any information about her. No one has said a thing."

Beau studied the crowd of people on the street. "You must remember the kind of people we're dealing with. They'll want to be very careful about being seen with either of us."

The loud shattering of glass startled Beau into turning around to stare at his friend, noticing the shiny fragments of crystal lying on the marble slab at his feet, and Radford's hand empty. "I never should have let her stay in town. I should have made her move to Briarwood Manor. Dear God, why didn't I?"

"Take it easy, Rad," Beau soothed from his vigil at the

363

window. "Whoever is responsible would have found a different way to lure her from you. Don't blame yourself."

"But why? What did Alanna ever do to anyone?" Radford demanded.

Their eyes met and held for a long while, until, unable to endure the torment he saw on Radford's face, Beau looked away. "I don't know."

Several minutes passed, and Beau quietly listened to Radford pour himself a fresh drink before coming to his side at the window. He, too, stared outside.

"You do love her, don't you, Beau?" he asked softly.

Beau could feel a quickening in his chest and a warmth spread throughout him to linger hotly against his cheeks. "It doesn't matter," he said.

"But it does. To me."

Beau glanced up, then back outside. "Why?"

"Because I want to know that should anything ever happen to me Alanna will be cared for."

Beau chuckled. "I'm sure you're aware of how I cared for her before. Doesn't sound like a wise request."

Radford studied the wine in his glass as he swirled it around. "Alanna never understood what caused you to react the way you did. But I do."

Beau looked at him, one brow cocked.

"She had gotten to you in a way no other woman ever had. You struck out at her trying to deny the fact, to do everything possible to prove she didn't mean a thing to you."

Beau's mouth twisted into a half-smile. "If that's true, then why did you offer her marriage?"

Radford's eyes sparkled for the first time in days. "I'm not a saint. I love her. And since you were stupid enough

364

to cast her aside, I stepped in." His gaze drifted downward. "Now I wish I hadn't."

Beau considered the man's face for several minutes, then looked to the toes of his boots and finally outside again. "I just don't understand why you make it sound so urgent."

"Because it is," Radford said, strolling back to the fireplace. "Briarwood Manor is near collapse."

"I'm afraid I already knew that."

Radford chuckled. "It figures. I never could keep my problems a secret, and you always warned me that I mismanaged my affairs. Now I'm paying the price. But if I know you'll not let Alanna suffer for my foolishness, I can marry her without worry. Oh, please, Beau. It means so much to me."

"She'd never agree," Beau warned.

"She wouldn't have to know. I'm positive you could hide it from her. Just as you hide your love." Seeing the expression on Beau's face, Radford grinned. "You never could fool me, Beau Remington."

A smile brightened Beau's eyes and he laughed. "No, I never could. And I promise that if the need arises, I will see to Alanna's care. Now are you satisfied, my big, dumb friend?"

Radford nodded playfully with a salute of his glass and an obvious look of relief on his face. However, it slowly changed into one of concern. "You know," he said, "standing around here isn't doing any good. Maybe we should go back and talk with Mrs. Allison again. Maybe there was something she forgot to tell us."

Beau shook his head. "She already said she didn't talk to Alanna that morning."

"Yeah, I know," Radford agreed, "but I'd feel better if

365

we were doing something other than standing here drinking wine. Who knows, maybe someone will try to contact us there."

Contemplating the idea, Beau realized the room had seemed to close in on him, too, in the past few hours. "All right," he said. "I'd like to have her tell us what went on the days before Alanna disappeared, anyway."

"Why would that matter?"

"If this thing was planned, it had to have started long before, and it's just possible something out of the ordinary happened to Alanna that would give us a clue. Get your coat," he said, reaching for his own.

A light snow blanketed the streets, marked by the telltale footprints of those who walked the waterfront in early morning. Stillness replaced the usual sounds, as, for the most part, everyone sought refuge inside by a warm fire. Cain pulled the collar of his coat in close to his chin, bracing himself against the cold as wet crystals flittered about, heading for yet another pub where he might sit and listen without notice. When he reached the door, he paused, glancing back down the street, a dismal look about him. His luck had not been good so far, and he could only hope it would change soon. Too many people depended on it.

As he had expected, the pub was filled with men, sailors mostly, and he pulled his well-worn hat down further over his brow, not wanting to run the risk of recognition by even a single man. What he wanted to learn must come from an unsuspecting source, from one who would not twist the truth for the mere pleasure of misleading.

He took a seat at the small table near a group, ordered a tankard of ale and waited, quietly sipping the brew and watching the men from the corner of his eye. They talked of the long journey they had just completed and the storms they had encountered at sea. They had only been in port a few hours, and Cain knew they were not the men he sought.

He focused his attention on another circle of ruffians and listened to their sordid exchanges about the night past, each trying to outdo the other in an exaggerated account of his manhood.

"Aye, and if ya hadn't had that aching in yer loins, ya'd be on yer ship now," one of them laughed.

The victim of his jest sent him a hate-filled glare before downing his drink. "How was I to know they'd set sail so soon?" he growled, wiping the drool from his chin with the back of his hand.

"I'll bet he ain't even missed!" still another laughed.

"You scum would be laughin' out the other side of your face if it was you," he hissed.

"Browny, my boy, none of us would be that stupid!"

Browny sat upright in his chair, his glazed eyes trained on the man who had insulted him. "Oh, yeah? What makes you think so?" he demanded.

The man looked at his partner, half chuckled, and leaned in on the table. "You're the one told us ya heard Gallagher order a couple of your mates to find the woman with a red bonnet and bring her back on ship quick as they could."

"Yeah, so?"

"Well, I don't think he's stupid enough to sit in dock for very long after that. You shoulda know'd that."

"We were sailin' to New Orleans. We didn't have

367

enough supplies to sail that long. I thought it'd be at least one more night."

Laughter broke out and Cain studied the men over the end of his mug, wondering if the lady of whom they talked had been willing to board or was someone who had sought the secrecy in leaving Williamsburg. Strange that she would trust herself to the hands of someone who commanded a crew with men such as Browny in it, Cain thought resting back against his chair. Gallagher, he mused, I wonder if it could be the same—

"Mr. Remington!"

Beau and Radford had just stepped from the Chesterfield House on their way to Mrs. Allison's when they heard someone call out. They stopped, turned around, and saw Cain running to catch up with them.

"Did you find out anything?" Beau asked once the man reached them.

"No," Cain replied with a disgusted shake of his head. "I've been to damn near every pub and whorehouse in the city, drunk more ale in the last six hours than I have in a lifetime, and all I have to show for it is a bad taste in my mouth."

"Now what?" Radford implored.

"We keep looking and we keep asking questions," Beau said turning back in the direction of the boarding-house. "And we'll start with Mrs. Allison."

The cozy little fire in the parlor of the boardinghouse greeted the men as they each took a seat and waited for Mrs. Allison to join them.

"She's in the kitchen," Elvira told them. "She's always in the kitchen. She never has time for me."

Beau and Cain exchanged smiles before looking away.

"She'd rather play nursemaid to any stray that came along," Elvira continued, taking a seat before the fire and, fortunately for the others, growing quiet as she studied the flames.

A few minutes passed before the sound of someone's footsteps clicked against the wooden floor of the hallway and the men looked up to see Mrs. Allison in the doorway, a tray filled with a silver tea service and sweet rolls in her hands. She smiled politely, glanced at Elvira, and entered the room.

"I hope she wasn't bothering any of you," she whispered with a nod toward the figure before the fire. "I'm afraid she has a tendency to rattle on about anything." She smiled. "Now, what can I do for you?"

"We're trying to find out if Alanna ever met with someone before she disappeared," Beau said.

"I'm sorry, Mr. Remington, but Alanna hardly went out. It's been so cold, and she heavy with child, it was too much of a strain," Mrs. Allison said, handing them each a cup of tea.

"Did she have any visitors?"

"No one, except the messengers Mr. Chamberlain sent. Would anyone care for a sweet roll?" she asked, resting her fingertips against the edge of the plate. All three declined. "I remember thinking it strange she would go out that morning," she continued, sitting down on the sofa. "She hadn't felt very good the night before. The babe's giving her trouble."

"She never looked sick to me," came a poutful remark from the corner of the room.

369

Mrs. Allison smiled. "Now Elvira—"

"Well, she didn't," the old woman scoffed, rising from her chair to shuffle across the floor toward the door. "She looked down right prissy in that red bonnet, if you ask me."

Choking on the sip of tea he had taken, Cain awkwardly replaced his cup in its saucer and wiped his chin with the back of his hand.

"Cain, are you all right?" Beau asked, coming to his side.

"A red bonnet?" Cain coughed, fighting desperately for air.

Elvira stopped just outside the door and looked back. "Yes. And I think it's much too gaudy a color for a woman in her way."

"Why does the color of her hat make a difference, Cain?" Beau asked.

Clearing his throat and wiping a knuckle to his nose, Cain swallowed a few times before he was able to speak easily again. "I didn't think much of it at the time, but I overheard some sailors talking about a woman. From what I could gather, one of them had missed his ship because it had sailed earlier than he thought it would. They had taken on a passenger and headed for New Orleans. The only reason I remember it now was because they had looked for a woman wearing a red bonnet."

"Alanna!" Radford cried out, coming to his feet.

"Did they say she had been kidnapped?" Beau asked.

Cain shook his head. "No, but they didn't say she wasn't, either. Do you suppose it was Alanna?"

Beau shrugged. "Won't know until we ask them," he said, heading for the door, pausing once he reached it. "Thank you, Mrs. Allison. You've been a great help." He

370

looked down at the small woman beside him. "And so have you, dear lady," he grinned, looking up to see that Cain lingered. "Something wrong?" he asked.

Cain fumbled with the hat he held tightly in his hands. "I think you ought to know," he said quietly, unable to meet Beau's eyes. "The men I heard talking mentioned the name of their captain." He looked up and saw Beau's questioning expression. "His name was Gallagher."

Cain's face faded into a sea of amber, orange, then red, as Beau's entire frame stiffened in rage, his chest tight with hatred, his nostrils flared, his mouth set in a hard, straight line. Dillon Gallagher!

"Radford, while Cain and I look for his sailor, you go and find a schooner that's willing to sail to New Orleans. Tell the captain we want to sail as soon as possible and we'll pay a good price for his haste," Beau said on their way to the waterfront. "If we find this sailor and he confirms our suspicions, we'll want a ship waiting."

"You got it, Beau," Radford said with a gentle slap to Beau's shoulder as he skipped from the sidewalk and broke into a run down the street away from them.

"What happens if we don't find him?" Cain asked.

"We'll take the chance it was she. Right now, we don't have any other leads. You'll stay here, see to the plantation and keep an ear open in case we were wrong."

"All right," Cain agreed, pointing out the pub a few buildings further down from them. "That's the one."

The pub was nearly empty save the one group of men seated around a table playing cards.

"Recognize anyone?" Beau whispered as they went to the bar and ordered a drink.

"No. I don't see him," Cain replied sadly. "Maybe the barkeep would remember him." He turned back, leaned his elbows against the wooden planks supported on either and by several barrels and waved a finger at the man. "Excuse me but I was wondering if you could tell me where I might find a sailor who was here earlier. He missed his ship this morning."

The barkeep shrugged. "I might," he said, drying the glass in his hands with a towel.

Cain dug into his pocket and slapped a coin on the bar. "Now can you?" he asked again.

"Sure," the barkeep said, quickly sliding the coin into his pocket as he nodded toward the stairs at the end of the room. "He's up there. Second door."

Beau and Cain wasted no time in climbing the stairs, pausing just outside the room. But when Cain put a hand to the latch, Beau touched his companion's arm as he pulled a pistol from beneath his coat.

"Just in case he doesn't feel like talking," Beau said with a lift to one brow.

The door swung open easily and both men filled the frame, Beau's pistol cocked and ready, pointing at the two figures tossing about in the bed.

"Look alive, matey," Cain mocked, a wide grin covering his face as he watched them scurry about to hide their nakedness beneath the thin blanket. Four widened eyes stared back at him.

"W-what do ya want?" Browny asked.

"A little information," Cain said, stepping inside and closing the door behind Beau. "And I suggest you be truthful or my friend here won't hesitate to put a hole in you big enough to walk through."

"Sure, sure. What do ya want to know?"

"Who was the captain of the ship that sailed without you?"

"Gallagher, Dillon Gallagher," Browny offered eagerly.

"And what about the woman?"

"What woman?" he frowned.

Beau raised the pistol.

"Oh, her," Browny half laughed. "Ah—I don't know nothin'."

Beau took a step nearer and Browny quickly raised a hand in front of him. "W-wait a minute. I meant I didn't know who she was."

"Did she hire Gallagher to take her somewhere?"

"Are you jestin'?" Browny shrieked. "Gallagher sent two of the crew to get her. Our ship was hired to take her to New Orleans, not ask if she wanted to go."

"Who hired you?"

"Don't know."

Beau took another step.

"Holy Mother!" Browny screamed. "I don't know! Honest!"

Cain looked at Beau and shrugged. "Could be telling the truth, I suppose. What do you think?"

"Well, if he isn't, I'll be back," Beau said, slowly releasing the hammer of his pistol as he stared at the man huddled in the bed. Cautiously, he backed toward the door as Cain touched a fingertip to the brim of his hat.

"Ma'am," he said with a smile to the woman at Browny's side. "I hope we didn't disturb anything."

The sails of the *Bay Loch* appeared transparent in the glow of the dying sun as it swiftly and quietly skimmed the waters of the bay off Williamsburg heading toward the open sea and the intense search for Alanna Bainbridge. Alone at the bow of the ship, a dark figure scanned the horizon, lost in thought and greatly troubled as he listened to the gentle slap of breaking water against the prow. Beau's head was filled with visions of a young woman with flowing black hair and soft brown eyes, wondering about her fate at that very minute and recalling his admission of love for her to her betrothed. He leaned forward against the railing and studied the trio of gulls soaring above him, wishing away the twinge of jealousy he experienced and cursing his stubbornness. As soon as they found Alanna, Radford and she would marry and after a while they would begin to raise his child. It is what I deserve, he silently confessed. Had I just once thought about another person, things wouldn't have turned out as they have. An angry frown contorted his face, masking his worry about Alanna, and the guilt he felt for putting her in such a way. "Dillon Gallagher," he hissed. "If it be the death of me, I shall see Alanna avenged."

Twenty-Six

A loud crack of thunder pierced through the stillness of early dawn, one marred with darkened, misshapen clouds, bringing Alanna out of a sound sleep. With eyes heavy from an unfinished rest and a slight pounding in her temples, she dragged herself from the hammock that had been strung up in the galley for her and stumbled toward the port to peer outside. Another thunderbolt sounded, preceded by a host of flashing lights scattering across the sky and disappearing again. She squinted in their aftermath, the blinding rays having sharpened the hammering in her head. With shaky fingers pressed against her temples, she turned away to seek what warmth her hammock had to offer, stumbling against the table at her side when the ship suddenly seemed to change course. The scrambling of feet outside her door alarmed her, and she quickly dressed, covering her tired body with the tattered remnants of her velvet gown. She went to the door and pounded a fist to it.

"Parker!" she called. "Parker, unlock the door. Please?"

Listening for him to acknowledge her request, she heard instead a loud splash as the sea anchor hit water. They were securing the *Sea Falcon*, making ready for the tempest, and Alanna trembled at the thought. Only a storm of great winds and high waves would warrant the need to drop anchor.

She beat against the door again. "Parker, please!" she screamed, tears of panic filling her eyes.

"Stay where ya are. It's safer," he returned,, and Alanna relaxed just a little knowing he had heard.

"No, please," she begged. "It frightens me to be locked in with danger so near." She stepped back, having heard the key turn in the lock and watched the door swing open. She smiled gratefully.

"Capt'n won't like it," he growled. "You know what he said."

"Yes, I know. I won't tell him," she promised. "And I won't leave the galley."

He eyed her a moment. "All right then," he said, glancing back over his shoulder, "take the key. If someone comes snoopin' 'round, lock the door. Ya hear?"

She nodded obediently, and when he turned to go she called his name. "Thank you," she smiled.

Quiet a moment, he turned and grunted as he walked away.

Feeling a little better with the key in the palm of her hand, Alanna closed the door again and leaned back against it, her eyes traveling the length of the room for the hundredth time. For the past two weeks, she had not seen anything else, except for the times she had been summoned by Parker to go to the captain's quarters a deck above her. On rare occasions, Dillon Gallagher had grown bored in the early hours of evening when sleep would not come and ordered her presence in his cabin to teach her a game he called chess. At first it had been difficult to learn, but, once she had mastered it, Dillon found her a challenge, and one he could seldom beat. Before long, she realized that he seemed to have a growing inability to rest, and she smiled, knowing that he would probably like to lock her in his quarters for the remainder of their trip.

A warm feeling of friendship flooded through her. The captain of a pirate ship had let down his guard in the presence of a woman half his strength and worldliness. She realized how lucky she had been that it was Dillon Gallagher rather than another who had taken the price offered for her kidnapping. She shuddered, thinking how it could have been, that instead of a hammock purposely strung up in the galley, she could have been sharing the hard wooden deck of the hold with the family of rats already living there, or, instead of having her job as the captain's cook, she could have been at the mercy of each and every mate on board, bruised and bloody, all sense driven from her. She closed her eyes, thankful that the only inconvenience he had burdened her with was keeping her locked in the galley at all times.

A thunderbolt crashed again, sounding like cannon fire on the deck above her, the tremor it caused shaking the entire ship and sending shivers up her spine. Frightened, she ran to the port and stared outside at the turbulent sky. It had yet to rain, but she was certain that at any moment the sky would open up and pour into the sea and onto the ship that lay waiting. Could the *Sea Falcon* weather against such a storm? she wondered. Would it stand tall against the waves of destruction that were sure to follow? Or would it bend and crumple, taking with it all the lives that fought so bravely to defend it? Lightning flashed, searing her eyes. Alanna turned and ran from the cabin.

The storm seemed fiercer on deck than in the safety of her cabin, its howling winds screaming in her ears and tearing at her clothes. She fought to keep from falling, one hand grasped about the railing, the other uselessly trying to pull the hair from her face as it whipped about her. She must find him. She must hear him tell her that everything would be all right.

The sky exploded in a blinding rage, weakening even the strongest of hearts in its wake. Alanna looked up, spotting Dillon at the helm, his dark-clad form silhouetted against the sky with each silver finger that kinked its way toward the sea. She called out to him, but her cries were lost in the roaring thunder that surrounded them. She tried again, and this time she was answered with the cold, stinging droplets of rain as the skies opened up with the fury of the storm. She turned for the ladder, knowing how foolish it had been for her to venture topside, and prayed she would make it below decks before she was swept overboard.

The rain beating down on the wooden planks beneath her instantly became as slippery as an icy pond in winter. Losing her footing, she fell. A sudden wall of water spilled over the railing, crashing into her and sweeping her across the desk to pin her against the railing on the other side. There was no time for her to scream as she fought desperately to grab hold of something. Every bone in her body ached and her strength seemed stretched to its limit, but Alanna would not give up. She had come too far to let her life slip through her fingers now. Reaching over

378

her head, she caught hold of the railing, giving herself time to catch her breath and regain some of her strength. She rested a moment until lightning flashed, brightening up the black sky and enabling her to see Dillon at the helm as he fought to keep the bow of his ship toward the oncoming swells, his years at sea telling him not to get hit broadside. She opened her mouth to call his name only to have it filled with the salty, wet taste of the ocean. The storm grew tenfold, and she realized Captain Gallagher's ship was more important to him at that moment than the life of a woman he hardly knew. Trying again, she dragged herself to her feet and started for the galley, but another wall of water threw her back against the railing, nearly tumbling her overboard, the balustrade digging into her stomach. Unbearable pain shot through her. She screamed once before she fell, unconscious, to the deck.

"Looks like we're in for a bad one."

Beau glanced back over his shoulder at Radford walking across the deck toward him. "Sure does," he said quietly, his gaze scanning the blackened horizon that masked the usual pastels of early dawn. "I wonder how the schooner will hold up under it."

"I'm more worried about me," Radford smiled, resting his hands upon the railing. He took a deep breath and let it out slowly. "The air always smells so fresh right before a storm." His mood changed. "Beau," he said quietly, pausing before continuing, "Beau, do you think we'll catch up to them before New Orleans?"

Beau fixed his gaze on the spiderlike delicacy of the riggings overhead. "I hope so. It will make our job so much easier. In fact, I pray we anchor long before them.

We can hide among the merchants at the docks and once she is free of them, we would only have to walk up to her."

"And what if we don't?" Radford implored.

Beau sighed heavily and turned to study the choppy water of the sea. "Then we search until we find her."

The men grew silent, each filled with worry and concern, never once feeling the cold, stinging droplets of rain beating against them.

"Hurry, Parker, me boy. I think she's comin' 'round."

Alanna could vaguely hear the captain's voice talking with his first mate. The chill she had felt no longer shook her, but the discomfort in her stomach painfully recalled the happenings on deck. Her eyes flew open.

"Easy, lass," Gallagher warned, pressing her back against the pillow of the bunk and placing a cool, damp cloth to her brow. "Ya gave us a fright."

"W-what happened? I hurt so."

"I'm afraid ya took a bad spill. Seems a wee lass like yourself shouldn't a-been topside in that storm." He nodded toward Parker who then handed him a tin cup. "Drink this," Gallagher said, holding it to her lips. "It will be makin' ya feel better."

"What is it?"

"Now don't be arguin' with your captain. Do as ya is told," he replied, a slight smile tugging at the corner of his mouth.

It pained her to rise even only a small distance, but she drank obediently, taking only a sip once she realized he had given her rum. It burned all the way down, but a

380

moment later she gratefully accepted the warmth it spread throughout her tired body.

"I'm sorry for taking you away from your ship, captain," she apologized, struggling up on one elbow. "I feel better now and I shall not neglect my duties. In all the confusion, you've probably not had your breakfast."

Dillon shook his head. "You're ta stay where ya are," he said firmly.

Even as he spoke, Alanna's head began to swim. Slowly, she fell back to the softness of the pillow, fatigue spreading to every limb. How could a fall cause her so much pain? Questioningly, she looked to Dillon for the answer.

He knew what she wanted. He could see it in her eyes. How could he bring himself to tell her? Looking to Parker for help, denied by the man's own sad expression, he sighed, took a deep breath and turned back.

"Alanna," he began, unable to meet her eyes, "as I said before, ya took a bad spill. When ya hit the rail—well, I'm afraid it was too much for ya. Ya lost the babe."

A cold, shocking wave of remorse swept over her. "No!" she screamed. "No! It can't be! Oh, God, no!"

With an affection he had not felt since that night with Bevin, Dillon Gallagher took the young woman in his arms, cradling her comfortingly against his chest as she wept for the loss of her unborn child. Sobs racked her body and it was all he could do to keep her held tightly within his arms.

"Dillon, why?" she wept. "Haven't I paid enough already? Must I be punished over and over again? Why, Dillon, why?"

"Hush, me child," he soothed, for what else could he

381

say? He had no answers.

Parker's attitude toward Alanna changed drastically
after her fall. He insisted she use his cabin, and he slept in
the galley. Every morning he fixed breakfast for her, not
allowing her to leave the bunk even to eat, nor leaving
her side until every bite was gone.

On the morning of the sixth such time, Parker entered
the cabin after a timid knock, placed the tray across her
lap as she sat propped up in the bunk, and left the room,
much to Alanna's surprise. A moment later, he returned
with a bundle of clothes draped over his arm.

"What have you got there, Parker?" she asked.

His cheeks reddened as he stood there awkwardly
fiddling with the garments and fought to regain his usual
hardened exterior. "The capt'n and I decided you need
something more proper and fitting to wear on board the
Sea Falcon," he answered, unfolding what appeared to be
a small boy's breeches. "Now I know a lady wouldn't
consider wearing these things, but you'll be able to move
about more freely in them. You can save your dress for
New Orleans."

Watching him unfold the garments, she appraised
their value. Brass buttons secured the waist and adorned
the knees of the buckskin breeches, and there was an
ivory-colored shirt trimmed in lace around the cuffs and
at the neck. She examined the items laid out before her,
discovering that neither of them had had much wear.
They were much too fine to belong to any of the men on
board the *Sea Falcon*.

"Wherever did you get these?" she asked.

"You don't want to know," Parker replied with a look of shame, and Alanna knew right away that some poor soul had fallen victim to the assault of this pirate ship. She hoped this was the only price he had had to pay.

"Thank you, Parker," she said. "And tell Captain Gallagher I'm grateful for his thoughtfulness."

"It's the least we could do for you after what's happened," he said softly.

Lost in her own world of memories, Alanna looked up to see the sadness on the old pirate's face. Smiling softly, she made room for him to sit on the edge of the bunk as she urged, "Tell me about yourself while I eat."

"About me, ma'am?"

"Yes. I'd like to know."

"There really isn't much to tell. I'm a pirate."

"But you weren't always a pirate. Where's your home?" she asked, sipping her tea.

Clayton Parker studied her quietly for a moment, his head tilted to one side, wondering if his life was really interesting enough to tell or if she really cared to know.

"Won't you tell me?" she pleaded as if reading his thoughts. "I truly want to know."

A tingle of warmth flooded him and he raised a knuckle to his lips, clearing his throat. "Well, I suppose I could," he said slowly, "if ya promise not to fall asleep."

Alanna smiled brightly. "I promise."

Rather than sit so near to her, he pulled a chair next to the bunk and straddled it, suddenly and unexplainably eager to relive his life in words. "I lived in England until I was twelve. My mother had died, and since I had no one to take care of me, I signed on as a cabin boy for an English navy ship. I loved the sea and had big dreams of

383

becoming an officer."

"What happened?" she implored. "You're a far cry from an English officer."

He laughed. "Aye, that I am. Our ship was attacked by pirates off the coast of France and I was taken prisoner. I was never able to escape them, and before long I realized I could never return to England. I was sure they'd hang me for a traitor. So," he said, reaching down to smooth a wrinkle from the thigh of his pants, "I learned their ways. Then one day I met Dillon Gallagher." He smiled, remembering. "He saved my worthless hide."

"He did? How?" she asked, setting aside the tray of half-eaten food, too engrossed in his stories to finish her meal.

"I was a young man then, filled with the notion that I was a great lover. I had fought a duel over a woman I thought was in love with me. I killed the man easily and then found out he was her husband, a man of great wealth. She had a lot to gain from his death. I wasn't part of it." His face suddenly went sober. "She told her husband's brothers I had murdered him and they set out to kill me. They would have if the capt'n hadn't been in port that night."

"Tell me about it," she begged.

"We had been at sea for a long time. My shipmates were either drunk in some tavern or bedded down with a wench. Her husband's brothers had cornered me in an alley just outside the pub where the capt'n was. They all three had knives and began circling me, telling me how they planned to cut me up piece by piece until I bled to death. I didn't stand a chance." He rose and went to the porthole to stare outside at the bright sunlight. Alanna watched him. "The biggest of them began to move in,

384

tossing his knife from one hand to the other. I don't mind tellin' ya, I was scared. He lunged at me and I jumped out of the way, but another brother swung his knife at me and slashed my arm. I was blinded by pain." Without realizing it, Parker reached up and held his arm, cradling it as if the pain had returned. "I stumbled back and fell over something. The next thing I knew I was laying on my back staring up at them. Only instead of three figures, I saw four. I thought I was near passin' out, seeing more than what was there, and then I heard a pistol fire, and one of the forms fell on top of me. I blacked out, and when I woke up again, I was laying in that bunk you're in now."

"It must have been horrible for you," Alanna said, her voice full of compassion.

Clayton sighed. "Nearly as bad as watching all my shipmates from England being massacred." He turned away from the porthole. "And I've been with the capt'n ever since," he smiled in a sudden change of mood.

"What do you know about him, Parker?"

"Nothing other than his name. And that he's from Ireland. He doesn't trust a single man. Not even me, and I've been loyal to him for twenty years. I guess that's why I respect him. He doesn't meddle in my affairs or burden me with his. You know," Parker said, scratching the growth on his chin, "he's never even asked why those men tried to kill me."

"Have you ever asked him about himself?"

"No. Figured he'd tell me if he wanted me to know," he said, coming to her and taking the tray from the bed. "And what of you? What are your plans now?"

Alanna shrugged. "I really don't know, Parker. I guess I'll work and save my money so that I may return to

England someday."

Parker lingered by the doorway a moment studying Alanna as she looked sadly toward the porthole, obviously wishing the *Sea Falcon* was trudging waters toward her home. "I hope you'll find happiness again, Miss Bainbridge." He turned and left the cabin.

Twenty-Seven

"I sure wish I was gettin' a little of what the capt'n gets every night."

"Yeah, and him tellin' us he'll keelhaul anybody who touches her. Figured to scare us off and leave 'er to him."

"Naw. I think it was her doin', seein' as how she ain't sleepin' in the hold. Maybe ol' Parker's takin' his turn too since it's his cabin she's got for herself."

Alanna pressed her body against the bulkhead at the foot of the ladder, hoping the men she heard talking on deck wouldn't see her. She listened, holding her breath so that even that would not reveal her hiding place, and waited for their fading footsteps to tell her that they had gone. Where was Parker? she frowned, praying somehow he would suddenly appear and walk with her to Dillon's cabin. It had been foolish, she realized now, to send him away, telling him she would go to the captain as soon as she finished washing the breakfast dishes and he needn't wait. Was this how all the men on board the *Sea Falcon* thought of her? That she was Dillon's and possibly Parker's mistress, and, worse yet, that it was of her own making? She shuddered, realizing the danger she was in.

All grew quiet on deck and Alanna summoned the courage to lean out and peer up the ladder, trying to see if it would be safe for her to climb topside. There was no movement, no shadows darkening the way, and, cautiously, she climbed the ladder, listening for any noise to tell her the men still lingered there. At the top, she paused, hesitant to step from the protection of the bulkheads, certain they were there but not really knowing. Finally, realizing she could not delay her journey by waiting for the darkness of night to conceal her, she stepped onto the deck.

"Well, well, well," a deep-throated, threatening voice said from behind her, "if it isn't Miss-Holier-than-Thou."

Alanna spun around, too petrified to find her voice. The two men she had heard talking stood boldly before her as different in appearance as the fog-laden skies of England in morning and the sun-drenched ones at Raven Oaks. The larger of them leaned his heavy torso against the bulkhead while he looked her up and down, his gaze lingering on the swell of her breasts. His dark, curly hair, unwashed and in need of trimming, stuck out from beneath the red bandana he wore. The strands resting against his brow lay matted, accenting his small round eyes and reminding Alanna of the rats in the hold. His mouth twisted into a sneer on his unshaven face and Alanna felt her heart quicken, realizing no amount of threats on her part would convince him to leave her alone.

The other, a smaller man in size and stature, stood behind him, staring wide-eyed while periodically glancing about as if fearing discovery and punishment for merely talking with the captain's woman. His tousled blond hair glistened in the sun, giving him a cherubic appearance and revealing his youth; he was hardly old enough to know the ways of a sailor, much less live them. If she was to save herself, Alanna knew he would be her only hope for salvation.

"On your way to the captain's bed?" the older man grinned viciously.

She glanced toward the ladder, wondering if she shouldn't just flee without a word. If she did they might follow. Any men as imprudent as they would surely not hesitate long enough to debate the consequences. She turned back.

"Please, sir. I do not wish to cause trouble—"

"Ya ain't causin' me no trouble," he laughed. "Maybe just a tightening in my pants."

Alanna's stomach knotted. Head down, she started past him, but a thick, muscular arm reached out to block her way. She looked up to find him smiling at her.

"Please, sir, allow me to pass."

"Ain't ya even got time to talk with us scum?" he sneered, glancing at his friend. "Or are ya in a hurry to warm Gallagher's bed?"

"Wilson," the young man warned, lightly touching the outstretched arm. "Ya better let her go. Someone might see."

"You gutless boob," Wilson growled, shaking off the hand on his sleeve. "I told ya before that I'm tired of sitting by while someone else has her. I think it's my turn now."

Alanna instantly stepped back, ready to run to her cabin, but a strong, painful grip seized her elbow, causing her to stumble.

"What ya gonna do?" the other nervously asked, shooting a worried glance toward the helm.

"What do you think?" Wilson asked sarcastically.

"Right here?"

"No, you stupid ass, below decks."

Alanna opened her mouth to scream only to have it stifled by a large hand as the man grasped her about the waist with his other arm. Lifting her off her feet with very little effort, he started toward the ladder, his friend close behind.

"She'll tell, Wilson," his companion warned with a panic-stricken frown.

"If you're scared, Rilley, go scrub the decks like ya was told," Wilson growled.

"I ain't scared."

"Then shut your damn mouth and help me."

"What do ya want me to do?" Rilley asked, his voice quivering.

"Make sure the way ahead's clear. We'll take her to her cabin." Wilson grunted when Alanna's elbow found his side. He squeezed tighter, nearly shutting off her breath. "Hold still, damn you, or I'll have my turn right here so's everyone can watch."

Her ribs threatening to crack from the cruel vise of the pirate's mammoth arms, Alanna hung limp as he carried her back down the ladder, Rilley leading the way. When their destination drew near, Alanna knew she would be helpless against Wilson's attack. Frantic, wanting desperately to voice an alarm, she dug her nails into the fingers clamped over her mouth.

"Go ahead, ya little bitch," Wilson hissed in her ear, his breath smelling of rum. "Don't hurt me any. I like a woman with spirit. And I'll show ya what a real man is like." His hand slid up to her breast, squeezing it painfully.

Determined not to cry, she blinked away the tears of agony, her mind clouded by the stench of the pirate who held her. Any victory she might claim would be achieved only if she remained calm, allowing herself time to think and act quickly should her chance to escape present itself.

Finding the cabin empty, Rilley motioned his friend inside and closed the door behind the trio, securing the latch before he turned back nervously to ask, "How ya gonna keep her from screaming?"

"Easy," Wilson sneered. "We'll gag her. Use my bandana."

Alanna struggled uselessly while Rilley did as told, binding a foul-smelling, rancid-tasting cloth tightly over her mouth, the knot at the nape of her neck entwined painfully with a few tendrils of her hair.

"Now what?" Rilley asked impatiently, his youthful looks suddenly distorted with his lust.

"You hold her while I strip her," Wilson answered, his voice thick.

When they moved to exchange places, Alanna kicked out, connecting the instep of her bare foot against Wilson's shin, causing her more pain than him, igniting his wrath. A huge fist smashed against her cheek in a bone-crunching blow. A thousand tiny lights mixed with excruciating pain bolted through her, leaving her dizzy and momentarily helpless. Two thick hands reached out to capture the collar of her shirt and rip the garment to the waist. Numb from the assault, Alanna sensed more than felt the hands move to the belt of her breeches. She moaned, fighting to clear her head, her arms pinned unmercifully behind her as the buckskin cloth was stripped away.

"Don't you dare swoon, ya little slut," Wilson growled, pinching Alanna's jaw in his thick fingers to pull her dazed eyes to meet his, his grip bruising her flesh. "I want ya ta watch. Ya hear?" He shook her cruelly.

Forcing her eyes open, she mustered the strength to glare back at him, her courage fading when his eyes lowered to view the thinness of her camisole. He licked his lips. Alanna's chin trembled. *Dillon. Dillon, please come looking for me!* her distraught mind called out.

Pudgy hands, their nails dirty, palms rough with callouses, claimed the strings of her camisole, tugging impatiently to free the full breasts hidden beneath. Alanna screamed, the alarm a muffled groan. She squeezed her eyes closed, the painful entrapment of her arms forbidding her to struggle.

Cold morning air seared her bare flesh, flooding her with shame, humiliation, terror. Then a new horror filled her when a hungry, pernicious mouth covered her breast, teeth biting her nipple brutally. Her throat constricted, tears flooded her eyes, she prayed she would faint, to bring an end to what she forcibly endured. Then, as if by the grace of God, her abuser withdrew. She opened her eyes, new torture cramping the muscles of her body as she witnessed the obese, guiltless pirate fumble with the buttons of his breeches. Bile rose in Alanna's throat, gagging her, tears blurring her vision. She shook her head, a silent plea to abandon his intent. He grinned viciously, kicking off his shoes and letting his garb fall to the floor, sneering at the shudder of repulsion he produced from the young woman. He stepped nearer, a malevolent twist disfiguring his mouth. Alanna's knees buckled, her shoulders threatening to crack when Rilley pulled her upward.

Wilson took her from his companion, clamping her wrists in one hand in an agonizing hold behind her, crushing her naked body to him. His stench filled her nostrils, sending a wave of nausea through her. His free hand clumsily fondled her breast, pinching, kneading, bruising, as if he could not get enough of her. His hand slipped to her buttock, pulling her bare thighs against his throbbing member. Her body convulsed. In the next instant, he threw her down, her spine aching when it connected with the unyielding wood of the deck. He fell on top of her, crushing her tiny form with unbearable pressure. Reaching out to tear away the gag, he stifled her screams with his mouth, drowning her in wet kisses, his tongue exploring.

Alanna forced her eyes closed, praying her death would free her. Hearing him grunt, his large fingers touching her everywhere, she forced her mind to think of pleasant things, any diversion until he had had his way with her. Visions of her red-haired friend broke the gray fog of terror, her smiling face, her consoling voice, and warm eyes. Oh, Cinnamon, Cinnamon. Somber shades of early morning blossomed in her thoughts, the mist of England, her homeland, her father, and dear, sweet Aaron. So young, so fair, so loving. Her eyes flew open. Rilley! Rilley would help her! Filled with a sudden glimmer of hope her gaze found him, her sanguine expectation shattered when she discovered the youthful innocence in his eyes gone, supplanted by burning lust. He watched the demeaning violation as if possessed, his hands fondling his growing manhood, his mouth open, saliva dripping from the corner, his tongue tracing the

393

outline of his upper lip.

Tears clouded her vision of him. Every muscle, every bone in her body ached, Wilson's malodorous stench engulfing her. What had she done to deserve such a degrading, brutal act? She was innocent, from the very first. Dillon understood. He knew. He would stop them. Sparked with a sudden urgency to prove her virtue, she twisted her mouth from Wilson's claim and screamed.

"You little whore!" he raged, lifting up. A meaty fist crashed against her jaw, snapping her head to one side. In the next instance, she fell limp beneath him.

"Damn it, Wilson, we gotta get outa here," Rilley whimpered, his desire to share the woman suddenly gone. "They'll be comin' now. They musta heard!"

"Shut up, will ya? Let me think," Wilson spat, angrily glaring at the unconscious girl, his lust dissolving with the need to come up with a useful plan.

"But what'll we do?" Rilley's hazel eyes fearfully glanced from the unmoving form to Wilson to the door.

"It's her word against ours," Wilson said, looking around for his breeches. "We'll just tell him we heard her scream and came to see what was wrong." His garments just out of reach, Wilson rolled from his victim to crawl toward them, his eyes nearly bulging from their sockets when he heard the rush of hurried footsteps coming down the passageway.

Every man on board the *Sea Falcon* crowded around the men bound in heavy ropes. Parker stood off to one side, a solemn, angry expression on his face. Above them all near the helm stood Dillon Gallagher, his back to them as he looked out across the sea. Before long all grew quiet, and Gallagher turned to face his men.

"I thought I made meself clear that no one was to be botherin' the woman," he graveled, standing above them, each hand resting on the railing as he leaned forward with the effect of the Almighty on Judgment Day. His face clearly marked the gravity of the matter in the blackness of his eyes. "Me orders are to be followed to the letter and if anyone be doubtin' it, let this be a lesson to them." He waved a hand, and Parker issued instructions to two of the crew.

Forced to stand aside, Rilley could do nothing but watch, unable to hold back the small cry of anguish within him as he witnessed the men drag Wilson to the bow of the ship. His hands were bound together at the end of a great length of rope, and a second one was tied about his ankles before several of the crew lifted him in their arms.

"Take a deep breath, laddie, me boy," Dillon hissed. "God willin', it will be your last." His once soft features turned hard, his eyes unreadable dark pools of clouded brown. His brows, drawn tightly down over them, shaded any chance the sunlight might have had to reflect the bright sparkle that until now had always been present. A fist rested on each hip, his feet spread apart. "Have ya nothin' ta say?"

"Aye," Wilson barked, his voice unwavering. "If I had the chance again, I would take the girl and make you watch!"

'Tis a shame ya will die for the lust in your loins, Dillon seethed inwardly, a sneer curling his lip. He straightened and drew in a slow breath. "'Tis clear ta me, me crew has gone soft in their thinkin' I'm not a man true ta me word," he said aloud, folding his arms in back of him.

"Maybe now ya will have second thoughts." He nodded to Parker, who made the sign of the cross and stepped up to the man held high above him.

"Two of you grab onto the ends of the rope. The rest stand clear." He waited until his command was fulfilled, then looked up at Wilson. "May God have mercy on your soul. Throw him overboard."

The sound of Wilson's body hitting the water echoed as loudly as a thunderbolt in a summer storm. Parker stood back to watch. "Hope he did as the capt'n suggested," he muttered indignantly.

The deck seethed with mass confusion as every man on board rushed to the railing to watch while the two rope bearers raced toward the stern. Half-heartedly, Parker joined them, looking over the edge of the ship at the long rope that disappeared below the green, foamy surface of the sea. At the end of that rope, he knew there was a man struggling to stay alive as he was dragged below the belly of the ship.

Clayton looked up to the helm and noticed that Dillon had not moved since issuing his order. His eyes were fixed on an object that was not there as he stared blankly out to sea, his chin set firm and held high, his shoulders squared and a slight flare to his nostrils. The black cape draped over his shoulders caught the gentle breeze, bellowing it about and giving him an almost sinister appearance. I wonder what he's thinking now, Clayton mused, crossing his arms and leaning a hip to the railing. When he had told Dillon what had happened, he'd thought Dillon would kill Wilson with his bare hands. Clayton frowned, recalling the name Gallagher had whispered. I wonder who Bevin is.

Shouts from the men penetrated his thoughts, shouts

of encouragement. He looked at the crew and found them all hanging over the railing as the rope drew closer to the stern. Curious, he strolled to join the men who now tugged firmly on the rope to pull Wilson on board again.

"He's alive, but God, look at him!" someone hollered, and Clayton pushed his way to the center of the crowd huddled around the man. On the water-darkened wooden planks lay a man, a disfigured man, for mingled with the salty ocean water was the diluted color of blood. Although the ropes were still bound securely around his ankles, Wilson's foot was all that remained of his left leg.

"Sharks," someone whispered. "He didn't stand a chance."

"Too bad," Parker said, walking away. "He's sure to die now." He returned to his place at the foot of the ladder leading to the helm, one hand resting on his hip, the other wrapped about the rope at his shoulder, watching two of the crew bind the stump of Wilson's leg with rags and carry him off. He shrugged. It was just punishment, he thought. I never liked the man, anyway.

"Parker!"

Clayton came to attention immediately with a salute and click of his heels. "Yes, sir," he said, looking up at the dark, scowling figure above him.

"Tie him to the mast."

Rilley broke out in wails the minute Parker reached down and hauled him roughly to his feet, resisting half-heartedly as he was dragged across the deck. He knew there would be no escaping his punishment and fought desperately to control his sobs in front of the men. His hands were bound to a rope that in turn was thrown over the yardarm and pulled taut to stretch his arms high above him, his shirt ripped from him.

"I will see ya bleed for your disobedience," Dillon condemned him as he marched down the ladder, a cat-o'-nine-tails dangling from his hand, "and then you and your mate will be set ta sea. I'll not have scum like you on board me ship!"

The entire crew stepped back, each silently thankful it was not he who was tied to the mast as Gallagher unfastened the strings of his cape in no apparent haste, whirling it from his shoulders at Parker. He stepped back, tested the whip with a quick shake of each knotted length of cord, then drew back his arm to administer the first lash against the exposed flesh bound tightly before him.

Dillon studied the bruised and swollen face that lay peacefully in slumber from the doorway of the cabin, praying that this young woman was somehow stronger than the one who had taken her own life some thirty years ago. Had she known what had transpired on deck only moments before she might not have rested so easily. Dillon knew the young girl to be soft of heart. He leaned a shoulder to the door frame, crossed his arms over his protruding belly, and idly strummed the length of his scar with one finger. Would she hate all men for what had happened? Would she ever find it in her heart to forgive? Would she ever be able to bear the gentle touch of a man who loved her, finding the reward it could give? He didn't know. She stirred in slumber and Dillon held his breath, hoping not to awaken her with his presence, and when she seemed to quiet again, he went to her bunk and knelt down.

"Sleep, lass," he whispered, lifting a dark curl from her cheek. "They'll not be hurtin' ya now."

Twenty-Eight

The golden streams of late-afternoon sun trailed in through the portholes, spreading across the surface of the desk to accentuate the small specks of dust that rose in the air in a fine curtain. Dillon studied the gentle movement, but his mind centered on the young girl locked safely in her cabin. It had been a week since the attack, and the two men had been put to sea in a rowboat, but Alanna had yet to say a single word, only the movement of her eyes telling him she had heard him speak. Dillon worried about her, wondering if by some unfortunate curse Alanna's mind had snapped, that she would never again smile or tease in the way only she could. Dillon slammed his book closed and went to the wall filled with a multitude of paned windows and looked outside at the dock of New Orleans. As soon as Clayton returned, they would take her to a convent he knew of on the far side of the city. Maybe the good sisters could help.

A firm rapping broke the silence and he looked back over his shoulder to see Clayton let himself in.

"The carriage is waiting, capt'n. Shall I get the girl?"

he asked.

"Aye," Dillon said with a wave of his hand and returned to his desk to rummage through the top drawer. "As soon as she's settled, we'll find the street wench we need." With the small bag of gold clutched in his hand, he lifted his tricorn from the bunk and followed Parker from the cabin.

The crew of the *Sea Falcon* stood aside to watch the trio descend the gangplank and board a carriage, each with somber faces and downcast eyes. The once well-fitted gown hung loosely from Alanna's shoulders, its waistline now much too large for her slender shape. Walking slowly, she stared straight ahead, and the men of the *Sea Falcon* could not bring themselves to watch any longer, casting their gazes to the shoreline or at their feet until the carriage had rolled from view.

Dillon and Parker sat across from her watching as she stared blankly out the window of the carriage. They traveled for quite a while until Dillon found the courage to speak. Slowly, he leaned forward and gently touched her hands lying folded in her lap.

"Alanna," he beckoned, waiting for her to look at him. "Child, I'll be takin' ya to a safe place. A place where only kind people will get near ya. Do ya understand, lass?"

Alanna blinked once before looking outside again, bringing a sigh from Dillon as he leaned back against the hard seat of the carriage. He sent the man at his side a weary glance, and Parker could only shake his head in silence, each filled with the feeling of helplessness.

The buggy rolled to a stop outside a stone building covered with a web of green, leafy vines that trailed their long fingers from the ground to the red tiled roof. It appeared peaceful in its solitude, and Dillon relaxed just a little with the comforting thought that he had made the best decision. He climbed down and turned back to help the young girl down, carefully guiding her up the long steps that led to the doorway covered with ivy, while Parker watched them, his eyes glistening.

The sound of the brass doorknocker echoed and then faded before the hurried clicks of footsteps against a stone floor greeted them. The huge wooden door moaned on its hinges as it opened ever so slowly.

"*Bon soir,*" a small voice addressed them. "May I be of some 'elp?"

Standing before the woman dressed solely in black, Dillon quickly snatched the tricorn from his head, crushing it to his chest. "I be thinkin' ya can, sister," he smiled politely. "We've sailed a long way and will be puttin' out to sea again soon. I'm afraid we've no room for the lass and wondered if ya'd take her in?"

"*Oui, monsieur. Entrez, s'il vous plaît* and take the chill from you by our fire. I will bring Mother Superior and wine."

"Thank ya, sister," Dillon nodded, taking Alanna's elbow and following the nun to a room down the hallway where they stopped just outside.

"Wait here, *s'il vous plaît*. We will be right back," she instructed.

Dillon made a short bow, watched the nun disappear into another room, and then turned back to Alanna. "Won't be long before ya will sleep in a bed again, lass," he said, leading her to a chair and gently pushing her down into it. "You'll be knowin' what 'tis like to have feathers beneath your head again." He smiled broadly at her, but when her gaze fell to the flames dancing in the hearth of the fireplace, his smile faded into a frown. "I

401

should have cut the bastards' throats meself," he muttered.

"Excusez-moi, s'il vous plaît, monsieur?"

Startled by the sound of a woman's voice, Dillon glanced up to find another nun standing in the doorway. Although her garb was identical to that of the nun who had met them at the door, he had a feeling by the way she carried herself that he now faced the Mother Superior.

"I was but talkin' to meself, sister," he apologized. "Me name is Dillon Gallagher, captain of the *Sea Falcon* anchored off the shores of your town."

The nun nodded and walked further into the room. "I'm Mother Superior Sister Marie Angeline," she said, glancing at the silent figure before the fire. "Sister Marie Thérèse tells me you wish to leave the girl in our care."

"Aye, Reverend Mother," he said, glancing down at Alanna. "But first ya must know of her situation."

"Oui, monsieur. Then let's sit and be comfortable. Sister will be along shortly with wine," she said, crossing to a chair to do as she suggested, her hands folded politely in her lap. She waited until Dillon joined her and smiled. "So you are a captain of a ship."

"Aye, Reverend Mother. That I am," he answered, somehow ill at ease in her presence, for every time she took a gentle breath the light from the fire sparkled against the silver cross hanging from her neck. It reminded him that it had been a long while since he had attended Mass.

"I have a brother who captains a ship," she continued, not seeming to notice his discomfort. "It is a hard life."

"Aye, ma'am," he agreed, looking to Alanna again. "Sometimes more than a man like meself can bear."

The Mother Superior, having noted his pained look,

followed his gaze. She, too, studied Alanna for a moment before asking, "Doesn't she speak, *monsieur?*"

"Not for a week now," he said with a sad shake of his head. "Ya see, the poor lass was attacked by two of me crew—and—well, 'tis afraid I am it had a great effect on her mind."

"Attacked, *monsieur?* You don't mean—"

"Aye, ma'am," Dillon cut in. "But we be findin' them before they—well, they did not accomplish what they intended, if ya be knowin' me meaning. I tried ta tell the lass that but as ya can see, she doesn't seem ta hear—or doesn't want ta."

"Oh, *mon Dieu*," the Mother Superior exclaimed, grasping the crucifix at her bosom. "How tragic!" Swiftly, she rose from her chair and went to Alanna's side where she crouched down to look into the girl's eyes, gently reaching up to pull the long curls from Alanna's shoulder. Hearing the hurried footsteps of someone in the hall, she looked up to see Sister Marie Thérèse, a decanter of wine and crystal goblets in hand, enter the room.

"Sister, we'll be having a guest for a while," she said before looking back to Dillon. "What is her name, *monsieur?*"

"Alanna Bainbridge, Reverend Mother," Dillon said, coming to his feet and pulling the bag of gold coins from his pocket. "And I'd be pleased if ya'd take me money. A gift to the church to help pay for her care. I'd feel better knowin' ya had, seein' as how I feel responsible."

Mother Superior gently stroked the unmoving hand that rested on the arm of the chair, noticing how Alanna didn't seem to be aware of the gesture. She stood up. "Sister Marie Thérèse. Take Alanna to one of the rooms.

She must be tired and hungry after her long journey."

"*Oui*, sister," the nun replied, setting the wine and goblets on a nearby table. With a swiftness to her step that only the gentle movements of her dark skirt revealed, the nun went to Alanna and pulled her to her feet. As they passed by, Dillon reached out and touched Alanna's arm.

"I'll be missin' ya, lass," he whispered. "And I pray ya won't always hate me."

"Where do we start?" Radford asked as they quickly left the *Bay Loch* and headed for the marketplace of New Orleans.

"I have a business associate here who could probably suggest a few places and point the way," Beau answered glumly. "We'll start with him."

Radford had to sidestep a chubby little woman pushing a cart full of fish, nearly colliding with another full of flowers, and finally managed to catch up with Beau again as they made their way through the crowded streets. "How long do you suppose they've been in port?" he asked, ducking out of the way of a basket perched on top of yet another woman's head.

"Don't really know," Beau answered, stepping around an old man hobbling down the sidewalk toward him. He stopped outside a hostelry and studied the faded sign overhead. "This is it," he said after a moment.

Radford laughed. "What kind of associates do you have, Beau? This place doesn't look too respectable."

"I go where I get a good price," Beau grinned, pressing his hand to the swinging door and allowing Radford first view of the interior.

The pub was crowded elbow to elbow with sailors and merchants reeking of liquor, sweat and fish while the air hung heavily with smoke from their pipes. The stench it created turned Radford's stomach, and as soon as he was able to order a drink he downed it in one swallow, hoping to bring some relief to his jittery belly and comfort to his aching muscles. They had traveled a long way in a short time, stopping only once for supplies, nearly running aground once, and bravely sailing through a rough storm. All of this was taxing for a man as gently raised as Radford, but he had come through it gallantly, never complaining, and winning the admiration of his friend. He deserved a drink. Beau smiled.

"Excuse me," he said to the barkeep after he had been served. "I'm looking for Jean-Paul Duve. Is he here?"

The man's brows furrowed in caution. "Who's askin'?"

"Beau Remington from the colonies. Just tell him I'm here. He'll know the name."

The barkeep paused a moment, looked Beau up and down, glanced at Radford, and then turned away, disappearing into the crowd of noisy customers. He returned a few minutes later and pointed out a door under the stairs at the far side of the room.

"In there. Says to go on in."

"Thanks," Beau nodded, touching Radford's sleeve as he started past him.

Duve's office was in startling contrast to the dingy, foul-smelling hall they just left. The interior had a French motif, exquisitely crafted in every detail. Heavy velvet draperies adorned the windows, and the air smelled fresh and sweet. In the center of the room stood a huge mahogany desk, and the man sitting behind it

405

smiled broadly as he rose to greet them.

"*Bonjour,*" he said, rounding the desk to stand before them, "and one of you is Beau Remington."

"Yes, sir," Beau said, extending his hand. "And this is a good friend and neighbor of mine, Radford Chamberlain."

Jean-Paul shook hands with both men, then extended an invitation to sit. "Would you care for a drink?" he asked. "I've some very fine wine from France."

"Yes, thank you," both men agreed, and Jean-Paul set about pouring three glasses.

"So what brings you to New Orleans?" he asked, handing each a glass of dark red wine before settling into his chair again.

"We're looking for someone," Beau said, taking a sip from his glass.

"Someone who cheated you?" Jean-Paul grinned.

One corner of Beau's mouth twisted upward. "Not this time. I wish it were. It wouldn't make the situation as grave."

Jean-Paul pressed his heavy frame back into the chair, his round belly covered in silk ruffles and protruding outward. He took a slow drink and studied his visitors from beneath thick white brows. "How can I be of help, *mon ami?*" he asked with guarded calm.

"We're looking for a woman. Her name is Alanna Bainbridge. She was kidnapped from the colonies, Williamsburg, to be precise, about three weeks ago, and we know her abductors came here to New Orleans."

The lines in Jean-Paul's brow deepened. "*Monsieur,* you are not suggesting Jean-Paul had—"

"No, no," Beau assured him, "I just thought you'd have knowledge of her whereabouts or at least give us an

406

idea where to look."

Duve shrugged his thick shoulders. "You'll have to tell me a little more about the *mademoiselle.*"

"We believe Dillon Gallagher is the culprit."

"Gallagher?" Jean-Paul said with new respect.

"Yes," Radford interjected. "Have you heard of him?"

Jean-Paul leaned forward against his desk. "Who hasn't, *mon ami?* Until England took him under wing he was one of the most feared pirates of the English sea. If Monsieur Gallagher is behind this, he shouldn't be too hard to trace. Describe the *demoiselle.*"

"She's very young, and at full height she barely reaches my ascot," Beau said. "Her hair is very dark and very long with golden streaks in it whenever the sunlight catches it."

"*Ce n'est pas bon.* I know many such *mademoiselles,*" Jean-Paul frowned, scratching his temple with the point of one finger.

"Except for one thing," Beau added. "She's heavy with child. In fact, it shouldn't be long, a month or less, before the baby comes."

"And how long have they been in port?"

"I'm not sure. Maybe only a few days.".

"Has Monsieur Gallagher contacted you about a ransom?"

"No. That's the strange part. We haven't any idea why he took her."

"*Ma oui,* but you can bet it was for money," Jean-Paul added. "Either someone in Williamsburg paid him or someone here will."

"But no one here knows Alanna," Radford broke in. "It wouldn't make sense."

"Some of the businesses here don't have to know the

victim, monsieur."

"What do you mean?" Radford asked.

"A brothel wouldn't."

"Oh, God, no!" Radford cried out, his face distorting in anguish.

"Take it easy, Rad," Beau soothed. "If a brothel wanted a new girl, Gallagher wouldn't be stupid enough to bring one as heavy with child as Alanna. It must be something else."

"*Oui, mon ami*," Jean-Paul added. "So let's assume someone in Williamsburg wanted her removed and Monsieur Gallagher has already been paid. This would just be the place where he would rid himself of her. Can the *mademoiselle* sew?"

Beau nodded.

"Then try every dress shop," Jean-Paul said, reaching for a quill and piece of paper. "I will list every one we have. It would seem a logical place to begin. Can she read and write?"

"Yes."

"Then try the school. They might have need of another schoolmistress." When he finished with his list, Jean-Paul folded the paper and handed it to Beau. "I'll spread word about the *chérie*, and if I hear anything, I will contact you. Where are you staying?"

Beau shrugged.

"Then I suggest the hotel across the street. Just mention my name," Jean-Paul added before rising from his chair. "*Bonne chance, mon ami.* I hope I have helped."

As they left the pub and started down the street toward the first shop named on the paper Beau held, Radford sighed. "You really don't think Gallagher took her to a brothel, do you?" he implored.

408

"No. First of all, you heard how the sailor Cain overheard said they were looking specifically for a woman in a red bonnet. How would anyone this far away know what she would be wearing?"

Radford shrugged his tired shoulders. "I guess you're right. It just alarms me to think she might be in such a place."

"Well, don't worry," Beau comforted him, pausing outside the storefront whose windows were filled with bolts of fabrics in assorted colors of the rainbow and an exquisitely tailored gown draped over them for display. "We'll find her, Rad. We won't leave until we do."

Radford smiled weakly and followed Beau into the shop, hearing the tinkling of a bell as he closed the door behind them.

"Alanna. Alanna, I've brought you something to eat," Sister Marie Thérèse said, placing a tray of soup and some hot rolls on the small table. She straightened and looked at Alanna, who sat crosslegged on her bed gazing out the window. "What are you looking at?"

With a measured slowness in her moves, Alanna looked back at the sister. "Birds," she said quietly and looked outside again.

"Birds?" Sister Marie Thérèse asked, coming to join her and peek outside. "Where?"

Nested in a tree only a few feet from the window, Sister Marie Thérèse saw a young family of sparrows noisily carrying on while their mother fluttered about them. A hopeful smile parted the nun's lips. "They are one of God's more delicate creatures, don't you think, *ma chérie?*" she asked, cocking her head to one side to study

Alanna's face. She sighed when she realized Alanna had slipped away again. As quietly as possible, she pulled up a chair beside the bed and sat down to observe her in silence.

Alanna had been with them for three days and in that time she had gotten Alanna to say only a few words, and that only after much prompting on the nun's part. But she had not lost hope, for she could see in Alanna's eyes that she wanted to speak but had resisted. Why she didn't know. She could only assume it was because she felt ashamed of what had happened. Sister Marie Thérèse smiled softly as she watched Alanna, thinking how beautiful the young woman was, and wondering if there was someone somewhere right at this moment who was worried about her. Surely there was, and it was this thought that gave the sister an idea.

"Alanna," she said, and waited until the dark, somber eyes found her. "If you wish, I'll send word to your parents that you're all right."

Alanna's gaze fell to her lap.

"They must be worried. It would be a kind thing to do to tell them you're safe," she added, encouraged by the pained look on Alanna's face.

"No," she whispered.

"But why, *ma chérie?*" Sister Marie Thérèse asked, leaning forward to touch Alanna's hand.

"Dead."

Sister Marie Thérèse's throat tightened. *Mon Dieu,* she thought, *ma chérie* hasn't a family. "Then someone else, *oui?*"

Alanna shook her head and studied the sparrows again.

"Alanna, are you of my faith?" she asked, waiting until Alanna shook her head again before continuing.

"Then living here in this cell will not satisfy you after a while. You will grow weary of the confinement. I never will because I've chosen this way of life. Look at me, Alanna, *s'il vous plaît.*"

Several moments passed before it appeared as if Alanna had heard the request and turned her head to stare at the nun.

"We are nearly the same age, *mon amie.* Too young for you to close out the world. What happened to you will not go away just because you refuse to think about it. You must accept it, forgive those who hurt you, and start living again. *Merci, mon Dieu,* you are alive!"

Sister Marie Thérèse searched the dark eyes staring back at her for some sign of understanding, something that would give her a clue as to how better to help Alanna. But it seemed as if the brown eyes only mirrored the hollowed shell of a woman who once had been vital and alert.

"If I only knew what meant something to you, *ma chérie,* I could talk of it to you," she whispered. "But I know nothing. I cannot help." Tears pooling in her blue eyes, Sister Marie Thérèse stood up and moved toward the door. "I have failed you," she said quietly, closing the door behind her.

A cool breeze drifted in from the sea bringing with it a smell of salt water and bellowing the full sleeves of Sister Marie Thérèse's habit as she reached up to lift a thin branch dangling in her way as she strolled in the gardens. It felt good to be outside yet it failed to cheer her. All she could think of was how she had labored in vain to bring Alanna out of her depression. She stopped by a huge willow tree and gazed out at the chapel sitting alone on the hill. Maybe she had failed God, for it was through her that He would reach His children. With heavy heart she turned back to go inside and stopped abruptly when she spied a thin figure standing in the pathway. Her heart pounded and she wanted to run to her, but she knew she must let Alanna be the first to make an overture. After what seemed an eternity, the frail form slowly stepped nearer until Alanna was within reach, and Sister Marie Thérèse could see the tears streaming down her face. Slowly, she held out her arms to her and a moment later cradled Alanna in her embrace.

Twenty=Nine

Dillon refilled his mug with rum, settling back in his chair again to stare at the docks and the bustling activity near the gangplank of the *Sea Falcon*. Since early morning he had tried to center his attention on anything but the dark-haired beauty who had plagued his thoughts for the last two days. The muscle of his jaw twitched, kinking the scar of his cheek into a zigzag line. If only he were twenty years younger, not so fat and ugly, he would contemplate going back to the convent and taking Alanna from it. He would sail her away to his homeland and care for her, and in time she would fall in love with him.

"Ha!" he roared, bolting from his chair to pace about the confining cabin. "A lass such as her would never love a rogue like me! Ya've gone mad, Gallagher!"

Angrily, he slapped the mug down on his desk and went to the paned windows where he could watch his crew half-heartedly loading the ship. In the morning they would set sail and he would leave New Orleans. His gaze traveled across the horizon until it fixed on the minute outline of the cross atop the steeple of the church nearly a mile away.

"I'll never forget ya, lass," he whispered. "And when we sail this way again, I'll be stoppin' by ta see how ya fare."

The click of the latch on his cabin door shattered the silence around him, and Dillon pressed a knuckle to the corner of his eye before turning back.

"Well, Parker, me boy," he grinned in a forced change of mood, "how 'bout goin' into the fair city and findin' ourselves a lass or two? Better yet, why not see if ya can still drink me under the table? I grow tired of rum and long for the better taste of me Irish whiskey."

"I'm more than willing to take you on, capt'n, but shouldn't one of us stay behind to keep an eye on the men?" Clayton asked. "You know they're not willing to leave yet."

"Aye, that they are not," Dillon winked as he reached out to grasp his first mate around the shoulders. "And let them go. We'll all be needin' one more night to ease our wicked desires."

Clayton looked at his captain suspiciously. "You're not thinking about the girl, are you?"

"What girl?" he mocked. "The one I plan ta bed?"

Before Clayton could answer, Dillon pulled him from the cabin and led him down the gangplank toward the first available whorehouse.

A shadow darkened the stream of sunlight falling against the stone floor in the hallway and Alanna looked up, brush in hand, to see who had caused it.

"Good morning, Sister Marie Thérèse," she smiled.

"*Bonjour*, Alanna."

414

"Where are you going?"

"To vespers. I thought maybe you would stop with your cleaning and come with me."

Alanna let the brush fall back into the bucket, wiped her hands on the hem of her gown, and stood up. "But I am not of your faith, sister. It would all seem strange to me."

Sister Marie Thérèse smiled cheerfully. "You would but have to sit quietly and watch. And besides," she added, patting Alanna's hand, "it might help, *non?*"

Alanna's gaze fell away. "Thank you, sister, but I'm much better now. The dreams don't last as long."

"I know," Sister Marie Thérèse whispered, looking about them. "And in time they'll go away." She straightened and started toward the chapel. "Well, maybe another day, *oui?*" she called. "Why don't you stroll about the gardens for a change? I can join you later and we'll talk."

"Yes, sister," Alanna said, watching the slim figure gracefully glide from view, realizing what a good friend she had found. Sister Marie Thérèse was only two years older than she and very naive about men and their ways. Alanna often wondered if, before the sister had taken her vows, of course, she had ever allowed a man to kiss her. If she hadn't, Alanna decided, she was better off. For Alanna the results had been nothing but pain. Returning her bucket and brush to the closet, she set out for the gardens as Sister Marie Thérèse had suggested.

Nearly an hour passed before Alanna spotted the dark-clad figure coming from the church. She smiled warmly at her and eagerly allowed the nun to link her arm with hers as they aimlessly walked along the path lined with brightly colored flowers.

415

"Comment allez-vous?" the sister smiled brightly, and Alanna failed to hide a smile of her own.

"You are determined to teach me French, aren't you?" she chided.

Sister Marie Thérèse grinned all the more.

"I'm fine, *merci*," Alanna obliged.

"Trè bien!" Sister Marie Thérèse sparkled. "You will speak my language in no time."

"If only to have peace from you," Alanna laughed. Then her mood seemed to change suddenly. "Sister, I'd like to tell you a little more of what happened to me. I mean I'd like to tell you from the beginning. For some reason I feel I must. Would you mind?"

"Of course not," Sister Marie Thérèse said, her bright blue eyes twinkling in the early afternoon sunlight. "Let's sit over there," she added, pointing to a wooden bench a few feet away.

The sister sat spellbound as Alanna related her story, starting with the ocean voyage that had taken the lives of her father and stepmother and proceeding all the way to the dreadful end and the reasons she spoke of Radford Chamberlain and Beau Remington with disgust. Sister Marie Thérèse's face seemed to pale even more.

"What happened to *le bébé?*" the sister asked when Alanna spoke of her child.

"There was a storm at sea. The waters threw me against a railing and the child came before it was time. Captain Gallagher buried it at sea."

Alanna heard the nun gasp before she quickly made the sign of the cross, clutching the silver crucifix tightly in her hand as she waited for Alanna to continue.

"It is best, I suppose," Alanna murmured. "Growing up without a father to guide you can be very difficult."

"Did you love the child's father, Alanna?" Sister Marie Thérèse asked hesitantly, watching the young woman reach down to pick a daisy at her feet.

In thought, Alanna slowly plucked the petals from it. "At one time I thought I did. But it seemed so hopeless when he never returned my love."

A gentle hand reached out and squeezed Alanna's arm. "In time you will love again," Sister Marie Thérèse said.

Alanna shrugged. "Maybe."

Having exhausted their supply of suggested businesses, Beau and Radford sorrowfully headed for a café they had spied earlier. None of the women with whom they had talked had seen or heard of a woman of Alanna's description. Dejectedly, they took a table near the window and sat in silence until after they had been served, had eaten, and the dishes were cleared away.

"What now?" Radford asked, swirling the coffee in his cup.

"Unless he just dumped her at the wharf, there's only one person who really knows where she is," Beau said, staring out the window.

"Gallagher?"

"Uh-huh. I guess we'll have to ask him."

"But have you ever seen him to know what he looks like?" Radford asked, the fair lines of his brow darkening.

"No."

"Then how will we know him?"

"Shouldn't be too hard. He's Irish. Aren't too many here who are, and you'll know it the minute he opens his mouth. Not to mention the fact that he has flaming red hair." Beau smiled oddly. "And if I'm not mistaken, he'll have a scar from one temple to his chin."

Radford laughed, feeling the scar was a justifiable emblem of the man's evil way of life. "I wonder who gave him that."

Beau looked at his companion with a lazy grin. "One of my men. A long time ago. Now let's get moving. We've wasted enough time."

The rest of the day passed unrewardingly, and the two men took a room at the hotel Jean-Paul had suggested only to sleep and begin again the next day. By the time the last rays of sunlight had faded they felt certain they had visited every shop, pub, and eating establishment in New Orleans, none of which turned up a single clue to Alanna's *or* Gallagher's whereabouts.

"Maybe we should check the boardinghouses. Alanna would have to have a place to stay, and maybe one of them would let her work off her board and room," Radford said as they walked randomly down the crowded sidewalk.

"Damn," Beau growled beneath his breath. "Why didn't we think of that before? Come on. We're going to see Jean-Paul again."

Alanna's chin fell in surprise at the thin face that stared back at her in the mirror Sister Marie Thérèse had somehow managed to procure for her. For some reason she had been unable to fall asleep that night and had left her room to go to the kitchen for a glass of wine to relax her. When she returned she found a small hand mirror and hairbrush on her bed, and knew immediately who had left them.

"Oh, sister," she murmured, "if you had known how awful I think I look, you never would have given me these."

Even her hair lacked the usual shine, hanging in long thin strings of muted brown. Pulling the sash of her robe more tightly about her waist, she began to brush the tangles from her hair, hearing it crackle with each stroke. Before long it fell in soft curls about her shoulders and when she looked in the mirror again, she felt comfortable with what she saw.

The wine slowly took effect, and she lovingly laid aside her gifts and crawled into bed. She had just closed her eyes when she heard the hurried footsteps of the nuns outside her door. Curious as to the reason they hustled through the corridor at such a late hour, she left her bed to go to the door and peeked outside.

"Excuse me, sister," she said to one who approached her.

"*Oui, ma chérie?*" the nun whispered.

"Is there trouble?" she asked. "Where is everyone going? It's so late."

"To the chapel. To pray for a soul."

Alanna gasped, thinking it to be one of the sisters she was just beginning to know.

"Do not fear, *ma petite*," the older nun smiled, reaching out to squeeze Alanna's wrist. "The *monsieur* was only a visitor to New Orleans, not someone you know. Go back to bed and do not let it trouble you."

"Yes, sister," Alanna sighed in relief.

She stood in her doorway until the last dark figure had disappeared before she returned to her room and bed. But she found little comfort there as she lay awake listening to the muted voices drift into her room from the chapel, her mind filled with thoughts of another who had been denied a proper burial. Tears welled up in her eyes as she thought of the infant, and she rolled to her stomach, buried her face in her pillow and cried herself to sleep.

"You must have gotten my message," Jean-Paul said as he let Beau and Radford into his office.

"Message?" Beau said, stopping just inside the door. "What message?"

"I sent a man to the hotel about an hour ago. Didn't you get it?"

"No. I'm afraid we haven't returned to our room all day," Beau said anxiously. "What was it?"

"Gallagher. He was here."

"Here?" Beau gasped. "Did you have him followed?"

"Yes."

"Well?"

Jean-Paul sighed and went to his desk. "I'm afraid you won't like it. He returned to his ship. Henri thinks they're making ready to sail. They might even be gone by now."

Beau whirled around and touched a hand to the door latch.

"Beau, wait," Radford called. "What are you going to do?"

"I'm going to try and catch him."

"Alone? We wouldn't stand a chance."

"We'll have to go alone. Who'd help us? The crew of the *Bay Loch* hired on to sail us here not fight for us."

420

"*Vous plaisantez,*" Jean-Paul intervened. "Monsieur Gallagher would just as soon shoot you as look at you."

"He's the only one who knows where Alanna is. We've got to get to him before it's too late."

"*Mon Dieu,*" Jean-Paul said, throwing his hands in the air. "Do you at least carry a weapon?"

Beau pulled back the edge of his coat to expose the pistol he wore in his belt.

"And you, *monsieur?*" Jean-Paul asked, turning to Radford.

Radford shrugged meekly. "I was hoping I wouldn't need it."

"Then I will loan you one of mine," Jean-Paul said, pulling open a desk drawer. "But *monsieurs,* be careful, *oui?*"

Both fully armed and ready, and having thanked Jean-Paul Duve for his help, Beau and Radford set off for the docks and Dillon Gallagher. Neither of them spoke, contemplating rather their next move once they reached the *Sea Falcon.*

The docks had grown quiet, and Beau could only assume that most of the ships' sailors were ashore in some pub or whorehouse, making their own movements that much more obvious. He frowned in the darkness, praying Gallagher had been remiss in ordering a crew member to stand watch as he followed the motions of a handful of men going ashore empty-handed to return a moment later carrying supplies. Duve's man had been right. The *Sea Falcon* made ready to set sail.

"What's your plan?" Radford whispered when they stopped a good number of yards from the ship.

Thoughtfully, Beau studied the caravan of men

steadily boarding and departing from the ship. "The easiest way I can see to get on the ship would be to walk on."

"But—"

Beau raised a finger to stress his idea. "Please, give me more credit than what you're obviously thinking, my friend," he grinned. "There is no one in New Orleans more eager to rid the town of unwelcome riffraff like Gallagher than I. In fact, I plan to help supply his ship."

An expression of relief flooded Radford's face with Beau's explanation since he had thought Beau mad in attempting to board the *Sea Falcon* unobserved. "An excellent idea," Radford concurred, "but I fear we shall be as obvious as two stalks of maize in a tobacco field dressed as we are."

Beau nodded. "Then we must borrow some clothes."

Radford's brow crinkled and Beau motioned toward the end of the pier where the sailors were lifting boxes from the end of a wagon. He nodded for Radford to follow and they quietly made their way toward them. They slowed their step to allow all but two sailors to start back toward the ship, and when they were all out of earshot Beau quickly stole up behind one of the two and struck him across the back of the head with the barrel of his pistol. The second man, who had stopped to adjust his belt buckle, had turned his back to them, and at the sound of his friend's moan turned back to see what was wrong. His eyes never had a chance to focus on the scene before a huge fist struck him against the jaw, sending him unconscious to the wooden planks. Quickly, Beau and Radford exchanged clothes with the sailors, hoisted boxes to their shoulders and started off for the gangplank.

As they neared the ship and some of the crew, they shifted their cargo to hide their identities, and boarded the ship without the slightest notice. Only one man remained on deck, but he, too, paid them no heed while he idly toyed with the dagger in his hands. They watched him, and when they felt certain he was too absorbed with his plaything to look their way, they put down their boxes and slipped down the passageway leading to the captain's quarters. Standing at the door, Beau pressed an ear to it, listening for any sounds coming from within. It wasn't long before he heard the muffled voices of two men, one of which carried a heavy Irish brogue. He straightened, drew his pistol, and raised a questioning brow at Radford. A quick nod told him that Radford was ready, and without another moment wasted, Beau lifted the latch of the cabin's door and hurled it open.

"Hold it right where you are, Gallagher," Beau warned, his pistol aimed at the man's belly as he stood beside his desk. "And tell your man to drop his firearm."

"Do as the man says, Benson," Gallagher instructed. "I believe he has us at a disadvantage." He watched the mate slowly pull the pistol from his belt and drop it to the floor before he looked back at Beau again. "And will I be havin' the honor of knowin' who 'tis that found himself foolish enough to be pointin' his gun at me?"

Beau stepped further into the room to allow Radford to join him, a slow smile parting his lips. He nodded. "Beau Remington."

A surprised frown flitted across Dillon's face, instantly replaced by a grin as he slowly crossed his arms over his chest. "Aye," he said, "and who else would be havin' the nerve?" He glanced at Radford. "And who might your friend be?"

"We haven't come for a social visit, Gallagher. I want to know what you've done with the girl."

Dillon moved to reach for his desk, stopped by the warning click of Beau's pistol as he cocked it. He raised a hand and smiled. "I only mean ta have a cigar, laddie."

"It can wait," Beau hissed, waving him away with the point of his weapon. "We don't intend to stay long enough to be discovered. Now what have you done with the girl?"

Dillon's face showed mock regret. "I think 'tis a wee bit late, laddie. Me first mate already has his pistol aimed at your back."

Fooled by his trick, Radford instantly glanced back over his shoulder, dropping his guard on Benson long enough for the man to pull a knife from the scabbard strapped to his back. But not quickly enough for Beau to miss the movement. With the hammer already cocked, Beau simply aimed and squeezed the trigger, striking the man between the eyes and killing him before he hit the deck while Dillon yanked open a desk drawer and withdrew his own pistol. He pulled back the hammer ready to fire when another round exploded and the ball whizzed by his ear. Instinctively, he aimed his pistol at his attacker and fired, hearing a man scream and watching Radford clutch his belly as he crumpled to the deck.

Horrified, Beau stared at Radford as his shirt front quickly stained with blood, a color that brought bitter reality crashing down on him. Overwhelmed with rage, Beau scanned the interior of the cabin for some sort of weapon, spying a saber that hung decoratively on the wall behind him. He ripped it from the hook and spun around.

"You son of a whore," he bellowed. "I'll kill you for this."

For only an instant, Beau's brow furrowed, wondering why Gallagher never flinched when he charged him. Then feeling a sharp pain to his temple before everything began to swirl, his knees buckled and blackness overtook him.

"Thank ya, Parker, me boy," Dillon breathed, falling into his chair. "Another minute, and he'd have run me through."

Clayton cautiously hooked the toe of his boot beneath the unconscious man's shoulder and rolled him onto his back before returning his pistol to his belt. "What do you want me to do with them?" he said.

"Are we ready to sail?" Dillon asked, pouring himself a mug of rum.

"Close enough."

"Then throw them all overboard."

"Why not finish this one off? The other's as good as dead."

Dillon took a big swallow of his rum. "The one you're referrin' to, me boy, is Beau Remington," he said, smiling when he saw the surprised look on Clayton's face.

"All the more reason."

"I haven't a grudge against the man. Not like he does ta me. And I rather enjoy the sport of havin' him spend his money tryin' ta catch me." Absently, he touched the scar on his cheek. "Maybe this time he'll come himself."

In a half-conscious state, Beau could feel himself being lifted, suddenly free of the hands that held him as he fell

425

through the air to be swallowed up by the sea. The water surged around him and he opened his eyes to discover he had been thrown overboard. Fighting to hold his breath, he began pulling himself toward the surface, gasping for air and hearing the blood pounding in his temples when he had reached it. He brushed the hair from his face and quickly glanced about him for Radford, looking up in time to see someone hurl another figure over the rail above him. The body hit the water a few yards away from him and disappeared without a fight below the white caps that swirled around him. He took a deep breath, dove under the water and swam as quickly as he could toward the shadow, grasping it under the shoulders when he reached it and straining to push it to the surface again. Spotlighted in the golden streams that came from the porthole, Beau suddenly realized the man he had tried to save was not Radford but the man he shot. He let go of him, watching the body disappear into the darkened depths of the water.

Frantic, he splashed about, twirling completely around and listening for a cry for help, instead hearing only the gentle slap of the water as it caressed the side of the ship. He looked up. Standing above him at the rail was the silhouette of a man with another man draped over his shoulder. He started to call out just as the body of the second man, the one who must be Radford, was heartlessly thrown to join the others, hitting the water only a few feet from him. In two powerful strokes, Beau reached him, keeping Radford's head above water as he studied the face for any sign of life. Radford's eyes fluttered open and then closed again.

"Hang on, my friend," Beau whispered, locking his arm around the man's chest as he began treading the water toward shore.

He could hear the excited voices of the men on the pier above him, knowing they hurried to set sail. Just as soon as he saw Radford in the hands of a doctor, he vowed to return and finish the job he had started. Dillon Gallagher would die before the night was out.

With Radford held securely under an arm, Beau floated then swam beneath the pier, staying out of sight until they reached dry land, where he carefully pulled Radford's motionless form from the water, easing him onto his back to better study his wound. Gingerly, he lifted the blood-stained shirt apart and frowned when he saw the extent of the injury. Radford had caught the lead ball in his stomach, a wound that meant certain death. He glanced about them looking for a carriage or anything in which he could lay Radford and take them to a doctor.

"Beau," a weak voice called, and Beau knelt down beside the stricken man.

"Don't try to talk," he said. "I'll get you to a doctor. We'll talk after you've rested."

Radford coughed, choking on his own blood, and Beau quickly raised the man's head in his arms.

"Alanna—will—"

Radford's voice grew weaker and Beau leaned in closer to listen. "Alanna will what, Rad?"

"I—love—" Radford's eyes found Beau's. He coughed again, sending a fine mist of blood splattering against Beau's shirt.

"Don't talk," Beau ordered almost angrily.

Clutched tightly in Beau's arms, Radford smiled up at him and reached out to grasp the stained shirt front in his fingers, strangling as he did and gasping for air, his glazed eyes looking through Beau as he took one final breath.

"No-o-o," Beau moaned in the darkness, wrapping his arms around Radford's lifeless form to cradle him and rock to and fro. "God, no!"

"Sister Marie Thérèse!"

"*Bonjour,* Alanna. *Comment allez-vous?*" the sister smiled brightly as she paused in the hallway to wait for Alanna to catch up to her. Reverently, she stepped aside to allow the others to pass.

"I'm fine, *merci,*" Alanna returned. "Are you going to chapel?"

"*Oui.*"

"To the funeral?"

"*Oui.* Why do you ask?"

"If you would permit me, I would like to come along."

"*Ma oui, ma chérie.* May I ask why you wish to?"

Entwining her arm with the sister's, Alanna studied the toes of her shoes each time they peeked out from beneath her gown as they walked along. "I would like to offer a prayer of my own for my child if I could," she whispered.

"*Ma, oui.* And I will do the same. Would you care to sit with me in the choir loft? We can always use another voice in song."

Alanna stopped abruptly. "But—"

"Do not worry. I will give you a book from which to read the words," Sister Marie Thérèse smiled comfortingly. "But we must not hesitate a moment longer. The Mass will begin soon and it is beginning to rain. If we wish to stay dry, we must hurry."

To Alanna, it seemed the chapel had a million candles all aglow and casting warm, comforting light all around.

428

In single file, the nuns climbed the narrow stairway that led to the loft and seated themselves quietly around the organ, books in hand and heads down in prayer. Alanna sat at the end of the row, too afraid even to breathe lest she make a sound and draw the attention of the figure sitting in a pew only a few feet away from the casket at the alter. A man, she thought, turning her head to study him. I wonder if the dead man is his brother or just a friend. Maybe his father. Alanna's throat tightened and she bowed her own head in prayer for the loss of the mother she never knew, her father, her stepmother, her aunt, and most of all, the baby she would never hold in her arms.

Thirty

A fine mist veiled the city within its damp arms, masking the dolorous passage of a man going to chapel. Beau looked up, letting the minute droplets of rain hit his face to study the gray sky overhead. A few hours before he had taken Radford's body to this place and left it in the care of the priest, knowing it was what Radford would have wanted, to be buried in the cemetery of the Catholic church. A shudder ran through him as he thought of leaving his friend in a strange city, but time would not allow him to take Radford back to Virginia and lay him to rest in the soil of Briarwood Manor. He had made a promise to Radford to care for the woman he loved, and Beau knew he could not leave until he had found her. He frowned, wondering if he ever would.

As he walked up the stairs leading to the chapel and quietly opened one of the double arched doors, he could hear the soft melody of a pipe organ drifting down from the choir loft. He paused just inside to listen and study his surroundings. At least a dozen stained glass windows stood tall and stately on either side of the numerous rows of pews, casting dull colored shadows to blend with the golden beams of candlelight. He watched the flickering movements of the flames and at last found a small measure of comfort, until his gaze fell upon the casket sitting before the altar in quiet solitude. He felt a tightening in his throat as he slowly approached it and sat down in a pew only a few feet away to quietly observe the funeral Mass of which he knew very little. He closed his eyes, listening to the verse recited in Latin, and let his mind wander back in time, recalling the days when he and Radford were boys playing outside the manor at Raven Oaks. He could hear the lighthearted laugher of his lifelong friend, knowing it was a sound he would never experience again, as he would never hear the carefree voice that always teased, that always made him happy, that was always there whenever he had needed him. God, how he'd miss him!

Soft voices raised in a harmonious song drifted into his thoughts, and for a moment he was enthralled by the melody. He opened his eyes and glanced back at the sound, spying the dark shapes clustered about the organ in the loft. He smiled one-sidedly, and bowed his head again as the pungent odor of incense filled his nostrils. It grew quiet in the church; there was only the voice of the priest citing the requiem for their lost brother. The chant sounded again with more fervor than before, compelling Beau to look upon the nuns once more. Seeing them truly for the first time, his thoughts fleetingly on the question of what had driven these women to a life of devotion to the church. He looked away, supposing the reasons to be just in their minds. Perhaps a vision, tradition, or possibly a form of escape from reality and the harsh bitterness of life. His expression changed. And why not?

he asked himself, glancing back hopefully as if to find the answer in the movement of the dark shadows. Perhaps a place such as this had been Alanna's sanctum.

"Maybe, Radford," he whispered, looking to the casket, "maybe this time I'm right."

"I wish to express my heartfelt sympathy for your loss, Monsieur Remington," Mother Superior said from her chair by the fireplace.

"Thank you," Beau answered quietly from the window where he gazed outside at the steady pouring rain.

"But you haven't come to hear that. Something else is bothering you."

"Yes, there is." He looked back, pressed a shoulder to the cold stone wall, and sighed. "My friend and I came to New Orleans because we were looking for someone."

"And you think to find him here?"

"Not him, madam, her. We were looking for the woman promised to marry Mr. Chamberlain. This is my last hope, since we exhausted all other possibilities."

"Tell me about her," the Mother Superior suggested, leaning back more comfortably in her chair, a guarded knot twisting her brow.

Beau began to stroll aimlessly about the room, studying his hands from time to time or crossing his arms in back of him. "Her name is Alanna Bainbridge. She was once an indentured servant of mine until Radford paid her debt and freed her. He asked her to marry him, and she agreed. Then she was kidnapped and brought here to New Orleans. We looked everywhere for her. We found the man responsible for her abduction, and when we tried to force him to tell where she was, Radford was killed."

He looked away, missing the slight frown on the woman's face.

"Can you describe her?" Mother Superior asked.

He returned to the window and watched the rain gather into streams trailing down the windowpane and puddle on the sill outside, silent for a long while. "She has a gentle manner, one becoming a woman of her size, with a heart that is warm and sincere. She will fight for what she believes and never back down even in the face of danger or harm to herself. She is small in stature, small enough that I could crush her in my arms if I so chose. Her hair is the color of the sky at midnight, with golden streaks when the sunlight touches it. And her eyes, her eyes are so dark—and alluring—and soft."

"Do you love her, Monsieur Remington?"

Suddenly aware of what he had said, Beau turned an embarrassed look toward the Mother Superior. Then his features softened and he smiled. "I guess I do."

"Then you should know the whole story," Mother Superior said, rising from her chair. "Wait here until I return."

Beau hardly had time to ponder the reason for the Mother Superior's sudden departure when she reappeared at the doorway followed by another nun. "This is Sister Marie Thérèse," she said, nodding to the woman at her side. "Sister, this man has come about Alanna."

"You mean she's here?" Beau cried out. "Take me to her. I must see her."

The Mother Superior raised a hand. "You will see her only if she wishes it, *mon ami*. But first you must know what troubles her." She firmly guided Beau back to a chair and motioned for him to sit down. "Go ahead, sister. Tell Monsieur Remington what Alanna

434

has told you."

Sister Marie Thérèse studied the hands folded in front of her for a moment, hesitant to begin. "You must understand, Monsieur Remington, that right now Alanna feels nothing but hatred for you and Monsieur Chamberlain."

Beau frowned. "For me, I can understand. But not Radford. He loved her and wanted to marry her."

"Alanna feels otherwise. When she was kidnapped, the captain of the ship gave her a note explaining why he had taken her."

"A note? From whom?"

"From Monsieur Chamberlain. He told her how he had had a change of heart and had decided not to marry her after all. That he loved someone else."

"That's not true!" Beau exclaimed. "The man laid down his life trying to find her. Someone else wrote that note. You must let me speak with her, to explain it was all some sort of awful trick played at her expense."

"In good time, Monsieur Remington. In good time," the Mother Superior warned. "Go on, sister."

"The captain had been instructed to sell Alanna to a brothel—"

"What?" Beau roared, bolting from his chair to pace the floor.

"But the good captain would not do it. Not with Alanna heavy with child. They decided to find another to take her place, one who was willing, and after she lost the child, it made it that much easier."

Beau stopped his pacing and stared wide-eyed at the nun, his mouth agape. "The baby is dead?" he breathed.

Sister Marie Thérèse and the Mother Superior made the sign of the cross before exchanging glances. "Yes,

Monsieur Remington," Sister Marie Thérèse continued.
"It was an accident. She fell. But that wasn't the end of it.
Several days later two members of the crew—" Sister
Marie Thérèse stopped and looked at her hands again.
"They tried to use her in a most degrading fashion, but
the captain found them before they—they could . . . the
captain had them thrown overboard for their deed, but it
was too late for Alanna. For more than a week she didn't
speak a word. It was Captain Gallagher who brought her
to us."

Beau slowly sank into a chair, his elbows pressed to his
thighs as he ran his fingers through his hair.

"She's much better now, Monsieur Remington, but I
fear what will happen to her when she sees you."

"But I can't leave her here. I made a promise to
Radford. And she knows no other home now than
Virginia. Please," he said, "let me talk with her. I must
not let her go on thinking Radford was to blame."

Sister Marie Thérèse looked to Mother Superior and
saw her nod. Without another word, they left the room.

Beau returned to the window again and placed the
palm of his hand against the coolness of the glass, flooded
with every emotion he could feel. Sorrow, pain, anger,
hatred, all whirling about in his head and confusing him.
Would he be able to convince Alanna of the truth, to
make her willing to return to Virginia? He looked outside
and saw the sun fighting to break through the dark
clouds. If he had only forced her to marry him when he
had found out about the child, none of this would have
happened. Radford would be alive and Alanna would
never have had to go through all that she had. He silently
cursed his own stubbornness, closed his eyes and leaned
back against the wall, wondering if his words would be

the right ones for the first time in his life. Then, feeling as if someone watched, his eyes flew open. Haloed in the doorway stood a slim figure with long, flowing, dark hair tumbling over her shoulders to her waist, her thin face solemn and unsmiling, her dark unreadable eyes trained on him.

"Alanna?" he whispered. Somehow she looked different. Older. He drew himself up when she came further into the room and went to the darkened fireplace. "Alanna, I've come to take you home."

"I have no home," came her bitter reply.

"But Virginia is the closest you'll ever come," he said softly.

"It only holds bad memories, not comfort."

"Please, Alanna, let me explain."

"Explain what?" she demanded, turning on him. "How Radford and you set out to drive me away? All you would have had to do was send me home again. That's all I ever asked of anyone." She looked back at the cold hearth.

"Alanna, the sister told me what happened. If you'll just sit down, I'll tell you our side of it."

"How did you find me?" she asked, ignoring his request.

"I'd rather start at the beginning."

"How did you find me?" she asked a bit more strongly, her eyes glinting with anger.

"By chance. When I was in the chapel—"

Her brow furrowed in puzzlement. "The chapel? What were you doing there?"

Beau's face reflected the pain he felt and rather than have her doubt its honesty, he looked away quickly, hoping she had not seen.

"Had you sought out the help of the priest?" she asked sharply.

"No," he whispered, unable to speak the truth so abruptly.

"Then what were you doing there?"

Beau found it difficult to tell her, wanting to explain everything step by step first, a little at a time, and not shock her with a cold, simple answer. But she gave him little choice. He drew a deep breath and braced himself for her tears.

"I was there to attend Radford's funeral."

He watched her, ready to move as soon as her grief overtook her. But to his surprise her face showed no emotion. She looked back to the marble slat at her feet.

"It's what he deserved," she said flatly.

Beau fought hard to contain his anger at her callousness, then realized she could feel no other way when she had yet to learn the truth. "Radford was not responsible for your kidnapping. Someone else hired Gallagher and sent the note."

Cold, hate-filled eyes found him. "Oh? Then how was it the message was penned by his hand?"

Beau shook his head and slowly walked closer to her. "I don't know. Until I find the person responsible, I never will. But I can tell you this. Radford died trying to find you, to bring you home again."

She eyed him suspiciously, but doubting her own certainty in the matter, looked away. "Then why bother now? He's dead," she said scornfully.

"Because I made him a promise."

"What promise?"

"I vowed to care for you."

"Oh, really?" she mocked. "And what of me? Don't I

438

have a say in what my future brings? Remember, Mr. Remington, I am a free woman now. I don't have to answer to anyone."

"Agreed," he concurred. "But why not go home to Virginia? You have friends there."

"I have made new ones here."

"The sisters? You wish to spend the rest of your days here within these walls, doing nothing, merely existing? It's not in your nature, Alanna." He drew up beside her, resting an arm across the mantel and studying her face. "If you fear what others will think, I can assure you they will never learn of it from me. What happened to you on board the *Sea Falcon* is our secret. You have my word on it." He could see a slight quiver to her chin and quickly added, "I'll give you a cabin of your own on Raven Oaks and pay for your services. In time you can save enough money to go wherever you please, should that be your wont." He frowned when he saw the odd smile on her lips and the way she looked at him.

"Right back where we started?" she asked, lifting a brow. "How convenient."

Being reminded of the truth pained him and he dropped his gaze to the floor before speaking. "On that I will give my word also. I shall never force myself upon you again." He looked to her once more. "Please, Alanna, say you'll return with me. I could bear Radford's death more easily knowing I fulfilled my promise to him."

Alanna quietly digested his words for a moment before turning for the door. "I will give you my answer in the morning," she said over her shoulder. When she reached the doorway, she paused and looked back at him, her gaze lingering on the handsome lines of his face. Then she turned and walked away.

Alone in her room that night after supper, Alanna sat by the small window gazing out at the sprinkling of stars dotting the velvet sky. She knew Beau was right, that in a very short time she would grow weary of the solitude of the convent no matter how kind the nuns were to her or how much she liked Sister Marie Thérèse. She leaned her head against the back of her chair, recalling the strange feeling she had had when she first saw Beau standing in the parlor. She had been flooded with relief, certain someone cared what happened to her, yet surprised it had been he. Then he admitted he had only come because he was committed to. One corner of her delicate mouth turned upward. I truly think he hasn't a heart, she mused. Not for me, anyway. I wonder if he was glad when Sister Marie Thérèse told him about the child. She rose from the chair and went to the bed to pull back the covers and slip from her robe. I guess I have little else here but this room, she thought, easing herself onto the hard surface of the bed and closing her eyes. Maybe he's right. If I save what he pays me, after a while I can return to England if I want. She yawned, realizing how tired she was. In the morning she would tell Beau of her decision.

Thirty-One

Having seen Alanna safely to her room at the Chester-field House, Beau started off toward the lawyer's office to advise him of Radford's death. His affairs would have to be settled before things could return to normal and the sooner it was done the better he would feel. He had already sent word ahead to Raven Oaks to advise Cain of his arrival and to make ready a cabin in which Alanna would stay. He did not, however, include the fact that Radford had not returned with them. He decided it was best told in person, since he knew how much Radford had meant to Cain.

Garrett Bosworth's office sat between a haberdashery and the bank, and only because Beau came upon it first did he decide to talk with the lawyer before seeking out Mr. Honeywell. The whitewashed sign hanging above the door swung in the cold sting of the late afternoon breeze, and Beau only glanced at it, wishing he was here for some other reason.

The man behind the desk looked up when he heard the office door open, and he quickly came to his feet when he saw who it was. "Beau," he sang, honestly pleased to see him as he reached out a hand to welcome his visitor. "When did you return?"

"Only this morning," Beau said, taking the chair Garrett offered. "And I'm not here for a social visit, I'm afraid."

"Oh?" Garrett asked, placing his crossed arms against the edge of his desk after sitting down again.

"It's about Radford."

"Radford? What about him?"

Beau took a slow, labored breath, knowing his news would come as a shock to Garrett, as it would to the rest of Williamsburg. The town would grieve his loss for some time to come. "He was killed in New Orleans. I had to leave him there."

"Oh, God, how awful," Garrett moaned, falling back in his chair. "How did it happen?"

A tired, painful sigh escaped Beau as he leaned forward to rest his elbows against his parted knees, his head hung low. "It was through my own stupidity," he confessed. "We sought to force the truth from a pirate's lips and found ourselves outnumbered. You know of Radford's easy nature. He was played the fool by the captain's trick and the scoundrel took his life."

"I'm so sorry, Beau," Garrett soothed. "I only wish there was something I could do—or say—to ease the hurt you feel." He fell silent, watching Beau. Then a frown shadowed his eyes. "What of Miss Bainbridge? Were you able to find her?"

Beau nodded. "But not until after—Radford never saw her again."

"Beau, don't blame yourself. I'm sure it was something that just happened. And I don't think Radford

442

would want you to feel like this."

A faint smile flitted across Beau's face. "Yes, I'm sure he wouldn't."

"Look," Garrett said, moving to the edge of the desk, "I'll take care of the legal end of things, and you come by tomorrow morning around ten. We'll discuss it then. All right? You look as if you could use a drink. Why don't you take a room at the Chesterfield House, if you haven't already, and rest up. I think you've done just about all you can for now."

Beau wearily rubbed the back of his neck. "Yes, I suppose you're right. But I must go to the bank first. I'll see you tomorrow."

Together they went to the door, where Beau stopped and extended his hand. "Thank you, Garrett."

"Surely, Beau," Garrett smiled comfortingly as he returned the handshake. "And, oh—bring Miss Bainbridge with you in the morning. What I have to say concerns her, too."

A slight puzzlement shadowed Beau's face, then disappeared. He couldn't imagine at first why Alanna would need to be present, thinking afterward that she had, after all, been engaged to Radford. He nodded, then stepped outside.

"Where are we going?" Alanna asked as Beau guided her out the front door of the Chesterfield House the next morning after a late breakfast.

"To see Garrett Bosworth."

"I'm afraid I don't know him," she said, hurriedly walking to keep up with Beau's long, effortless strides.

"He's Radford's lawyer."

"Lawyer?" she frowned, stopping in the middle of the sidewalk. "But what need is there for me to see him?"

Beau came to an abrupt halt and turned back to face her. "Because he asked if you'd be present when we discuss Radford's affairs."

The lines faded from her face. "But why me?"

"You'll find out in a few minutes if you'll hurry up," he growled impatiently, reaching out to take her elbow and hustle her along again.

Apparently Garrett had been watching for them from the window of his office, for once they reached the door he opened it to greet them. After taking Alanna's cloak, he turned to her.

"Miss Bainbridge," he said, taking her hands in his, "please let me express my sympathy at your loss."

I grieve only for my child, she thought bitterly, but rather than cause the man undue embarrassment for his ignorance of the truth, she smiled a weak nod of acceptance.

They each sat down on chairs precisely placed around Garrett's desk and waited while the lawyer pulled a pair of thin wire-rimmed glasses from his pocket and perched them on the end of his nose. Studiously he searched the desk top, which was filled with a large collection of papers, until he found the document he sought, and smiled as if surprised to have achieved such a feat. He glanced up at his audience, cleared his throat, and said, "This is Radford's will. Since the two of you are the only ones named in it, I see no reason to delay in reading it." He repositioned his glasses, concentrating on the penscript of the document, and missed the confused expression on Alanna's face.

Radford's will? Her lips moved with the question but

no sound escaped them. Me? But I don't understand. A slight frown wrinkled her brow, and she turned a suspicious gaze upon Beau. Is this another sordid trick he's playing? She opened her mouth to confront him, hearing instead the unvarying inflecton of the lawyer's voice as he read.

"I, Radford Meredith Chamberlain, this fifth day of December in the year of our Lord seventeen fifty-seven, under the sovereign rule of King George of England and being of sound body and mind do bequeath—"

Beau closely watched Garrett's face as the lawyer recited the words written on the page he held before him, not really hearing what the man said but recalling instead the last moment he had spent with Radford. He glanced at the woman at his side only briefly and then back at Garrett. It surprised him that Alanna should be a part of this. When had Radford decided to change his will and include her?

"To Beauregard Travis Remington: his choice of seven of my finest stallions, mares or both, and my father's gold watch."

Still Beau did not hear the lawyer's proclamation as his unconscious mind evoked an image of the pale and pain-filled face that declared his love for a woman with his dying breath. But what else had Radford tried to tell him? Beau closed his eyes, woefully searching his memory for the words Radford had spoken so ardently.

"The estate of Briarwood Manor, its servants and slaves, and any money I might have at the time of my death, I leave to my beloved Alanna Elizabeth Bainbridge."

Beau's eyes flew open. Now he remembered. The will. Radford had tried to tell him of the will.

445

"So attested and witnessed by one Garrett Bosworth, Attorney at Law."

Garrett laid aside the document, folded his hands and looked up, frowning when he saw Alanna. Her thin face wrinkled in lines of confusion. "Is something wrong, Miss Bainbridge?" he asked.

Alanna glanced up at him, her mouth opening and closing as if she hadn't the right words. Finally, in a voice choked with pain, she asked, "When was this written?"

Garrett looked back at the paper. "December fifth."

"Before I was kidnapped?"

"Yes."

Alanna's chin quivered. "Tell me how he acted."

"Acted?"

"Yes. What did he say?"

Puzzled, Garrett looked at Beau for understanding, only to find him absently studying the nails of one hand. He looked back at Alanna. "He—he was happy. All he talked of was marrying you and how fortunate he was to have found you. Why do you ask, Miss Bainbridge?"

Tears welled up in her eyes, and before she would allow either of them to see, she quickly rose, snatched her cloak from the hook on the wall and fled the office.

In a near run, she fought to wrap her garment about her, hardly aware of the crisp bite of the wind that whipped about her, and quickly made her way back to the Chesterfield House. She raced up the stairs and into her room, slamming the door behind her. Pressing her small frame against it, she was overcome by tears, and she sobbed uncontrollably. It was a great while before she could calm herself and, when she had, she went to the window and stared outside. Why would Garrett Bosworth lie to her? He had nothing to gain by it. No, it was

446

the truth. Every word Beau had said was exactly the way it had been. It hadn't been Radford who had had her kidnapped, nor he who had sent the note. She went to the valise that lay upon her bed and rummaged through it until she found the wrinkled piece of paper. She read it again. It had to be his handwriting. But how? Suddenly filled with anger and more confused than ever, she crumpled up the note.

"Oh, Radford," she wept, "please forgive me. How could I ever have doubted you?" She threw herself across the bed and buried her face in the pillow. If he had wanted Briarwood Manor to be hers, then she would accept it gladly and, as one last tribute, she would see it prosper, honoring the man who had laid down his life for her.

Thirty-Two

"Beg pardon, ma'am."

Alanna looked up from her work at the desk and laid aside her quill. "What is it, Maybelle?"

"Masta Remington's here ta see yo'."

The fine line of Alanna's brow arched slightly. "Show him to the parlor and tell him I'll be there directly."

"Yes'm." The maid curtsied and quietly closed the door again.

Alanna leaned back in her chair and gazed out the window, thinking how spring had come early this year, turning the dismal brown colors of the land into bright crisp greens. She had been mistress of Briarwood Manor for nearly three months, loving every minute of it, yet finding the loneliness of it at times overwhelming. She never went anywhere, except into Williamsburg occasionally to oversee the purchase of supplies for the house. She frowned, recalling one of those trips when she had unfortunately met Melissa Bensen and Blythe Robbins in the general store. Melissa's behavior had surprised Alanna, extending her good wishes for success in running Briarwood Manor and then suddenly asking if Alanna had ever discovered the culprit responsible for her abduction so many months before. Forced to remember the horrifying experience, Alanna crisply informed her that she hadn't, but with the evidence she had in her possession, it would only be a matter of time.

"You must come for tea sometime, Alanna. You can't lock yourself away forever," Melissa had said.

Reluctantly agreeing to do so at the first opportunity, Alanna had stood back and watched suspiciously as the two women walked away chattering quietly to themselves.

When she returned home that afternoon, she spoke with Lilly, her rather plump black cook, about the incident, wondering if she thought Melissa's attitude as strange as she did. Assured that it was nothing out of the ordinary where Melissa Bensen was concerned, Alanna dismissed the meeting, concentrating on matters more pressing. With the burning of the barn last fall, most of the cotton Radford had intended to sell had been destroyed, leaving the plantation short of funds and with the constant fear of whether or not they would make it through the next month. She had closed herself off in the study for days trying to devise a way to save money and not be forced into going to the banker for help.

The butler, Amos, a stout little man, had argued heatedly with Alanna the day she decided to fire the overseer.

"But ya need 'im, Miss Alanna," he had said. "Them's nothin' but lazy niggers and ya have ta beat 'em to get 'em ta work!"

"I don't agree, Amos," she said, shaking him off. "You'll see. If they want to eat, they'll have to work. Now

I'll hear no more about it." She wouldn't admit that, come spring and planting time, if her idea proved wrong she would hire another overseer. But for now she wouldn't think of it, putting Amos in charge of the servants instead and refusing to call them slaves.

A cloud drifted across the face of the sun and cast a shadow into the room. Alanna blinked, realizing she had been sitting there for several minutes while Beau waited in the parlor. Beau, she mused, wondering what reason had brought him this time. Hardly a week went by that he didn't suddenly appear on her doorstep with some sort of excuse or another. Most of the time he would say it was a custom not to pass by a neighbor's house without stopping, and Alanna grunted, wondering how many other, if any, neighbors were graced with his appearance. She rose, crossed the room and stepped into the foyer, pausing before the small gold-framed mirror that hung there to study her reflection. The corner of her lip curled upon seeing it, realizing how much she missed Tilly's hand at coiffuring her great lengths of hair. Poor Maybelle, she thought, she does really try, but she'll never be able to match Tilly's skill. With a tug at the bodice of her gown, she turned and went into the parlor.

"Good afternoon, Beau. Just passing by?" she mocked.

"Not exactly," he said, turning away from the window to look at her. "I'm actually here on business."

"Oh?" she said with a raised brow.

Beau waited for her to sit down before he joined her, taking a chair opposite her. "I'll come right to the point. I was talking with John Harrison at the general store today," he said, focusing his attention on the floor at his feet. "He told me—reluctantly—how deeply in debt you are to him."

451

"What?" she demanded angrily. "How dare he discuss my personal affairs with anyone else!"

"I also talked with several other businessmen and the banker. They all tell me the same."

"How dare you!" she screamed, jumping to her feet in a rage. "You have no right!"

"Alanna," he coaxed, coming to her side and attempting to take her hand in his, but she jerked free of him. "I made a promise to Rad. He—"

"He what? Asked you to spy on me?"

"No, of course not. He told me how much trouble Briarwood Manor was in and asked that I would take care of you. I wasn't spying. I was only fulfilling his request."

"And you think I cannot manage on my own. Well, you're wrong," she seethed. "I can manage quite well, thank you."

"Then why did you fire the overseer? And why do you ration the food? I'm not blind, Alanna. I know you're in trouble and I've come to offer a solution."

"Which is?" she demanded hotly.

"To buy Briarwood Manor."

She laughed almost hysterically. "And leave me homeless?"

"It wouldn't leave you homeless!" he argued. "You'd be a very wealthy woman. I just mean not to let Radford's estate be divided among the merchants in Williamsburg, that's all!"

"Radford this, and Radford that," she screamed. "Do you ever think of me?"

He opened his mouth to respond, but snapped it closed and started for the door. "After you've thought about it," he threw back over his shoulder, "you'll see I'm right. You know where to find me."

"Don't count on it!" she called after him.

"You did what?" Joshua Cain bellowed.

"I offered to buy her out," Beau growled, pouring himself a glass of brandy as the two men discussed the rewards of Beau's trip into Williamsburg.

"That's just fine," Cain scolded. "And what have you left her?"

"What do you mean, what have I left her? The sale of her plantation would leave her a great deal of money. Not many women around here can say that."

"And what good is wealth if you are alone?"

"I'm alone!" he stormed in protest.

"Yes, and see how you behave."

Beau glared at Cain for a moment, contemplating the idea of reminding the man that he was merely an overseer and not his judge, but changed his mind, going to the sideboard instead to replenish his glass. "It won't be long before some gentleman will call on her. She's young and beautiful, and wealth can be enough to entice any man. She won't be alone for long."

"Enough to entice you?"

"I don't need wealth," he snapped. "I already have it."

"Yes. But you need Alanna," Cain said, casually strolling to a chair by the fireplace and sitting down.

"Oh, I do?" he peeled, glaring at Cain's back. "And just what makes you say that?"

"Beau, I've known you all of your life. There isn't a person around that can read you better than I. The day Alanna was kidnapped you nearly went to pieces. Was it because you sympathized with Radford? No. It was because you felt something deeper for that young woman than friendship to Radford. You cared for her, feared for her, but most of all you loved her. Deny it, if you can." He turned slowly in his chair to confront Beau. "Look me in the eyes and say it."

Beau stared at him a moment then turned and went to the window. "So what if I do love her? What does it matter?"

"What does it matter?" Cain echoed angrily. "It means you should ask her to marry you and solve two problems at one time!"

Beau turned back, a dark scowl hooding his eyes. "Damn it, man. Stop trying to run my life! You talk as if you think you're my father."

Cain left his chair and drew nearer, the deep lines of his face softened in the candlelight. "That's because I am," he said quietly.

Beau's dark eyes widened in surprise and confusion. He turned his head from one side to the other, his lips parted, unable to comprehend what Cain had said. "What?"

"I said I'm your father," Joshua answered, his eyes never leaving Beau's until the younger man turned away with a shake of his head.

"I don't believe you."

Perching on the edge of the desk, Cain studied his hands folded on one knee. "Can't say I blame you. But whether you like it or not, I am."

Beau spun around. "You're lying. They loved each other."

"Yes, they did."

"Then how can—"

"There was a time," Cain broke in, "when Andrew was away more than he was home. Your mother grew lonely

454

and sought my company to pass away the time. At first I went to the house to share a glass of wine with her after dinner. It became as regular as the passing of seasons. Nothing more ever happened between us than casual conversation. Then one night when Andrew had been gone for nearly two weeks, your mother suddenly appeared on my doorstep. She was frightened. I could see it in her eyes. She had had a bad dream, one where she feared her husband's death. She came to me for comfort." Joshua rubbed the tired line of his jaw. "If anyone is to blame, it is me." He glanced up to find Beau glaring at him.

"Well?" Beau demanded.

"Well, what?"

Beau slapped his glass of brandy down on the desk with such force it rattled from the abuse. "Well, don't stop there. What happened next?"

"I—I really don't think I need—"

"You seduced her. Or was it rape? Maybe that's why she hated me. Because I was conceived from violence."

"No. It wasn't anything like that," Cain answered sharply. "And you're a fine one to talk."

The color drained from Beau's face almost instantly. "That was different."

"Yes, it was," Cain agreed. "What your mother and I shared that night was love. Even though for her it lasted only a few hours, *it was love.*" He left the edge of the desk and moved closer. "In the morning light she knew she had sinned, although I never felt the same. She had been unfaithful to Andrew, the man she truly loved. You, unfortunately, were a constant reminder of that fact. That's why she turned against you."

Beau's shoulders trembled with the breath he took.

"But why, after all this time, have you chosen to tell me?"

"Because I refuse to sit by any longer and watch you grow more miserable for something I did," he said. "You're afraid to love, afraid you'll be hurt again. And all because of something I created. Monica didn't hate you. She hated herself and took it out on you. All women aren't like that, Beau. Alanna isn't."

Beau grunted. "She has every reason in the world to hate me. More than my mother," he frowned, staring out the window again.

"Then change her mind."

"How?"

"Make her fall in love with you all over again."

"Again? What makes you think she ever did?"

Cain smiled. "You're the one who's blind. Not me. And if my hunch is right, it won't take much doing. Look, Beau, right now there are two things that mean the world to you. Saving Briarwood Manor for Radford, and that stubborn little woman living there. God knows you two deserve each other! And I'll do anything I can to help."

A lazy smile spread across Beau's face. "I should have known."

"Known what?" he asked.

"That I was from your loins. No other man but a father would have such patience."

"And love," Cain added with a smile.

"Miss Alanna?" Amos called. "Someone's coming."

Alanna stood up and removed her gardening gloves, studying the horizon and the shadowed figure riding in.

"Take those inside," she said to Maybelle, pointing to the tulips they had cut, "and put them in a vase."

"Yes'm," Maybelle answered, hurriedly doing as she had been told.

It couldn't be Beau, she thought, shading her eyes from the sun. He was just here yesterday. Suddenly remembering that she was kneeling in the dirt near the flowerbed outside the house, she glanced down and saw the smudges on her gown. She quickly brushed them away as best she could and looked up again, recognizing the proud figure as he rode nearer. Now what does he want? she sighed.

"Good morning, Miss Bainbridge," Beau smiled. "You're looking quite lovely."

She stared at him suspiciously, absently chewing on the inside of her lip. "Why have you come?" she asked after a while. "To make another offer?"

Beau's grin widened. "You could say that."

"Well, I'm not interested," she said, turning away to pick up her basket of gardening tools and start up the stairs.

"Please," he begged. "Hear me out."

At the top of the stairs, she stopped and looked back. "If I must."

Awkwardly, he glanced about them, spying several of the servants who stood watching in curious silence. "Must we talk here?"

"If what you have to say is what I think it is, then you mustn't waste the energy in getting off your horse. You'll only have to get on again once I've asked you to leave." She grasped the handle of the basket in both hands and set a hard look upon him.

He smiled softly, crossed his wrists against one thigh

457

and relaxed. "I apologize for yesterday," he said. "I shall never suggest it again. In fact, there's no possible way I could afford to do it now. All I ask is a moment of your time." He looked about them again. "In private, if I may."

Alanna eyed him a moment, and when she could not find the arrogant gleam in his eye that usually caused her to bristle, she nodded and went inside without waiting for him to dismount. She set her basket and gloves on the table in the foyer, called for Maybelle to serve tea, and went into the study before Beau had even entered the house.

"In the study, Mr. Remington," she called, sounding more like a nanny than a prospective business partner.

Beau grinned, knowing this would only be the first of many such confrontations.

Radford's tall wing back chair seemed to engulf the small figure sitting in it, but when Beau first stepped into the room he thought how natural she looked, as if she had been born to it. He hid his smile and took the chair she pointed out for him.

"Now, what is so urgent that we must speak in private, Mr. Remington?" she asked, her elbows resting on the arms of the chair, her fingers entwined.

"Beau," he said. "I wish you'd call me Beau."

She shrugged indifferently.

"I'm here to offer a deal," he said, quickly raising a hand to silence her when he saw the sudden knot of her brow. "I am in need of a job and you need someone knowledgeable in running a plantation."

Alanna laughed suddenly. "A job?"

"Yes. Since I no longer live at Raven Oaks, I must find some other means of support."

"Is this some sort of trick?" she demanded, leaning forward on the desk. "I do not find it amusing."

"We both know how much trouble the plantation is in and I'm willing to help solve your problems," he replied, ignoring her pointed words.

"Oh, really? And just how do you plan to do that? You have your own to manage."

"Not anymore."

Alanna fell back in her chair. "Not anymore," she said. "And what's that supposed to mean?"

"I sold it," he said flatly.

"Sold it? To whom?"

"To my father."

Heatedly, she rose from her chair and pointed a shaky finger at the door. "Get out! I haven't time for games."

Beau smiled to himself when he realized how it had sounded. "If you'll just sit down, I'll explain."

"Get out!" she demanded, and all of a sudden Beau's mirth vanished.

"And I said sit down!"

Alanna felt as if a cold wave of winter wind had whipped into the room, and without much hesitation she did as he bade, more surprised by his outburst than at her own cowardice.

"That's better," he said, relaxing in his chair and crossing his ankle to one knee. "For seventeen years I thought my father dead. Then last night Cain told me otherwise."

"Joshua? How would he know?"

"Because *he* is my father," he said, watching the fair lines of her brow wrinkle. "I couldn't believe it at first, either."

"And what changed your mind?"

"Something he said." He looked away to pluck a piece of lint from his coat sleeve, obviously not wishing to volunteer another word.

"And will you not share your understanding with me?" she asked.

He looked back at her. "No," he said simply. "It's of no importance to you. I only tell you this much so you will understand why I turned over Raven Oaks to the man who deserves it."

"But Joshua hadn't the wealth to purchase such land, and if he did you wouldn't be here seeking employment."

"I guess one would call it a trade rather than a purchase," he added.

"You're confusing me," she said, pressing her fingertips to her temple.

"For more than a score and ten years, he hid the truth from everyone to save us all a lot of pain and sorrow. In doing so he had to veil his love for me lest someone suspect the truth. Giving him the land that he loved as well wasn't nearly enough to equal what he had forfeited."

"And in telling the truth he drove you from him," she added with a lift to one brow.

"Quite the contrary. The deal was that if you allowed me to help get Briarwood Manor on its own again, I would return to my home and we would live as father and son. But either way, I am a pauper until I inherit the land of my father.'

As Alanna grew quiet, idly toying with the base of the candelabrum sitting on the desk, Beau watched her, wondering what it was that she was thinking. Then a smile flitted across her face and vanished before she looked up again.

"And if I hire you—to help in the management of Briarwood Manor—you will follow my orders to the letter?" she asked cautiously.

"To the letter, Mistress Bainbridge," he nodded.

"And you will follow the rules I have set down for all my servants?" she said, growing more daring with each question.

"Whatever you wish," he agreed.

She leaned back in her chair and let one hand dangle over the arm while she rested her chin against the knuckles of her other hand. She contemplated the idea, growing acutely aware of the position in which she would have him should she agree. And why not? After all these months, and everything she had had to endure at his hands, he would finally work for her. She would give him a taste of how she had lived under his rule, not to mention the fact that Briarwood Manor really needed him.

"What kind of payment do you ask?" she said after a while.

"None. Only a place to live and food to eat."

"That's nonsense! You'd be nothing more than a—" She caught herself before she had finished.

"My payment will be to see the plantation prosper again. It's all I want."

"You have never lived in poverty before, Mr. Remington," she noted. "You will be uncomfortable."

"But I will survive. You have, Mistress Bainbridge. And please skip the formality. Call me Beau," he instructed again.

"If you are to work for me, I can have it no other way. We are not friends, Mr. Remington, and I shall not lead the others to think we are." Loving the sense of power

461

over him she experienced, she rose and casually wandered about the room. "You shall have a free hand in deciding what is best for Briarwood Manor, Mr. Remington, but under no circumstances will you follow out your ideas without first checking with me. I am in charge here and I would appreciate it if you kept that in mind."

"Yes, ma'am," he agreed with a soft smile, one she failed to notice as she eyed him up and down. Her gaze lingering on his garments, she raised a single brow.

"The first thing you shall do is to have a change of clothes. If you're serious about this undertaking and wish others to know it, you will have to shed your silks and velvets." She looked away, crossed her arms in back of her and began to pace again.

"The only time you will be allowed to enter this house is when we discuss your ideas. You may have the overseer's cabin, but you shall have to see to its upkeep yourself since, I cannot afford someone to do it for you." She paused a moment before another idea came to mind. "As for your meals, I realize very few men are able to cook so I will allow you to eat in the kitchen as long as Lilly approves. She is very important to me so tread lightly, Mr. Remington. I would not hesitate to sever your employ before endangering Lilly's happiness. Do you understand?" she asked, turning on him once more.

The nod of his head was his only answer.

"Good," she smiled in satisfaction, returning to the desk where she pulled open the top drawer just as someone knocked on the door.

"I have yo'r tea, Mistress Alanna," Maybelle smiled after Alanna motioned her inside.

"Thank you, Maybelle. Just leave it here," she said,

462

pointing to the corner of the desk before she searched through the drawer again. "And tell Amos I wish to speak with him."

"Yes'm." Maybelle curtsied and quickly disappeared.

Alanna extracted a leather-bound book from the drawer. Awkwardly, she laid it upon the desk top and centered her attention on Beau again. She noticed how his eyes had grown hooded as he rested his chin on his thumb, a knuckle pressed to his lips while he leaned against the arm of his chair. It sent a chill through her, and she realized she would have to be very careful in the way she handled him. He might be a pauper as he had said, but he was still Beau Remington. She swallowed the sudden lump in her throat and pushed the book his way.

"It's Radford's ledger. I'm afraid I can't make heads nor tails of it, but I'm sure it will be of importance to you. You may take it and keep it with you if you like," she said, spotting Amos in the doorway. "Come in, Amos."

The round-figured butler shuffled into the room, his frosty white hair contrasting brightly with his wrinkled ebony brow, and his face marked his wonderment at having been summoned. He presented quite a stately appearance in his dark gray suit, white ruffled shirt and gloves, remaining silent, his posture erect, despite his age.

"Amos, Mr. Remington will be living with us for a while. Show him the empty cabin and tell Lilly she will be sharing the kitchen table with another." She looked at Beau. "If there's nothing else, I have work to do."

"I think you've covered it, Mistress Alanna," he said, leaving his chair and taking the ledger from her desk. "I'll send word when I've decided on something." With a polite nod, he turned around and headed from the room,

463

Amos respectfully following several steps behind.

From the large window of the study, Alanna stood off to one side, watching the two men walk across the yard toward the overseer's cabin. Only time would tell, but she felt certain she could repay Beau tenfold for all the discomforts he had bestowed upon her. Her smile turned to one of pure mischief as she spun around and bounced from the study.

Thirty-Three

Thunder exploded. Two faces loomed above her. Alanna fought desperately to rise, feeling the icy fingers hold her down. She screamed, but no sound erupted, hearing instead only the wicked laughter of the men. Someone called her name. Finding herself suddenly free, she rose, studying the shadowed figure in the distance.

"Alan-n-n-na," the voice beckoned again.

"W-who are you?" She heard her voice, but knew her lips had not moved.

"It's me, Radford."

Tears of joy burned her eyes. "Oh, Radford. I thought you were dead."

As she moved nearer, a haze floated over him, distorting his tall, lean figure. She stopped, confused by the startling occurrence and cringing when the fog seemed to choke the breath from her. She coughed, rubbing the moisture from her eyes. Reaching out a hand to him, she pulled back sharply when she discovered he had changed. A smaller, darker shape stood before her, holding something out to her. An infant's wail broke the eerie stillness. Before she could grasp the child, the shadow tossed the baby away. The splash the body made hitting water reverberated in Alanna's ears.

"No-o-o," she screamed, running frantically in search of the infant.

An arm reached out in front of her, stopping her short, and thrust a wrinkled paper in her hand. She looked up. Only the green fog floated about her.

"W-wait," she cried. "Who-who are you?"

Unfolding the paper, she gasped when she recognized Radford's handwriting. Then, as if consumed by the devil, the letter burst into flames. She screamed.

Alanna lazily rolled over on her back and stretched in the warm comfort of her four poster bed. It felt wonderful to relax in the thick pillow of feathers beneath her, and for only a moment she felt a twinge of guilt for her indolence before an unexpected yawn captured her full attention. Cradling her head in her arms folded behind her, she studied the ceiling overhead, recalling the nightmare that had awakened her in the darkness of early morning. It had been nearly a month since the last one, giving her false hope that they were over for good. Why all of a sudden would one happen again? Dismissing it as best she could, she frowned, wondering where Beau might be at this very moment. It had been two days since he left the study with Radford's ledger tucked beneath his arm, and she had yet to see him. In fact she wasn't even sure he had eaten in the kitchen with Lilly each morning as she had allowed him to do. It mustn't appear that she cared one way or another, but curiosity bade her to inquire if he had had a change of heart about leaving

Raven Oaks. Her dark eyes shadowed as she thought how it must have taken a lot of courage simply to turn over to Cain the land he had built from very little into one of the richest plantations in Virginia without some sort of misgivings.

A splattering against the windowpane penetrated her thoughts and Alanna sent a questioning look in its direction, leaving her bed to investigate the sound. Pulling back the lace curtains, her shoulders drooped when she discovered the gentle rain that trailed minute droplets against the glass and distorted the view of the yard below. Surely it meant she would be confined to the house for the day. She sighed, wondering if she should spend the better part of it in bed, only to hear her stomach rumble its hunger. Deciding not to wait for Maybelle to bring breakfast to her, she lifted a white silken robe from the foot of the bed and headed for the kitchen.

Barefoot, she padded noiselessly down the long carpeted staircase, a chill running through her once she pressed a foot to the marble floor in the foyer. She pulled her robe more tightly about her and went into the kitchen, not once considering the way she looked with her unbound hair cascading to her waist and bare toes peeking from beneath her gown nor expecting to find someone already there having breakfast. She froze the instant she saw him, wishing somehow she could turn and run without his noticing her, but knowing it was too late when he sat his cup in its saucer and smiled up at her.

"Good morning, Mistress Alanna," Beau said softly, rising casually to draw out a chair for her at his side.

She swallowed the lump in her throat, unable to mutter a greeting of her own, but did somehow manage a weak smile in return before crossing to the cupboard. Nervously, she opened the tin of tea leaves, sprinkled a few into a cup and went to the hearth where she carefully lifted the kettle of hot water from the fire.

"I was hoping to see you this morning," she heard him say. "I have a couple of suggestions I would like to discuss if you have the time."

With the kettle safely hung on its peg again, she drew in a breath to calm her rapid pulse and returned to the table where she sat down across from him. "Where's Lilly?" she asked, hoping to sound light, but in fact sounding rather shaky.

"In the root cellar selecting a ham for dinner," he said with a frown. "Is something wrong?"

Alanna couldn't bring herself to meet his eyes. How could she explain the strange sensation that overtook her the minute she found him sitting so comfortably in the kitchen as if he belonged there? How could she tell him that, for some reason, spotlighted in the bright orange glow of the fire he seemed more handsome than he ever had before? Having shed his finery for a homespun shirt, breeches, and dark leather boots that came to below the knee, he had lost what small degree he might have had of the dandy she had mistaken him for so many months ago. It was easy to see why Cinnamon and so many others had fallen in love with him. She took a swallow of tea and courageously looked up. His dark hooded eyes engulfed her, sending that queer response over her once more. As if seeing the handsome features of his face for the first time, she stared openly, appraising the lean line of his jaw, the drawn brows shadowing the intenseness of his hawkish gaze, a thin, straight nose and a firm, but almost sensuous mouth now slightly curved into a mocking smile. She could feel the blood rush to her cheeks.

"No," she said looking away. "I was merely surprised to find you here."

"You shouldn't be," he said, cradling his cup in both hands. "It is by your word."

"I know," she corrected him. "I only thought you'd have gone by now."

He leaned back in his chair and laid one arm along the edge of the table, the elbow of the other hooked over the finial at his shoulder. He studied her intently. "You look quite lovely this morning. I had forgotten how beautiful you are when rousted from slumber."

Shocked by his boldness and lack of concern for the ears that might hear, she sent him a contemptuous glare before quickly scanning the room to see if Lilly had returned. "Please, Mr. Remington," she warned, "have the decency to keep the past just that!"

He shrugged heedlessly. "It was only meant as a compliment."

"I can do without them," she snapped, concentrating on the teacup in her hands.

A wry grin spread across his face, and he tried unsuccessfully to hide it. "Would you prefer to have breakfast or discuss business?" he asked. "If it's more to your liking, we can meet in the study later, after you've dressed properly."

Alanna felt as if her entire body was aflame with his remark, and she instinctively clutched the neckline of her gown to pull its lace collar tightly beneath her chin. Clumsily, she rose with teacup in hand and moved toward the door.

"We'll discuss your ideas in the study in one half-hour, Mr. Remington," she said unnerved, pausing long enough to draw in a slow breath before continuing. "Don't be late. I've important things to do today and cannot afford your tardiness."

"Yes, madam." He bowed as she passed by him. "In one half-hour."

The teacup rattled against the saucer in her trembling hand. It was all she could do to stop herself from glancing back at him while leaving the kitchen. She knew he watched, but rather than let him know how much he affected her, she squared her shoulders, raised her quivering chin in the air, and strode from his sight. When she reached the staircase, she hurriedly ascended, splashing tea over the edge of the cup without any degree of concern. With the door to her room closed safely behind her, she pressed her back against it and breathed a sigh of gratitude for her privacy once more.

"Damn him," she growled, going to the bedside table and setting her teacup upon it. Why did he have to come here? I was better off without him. Angrily, she threw herself across the bed, rolled onto her back and stared up at the ceiling. And why does his nearness touch me so? I do not care for him anymore yet I behave like a young maiden experiencing her first love. Does he suspect? She shook her head. He doesn't! He couldn't! It was only the surprise of seeing him there that caused me to react so. Of being alone with him! Absently, she touched the lace trim on the sleeve of her robe, remembering the absence of similar cloth on his garb and deciding how much more masculine he was without it, how much better he looked. Her eyes widened with the growl of frustration that exploded from her, and she flew from her bed and stormed the wardrobe. I won't think about him! I won't! she vowed, tearing open the doors

470

and whipping about the gowns hanging inside.

Selecting a plain worsted with long sleeves and high collar, she irately put it on and went to the mirror hanging above the dresser. With vigorous strokes, she brushed the tangles from her hair then twisted it into a knot high upon her head and secured it with several hairpins. She stood back and appraised her task with a look of satisfaction before she stalked from the room to descend upon the study.

"Come in, Mr. Remington," she said, sensing his presence in the doorway several minutes after she had sat down behind the desk. She kept her eyes trained on the paper she held. "And close the door."

"Are you sure?"

She looked up with a frown. "Of what?"

"Well, I think for appearances sake we should not be alone with the door closed," he said, fighting down a smile that tugged at the corners of his mouth.

"Close—the—door," she said slowly, her voice low and articulate. "I assure you nothing more than conversation shall ever transpire between us."

He shrugged and gave the door a gentle push, letting it shut before he walked further into the room. "I was only concerned with what others might think," he said.

"They are not allowed to think, only do their job. As are you," she reminded him. "Now do sit down and tell me what it is you want."

He stared at her a moment, wanting very much to tell her exactly what he wanted but knowing it was too soon. Mentally shrugging off the feeling, he took a chair beside the desk. "I wish to go to Raven Oaks and speak with Joshua."

"When?" she asked, her interest piqued.

"Today, if you will allow it."

"But it's raining," she protested.

Beau's dark brows knotted. "It usually does this time of year."

"Oh, I didn't mean that the way it sounded. I only thought to go with you. It's been such a long while since I've seen him or Tilly or Bessy or—"

"I don't think it will last long," he broke in. "The sky is already beginning to clear. If you dress for it, I don't think we'll get too wet."

Alanna's mouth suddenly curled upward with a thought—

Beau had been right in saying she wouldn't get too wet. She was as dry as when she sat talking with him in the study. A devilish smile twisted her mouth and Alanna reached up to pull away the leather flap that covered the window of her carriage. Ahead she could see blue sky and the cheerful rays of golden warming sunlight, although the steady downfall of rain continued to beat against the roof of the coach. Occasionally she heard a disgruntled curse directed at the horses for slowing their pace and she grinned all the more knowing Beau was probably soaked to the bone by now.

A loud thunderbolt cracked overhead, and of a sudden the horses broke into a frantic gallop. With one small hand clamped onto the edge of the seat, the other to the leather window-covering, Alanna hung on for dear life as they raced down the potted road. She opened her mouth to call out to him, but instead when the wheels hit another rut, she was thrown roughly to the floor, her skirts flying up about her waist. Her temper raged.

"Beauregard Remington," she screamed. "I demand you stop—"

The carriage suddenly veered to the left and Alanna then bounced against the door. Pain shot through her and, deciding to stay on the floor rather than fight for the narrow seat of the coach, she resigned herself to the position on the floor, each hand grasping the thickly cushioned seat on either side, her feet spread apart to balance her. The ride continued on for a great length of time, and she became gradually aware of the fact that he did not intend to stop until they reached their destination. In the shadowed darkness of the coach, her sultry eyes burned with rage.

The carriage turned sharply up the road lined with black oaks and slowed to some degree as it approached the manor. Its driver sawed against the tension of the reins, and a moment later the exquisitely styled coach from Briarwood Manor rolled to a stop.

The rain had diminished to a drizzle and, wiping the droplets from his brow with the back of his hand, Beau jumped down from the coachman's perch, waved a greeting to Joshua who watched from the veranda, and proceeded to open the carriage door. A low growl sounded from within the darkened cubicle, and Beau instantly retreated a step.

"You irresponsible clod," shrieked a voice from inside.

Beau withdrew even further when the small figure seemed to catapult from within, her hands up, nails ready to claw his face. He caught her only inches from her goal and crushed her to his chest.

"I humbly apologize for the ride, Mistress Bainbridge, but it has been a long while since I mastered a team."

"Let go of me!" she screamed, struggling against the dampness of his shirt and feeling the moisture quickly absorbed into the bodice of her gown.

"Certainly, ma'am," he concurred. "But not until I see you on dry ground. We don't want to ruin your slippers."

A shriek exploded from her as Beau agilely lifted her in his arms, turned about, and headed for the stairs of the veranda and Joshua who stood in amused awe at the situation.

"Put me down, you insensitive knave," she wailed. "You're soaking my gown!"

"Yes, ma'am," he grinned, pulling her closer to him, the fingertips of his hand beneath her arm intimately pressed against the fullness of one breast. "Had we obtained the skill of a coachman instead, none of this would have happened."

"So that you could ride inside with me?" she squealed, pushing against his hard chest in an effort to free herself. "You forget your place."

He stopped abruptly several feet away from the steps and let the sprinkling of rain hit against her nose and cheeks. "Would you prefer to walk?" he speculated with a glance at the puddle beneath him.

"I prefer you not hold me in this manner!" she stormed.

Beau glanced up at Joshua, shrugged, and promptly slipped his arm from beneath her knees.

"No-o-o," she wailed, clutching him.

"But I see no other way to hold you than in this manner," he teased, letting her feet dangle only inches above the mud and water.

474

"Ohhh!" she growled. "Sit me on the steps, you idiot!"

After a moment and a lift of his brows, he again caught her knees in the crook of his arm, but somehow managed to look as if he might stumble in the slippery underfooting, producing a squeal of helplessness from his small burden.

"Do not fear, madam," he chided, "you are safe in my arms."

"Ha!" she growled. "I fear for my life. And if you do not make haste, I shall catch a chill and surely die of fever."

Silently, but not without a smile on his face, Beau reached the first step in two easy strides, gently putting her down with a wide sweep of one arm. "At your beck and command," he bowed.

A low, throaty growl sounded within her, and she whirled from him to confront the grinning face of the man who had witnessed the entire scene. "If it's not too much trouble, Mr. Cain," she spat, "I would appreciate a warm bath and a gentle fire to dry my clothes."

"Certainly, madam," Cain nodded, having quickly swallowed his amusement. "I'll have Tilly see to your care." He stepped aside in time to allow her to pass and looked back at Beau with a wide grin and shake of his head once she had gone inside. "This is not exactly the way I would have wanted to see you treat her. But I suppose you have a good reason."

Beau lifted his wide shoulders, reached up to run his fingers through his damp hair, and climbed the remainder of the steps. "I merely thought to get even with her for making me ride all the way in the rain."

"Well, I would say you've accomplished your goal. And a little more, I might add."

"She's a difficult woman, Josh. It's easier to anger her than make her smile."

"She has good cause not to," Joshua reminded him.

"Yes, I know. But I can't just tell her I love her. She wouldn't believe it, and with the state she's in now, she'd only use it against me."

"Do not lose faith," Joshua urged, reaching up to put an arm around Beau's shoulders only to change his mind. "I think you could use a bath, too, or at least a drink."

"Both," Beau grinned. "And not necessarily in that order."

"Alanna, it's so good to have yo' here again," Tilly beamed as she helped Alanna slip from her gown.

"Thank you, Tilly. It's good to see you, too."

The young maid waited for Alanna to finish disrobing and slide beneath the surface of the hot sudsy water before she added another warm bucketful to the copper tub. "When Masta Beau sent word yo' be livin' here again, I was so happy. Then I hear yo' got Masta Chamberlain's land, and I was happier. I knowed it was what yo' wanted." She stepped back, bucket in hand, and fearfully bit at her lower lip. "It is, ain't it?"

Alanna vigorously lathered her neck with the soap-filled sponge. "Yes. You and I both know what would have happened if I had returned here."

Tilly looked away, her dark eyes sad. "Yes'm. Yo' probably would have fallen in love with him again."

The sponge fell into the bathwater. "Tilly!"

"Well, it's the way it should be," Tilly said.

A disgusted curl appeared on Alanna's mouth as she secured the sponge again and began scrubbing her knees. "It would have been one-sided."

"Oh, no, Miss Alanna," Tilly argued excitedly. "He's loved yo' for a long time."

"Have you lost your senses? He's never loved anyone!" Alanna said with an angry slap to the water that sent droplets flying everywhere. "He proved that the day he saw me to the door with another woman draped on his arm."

"Cinnamon?"

"Yes, Cinnamon," Alanna said without jealousy or rancor. "And it mattered not who she was, just that he wasted no time in finding a replacement. No, Tilly," she added, reaching for her sponge, "I will not believe he ever loved me."

Tilly quickly came to the edge of the tub and knelt down. "Then why has he not got a mistress after Cinnamon? I can tell yo' true he only used her to hurt yo'. 'Cause yo' hurt him."

"I hurt him? How?" Alanna demanded.

"'Cause yo' was willin' to marry Masta Chamberlain. I hear him rantin'. I knows!"

Alanna looked away angrily. "I only hurt his pride. Not his heart."

"Is that why he fills his days and nights with work? To ease his pride?" Tilly demanded. "Miss Alanna, I work for Masta Beau a long time. I know when he hurts. Do yo' think he only come to Briarwood Manor to help? No. He wants to be close to you."

"Tilly, this is absurd," Alanna said, refusing to believe another word. "Now cease this senseless talk and see an iron pressed to my gown. I will finish my bath alone."

Tears welled up in Tilly's eyes and her voice came out weak and sorrowful. "I's sorry I make yo' mad."

Alanna turned a surprised look upon the girl, instantly aware how Tilly had mistaken her anger. She smiled softly. "You haven't. It's just—well, something you'll never understand. Now hurry. I'd like to renew some old acquaintances."

"Yes'm," Tilly grinned brightly. Rising, she retrieved Alanna's gown from the back of the chair by the fire and left the room.

Alanna leaned comfortably back in the tub, her gentle, apologetic smile fading into a troubled frown. Tilly was wrong, frightfully wrong. Beau came to Briarwood Manor only to save it, not because he saw no other way to be near her. Just speculation would not prove truth, she mused. To hear the words upon his lips would be the only way.

Thirty Four

"Good morning, Joshua," Alanna smiled brightly when she found him alone in the study a short while later.

He rose to greet her with outstretched arms. "And good morning to you. You look as lovely as ever. I'd say running a plantation agrees with you."

Alanna laughed. "A fine turn of events, don't you think?" she asked, glancing up at him from the comfort of his embrace. "At one time we worked here and now we *both* own plantations. I hope you're doing better than I."

Cradled in his arm, he led her to a chair and watched her sit down before he drew up another to face her. "Raven Oaks does well. Of course, it always has. It had a good leader to run it."

"As it does now, I'm sure," she protested gaily.

He nodded gratefully for her faith in him. "And one day yours will prosper, too. Beau will see to it. Would you care for a sherry?"

"Mmm, yes."

Joshua went to the sideboard and filled two glasses. "I wanted to see you long before this," he said, returning to her side and handing her a glass, "but you know how busy a plantation becomes in spring. I apologize for my rudeness."

"No need," she told him. "I am just as guilty. And that's why I was elated when Beau asked to come." She looked at the crystal stemware in her hand. "And *I* apologize for our rude arrival."

Joshua hid his amusement behind his glass as he took a sip of sherry. "Don't. I rather enjoyed it, I must admit. There never has been a woman who could return his favors before you. It does him good. Of course, there was a time when such actions would have angered him. I think he's mellowed."

Alanna lifted one brow. "Possibly, but I wonder how he would react now if he suddenly found himself covered with flour?"

Joshua chuckled. "And if a woman doubled up her fist to strike him?"

"Yes," Alanna laughed openly. "If I had only known who he was."

He studied her awhile, hearing a sound from her he heard far too seldom and sensing an emotion in her she fought to conceal. Without a word he sat down next to her. "I wish you could know him as I do."

Alanna's brow crinkled in surprise. "Whatever for?" she asked.

Spurred by her interest, he sat his glass on the nearby table and took her hand in his. "You do trust me, don't you, Alanna?"

She cocked her head to one side rather suspiciously and nodded.

"And that I wouldn't lie to you?"

"Yes," she replied cautiously.

He smiled softly, then sighed before going on. "Beau was a very unhappy youngster where his mother was concerned. For reasons of her own she shunned him, and he grew to hate all women thinking them all the same. But with you I saw a change in him. He fought it at first and then, in time, softened, even though he tried to hide it from everyone, especially from himself."

Alanna drew back slowly, hesitant to hear any more yet wondering what forced him to speak. She listened intently.

"I've never seen him as angry as he was that day you announced your plans to marry Radford. I couldn't decide at first if it was because the two of you had snuck behind his back to trick him or because he truly didn't want to lose you. I was sure, however, the morning Radford came to tell us you'd been kidnapped. I could read it in his eyes." Letting go of her, he rose and crossed to the window to gaze outside. "He's a proud man, Alanna. Too proud, I'm afraid, to voice his feelings for another."

"Why are you telling me this?" she asked impatiently.

He turned back. "Because I can't bear to see the two of you suffer."

"The two of us?" she squealed, her anger quickly rising. "I do not suffer! Only when a meddling old man and a nosy housekeeper interfere where they shouldn't." She leaped from her chair, slapped her half-empty glass of sherry on the table next to his and headed for the door. "Thank you for the drink, Mr. Cain. I shan't keep you from your work any longer." She gave him one last dark scowl before turning back, nearly colliding with Beau stepping into the room.

He smiled down at her, but got only an icy glare in

return. He stood in awe, watching her stomp from the room and out the front door. He chuckled.

"I guess she's still upset with me," he said with an impish grin and walked further into the study. "Mind if I help myself to a drink?"

Joshua shook his head and retreived his own from the table. "Alanna tells me it was your decision to come."

Beau replaced the crystal stopper to the decanter, swirled his drink and swallowed it. Sitting down on the corner of the desk, he settled himself comfortably and crossed his wrists on one knee. "Yes, it was. I need your help."

I've done enough, Joshua thought, downing the remainder of his sherry. "All you need to do is ask."

"We need a barn. There's trees enough and I think the old sawmill will run, but I need a few extra hands."

"No problem. When do you want to start?"

"Just as soon as we've cleared away the remains of the last. How is the supply of hams and such?"

"We've plenty. Why?"

"I'd like to borrow enough to have a barn raising. It would do the plantation good to make the merchants of Williamsburg think we're getting on our feet again. As soon as we show a profit I'll pay back the cost."

"No need," Joshua argued. "Consider it a gift."

Beau chuckled. "A gift? You're beginning to act like Radford."

Joshua shook his head. "No, not this time. Consider it a premature wedding gift."

Beau grunted, scratching his temple with one finger. "You have more faith than I, I'm afraid. Sometimes I think I've driven her further away by being underfoot."

"You aren't giving up?"

"No, not yet. I only wish I had the opportunity to be alone with her. But she has carefully avoided that, as you can see by our ride here this morning."

Joshua's dark eyes took on a sparkle that Beau did not miss.

"What are you thinking?" he asked tentatively.

"Just never you mind," Joshua grinned.

Although the sun stole undeniably between the remaining dark clouds, it failed to dry the sodden earth, and Alanna found herself carefully avoiding a number of puddles in the yard as she walked away from the house. She had no idea where she was headed, only that she knew she must get away from the very people she had come to visit. The aroma of fresh-baked breads gladdened the air, suddenly filling her with memories. Looking up, she spotted the cabin that had once been hers. Happily, she lifted her skirts a little higher and quickly walked in its direction, unaware of the puddles that only a moment before had been so important.

The door of the cabin stood open, and from the porch Alanna could see the young woman with sun-lightened hair busily at work near the oven. Quietly, Alanna stepped into the doorway to watch unobserved. Having removed a finished loaf of bread from the rack and setting it out to cool, Cinnamon took another to replace it, wiping her damp brow with the back of her hand when it was done. She stood up, pressed her hands to the small of her back, and stretched.

"A task that never seems to end."

Cinnamon turned abruptly at the sound of the familiar voice. "Alanna," she called excitedly. "Is it really you?"

"I think so," Alanna grinned with a sweeping look over her frame. "Have I changed so much?"

"Oh, no. Only more beautiful, if that's possible." Cinnamon hurriedly wiped the flour from her hands on the edge of her apron and came to meet her. "Come in, won't you? I'll heat water for tea. Or would you prefer to go for a walk? The bread won't be done for a while, and it's rather hot in here."

Alanna laughed. "Whatever you'd like to do."

"Then let's walk. I grow weary of this cabin."

Their arms linked, they started off across the yard.

"I was afraid I might never see you again," Cinnamon admitted with a smile.

Alanna patted Cinnamon's hand resting against her arm. "I apologize for not coming sooner. I had a lot to forget and a new life to which I had to adjust. And, of course, the fact that my plantation was near collapse demanded my full attention." She looked upward with a sigh. "I'm afraid I'd still be there if Beau hadn't come to my rescue."

"I'm glad to hear you two are friends again."

"Oh, we're not friends," Alanna stated coldly. "Far from it. I simply mean he took over the worries of the plantation and freed me to do the things I wanted. Like being here with you," she grinned.

"You mean you came here alone?"

"No. I had Beau bring me."

"He did?"

"Ah-huh."

Cinnamon's pace slowed a bit.

"Something wrong?" Alanna asked, feeling the hesitation in her companion's step.

"He sounds like—like—"

"Like what?" Alanna asked, stopping suddenly to stare into the face framed in auburn hair.

"Like he's a servant."

"Well, he is," Alanna laughed, starting off again without Cinnamon.

"But he didn't give up his plantation just to be a servant to you."

Stopping instantly, Alanna turned back, meeting Cinnamon's gaze with equal determination. "And what is that supposed to mean?"

Cinnamon threw her hands in the air. "Well, hasn't he asked you to marry him?"

"What?" Alanna exploded.

Cinnamon sighed heavily. "It seems only logical, since the man loves you."

"Oh, not you, too," Alanna moaned, turning away toward the stable.

"Well, it's true, Miss Know-It-All," Cinnamon shouted, running to catch up with her friend. "He's loved you from the very first."

With an aggravated drop of her shoulders, Alanna stopped again to glare at Cinnamon. "If I hadn't just decided this morning to come, I'd swear the three of you had this all planned." She stalked off again in a more heated pace than before.

"The three of us? What are you talking about?" Cinnamon called angrily. She watched Alanna until she had traveled a good distance from her, feeling her own temper flare with each step Alanna took. "If you'll stand still a minute, I'll prove it to you."

"How?" Alanna called back over her shoulder.

Cinnamon gritted her teeth, suppressing her irritation. "Do you want all of Raven Oaks to know?" she

485

threatened, stopping Alanna almost immediately. Taking her own good time, she strolled up beside her hot-tempered friend. "Remember how I said I would make Master Beau fall in love with me?" She waited for Alanna to shrug one shoulder before she continued. "Well, I didn't stand a chance. You had already won his heart."

"You're not proving anything. You're just babbling on about your fantasies," Alanna said crossly.

"I'm trying to tell you that Beau Remington *never* made love to me. And after I moved back into the cabin, he never took another mistress. Ask Tilly!"

"She already told me!"

"Well, then?" Cinnamon demanded.

"Well, it doesn't matter!"

"How can you say that? Don't you love him?"

Alanna's eyes widened. "No."

"I don't believe you. How could you not love him? He was the father of your child."

Cinnamon's words bit like a winter wind, cutting through Alanna to the bone. Her throat tightened, unable to respond or deny the truth. She blinked back her tears, whirled about, and ran for the stable and escape.

Her pace did not slow until she reached the open stable doors, where she paused long enough to wipe a stray tear from her cheek. She glanced about her and saw that Cinnamon had not followed. A few confused looks were cast at her from workers who stood about watching in silence. She threw them all a warning glare to be about their duties, sending them off in various directions before she turned and went inside the shadowed doorway.

A voice raised in song drifted toward her from the back

of the stable, the soft, deep tones of a man and Alanna found herself captivated by the melody, absently following its sound. She paused in surprise to find Jeremiah bent down near the wheel of her carriage.

"You sing beautifully, Jeremiah," she said softly, disappointed when the song came to an end.

"Thank yo', Miss Alanna," he smiled quickly rising to his feet. "I heard yo' was here. Yo' look good as ever."

"Why, thank you. And so do you, I might add. Is something wrong with the carriage?" she asked, watching him wipe the grease from his hands on a small cut of cloth.

"Ah-no," he replied, glancing back at it. "Masta Beau asked me to take a look. Thought he heard somethin' that shouldn't a-been. Turned out to be a nice day," he added, changing the subject. "Yo' plan to be here long?"

"No, I don't think so. We've plenty to do at the plantation and can't afford to be gone long. How have you been?" she asked, walking with him toward the stream of sunlight flooding in through the open doors.

"Just fine. We all is. It's good ta see Masta Beau better, too."

Alanna stopped and touched his arm in alarm. "Was he ill?"

"Oh, not so's we'd fetch a doctor. Herbs wouldn't cure his problem."

"Whatever do you mean?"

Jeremiah patted his broad muscular chest. "Hurt in here," he said, pointing to his left side. "Ever since you went away."

Every muscle in her small frame tightened in an instant. "If the carriage is ready, hitch up the team," she said. "We will leave immediately!"

"Yes'm," Jeremiah nodded, watching her stomp from the stable, the agitated swish of her skirts stirring up the thin bed of straw beneath her feet.

Alanna stared angrily out the window of her carriage. What had started out as a pleasant idea of renewing her friendships with the people at Raven Oaks had turned into total mayhem. Not a single conversation with any of them had been what she intended. And all because of him! She glared at the wall of the carriage in front of which Beau rode in the coachman's perch. I wouldn't put it past him to have connived the whole thing.

The carriage wheel hit a rut jostling her about to such a degree that she was certain she heard her teeth rattle. She seized the leather window-covering determined to reprimand him, when the wheels hit what seemed to be a larger hole in the road, throwing her against the wall of the carriage on the other side and hearing Beau's urgent call for the horses to stop. Alanna didn't have to guess that the carriage had lost a wheel.

Struggling upright, she opened the door and leaned out. "Now what?" she demanded sharply.

"I'd say we have to walk," Beau said after a quick examination.

Looking up at the dark clouds growing in number again, she clicked her tongue in disgust. "How far is Briarwood Manor? I fear we shall get wet if it's any distance."

"A chance we must take. Unless you'd prefer to wait here alone while I go for another carriage. Of course—" he paused, letting his voice trail off.

"Of course, what?" she snapped.

He shrugged a shoulder as if it didn't matter. "Hard to say who might pass down this road."

Alanna's eyes widened, and she hurriedly climbed from the carriage steps. "But I could ride the other horse. I wouldn't have to stay behind."

"Bareback, Miss Alanna?"

An aggravated pout formed on her lips. "I've done a lot more that would surprise you," she said caustically.

"Really?" he asked, his voice taking on a rather suggestive tone.

She glared disgustedly at him, then set off for the front of the carriage. "If you wait much longer, we're sure to be soaked."

"I'm used to it," he reminded her, and nodded with the unflattering smirk he received for his comment.

"I think I should tell you," he added as they unhooked the harnesses from the tongue of the carriage, "these horses were not meant for riding. They are not used to weight upon their backs. You could be thrown."

"Worse than the fall I took inside the carriage?" she grinned sarcastically.

"I only thought it wiser if you ride with me," he replied, ignoring her jest.

"Thank you, but no," she told him firmly. "I'd feel safer on my own horse."

He shrugged good-naturedly, certain time would prove her wrong. He only hoped that just her pride would be harmed.

The moment Beau helped Alanna onto the broad, muscular back of the dapple gray, the mare reared excitedly, bringing a squeal from her rider.

"Take it easy, girl," Beau soothed with a gentle stroke to the mare's neck. "It's all right."

489

But the animal continued to shy, denied free rein by the strong hand that held the bridle. Finally, certain the mare would not calm unless shown a firmer restraint, Beau easily swung himself up on the animal's back behind Alanna.

"What are you doing?" she hissed, feeling the firm muscles of his chest and thighs molded against her. "I said I would ride alone."

"The filly is frightened. More so than you. I merely intend to calm her so you won't be thrown on that stubborn head of yours," he growled, having lost all patience.

"I can manage alone," she snapped, struggling to pull the reins from his grip.

"Stop it, Alanna! Before you—"

The animal reared instantly, catching Beau off guard as he fought not only the mare but the hot-tempered woman between his arms. In the next moment they both found themselves on the ground watching the rapid hoofs galloping away flinging clumps of mud in the air. Beau scrambled to his feet determined to catch the other horse before she, too, decided to run. As he reached out a hand for the bridle, the mare reared back its head, whirled around, and bolted off after the other.

"Damn," he growled, kicking at the ground beneath him. "Now we shall have to walk."

"Well, it's of your own doing," Alanna snapped, coming to her feet to brush away the dirt and leaves from her skirt.

"My doing?" he bellowed. "If you had sat still, none of it would have happened."

"And if you could manage a carriage one-tenth as well as you do a plantation, we wouldn't be afoot now."

"Woman, you do push me to the limits." His nostrils flared, and he restrained himself from saying more before he turned abruptly and started down the road.

"Wait for me!" Alanna called after him, but when she took a step to follow, she tripped over a decayed tree branch laying in her path and fell, twisting her ankle. "Ohhh!"

"Now what have you done?" he barked, standing in the middle of the road, a fist knotted against each hip.

"I hurt my ankle," she moaned.

"Fine," he grumbled, walking back to her side to kneel down. "Now I suppose I must carry you."

"Well, don't trouble yourself!" she remarked heatedly, pulling away from him.

"I only want to see what damage has been done. You may only have twisted it and will be able to walk on your own." He lifted the hemline of her gown. "Remove the stocking and slipper," he ordered, and Alanna glumly obliged. "As I thought," he hummed after a thorough examination, "you've only twisted it. It's not even swollen. Rest a moment until it stops hurting." He stood up and surveyed their surroundings until he spotted something a few yards away. He crossed to it and picked up a long gnarled stick. Leaning on it, he tested its weight, and then nodded his satisfaction. "Use it as a cane," he said, tossing it to the ground next to her.

"Thank you," she returned in an equally dark mood.

"You're welcome," he said flatly and went to a tree stump and sat down. Quietly brooding, he picked up a twig and began snapping it into little pieces, tossing each away one at a time.

Thunder rumbled in the distance, and he looked up in time to be assaulted with numerous droplets of rain.

Cursing beneath his breath, he hurriedly went to the carriage, opened the door, and returned to Alanna. Without invitation or her permission, he bent down, scooped her up in his arms under protest and carried her to the carriage without a word. Having dumped her inside, he climbed in after her and closed the door only a moment before the clouds rifled off their attack.

Settling himself in one corner opposite Alanna, he stretched out his legs before him and crossed his arms over his chest to concentrate on the intricate lines of graining on the wall ahead of him. *If I had left her at the plantation, I wouldn't be sitting here now,* he thought bleakly, casting her a sideways glance. He frowned when he discovered her staring at him in an almost fearful manner.

"Why do you look at me like that?" he asked crossly. "You act as if you're afraid of me."

"I always fear being alone with you," she responded softly, but with a sharp edge to her words.

He grunted. "Don't worry. I'm not in the mood to come any closer." He settled his gaze on the graining again. "Besides, if I were, I'd prefer a soft woman in my arms instead of a wildcat."

Piqued by his comparison, she sat upright. "Well, maybe I'd have responded differently if you had been gentle."

"I doubt it," he mused, settling deeper into the leather seats.

"Oh, do you?" she chimed. "Doesn't speak much for your charm. I had always heard what a great lover you were. But I could not attest to the fact. Quite the contrary. I see you as a stumbling boob."

"Even the greatest of lovers would have difficulty in

retaining the title when his partner fought him the whole way."

"A *great* lover would tame her," she hurled defiantly, lifting a delicate chin in the air.

Only his eyes moved to her. "Is that an invitation to try?"

Alanna experienced a sudden rush of fever to her cheeks, having realized what she had said and the way he mistook it. She swallowed the lump in her throat. "No," she said hoarsely, forcing her eyes to stare at the seat across from her.

A low rumble of laughter filled the small space they shared and, startled by the sound, she unthinkingly looked at him. He had uncrossed his arms and now sat forward in the seat watching her.

"Do you truly find me so unappealing, Alanna?"

She looked back at the seat, feeling as if her pounding heart might explode. "I try not to find you anything," she whispered, damning that all too familiar sensation rising within her.

"Why?" he asked, moving to sit next to her. "Does it worry you that for once in your life you might allow your heart to overrule your head?"

Fiery eyes flashed at him. "You conceited ass! If I let my heart tell me what to do, I would have thrown you off Briarwood Manor the first time you set foot on it."

"I would have returned," he stated, leaning back in the seat, his arms crossed in front of him while he purposely touched a shoulder to hers.

Alanna tried unsuccessfully to retreat from the contact. But he had forced her to the corner and her only escape from his nearness would require her leaving the carriage completely. Hearing the steady rhythm of rain

493

pounding against the rooftop, she resigned herself to endure the torment she suspected he enjoyed. "I would have sent you away again," she reiterated, her voice lacking its prior bravado.

"And the road would have known my weight upon it time and time again, for as often as you turned me out, I would have come again."

A nervous laugh escaped her. "Of that, I have no doubt. You seem to revel in causing me distress."

"Strange," he hummed. "I thought you more wise than that."

Alanna's brows drew together. "I see no ignorance there."

"Then you hide the truth in your words."

"I think not," she argued. "You only wish to plague me."

"I only wish to show my love."

The muscles across her chest tightened instantly, seeming to choke off her breath. She twisted in the seat to look at him. "You play games."

"Only to break down the barrier you erected between us."

"If there is such a barrier, it was put there by your hand."

"Then let me be the one to dismantle it," he said, all sign of mockery gone from his eyes.

She looked away. "You seek to court me?" she asked, her words tipped with coolness.

"If I must."

She laughed. "You think because you admit a love for me, I will fall victim to your charms." She looked back at him. "I have great cause to doubt your honesty. Several times you raped me without a single pledge of emotion of any kind. You made me heavy with child and denied the responsibility of fatherhood. You watched me walk away, your child in my womb, while you flaunted another woman on your arm. The only time I foolishly thought you cared was the day I found you in the drawing room at the convent. But you quickly shattered that illusion when you spoke only of a promise to Radford. I have not grown to doubt you overnight, and for you to change my feelings will come just as slowly. I am not like all the others you have known, for I will not again be wooed into your bed without the seal of wedlock. Now—do you think the task too much?"

A smile played softly on his lips. "I think it a great challenge, but one I decided long ago to take. I cannot deny your words, for they are truth—as you see it. My reasons for such behavior are known only to me, and no amount of argument on my part would convince you that they were valid ones. Although you think me false, I tell you true, I love you and vow to prove the fact no matter what length of time it requires. I have played the part of monk for many months, and though it is a strain to keep from reaching out for you, I pledge to stay away and let it be in response to your request the day I hold you in my arms."

Never having expected to hear such words upon his lips and still full of uncertainty, all she could do at the moment was stare at him, wanting desperately to believe everything and knowing she mustn't. The hammering of raindrops ceased, flooding the carriage with tense stillness. She turned away and lifted the leather window-covering. The sky was fresh, as if it had been cleansed by the downpour and as if, for some reason, it seemed to herald the start of a new beginning. Was it her imagination? Or did the heavens beckon her to forgive the man at her side? She sighed. Only time would tell. There were still a lot of questions unanswered.

Silvery moonlight trickled into Alanna's bedchamber through half-drawn draperies, flooding the room with romantic illusion. She lay awake in the huge four-poster bed, watching the platinum beams caress all they touched as they spilled out across the foot of her bed. Sweet smells of jasmine drifted up to meet her, attack her senses, and catapult her sanctuary into a narrow space, its walls and ceiling seemingly closer than a moment before. Sleep would not come. Midnight chimed its hour on the hall clock, and the methodical ticking pierced the quiet until she felt she would go mad. Rolling onto her stomach, she covered her head with the pillow, praying to block out the sounds, the smells, the sights. They burned vividly in her mind.

A throaty growl erupted from her. Tossing aside the bedcovers, she left the warmth of her haven and crossed to the window, slamming down the sash and flinging the heavy draperies shut. She returned to the bed and threw herself upon it, a muffled oath cutting into the stillness with the knowledge that no amount of darkness or lack of fragrant blossoms would ignite her dreams. Nothing she had tried chased away the visions or stilled the words she kept hearing over and over in her mind.

I tell you true, I love you . . . hold you in my arms . . . show my love . . . love you, love you, love you.

"Stop it!" Alanna screamed, bolting upright in the bed, her hands clamped over her ears. "They're lies. All of them. You can't love me. You don't!"

496

I tell you true, I love you.

Suddenly the room seemed to stifle the breath from her. She must leave it, get away, walk in the gardens to clear her mind. Groping in the darkness, she found her robe and stumbled to the door to fling it wide, not caring about the thundering crash it made slamming against the wall. She hurried down the steps, across the foyer, and through the front door, tightly wrapping her silk robe around her slim figure. Her pace slowed once she reached the path that wound its way through the beds of flowers and rows of bushes, and she sucked in a deep breath to calm herself. Savoring the sweet night smells, she looked skyward to study the multitude of twinkling lights laid out in patterns as if beckoning her to reach out and touch them. She smiled, relaxing in the serenity of the moment. She wandered aimlessly and, before she realized it, she had left the gardens and started down the road toward the servants' cabins. She stopped suddenly, realizing where she stood, for only a few feet ahead, shaded beneath a huge oak tree, a tiny cabin loomed out at her, the place that held the cause of her unrest within its walls.

Unable to stop herself and truly finding no desire to try, she traveled the short distance and paused outside the door. As if hypnotized, she lifted the latch and let the door swing open. A small room with only a table and chair and bed in one corner. She knew instantly that sleep had not eluded *him*. Streams of moonlight fell across the floor and revealed the presence of someone resting quietly on the straw mattress. She stepped forward, the overpowering desire to call his name tempting fate. He moved soundlessly and in the next instant, before her befuddled mind could react, Beau stood before her, his warmth touching her everywhere. She raised a small hand to his chest to stop him when he made to hold her, the dark curls and strong muscles beneath her fingers sending a chill through her.

"I-I've come to find out the truth," she whispered.

He reached up to gently brush a tendril of hair from her cheek. "Then you shall have it."

Her chin trembled and she swallowed hard. "Why did you let me go, knowing I carried your child? Didn't you care?" She stared up at him, his dark features enhanced in the glow of moonlight.

"You were promised to another," he answered softly. "Had it been anyone else and not Radford, I would have fought for you. But he loved you and I felt I hadn't the right. Even you told me as much."

"When you searched for me—"

"I would have traveled the world for the rest of my life until I found you. And not because of the promise I made my friend, but because I wouldn't have rested until I knew you were safe."

Moving away, Alanna stood in the shadows, her back to him. "You say these things, but how do I know they're truth?"

Coming up behind her, he touched her shoulders to turn her around. "Alanna, what could I possibly gain by giving up my home and coming here to work? If I didn't love you, want to be with you every moment of my life, there would be no need." Her gaze was averted, and he caught her chin in a gentle hold and lifted her eyes to meet his. "If you doubt me, ask my father. He knew how much I cared long before Radford asked you to marry him."

"Joshua?"

He nodded.

"But—"

"He'd have no cause to lie." He smiled softly. "Nor would I."

Whether he spoke the words of his heart or only those Alanna wished to hear mattered little to her. She had loved him from the first, through all the trials, misdoings, and even when she claimed she didn't. She loved him now, and she knew in her heart that she could never let him go.

"Oh, Beau," she half wept, reaching out her arms to encircle his neck.

He crushed her to him, his long-starved passions flared high, his lips hungry for the taste of her, and she met him with equal ardor. Their hands moved, searched, touched, unable to sate their need to explore, a wild explosion of desires burning within them. Beau easily lifted her in his arms and carried her to the small bed. Slipping his arm from beneath her knees, he let her feet slowly glide to the floor, his free hand undressing her in haste, as though he feared his dream would vanish. He kissed her throat, nibbled at her earlobe, buried his face in the long, dark tresses cascading over her shoulder before his mouth found her breast, his tongue teasing its peak. He lifted her again and gently laid her on the bed, falling at her side to trail a path with a fingertip along her shoulder and the valley between her breasts. She moaned, the embers of her passion fanned aflame with his touch. She could not stop the tremor that seized her body.

He pulled her beneath him, their kisses now fierce and savage in hungry impatience to be as one. Without shame or gentle nudging from her lover, Alanna opened her thighs to welcome him, knowing then there could never be another who would touch her so deeply, so passionately, with such finality. He had captured her being, but, more important, her heart.

He moved faster, deeper, his ragged breathing nearly a moan, and she matched his fervor eagerly until, their passion spent, they lay exhausted in each other's arms. Snuggled warmly in the circle of his embrace, Alanna laid her head against his chest, feeling the steady rhythm of his heart. Neither of them spoke, content to share in silence, the eastern sky stained pastel yellow with the early coming of dawn.

Thirty Five

From the window of her study, Alanna watched the
activity on the front lawn. A goodly number of long
tables joined end to end covered with white tablecloths
spread outward from the veranda steps. Only Joshua and
his crew had arrived to help with the barn raising, but
Beau had advised her to prepare for the great number of
guests he felt certain would appear within the hour. She
pressed a temple against the window frame absently
watching Beau unfold a large paper and lay it on one of
the tables for Joshua to see. After a moment's
examination, they turned, and Beau pointed toward the
spot where the remains of the old barn had been cleared
away. Joshua, too, pointed in the same direction, which
instantly brought a negative shake to Beau's head. They
looked back at the paper.

It had been nearly two weeks since Beau's declaration
of love for her and the blissful moments they had shared
in his cabin. They never spoke of it, nor had Beau broken
his word. She must be the one to open her door and her
arms to him, to be certain of her feelings and his love. But
at every available moment he showered her with verbal

affection, bringing the laughter of resignation bursting from her whenever she grew overwhelmed with his flattery. It felt good to laugh with him. It seemed to chase away some of the bad memories that surfaced now and then. But would the good times last? They were not meant for each other, she told herself. They were too much alike for peace to last for long. How different he was from Radford. She frowned, wondering why she had thought of him at this particular moment. She looked back outside at the men.

They still studied the drawings on the oversized piece of paper spread out before them, and she recalled the hours Beau had spent at the kitchen table in preparation of the diagram. Many times late at night when sleep would not come easily, she had risen to go to the kitchen for a warm glass of buttermilk only to find the room already occupied. Beau, too, had ventured there with much the same intent, choosing to stay a little longer as he toiled with the plans for the new barn. Even alone as they were, he never once made any advances toward her, reconfirming his oath that when he held her tenderly it would be by her choice and not his. She respected his restraint at first, later wondering if he had indeed had a change of heart when it seemed that nothing she said or the manner in which she dressed had any affect on him. Thinking of it now, she smiled. Maybe it's what he planned. Odd, she thought, at one time I would have welcomed his affections—whether truly felt or falsely given.

As she watched them, Joshua suddenly stood erect, a fist on each hip. They argue, she grinned. I wonder who will win. Now that Joshua has announced his parenthood, he has the right not to remain silent. I wish I was close enough to hear. It would be enjoyable to see their roles exchanged. Her eyes clouded, recalling the conversation she and Joshua had had that morning in his study. He had spoken of Beau's anger when she left him and of his concern when she was kidnapped. Her frown deepened and she went to her desk and pulled open a drawer, searching through it until she found a wrinkled and worn piece of paper. Maybe now, with Joshua there to help, she could show Radford's note to Beau. She glanced back outside, then heard the urgent rappings at the door.

"What is it?" she called.

"Come quickly, Miss Alanna," Maybelle pleaded as she stepped into the room. "I fear the worst."

"Good heavens, what is it?"

"Lilly and Masta Joshua's cook is fightin'."

"Fighting? Over what?"

"Oh, yo' know Lilly. She resents anyone usin' her kitchen."

"Oh, good gracious," Alanna moaned, coming to join Maybelle. Her discussion with Beau and Joshua would have to wait. She laid the note on the small table standing just inside the door and escorted her maid from the room.

"You haven't changed a bit," Joshua growled. "Just as hot-tempered as ever."

"When I'm right and someone tries to tell me otherwise, I usually am."

"I hope you don't show that side of you to Alanna."

Beau smiled, the heat of their discussion gone with the mere mention of her name. "No. I try very hard not to." He leaned back against the table and let his gaze drift toward the house, unaware that Joshua was studying him.

"If I had known the magic of her name sooner, I would have stopped our argument long before this," Joshua needled him. "Pray tell, does she act the same way when your name reaches her ears?"

"I would be lying if I said she does."

Joshua's gray brows knotted. "But I thought—"

"Thought what?"

"Are you sure? I mean after your trip home from Raven Oaks, she still behaves the same?"

Beau cast him a sideways glance. "What has our journey to do with it?"

Joshua instantly straightened and turned away. "Nothing, really."

"But I think it has or you wouldn't have mentioned it," Beau added, reaching out to firmly grasp the crook of Joshua's arm as he started to walk away. "I didn't think much of it then—carriage wheels have been known to work loose—but it seemed to happen at such an opportune time. You wouldn't by chance have had a hand in our misfortune?"

"Most assuredly not," Joshua rebuffed him sharply.

"Then by your word, perhaps?"

Joshua began to squirm under Beau's penetrating stare.

"Were you meddling?"

"Meddling?" Joshua barked, suddenly coming to life. "I merely thought to give you both a little help. I beg forgiveness if my intentions failed, but if I wait for you or Alanna to make the first move, I shall die before I have a grandchild."

A slow smile of genuine glee spread across Beau's face, his eyes twinkling his amusement at the man's discomfort at having been discovered. He reached up, encircled him within his arm and laughed. "I can't begin to count how many times you've saved my tail for some reason or another. And since you have no way of knowing the outcome of that trip, I think it only fair I tell you the gist of it. We've signed a truce, so to speak, and I've been given permission to court her."

"Praise the Lord," Joshua sighed. "Now we're getting somewhere."

"Not so fast, my worried trickster," Beau warned. "We've a long way to go. She's still full of doubt and misgivings, so don't start planning the ceremony."

"That's quite understandable. I've known you all of your life and have yet to figure you out."

Beau laughed again, and the two of them turned back to study Beau's sketch of the new barn, spying Alanna walking toward them.

"It's good to see you two aren't fighting anymore," she smiled once she reached them. "I've had enough for one day."

"Fighting?" Joshua teased. "You misunderstand, my dear. We were simply discussing our differences of opinion."

"Oh?" she laughed. "Then I would truly hate to see you argue." She stepped closer to examine the paper. "Do you think a barn this size will be completed in one short day?"

"No. That was never my thought. But if all of those I expect to come do come, we should at least have the roof on before sunset. Besides, should we not, Joshua will stay and help."

"Guess again, oh, Masta Overseer," Joshua chided. "I shall leave with all the others. I've noticed a rounding to your belly and think you could use the extra work before you grow fat and lazy."

Beau drew back. "Listen to who spills the words so

505

freely. It will take me many years for me to grow to look like you!"

"Please," Alanna broke in, "if you continue to stand here and banter words, not a single board will be put in place."

The rattling of a carriage intruded upon their merriment, and Alanna looked its way.

"See there. You've both been saved. The first arrives and you shall have to get to work." She cast them both a playful grin and set off to greet her visitors.

"I hope she mellows you," Joshua sighed happily, watching the gentle sway of skirts moving away from them.

"Why? Are you getting too old to mix words with me?"

Joshua flashed him a look of outrage. "Old, is it?" he fumed. "We'll just see who's old." In a huff, he set off toward the site of the new barn and the stack of fresh cut lumber.

Within an hour the front lawn of Briarwood Manor teamed with carriages, buggies, and wagons, and their wide assortment of passengers. It appeared as if nearly everyone for miles around had turned out for the event, and Alanna wondered how many had come out of friendship and how many out of plain curiosity.

"Isn't it wonderful?" she asked Beau when she found him at the well having a dipperful of water. "I never would have believed this if I hadn't seen it with my own eyes."

He smiled. "We colonists, as you shall find out in years to come, usually join together to help each other. If we didn't, none of us would last very long." He scanned the crowd of people bustling about. "Have you seen Joshua of late?"

Alanna laughed. "He is probably hiding from your torment. Won't you ever let him rest?"

Beau's wide grin faded slowly before he answered. "No. It's one of my faults. I make a nuisance of myself with the people I love."

Alanna could feel a tingling in the flesh of her cheeks. She looked down. "I'm glad," she whispered.

Placing a fingertip beneath her chin, he carefully directed her eyes to his. "Are you truly?"

A smile lightly touched her lips. She nodded. Then her gaze went past him and a frown replaced the happiness of the moment.

"What is it?" he asked.

"I've new guests to greet."

Beau quickly glanced back over his shoulder unable to comprehend who might spoil their pleasure, spotting the carriage and the reason almost immediately. Being assisted from within by the helping hand of her father, arrogantly swished the shapely and lavishly adorned figure of Melissa Bensen, followed closely by her equally patronizing mother and Blythe Robbins.

"Oh, well," Beau confessed, "we knew she would come sooner or later."

"Yes," Alanna sighed. "I only wished it later. Or not at all. I truly don't understand how a man as gentle and sweet as Mathew could have sired an offspring like her."

Beau laughed. "I think that thought has run through Mathew's mind a few times, too."

The corner of her mouth twitched. "And listen to me! I have never talked of another in such a way before. I must be careful not to fall in the way of gossips. It's a trait I truly despise."

Beau smiled, reaching out to tuck her hand in the bend of his arm. "Do not fear. If it be the case, it will be your only fault."

Unable to contain her laughter, she smiled up at him. "If you continue to fill my head with such thoughts, I *will* think I have none."

"That would not be a bad idea. It would drive all men away and leave you solely to me."

Alanna shook her head. "If I stand here much longer, I fear I shall believe every word you say and forget that other women are walking about." She pulled free of him. "Now return to your work lest Joshua call you lazy and be justified."

He made a sweeping bow. "At your command, m'lady," he grinned before turning on his heel and walking away.

She stood watching him until he joined the others at the roughly constructed beginnings of the barn, then turned away to greet her newest guests.

"Alanna," Mathew sang cheerfully once she had joined them. "It's good to see you."

"Thank you," she smiled in return, eagerly accepting his embrace before readying herself for the next encounter. "Good morning Mrs. Bensen, Mistress Bensen, Mistress Robbins," she said with a nod of her head to each. "Thank you for coming."

The stout elder woman cast a haughty glance about the yard surveying those present as if they were below her dignity, then fixed her gaze on Alanna. "You may thank Mathew for our presence. Had I the choice, I would be sipping tea in my parlor." She irately fanned herself with the lace handkerchief she held. "It's much too warm to stray from home today."

"Beatrice, please," Mathew moaned. "Had the situation been reversed, I'm sure Alanna would grace us with her presence."

"Well, must we stand in this awful heat? Or will we be allowed a place to freshen up?" Mrs. Bensen went on, ignoring her husband.

"Maybelle," Alanna called. "Please see our guests to a room where they can rest awhile."

"And while they rest, I'll get to work," Mathew smiled, rolling up his sleeves. "Just show me where Beau is."

Certain that Maybelle had set out to fulfill her wishes, Alanna turned her back on the women. "Over there, Mathew," she said, pointing to Beau's tall figure towering over the other men around him. "But do take it easy. It's awfully warm today."

"Don't worry," he assured her with a gentle pat to her hand.

She stood watching the gray-haired figure join the other men, then turned to go to the kitchen to be of what help she could. She suddenly noticed that Melissa and Blythe had lingered. She stopped abruptly, suspicious of the smile that spread over Melissa's face.

"You never did come for tea," she said sweetly. "I should be hurt."

A flicker of bewilderment dashed across Alanna's brow and disappeared. "I-I'm sorry. I just couldn't seem to find the time."

"Oh, that's all right," Melissa cooed, reaching out to take Alanna's arm and draw her toward the house, Blythe following closely behind. She looked about the yard. "It appears you do quite well alone. The place never looked so good."

"Thank you," Alanna mumbled.

"How are you feeling?"

Alanna glanced at her then quickly looked away. "Fine."

"You know, it must have been an awful experience for

509

you. Being kidnapped, I mean. I'm sure I never would have lived through it. And to think someone planned it all." She fluttered her handkerchief beneath her chin. "I'm so happy you have proof of the villain. We must see him brought to justice."

"Well, it's not exactly proof," Alanna admitted. "I only—hope—to find out who was responsible."

"You hope—" Melissa stopped abruptly, casting a sharp glance at Blythe. "But—"

"But what?"

Laughing nervously, Melissa started off again. "But of course, you do," she smiled encouragingly. "We all do. Well, I better see to my mother's needs. We'll talk later." She gave Alanna's hand a gentle squeeze and started up the veranda steps watching Alanna from the corner of her eye. When her hostess turned and walked away, she paused, pulling Blythe in close to her.

"What did I tell you?" she whispered triumphantly. "She really has no idea. Just speculation."

"It still frightens me," Blythe exclaimed, touching her brow with the back of her hand. "I just know someone will find out. I just know it!"

"They won't if you stop acting like this. You're such a coward, Blythe. No wonder you're still not married. If a man asked you, you'd run away and hide."

Blythe's mouth darted open to dispute the statement, but closed again when Melissa turned her back to her and went inside. Someday she'd have the courage to voice her feelings. And Melissa would be the first to hear them. Maybe—

By midday the new barn cast an eerie shadow akin to the skeleton of a monster, sunlight stealing between the rafters of its roof and the studs of its walls. The continuous chatter of dozens of men filled the air, while their women bustled about them to refill mugs with ale to cool them in the hot spring sunshine. Nearly all of the men had rolled back their sleeves, seeking what comfort it might bring to their perspiring bodies. Their faces glistened, muscles straining, yet not one pleaded surrender before the job was done. In the center of them all towered Beau, an example of strength and determination as he strained to lift the heavy planks into place, securing them with pegs. The pounding of mallets sounded like the musket fire of an army.

Alanna lovingly watched Beau and Joshua work side by side, feeling the devotion each felt to the other radiate with every move they made or banter they exchanged. Her eyes sparkled with the merriment they shared, playfully insulting each other then glancing her way with the wink of an eye. She sighed, realizing how much things had changed in one year, and wished she had known a year ago what the outcome would be.

"I'm afraid I'm no match for those two," Alanna heard a voice behind her admit. She turned to see Mathew ease himself onto the end of a wagon, a wrinkled handkerchief mopping his brow. His tired face, burned slightly across the bridge of his nose, glimmered with perspiration, and she worried he had done too much.

"I'll get you a dipper of water," she said, starting off, but he raised a hand to stop her.

"Thank you, no," he grinned appreciatively. "I simply need to rest a minute. Have you seen my wife or Melissa?"

Alanna quickly glanced about, finding the pair sitting in the shade of the veranda.

"Near the house," she told him.

"I would expect as much," he sighed, disheartened. "While all the other wives help their husbands, mine sits comfortably by without the slightest care for my well-being. Any other daughter would be standing where you are now, but Melissa can only think of herself." He smiled with a thought. "I can't imagine ever seeing her do more than brush her hair or soak in a scented tub for hours. She certainly isn't like you," he added when he glanced up to see the smudge of dirt on the end of Alanna's nose.

"Do not blame yourself. She has never known another way of life. She would act differently if she had."

Mathew chuckled. "I apologize for her shortcomings and you defend them. I wish I'd had a son so he could court you and win your heart. I would settle for a daughter-in-law, since I've failed with my own."

"And I'm sure if you had had a son, and he the image of you, I would have easily fallen for his charms," she grinned happily.

"Oh, I envy the man who captures your heart," he sighed, reaching out to take her hand.

"Now I understand why you pleaded fatigue," came a deep voice behind them. They turned to watch Beau amble toward them, a roguish grin curling his lips. "Can't turn my back on you for a minute or you're off somewhere wooing a beautiful woman."

Mathew laughed loudly. "And if I were twenty years younger, I would give all you young men a run for your money. I never would have let a beauty like this remain unwed for so long. But then again, you never were too smart, Beau Remington. You had her in your fingers once before and let her slip away."

"She was stolen from me," he corrected. "By the only man I would have ever allowed to do so. You I would merely put a lead ball into."

"Is that so?" Mathew rallied. "You might think me too old now, but let me assure you if I was single and Mistress Bainbridge would have me, I would meet you at dawn to argue the point."

"Joshua," Beau called back over his shoulder to the man filling his plate at one end of the tables.

Hurriedly, Joshua grabbed another biscuit and rushed to join them, devouring most of it before he reached them.

"What do you think of this?" Beau rebuked. "Mathew, here, thinks he could win Alanna's heart were he not already spoken for."

Joshua took a long swallow from his mug, eyeing first one and then the other before wiping his mouth with the back of his hand. He shrugged. "He isn't the first who entertained the thought."

"And what does that mean?"

"It means, my dear boy, I, too, have thought of courting Miss Bainbridge. Why should I simply stand by and let you have free rein? Remember, I have more to offer than you. Have you any coins in your pocket? Or just promises on your lips?"

Beau exploded into laughter. "Well, at least with me she's certain not to be a widow shortly after taking her vows. But you, old man, would surely die just thinking of your wedding night."

"Oh, really?" Joshua returned. "I will outlive you."

"Please, gentlemen," Alanna intervened, "not one of you has asked what I think. Not to mention the fact that no one has asked for my hand in marriage. Besides, what makes any of you think I would agree? I have my own wealth, so I would not need it from my husband. Nor do I want a man who would infringe upon my good fortune

513

merely to advance himself," she added, eyeing Beau tauntingly.

Mathew and Joshua broke into laughter, the latter placing a stinging slap on Beau's shoulder. "Sounds to me like you don't stand a chance, my boy," Joshua chuckled with a wink to Alanna. "Or, at least, you have your work cut out for you."

A mischievous gleam danced in Beau's eyes. "Of that, I'm certain," he agreed. "But I think my ways are more convincing than those of an old man."

The two elder of the group chorused laughter, bringing a sudden rush of color to Alanna's cheeks.

"Is this a private party or may anyone join?" came the nasal tones of a high-pitched voice.

Their gaiety instantly shattered, Beau moved in to stand at Alanna's side while Mathew rose to greet his daughter and her friend.

"Certainly you may join us," he said. "We were only discussing Alanna's future husband."

The wide-brimmed straw hat cast a shadow over Melissa's pale complexion and hid the darkening of her sea-green eyes from everyone except Blythe. "Oh?" she asked with guarded resolve. "And who might that be?"

"Well, we haven't decided," Mathew laughed, failing to see how the others had grown quiet with Melissa's presence.

"A little soon, don't you think?" she added with a twitch of one brow and a sideways glance to the woman at her side.

"Oh, we were only playing. Besides, it's not as if she was a widow," Mathew argued half-heartedly.

"She only lacked a few days," Melissa amended with a fluff to a yellow curl at her shoulder.

"Yes, we know," Mathew said sadly, remembering

what the outcome of that unfortunate engagement had been. Totally forgetting his daughter and Blythe, and not noticing that his wife had joined the group, he turned to Beau. "Did you ever find those responsible for Alanna's kidnapping?"

Melissa hid her smile of confidence.

Beau shook his head, an old, angry hurt surfacing again. He hated remembering the way Radford had died, just as he was certain Alanna did. Maybe more so, since she probably felt to blame. "No," he said. "And after all this time, I wonder if we will. If there had only been a clue—"

Remembering her aborted mission of the morning, Alanna reached up and touched Beau's arm. "I know we talked of it once, but I never actually showed it to you."

"What, Alanna?"

"The note Radford was supposed to have written. The one someone gave to Dillon. Maybe if we all look at it, one of us can find the answer," she added hopefully.

Melissa stiffened, glancing at each member of the party and retreating a step.

"Note? What note?" Joshua asked.

"After we were at sea, the captain had me brought to his cabin. When I asked how much ransom he sought for my freedom, he told me he had already been paid. Then he gave me the note. I still have it. It's in the study."

Melissa shot a frantic glance toward the house.

"I don't understand," Joshua continued with a shake of his head. "If he didn't seek a ransom and had already been paid, what could the note have said to clarify it?"

Melissa slowed inches away, pausing periodically to mask her departure from the group. If only Blythe didn't notice.

"For weeks I believed Radford was responsible."

"Radford?" Mathew echoed.

"Yes," Alanna said emphatically. "The note was penned by Radford's hand, and I could only assume it was for me."

"What did it say?" Joshua asked.

"He apologized for what he had done and said he hoped I would understand."

"I don't know about the rest of you, but I'm more confused than ever," Joshua said, scratching his temple.

"And I'm uncomfortable," Beatrice interrupted, her pudgy features shining with perspiration. "It's hot in the sun. Must we talk of this, anyway? It's over and done with."

"Yes, we must!" Mathew barked with an angry glare at his wife. "If you're so uncomfortable and unconcerned, why not return to the rocking chair on the veranda where you've been most of the day, anyway?"

Outraged, Beatrice raised her nose in the air. "Well—"

"Why don't we all go inside," Alanna soothed, hoping to dispel the forthcoming argument between the two. "It will serve two purposes. I can get the letter and we can all share a cup of tea where it's cool."

"I think that's a good idea," Beau quickly added with a light touch to Alanna's elbow to escort her and the party toward the house.

Falling to the back of the group, Blythe surveyed the area. Where had Melissa gone? Was she going to try to do something about the note?

From the veranda, Melissa looked back at the small gathering she had just left, breathing somewhat easier when she discovered they hadn't moved. In fact they

516

appeared to argue; her father and mother anyway, and Blythe seemed totally enthralled with it all. Hopefully they would allow her time to go inside. She looked about to see if anyone else paid her any heed, her confidence building when no one even looked her way, and left the porch.

"Masta Beau?"

They had nearly crossed the yard toward the house when Jeremiah's voice stopped them.

"Something wrong?" Beau asked, spying his diagram in the man's hands.

"Yes, sir. Could yo' look at this? I was sent to have yo' settle an argument," Jeremiah apologized, unfolding the paper for Beau to see. "Here," he pointed.

Beau stepped nearer, leaving Alanna in Joshua's care for the moment until he straightened again with a shake of his head. "Excuse me a moment, will you? With all the hours I spent working on this, I still managed to overlook something. I'll be right back."

"Can I help?" Joshua offered.

"Won't take a minute," Beau smiled and started off toward the barn with Jeremiah at his side. He returned a short time later before Mathew and Beatrice, deeply engaged in a heated conversation, had missed him. "Shall we go?" he smiled.

Starting off toward the house again, Beau glanced back over his shoulder at Mathew and his wife. "I hope you never turn into a shrew as Beatrice has," he whispered playfully.

"Shhh!" Alanna warned dutifully, looking back at the couple to see if the woman had heard. Seeing that she hadn't, Alanna turned back with a smile of her own on

517

her lips.

"Of course, I suppose she has good reason. Any even-tempered woman would change if she had a daughter like Melissa to contend with." His expression changed as he curiously glanced about. "Where is she, anyway?"

"Who?" Joshua asked, not having heard the entire conversation.

"Melissa."

Joshua snorted. "Count your blessings."

"Yes, I guess I should," Beau grinned with a lift to one brow.

As they reached the veranda steps, Maybelle suddenly appeared from out of nowhere, her dark skin glistening in the sunlight, a look of urgency on her face.

"Beg pardon, Miss Alanna," she squeaked with a short curtsy.

"What is it, Maybelle?"

"It's Lilly and Masta Joshua's cook again. I's afraid they kill each other!"

Alanna's shoulders drooped. "Honestly. What more can happen to spoil a beautiful day?" She smiled apologetically to her companions. "I won't be a minute," she said, starting off toward the back of the house and the kitchen.

Although Melissa tiptoed across the marble floor of the foyer, her footsteps seemed as loud as cannon fire. Or was it only her nerves that made it seem that way? Continually, she glanced about, praying no one would suddenly appear. The door to the study stood open, and she silently thanked whomever was responsible. A heavy door like that would surely moan on its hinges. If only she could control the pounding of her heart. Why did she have such a pain in her chest?

Touching her fingertips to the door frame, she paused and looked about again. She could hear voices raised in anger drifting in from the kitchen and the laughter of many near the veranda, but none appeared to draw nearer. With a quickness to her step, she disappeared inside the study.

From the doorway, she scanned the room. Where could it be? she wondered. I haven't much time. A stream of bright sunlight fell into the room and rested on the huge mahogany desk before her as if beckoning her to come to it. Of course! Where else would it be? Clutching a handful of skirts, she quickly moved to the desk where she paused to listen again. Other than the ticking of the hall clock and muffled voices from a distance, she heard no other sounds. Reaching out a trembling hand, she shuffled the papers and books lying on the desk. Where could it be? Panic rising, she pulled open a drawer and searched inside. Nothing. She tried another drawer. Then another. Her exquisitely clothed figure stiffened in outrage. *She's hidden it!* Whirling about, she crossed to the bookcase, pulling its contents from the shelf one by one, carelessly tossing them to the floor after searching between their pages. From somewhere in the house, she heard a door slam. She froze, her fingertips reaching for the last book. The voices in the yard seemed to intensify, and she frantically looked to the window half expecting someone to be peeking in at her. Drawing back her hand, she clutched it to her chest, forcing herself to breathe again. She tilted her head back, closed her eyes and calmed herself. She mustn't panic. The note is here. Alanna said it was. But where? she growled silently. Her eyes flew open and she concentrated on the room, eyeing every inch of it, trying to imagine where *she* would hide such a thing. Then her gaze fell on the minutely carved wooden table standing just inside the door. On top she could see a yellowed, wrinkled piece of paper.

Grasping the fingers of one hand, she reached up to nibble on the nail of a thumb, a vicious smile of satisfaction and triumph curling her darkly painted lips. Her sea-green eyes narrowed, devouring the sight of it, knowing at last she was safe. With an arrogant lift of her nose, she dropped her hands to her sides and slowly walked toward the table and the possession she longed to hold again. She will pay! Time and time again, Melissa vowed. She will *never* know who did this. It will drive her sanity from her! Then a movement at the door caught her eyes, intruding on her vengeful thoughts, and Melissa felt as if a knife had found its mark, imagining the pain it might cause burrowing into her chest. Haloed in the heavy frame of the door stood Alanna.

At first Alanna could not imagine why Melissa was in the study. Then she saw the books strewn about the floor, the papers scattered about the desk top and the wild, almost frightened look on Melissa's face. She frowned, opening her mouth to question Melissa's reason for the search, and then noticed the way she frantically glanced from her to the table at Alanna's side and back again. Cautiously, for she feared to take her eyes from Melissa in apprehension of the woman's actions, Alanna looked to the table. Dear God, she moaned inwardly, Radford's note! Slowly, she picked it up, feeling as if it radiated the heat of a hundred summer days.

"You?" Alanna whispered. "All along, it was you?"

Feeling trapped, with no way to escape, Melissa urgently stepped backward, bumping into the desk and the candelabra sitting on top of it. The brightly polished instrument teetered precariously, nearly catching its balance then suddenly tipping over. Hitting the floor, it made a thunderous clatter, filling the silence of the room and bringing panic to Melissa. She raced to the other side of the desk, keeping it between her and Alanna.

"How could you?" Alanna asked, never moving nor hearing the hurried footsteps of several people in the hall.

Melissa's lip trembled. She brought up a hand, pressed the back of it to her mouth to hide her fear, and stared wide-eyed, not willing to answer and realizing she didn't really know why herself.

"Alanna, are you all right?" Beau asked, bursting into the room, Joshua close on his heels. "We heard a—" He stopped, glancing about to discover the upheaval of the once neatly kept study.

"What's happened?" Joshua asked, looking from Alanna to Melissa.

Feeling as though every ounce of strength had been drained from her, Alanna weakly handed the paper to Beau. "She was looking for this," she said quietly.

"What is it, Beau?" Joshua asked, straining to look over Beau's shoulder at the paper he held.

"The note from Radford," Beau answered after briefly glancing at it.

"But why would she want it?"

"Because it belongs to her."

"Melissa, is this true?"

At the sound of Mathew's voice, everyone turned to look at him standing in the study doorway, Beatrice at his side, and Blythe staring wide-eyed. His tired face mirrored his suspicion and his pain as he quietly eyed his daughter from across the room.

"Well, is it?"

Tears welled up in her eyes and, finding it impossible

to speak, Melissa simply and desperately reached out a shaky hand toward her father, a silent plea for understanding and forgiveness. But Mathew only shook his head and sighed. Turning away, he took Beatrice by the arm and disappeared from the room, leaving Blythe haloed in the doorway. Her own eyes filled with tears, her chin trembled. But the look on her face announced her long-hidden determination to finally abandon her relationship with Melissa. A woman who would go to such lengths as to be finally responsible for a man's death would not hesitate to turn on her only friend. Fighting back a flood of tears, she lowered her head and walked out.

"Maybe now your nights will pass in peace, Alanna," Beau whispered. "The truth is known."

She raised tear-filled eyes to his and smiled. "They will only be that way if you are at my side to give me strength."

He grinned. "Until I breathe my last, Alanna, I will never leave you."

Without the slightest hesitation, she reached out and slipped her arm into his, pulling him away. "A promise I shall see you keep," she said, glancing over her shoulder at the woman crumpled in the corner of the room. A tired sigh shook her and she turned back, finding Joshua standing near the door, his head down, hands folded in front of him. She smiled.

"We have work to do, Mr. Cain," she grinned, wrapping her other arm around his. "And I am most anxious to see which of you outlasts the other." She looked up at Beau. "I think we can go now. Everything here is finished."

Epilogue

"You may go to her now," the doctor said, then stopped him with a raised hand. "But remember—she's still very weak."

"Thank you, doctor, I will," Beau assured the man, then opened the door to the adjoining room.

A tiny whimper sounded in the soft shadows of the candlelight. His eyes were drawn to its source immediately. Cradled in its mother's arms lay a baby, a small, helpless infant, its dark curls reminiscent of its mother's. He approached the bed hesitantly, wishing not to disturb either one, but longing to reach out and hold them both. He had waited such a long time for this moment, dreading it, thirsting for it, fearing it, but wanting it. Now that it had come, could he endure it? He knelt down quietly and reached out to touch a giant finger against the delicate hand knotted tightly in its first few minutes of life. He smiled when the baby yawned, its eyes squeezed tightly closed, its face contorted. God, how he would love this child! He looked up, having felt another's eyes upon him, and found the mother staring quietly.

"Are you all right?" he asked.

"Yes."

"I hope someday you'll forgive me for putting you through all this pain."

She sighed and closed her eyes. "Never," she whispered.

Filled with grief, he looked away, unable to bear the thought of her hatred for what he had done. He must not let her feel that way. A plea of forgiveness on his lips, he looked back, finding her eyes upon him once more, a smile touching her lips. He frowned, bringing laughter from her.

"You tease me," he scowled.

"And have you not the strength to temper it, my husband?" she laughed.

"Not when I worried the whole night past that I might not ever speak with you again or hold you in my arms. The doctor said you were having a hard time of it."

"And you should know better, Beau Remington," Alanna scolded. "I would never turn you free. I will haunt you 'til your dying day."

Beau threw back his head and laughed. "Yes, my little witch, I'm sure you will."

Alanna giggled, feeling his weight upon the bed as he lay down beside her. "What shall we name your daughter?" she asked, snuggling up in his embrace.

For a long while, he stared quietly at the ceiling above them, listening to the gentle gurgles and suckings his child made when she attempted to find her mouth with her fist. He smiled softly.

"Victoria," he announced suddenly.

"You sound so certain of the choice. Why?"

"Whenever I call her name, I want to be reminded of

524

you, and since I feel that to have won your heart is a victory, I wish our child's name to reflect that feeling. Victoria Remington," he said proudly, testing its sound on his lips.

"And will there be other victories, my love?" she whispered temptingly.

His laughter rumbled in his chest. "Just as surely as the snow falls in winter."

MORE RAPTUROUS READING
BY SONYA T. PELTON

MORE ROMANTIC READING
by Cassie Edwards

SAVAGE OBSESSION   (1269, $3.50)

When she saw the broad-shouldered brave towering over her, Lorinda was overcome with fear. But a shameless instinct made her tremble with desire. And deep inside, she sensed he was so much more than a heartless captor — he was the only man for her; he was her SAVAGE OBSESSION!

SILKEN RAPTURE   (1172, $3.50)

Young, sultry Glenda was innocent of love when she met handsome Read deBaulieu. For two days they revelled in fiery desire only to part — and then learn they were hopelessly bound in a web of SILKEN RAPTURE.

FORBIDDEN EMBRACE   (1105, $3.50)

Serena was a Yankee nurse and Wesley was a Confederate soldier. And Serena knew it was wrong — but Wesley was a master of temptation. Tomorrow he would be gone and she would be left with only memories of their FORBIDDEN EMBRACE.

PORTRAIT OF DESIRE   (1003, $3.50)

As Nicholas's brush stroked the lines of Jennifer's full, sensuous mouth and the curves of her soft, feminine shape, he came to feel that he was touching every part of her that he painted. Soon, lips sought lips, heart sought heart, and they came together in a wild storm of passion. . . .